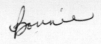

 Praise for *Healing Waters*

"The authors use a mix of humor and grace to tell a meaningful story that many readers will be able to relate to in their own struggles with size and image."

—*Library Journal*

"Evangelical Christian writing duo Rue and Arterburn collaborate again in this follow-up to *Healing Stones,* the first of many (one hopes) Sullivan Crisp Novels . . . This well-written tale will move and engage readers in its volatile mix of questionable religious healing claims and the real deal—inner restoration of the soul."

—*Publishers Weekly*

"*Healing Waters* washes over you, leaving you gasping for air . . . an intriguing must-read."

—*CBA Retailers+Resources*

"The characterization is so complete and compelling, it's hard to believe any reader can close the cover unchanged . . . Anyone who's ever questioned their faith because life seemed to reward the wicked and smash the faithful needs to read *Healing Waters* and recalibrate their beliefs about God's character."

—*Titletrakk.com*

"The second book featuring quirky psychologist Sullivan Crisp is as stunning as the first. The shocking, gripping story, coupled with realistically broken characters, adds up to another triumph. The clear spiritual message about God's love despite our weakness is stellar."

—*Romantic Times*

HEALING WATERS

Nancy Rue and
Stephen Arterburn

THOMAS NELSON
Since 1798

NASHVILLE   DALLAS   MEXICO CITY   RIO DE JANEIRO   BEIJING

Published in Nashville, Tennessee, by Thomas Nelson. Thomas Nelson is a registered trademark of Thomas Nelson, Inc.

Published in association with Alive Communications, 7680 Goddard Street, Suite 200, Colorado Springs, CO, 80920, www.alivecommunicaitons.com.

Page design by Mandi Cofer.

Thomas Nelson, Inc., titles may be purchased in bulk for educational, business, fund-raising, or sales promotional use. For information, please e-mail SpecialMarkets@ThomasNelson.com.

Publisher's Note: This novel is a work of fiction. Names, characters, places, and incidents are either products of the author's imagination or used fictitiously. All characters are fictional, and any similarity to people living or dead is purely coincidental.

Library of Congress Cataloging-in-Publication Data

Rue, Nancy N.
  Healing waters / Nancy Rue & Stephen Arterburn.
     p. cm. — (Sullivan Crisp ; 2)
  ISBN 978-1-59554-431-5 (trade pbk.)
  1. Sisters—Fiction. 2. Eating disorders—Fiction. 3. Aircraft accidents—Fiction. 4. Counselors—Fiction. I. Arterburn, Stephen, 1953– II. Title.
  PS3568.U3595H433 2008
  813'.6—dc22

                                        2008042008

Printed in the United States of America
09 10 11 12 13 RRD 10 9

Sometimes a work of fiction is so achingly real it reads more like a conversation with a close friend than a story. *Healing Waters* is one of those books. We chose it as Women of Faith's 2009 Novel of the Year precisely for that reason.

The main character is like many of us, our friends, and the women who join us every year at Women of Faith events. Lucia is concerned about her weight and her marriage. She has unresolved issues with her family. Her relationship with God is shaky. And she's desperately trying to keep it all together so she can take care of everyone else.

Sound familiar?

Here's the beauty of *Healing Waters:* Lucia starts where many of us live. But she doesn't stay there. Through a series of events—some shocking, some beautiful—Lucia grows into a much healthier woman. Not a perfect woman, by any means, but one who is definitely farther along the road to recovery. She does this with the help of a counselor named Sullivan Crisp, a man who has to do some healing of his own.

Stephen Arterburn and Nancy Rue have crafted a wonderful book that uses a fictional story to address very real issues. If you're like me, you'll be so engrossed in the lives of Lucia and her family you may not realize at first all you're learning about relationships, about faith . . . possibly even about yourself.

For every woman struggling with self worth, here's *Healing Waters.* I think you'll find the water is just fine.

In His Love for You,
Mary Graham

For the brave and honest participants of Lose It For Life,
who have made healing their choice.

CHAPTER ONE

I had done everything on my list. Everything but the last item. Neat black checks marked the first five to-dos:

✓ *paint bathroom*
✓ *put last layer on torte*
✓ *redo makeup*
✓ *call modeling agency—say NO*
✓ *shave legs*

Before the traffic moved again and I made the turn into tiny Northeast Airport, I put a second check beside number five. I'd shaved twice. Chip liked my legs hairless as a fresh pear. Not that I expected him to be interested in them or in any other part of my ample anatomy, but it couldn't hurt to be prepared for a miracle. In truth, I'd probably broken out the razor again just to procrastinate—because I wasn't sure I could do the sixth thing on the list.

I snatched the paper from the seat next to me and folded it one-handed as I pulled up to the gate marked *EXECUTIVE AIRPORT PARKING*. I was still trying to stuff the thing into my purse when an attendant marinating in boredom slid open the window in the booth. She drew sparse eyebrows together and mouthed something I couldn't hear. Of course. My car window was still up.

I pushed the button and felt like I'd just opened an oven door. As the aroma of jet fuel joined the July heat, the makeup melted from my face.

"Help you?" the woman said.

"I'm meeting my sister's private jet," I said.

"Name."

"Lucia Coffey. Oh—did you want my name or hers?"

"Don't need your name."

Staring vacantly at some point beyond me, she smeared her wrist across her forehead and produced a damp cuff. My mascara gathered in puddles at the corners of my eyes. I didn't even want to think about the damage in my armpits.

The woman shifted her gaze to a computer screen. "Who's it you're meeting?"

"Sonia Cabot," I said. "Abundant Living Ministries?"

The attendant's colorless eyes met mine for the first time. "She that woman on TV? Does the show for people got somebody dyin'?"

I gave my watch a surreptitious glance. I would be the one dying if I had to run from the car to the terminal to meet them on time. Just sitting there I was already dissolving like a pat of butter in a skillet.

"She's your sister?"

I looked up, unsurprised at the sudden interest on Apathy Woman's face. The tinge of suspicion didn't shock me either. I waited for the usual next question: *Are you sure?* To be punctuated with: *You don't look anything like her.*

I was tempted to save her the trouble and say, *Sonia's adopted,* which wasn't true. Or, *Usually I look more like her than this, but I'm pregnant,* which wasn't true either. The bulge hanging over the elastic in my pants resulted from pure mashed potatoes and gravy.

"Where do I park?" I said instead.

She perused the clipboard and, the epitome of servanthood now, pointed. "Just to the left of that building. Door's on the end. You better hurry. Plane's due in about five minutes."

I resisted blurting out a *No kidding?*

She knew who Sonia was, which meant I should be careful not to smudge the image. Besides, as I headed for the small, unimpressive terminal building, I had other things to deal with. Like the fact that my hands were now sliding off the steering wheel and my face felt like I'd baked it in the aforementioned oven.

When I parked, a glance in the rearview mirror confirmed it. My cheeks were the color of a pair of tomatoes. I pawed in my purse for Kleenex, found none, and grabbed the list. I tamped it against my forehead, my vine-ripened cheeks, my neck, and then viewed the half bottle of L'Oreal foundation I'd spread on them so carefully just an hour before. So much for the 'do as well. Dark curls, the only thing on me that I *wanted* to be plump, had flattened to my head in strips.

A jet taxied in already, white and sleek, the sun glinting from it like an insult as it made a ninety-degree turn to come perpendicular to the terminal.

The hair was hopeless. Ditto for the sweat situation. My black tunic, permanently glued to the Spandex shaper beneath, cooked my skin and did little to keep the fat under control. I dabbed at my raccoon eyes with my fingers, wiped them on my black pants, and climbed out of my PT Cruiser.

The list dropped at my feet and I would have abandoned it, except that all I needed was for Sonia or someone from her entourage to see it when we got back to the car. Especially the last entry:

• *tell Sonia I want my husband back*

I debated whether to grab the Tupperware of truffles I'd planned for Sonia and whoever to have for the ride to my house. My cookies would be a soup of chocolate and coconut by the time we got back here anyway.

Oh, let it go, Lucia.

A guy in one of those sketched-in-with-a-pencil goatees and a dark blue jumpsuit he'd rolled up to his knees and elbows opened the door for me, then pushed it further, as if he could somehow make the doorway expand. He avoided meeting my eyes as he slipped out.

"Is that the plane from Nashville?" I said. "Sonia Cabot's plane?"

He didn't impress as easily as the lady at the gate. Probably didn't pause on the Christian Broadcasting Network while channel surfing.

"Guess so," he said before he disappeared.

My heart immediately slammed against my chest wall. ·

My husband was home.

I got through the empty waiting room—a miniature version of any I'd ever been in—to a row of seats that faced the window overlooking the tarmac, and perched on the edge of one. An image of getting stuck and having to Crisco my hips in order for emergency personnel to pry me loose while I watched my svelte sister descend the steps from the plane plastered itself across my mental screen. Behind her would be Chip, shading his eyes with his hand and, I hoped, looking for the wife he hadn't seen in three months. He'd have a hard enough time disguising his reaction to my recently acquired thirty pounds, layered over the extra fifty he surely hoped I had shed by now, without finding me trapped in a chair, awaiting the Jaws of Life.

I tried to breathe in the blessed cooled air, tried to erase the screen and form a cheerier picture. One of me running into his arms and finding the grizzly-bear chest and sinking into his smell: Downy fabric softener and spearmint gum and something musky and masculine I could never define. Then he would look into my face in that searching way, trying to memorize it, he always said.

I wilted further. Would there even be an embrace? Or would I draw back from a peck on the cheek? A backslapping hug with a quick release?

I opened my purse and groped for my Snickers, then remembered that I'd already polished it off driving down I-95. I was about to look around for a vending machine when the high-pitched whine of the jet engine pierced the glass. The plane made a maddeningly slow turn toward the crew of two that awaited it, almost as if Sonia were *sneaking* into Philadelphia.

Her assistant had said she wanted our visit to be quiet. She didn't have much time before she had to fly out to Pittsburgh, and she wanted us to have some "just family" togetherness—the implication being that I shouldn't invite any celebrity hounds over. I didn't tell her that none of my acquaintances were into Abundant Living. I wasn't even into it. I wanted to see Sonia-my-sister.

And then again, I didn't want to see her.

I stood up as the wheels finally stopped rolling and the engine wound down. Two crewmen, one of them Pencil Whiskers, moved in and placed yellow blocks under the wheels. No one's face pressed against a window, no hand waved an eager greeting. I tried not to sag. Maybe Chip was too busy grabbing his overnight bag—

The thought that my husband might come home after three months with only enough clothes for a weekend brought on a new onslaught of sweat.

The jet door popped open and began the slow hydraulic fall downward to become the stairs. A girl who looked to be about sixteen scurried out and down the steps like a startled squirrel. Pencil Whiskers swaggered over to her, and she scooped a mane of brunetteness into a handheld ponytail as she chattered at him. He slid his earmuff off one ear and chattered back. So he did actually have a vocabulary beyond "Guess so."

The girl hurried toward the building, letting the ponytail loose, and my eyes went back to the jet's open doorway. No one else appeared. I could feel bubbles of sweat forming on my upper lip.

Chip hadn't come. He'd sent this teenager to tell me we were done. She pulled open the door and scanned the waiting area. Her eyes skipped over me at first and then tripped back with unmasked disbelief.

Yes, believe it or not, I'm Sonia Cabot's sister.

"You're not Lucia, are you?" she said.

Everything in me wanted to scream that, no, I was not. That the real Lucia Brocacini Coffey stood as tall and slim and poised and stunning as her sister. That this dumpy woman whose waist had long since disappeared, whose chins repeated themselves, whose long sleeves in the ninety-degree heat didn't disguise the dangles of fat that hung like bags of pudding from her arms—this woman was no relation to the famous Sonia Brocacini Cabot at all.

"Yes," I said. "I am."

"Oh. Awesome."

I had to hand it to her: she recovered nicely. She came at me like Mary Lou Retton in her prime and extended a slender arm that flowed from the strap of her sundress.

"I'm Marnie," she said, in an accent so Southern I was sure she was putting me on. "Sonia's personal assistant? We e-mailed back and forth?"

I skipped the *Nice to meet you* and looked through the window at the jet.

"Where's Sonia?" I said. "Where's Chip?"

She smiled, revealing almost blue-white teeth, and wrinkled her pert nose. "Oh, they're here. Yeah, they can't wait to see you."

Obviously. That would explain why I saw no sign of them.

"Sonia wants you to come aboard." Dusty or Bambi or whatever her name was glanced around the terminal, this time giving her nose a more disdainful crinkle. "Yeah, it's way nicer on the plane."

It was also "way nicer" at my house, but discussing that with this child was pointless. As I followed her to the door, I decided she was at least in her early twenties, but she couldn't have weighed more than a Big Mac or two, most of which was firmly shaped into her breasts.

Again she told me that Sonia and Chip couldn't wait to see me and that it was much nicer on the plane than in the terminal, and I began to wonder if she were actually a robot who had been programmed with only four sentences. She finally varied that with, "So, you're a nurse. That's awesome"—but by then I was chugging up the steps behind her and could only grunt.

Good. Already a soggy mass of sweaty flesh and ruined makeup, now I'd be a soggy mass breathing like a locomotive. By now Perky

Patty stood at the top, wrinkling a smile as if I didn't look and sound about to go into cardiac arrest.

"Here she comes," Perky said into the plane, and then, with a waft of her arm, stepped back to allow me to pass. I had to press against her to get through. She flattened herself prettily against the bulkhead.

Whether it was nicer inside the jet than in the terminal, I couldn't say. I only saw Chip, ducking his head to emerge from a doorway and still grazing the top with his sparse, spiky, sandy hair. How could I have forgotten how his eyes had faded? Why was I surprised that those square shoulders that used to balance his head as if he were wearing a crown were still slightly slumped? Why had I expected that he would have changed back to the Chip I first knew?

"Hey, babe," he said. At least his voice was still a sandpapered tenor.

With a steaming cup in one hand, he pressed me to him with the other arm.

"Let me take that," Perky said.

She rescued the mug, and Chip folded me to his chest. My husband held me.

And I measured the hold, trying to tell if this was a beginning or an end.

"What does a person have to do to get one of those?"

I recognized my sister's cream-filled voice . . . but when did she get a south-of-the-Mason-Dixon accent? She was born and raised in Pennsylvania just like me, but she sounded like a character from *Gone with the Wind.*

Chip released his arms and stepped aside. Sonia slipped by easily and wrapped her long, lithe arms around my neck. Smooth move. She knew they'd never circle my girth. I felt a soft kiss on my cheek before she stepped back so I could look at her.

I had forgotten nothing about Sonia. Her hair-the-color-of-maple-syrup was as sleek as always, defying the humidity that frizzed mine. She'd pulled it into a shiny bunch at the crown of her head, giving her exquisite cheekbones and full, sensitive mouth center stage. Those weren't my words. I'd read them in *Today's Christian Woman,* where an admiring journalist had compared her to Esther in the Bible.

She surveyed me with her gold-brown eyes, which I hadn't forgotten either. The windows of her beautiful soul, that same journalist had said. Right now her soul looked sad. No, pitying. Disappointed—but not surprised.

Like little Perky, Sonia managed not to gasp and instead flashed me the smile that had won her every magazine cover from *TCW* to *Focus on the Family.*

"It is so good to see you, *sorella*," she said. "And your face is just as beautiful as ever."

I heard the unspoken *If only you'd lose some of that ugly fat.*

"It's been two years, *sorella.*"

It took me a few seconds to recover from her use of our pet name for each other. The Italian word for *sister* didn't quite translate into Scarlett O'Hara.

She shook her head. "It isn't going to be that long this time. When I come back, we are going to have some sister time."

My mind tangled. "I thought you were coming over to the house. Everything's ready. I painted the bathroom."

Good. *I painted the bathroom.* Add that to the list of pathetic things I have said to my sister.

"Darlin', I'm sorry." Sonia put her hands on my shoulders. "We've had a change of plans."

My eyes followed as she looked past me at Perky. She and Chip were by the door to the cockpit, Chip with his hand on the wall above her head, scanning her face with his eyes. Like he was trying to memorize it.

He whispered something to her, except that Chip Coffey had never been able to pull off anything quieter than a stage whisper. His "You have to change your mind" might as well have been broadcast on the airwaves.

"Hello," Sonia said.

They looked up. The girl and my husband both flicked on smiles.

"Marnie, didn't you send Lucia that e-mail with my new itinerary?"

Marnie didn't have a chance to answer before Sonia turned back to me.

"We have to go right on to Pittsburgh," she said. "I am so sorry. I thought you knew. Marnie, get Lucia a coffee—do you want a coffee?"

I shook my head.

Sonia threw out a smile that lassoed Chip and me. "I know ya'll need as much alone time as you can get this weekend. I'm not part of that."

When did she start saying *ya'll*? When did she *stop* making herself a part of *everything* that happened to me? And what exactly *was* happening to me right now?

Sonia brushed her lips against my cheek again and let go of my shoulders.

"Remember," she said to Chip, "I want you to pray hard before you give your final answer." She pushed back the diaphanous sleeve of the tunic that outlined the curves of her slender shape and shook a gold Rolex down over her hand. "I wish we had time to pray now, all of us." She smiled over my head. "I know, Otto, I know."

I only looked back at the man she spoke to long enough to see that he wore a pilot's uniform and that he had a brilliant shock of white hair, disconcerting on someone about to take a plane into flight. Beyond that, I didn't care. I was aching with the idea of Sonia and Chip praying about some issue I wasn't privy to, dying under the image of his whispered exchange with a waif half my age. And weight.

I might have him for the weekend, but he clearly wasn't mine.

As I watched Chip squeeze Sonia and give Marnie a lingering hug, I knew why I'd been surprised that my husband still looked the same. I'd been so sure Sonia would have changed him, taken some damaged piece of him and reshaped it. Of all her many talents, she excelled at that one.

I clung to the cable handrail as I navigated the steps, but I still managed to stumble.

"Babe, you okay?" Chip said behind me.

No, I wasn't. I wanted to roll into a ball and bounce across the tarmac, away from the inevitable.

Chip groped for my hand when we got to the bottom of the steps, but I shifted my purse to that side and risked more breathing-like-a-freight-train to hurry ahead of him. When the door to the terminal sighed shut behind us, I stopped, even turned his way, but I didn't look right at him. Out of the corner of my eye, I could see the steps folding back up into the plane and Pencil Whiskers retrieving his yellow chocks.

"Are you sure you don't want to go with them?" I said.

"Excuse me?"

The sandpaper edges of Chip's voice were raw. When he held me on the plane, I thought that meant he felt as frightened as I did about going back to our home and deciding whether we could live there together again—there or anywhere. I would have embraced his fear. Taken it home and fed it the five-course dinner I'd planned like the president was coming. Just like I always had.

Now those rough edges only sounded annoyed, the irritated last strings of a man anxious to tear away.

The engine roared to life, and Chip looked toward the window, eyes engrossed as the jet turned toward the taxiway. Slowly. As if it were dragging its wheels, giving him one more chance to change his mind. Or Marnie to change hers.

"Do you want to go with her?" I said. "Is that what you want?"

He whipped his face toward me. "What are you talking about?"

I shook my head, felt the limp panels of heavy hair threaten to stick to the sides of my face. I must make a stunning picture. How could I expect him to do anything but run after the plane that was leaving with the pretty women? The skinny twenty-something and the gifted sister. The God-connected sister.

I had never known Dr. Chip Coffey to be a party to prayer before, but he evidently bowed his head with Sonia these days, even while his whispers sought the ears of her assistant. I had made a list of possible scenarios for this meeting, many of them ending in a pained good-bye I would hide behind my pads of flesh. But this—this hadn't been one of them.

I watched the jet turn onto the runway and stop.

"Are they coming back?" I said.

"They're waiting for clearance for takeoff. Look, I just want to go home."

Chip took hold of the back of my arm, and I felt his fingers slip until they were clutching a loose fold of fat. I pulled away.

Beyond us the jet engine whistled, louder and stronger until the jet suddenly raced down the runway. I kept my gaze glued to it, watched its light lift, listened to the billowing thrust. They were leaving, and Chip wasn't running after them. Crazily, I had to make sure Sonia and Perky Marnie and half of what I feared had truly taken off and left us before I could move toward the door.

The nose of my sister's jet lifted and pointed upward, starting to make a sharp ascent, and Chip took a step toward the window, murmuring a curse.

"What?" I said.

His answer was lost to me as the plane virtually fell from the sky. Like a toy being thrown to the ground by a child, it slammed against the barriers at the edge of the airfield and erupted. Ripped in half. One piece slid through the grass on the other side of the fence.

The other erupted in flames.

CHAPTER TWO

A moment seared into me, a paralyzed moment when nothing happened and I knew something should have. The back half of the plane writhed in flames, and yet no one moved, no one spoke, as if we had burned to the spots we stood on, gasping for air. *Do something. Someone, do something.*

I was out the door before I realized I was screaming it, with Chip snatching at me as I hurled myself across the tarmac toward the runway.

The air was too angry to breathe in, and I flung my arm across my nose and mouth as I charged forward until the heat rose up before me like a wall. I could only stand, helpless, a cacophony of jet fuel and burning rubber and melting plastic searing inside my nose. The flames lashed upward and left me only distorted glimpses of blackening metal through the heat waves—the tail, the wing, a gaping hole where a window had been. Then, as if a giant voice had scolded them, the flames cowered before a twisted mass of horror that pushed another scream from me.

I started forward again and felt Chip's arm come around my chest from behind and clamp me against him.

"Sonia's in there!" I cried.

"You can't get her out—"

Sirens wailed from somewhere, and more people scattered like ants from a burning log, but no one went near the plane whose tail melted and twisted and wrestled with the flames.

A fluorescent yellow van cut through the smoke and halted just short of the fence. Movement caught my eye at the front half of the jet, which lay silent and still in the field. A waif appeared in the unnatural opening that should have been the rest of the plane and pleaded frantically with its arms.

Chip let go of me, screaming Marnie's name, and tore toward the aircraft, straight into the path of a fire engine. Someone hurled himself from the truck, tackling Chip and rolling him away from the fuselage. He shoved off a fireman, struggled to get up, still screaming for the girl above the din of burning and sirens and shouts.

Two more firemen ran with Sonia's assistant cradled between them, and Chip bolted for them with me at his back. When he stopped abruptly, I slammed into him.

"I can't do anything," his voice croaked through the smoke. "You go, Lucia."

"But Sonia—"

"I'll see about Sonia. You can help Marnie. Go!"

Some health-care professionals would tell you that their training completely takes charge of their emotions in a medical emergency—that in essence they have no personal feelings when their skills are needed. They have obviously never watched an airplane melt around their sister and known she couldn't possibly survive it.

I was nothing *but* raw gut as I chased the men to one of the parked yellow vehicles and forced myself not to look back. *Dear God, let Sonia be in that half of the plane—dear God, let her be alive.*

My prayers were as chaotic as the scene around me. Demands for information were shouted over the roar of vehicles that catapulted onto the field and the end of the runway. Foam swallowed the ground around the still-smoldering rear of the plane. Bodies in helmets and leaden-looking coats shot back and forth in a dizzying zigzag that pumped my fear up into my throat.

"I'm a registered nurse," I said.

"Can you stay with her till I get a paramedic?" one of the firemen muffled to me from behind the shield covering his face.

I pushed him away from Marnie and slid my arm around her waist. "I've got her—go get my sister out."

"Paramedics are on their way."

"Go!"

A fat lady's voice can be vicious. He fled.

I tried to focus on the next thing to do, and the next, as I got the oxygen mask someone handed me over Marnie's face and tore off the bottom of my tunic to staunch the bleeding above her eye. More sirens screamed in until a haphazard crowd of fire engines and ambulances blocked my view of the burning back of the jet. Smoke continued to heave, and the heat distorted the sky.

Marnie's eyes were wild.

"It'll be all right," I lied.

A paramedic emerged from the smoke and went to his knees beside us. "What have you got?" he said.

As I looked up, I caught sight of a tight knot of people in uniforms between us and the smoldering skeleton of the jet's tail. Their movements were quick and tense. Critical.

I heaved myself to my feet. "Sonia?" I said. "Is she alive?"

"Babe, come on," Chip said out of nowhere. "You need to get back."

"We have to help her."

I strained to pull away, but Chip pressed me close to him.

"You know I can't touch her," he said. "Let the paramedics do their job."

I stared up at the face smeared in soot and sweat. Their *job*? That was my sister—this was *my* job.

I hauled myself away from him and ran for the paramedic knot, clawing through the smoke until I nearly plowed into a figure tearing open a bag.

"How bad?" I managed to get out.

"You need to get back."

"I'm a registered nurse."

"Looks like full thickness burns," one of them said into a cell phone. "Face and neck. Probably second-degree on her hands from recoil."

I looked down at the gurney, still at ground level, where Sonia lay. I couldn't tell what part of her face was her nose, which part her mouth. She was as twisted as the plane they had pulled her from. Panic rose in me as I realized her eyes were open. They had to be. Her lids were no longer there.

The paramedics spoke in staccato. "BP 90 over 50—respirations faint—32—pulse tachycardic—130."

My own pulse pounded at me and brought me down to my knees. One paramedic squeezed a bag valve mask over her mouth. I watched another start an IV in her arm, tossing wrappers aside. And I saw Sonia's charred fingers move.

"Sonia!" I said. "*Sorella,* can you hear me?"

"We're going to have to intubate," the third one said into the phone.

"Got the Albuterol going."

"Sonia?" I said.

Her fingers tapped me, like the tentative touch of a baby's hand. I wanted to stroke her hair, but I was afraid I would draw back her scalp in tattered sheets.

"It's Lucia—I'm here—it's okay."

"You know her?" the female paramedic said.

I wasn't sure. That mass of white ash and grayness and soot could not be my sister.

CHAPTER THREE

From the time we rolled into the emergency room at Crozer-Chester Medical Center in Upland until Sonia was embedded in intensive care at Nathan Speare, their burn center, every face that turned to her showed a degree of horror before achieving professional cover. And these people saw over three hundred tragically burned patients a year.

I stayed with her until a nurse from ICU ushered me into a family waiting room and parked me in a chair.

"Is there anyone with you?" she said.

"I'm fine," I said. And I sounded so. Cool, pulled together, as professional as she.

The moment she left and I had nothing to do to shove away the flames and the fear and the future, it all assaulted me, and I came apart in pieces. I groped at them, tried to find my own senses.

I plucked frantically at my tunic and found the strings of my tattered hem. I was tying them together when Chip found me.

"Babe," was all he said. I let him pull me against his chest, but I couldn't cry. I went numb, and I thanked God for that.

"It's not good," I said into his shirt. "Her whole face—"

"Don't, Lucia. She'll get the best treatment here. Just think about that."

"They had to intubate her—I don't know if there's damage to her lungs."

Chip pulled me in tighter. "You can stop being the nurse now," he said.

"If that were your sister, could you stop being the doctor?"

It was out before I could catch it and stuff it back in.

"I already stopped being a doctor," he said.

I made a halfhearted attempt to pull him back to me as he stood up. We must have cut a pathetic vignette for the doctor who appeared in the doorway.

"Dan Abernathy," he said, putting out his hand. "I'm a burn surgeon. I'll be taking care of—your sister, is it?"

I nodded as I put a clammy palm in his. When he reached for Chip, I saw the flicker of recognition.

"Chip Coffey," Chip said, even though there was no need. Dr. Abernathy's eyes had already narrowed.

"I'm just here as the brother-in-law," Chip said.

I plastered both hands to my forehead. "Okay, so—what's the prognosis?"

Chip folded his arms, took a step back. Dr. Abernathy turned his attention to me and motioned us to chairs. Chip moved against the wall.

"I know it's bad," I said. "I'm a nurse. I want the full story."

The "story" unfolded with increasing degrees of horror, from possible injury to Sonia's lungs, which they would know more about in forty-eight hours, to second- and third-degree burns over 9 percent of her body, including the hands that she'd used to try to cover her face. That was only Chapter One.

Chapter Two still lay ahead, in waiting at least two weeks for the wounds to close and a few more months after that for scars to completely set up. The doctor tried to convince me he had some good news. The face regenerates well, he said, so once her body started healing itself, they could excise and graft. Because her injuries were limited to her upper extremities, they'd have plenty of donor sites elsewhere on her body.

If that was the good news, we were in trouble. Still, as long as we talked in clinical terms, I could stay numb and pretend to be the unflappable nurse.

But when Dr. Abernathy took off his glasses, rubbed his eyes, and put the specs back on, I caved. He was stalling.

"What else?" I said.

"Her eyelids have been compromised."

"Meaning—"

"They've retracted."

"Will she be blind?"

"No. But her eyes will always be open."

He seemed to wait for that to sink in before he went on about keeping her corneas moist, and using a prosthesis to hold her mouth open so it wouldn't draw down.

I remained trapped in the image of my sister, unable to close her eyes to sleep or listen or capture her own vision when she sang— out of a mouth that wanted to lose itself in her chest.

"It's a lot to take in, I know." Dr. Abernathy regarded me with soft eyes. "This kind of injury can be as difficult a loss as a death."

"The loss of her face."

I didn't mean to sound hard and flat, but I had to remain a board that could only handle Post-it notes—basic facts in small pieces that I would organize later.

"I don't know how much experience you've had with burn patients—"

"Almost none," I said.

He dragged in a breath. "She's lost a lot of facial function, and I'm not going to lie to you, her appearance is going to be drastically altered. Returning her to any semblance of normality is going to mean multiple procedures by a number of different specialists as time goes on."

"What about right now?" I said.

"The nurses are debriding the wounds in hydrotherapy. I prom- ise you that we will make this hurt as little as possible. Forget any draconian stories you've heard, anything you've seen on TV about people screaming while a team scrapes off their skin. That doesn't happen here. We'll use as much Ketamine as we need to keep the pain at a minimum."

Good. Can I have some? I was scraping my thumbnail across my palm, over and over.

"That's all I can tell you at this point," he said. "We'll sit down, the family and the team, when Sonia is able to, and come up with a master plan." He stopped and cocked his head. "One of the nurses filled me in about her professional background. This will definitely be a chance for her to apply her own faith, won't it?"

I couldn't answer that.

"Still—you'll have access to Sonia's psychiatric liaison nurse, and I encourage you to talk to her. This affects the whole family, and your sister is going to need you to be strong for her."

I was incapable of anything but a wooden thank-you and an acknowledgELDment nod at the hand he pressed briefly over mine. If I'd done more, I would have splintered.

"If you have any questions or concerns, don't hesitate."

Chip straightened from the wall. "Do you know anything about Marnie—Margaret Oakes? The other girl in the plane."

"Was she burned?" Dr. Abernathy said.

Chip looked at me. My head turned to wood as well. I couldn't even shake it.

"Our social worker can help with that. She'll be checking in." As he headed for the door, his last words were for me: "Get some rest."

The squeaking of his soles down the hall faded before Chip eased into the seat next to me, hands cool through my top as he ran them down my back.

"You okay?"

Was I okay? No. My sister's beautiful face was being scraped off, but my husband showed more concern for the little vixen he'd—

I stuck out a mental hand and sent all of that falling over itself. Let that in, and the pieces I would break into would be impossible to reassemble. No. I had to do what I did so well.

"Are *you* okay?" I said.

Chip's hand stopped on my back. "I don't know what I am. How do you get your mind around this? Or your heart, yeah?" His voice went husky. "She's our sister. We're both pretty shook." He kneaded the muscles at the tops of my shoulders. "I think I should take you home so you can get cleaned up."

I twisted to face him. "Home?"

"You won't be able to see her for a while."

"Are you serious?" I said. "I'm not leaving."

He peeled a hunk of hair from my cheek and tucked it behind my ear. His eyes looked washed out as they searched me.

"I could go home, then," he said. "Get you some clean clothes and whatever else you need."

"I look that bad?"

"Not to me. But you don't want to show up looking like a trauma victim yourself when you see Sonia." He rubbed gently at something on my chin. "You heard Abernathy. She's going to need you to be strong."

"Sonia hasn't needed me for years," I said. "I can't see her starting, even now."

Chip took my head in his hands and pressed it to his chest. "Well, I need you," he said.

I shook away and struggled up from the chair. "Maybe some coffee would help."

He gave me a long look before he said, "I'm on it."

As he strode off, my thoughts crowded in. He looked like he should belong here and didn't. He said he needed me. He was probably going to go check on that Marnie child.

I shut them all down and poked into the smoke-drenched pocket of my tunic. I withdrew two cracked M&Ms and looked at them. I wished they could erase everything, the way I always counted on them to do.

# CHAPTER FOUR

Chip had only been gone a few minutes when a tiny Asian woman with a walk like a farmer stalked into the waiting room and dragged an upholstered chair over to face me.

"You're Lucia Coffey," she said as she propped herself on its arm. She pronounced it Loo-CHI-a. I shook my head.

"LOO-sha," I told her.

She gave me a miniature hand to shake. "No one can ever say my name either."

She pulled at her top so I could get a close look at the tag pinned to it. *KIM AHN NGUYEN. PMHNP-BC.*

"I see your point," I said. I also saw from the letters that she was a psychiatric nurse practitioner.

"Do not even try to say it," she said. "Just call me Kim. I am your liaison with the medical team. Think of me like a concierge. And punching bag, if necessary."

"Oh," I said. "I don't feel like punching anybody at the moment."

"You will."

I shifted in the chair. The stench of my clothes was now beyond nauseating, and the aftertaste of smoke lined my mouth like bitter cotton. I didn't want to be around anyone.

"I understand that you are one of us."

I glanced at her, probably too sharply.

"Since you are an RN, we can let you stay closer to your sister than we usually do." She moved her head side to side. "It is what you are comfortable with."

I couldn't imagine being comfortable with any of it.

"I'm sure her entire staff is going to show up here pretty soon," I said. "She's a Christian, uh, I guess you'd call her a celebrity. She has a whole entourage of people who probably know her better than I do."

"But you are her family. She will want you, believe me."

I didn't, but I let it go.

"So." She looked at me earnestly. "What do *you* need?"

"Me?"

"We are a holistic burn care center. You are my patient too. And whatever other family."

"I'm it, basically." I churned again in my seat.

"Tell me. You mind? I need to know about her."

I did mind, but it seemed useless to argue. "We're the only two." My voice flattened. "Our mother died several years ago. Our father is—not in the picture."

She didn't chase that—fortunately, since there was nowhere to go with it.

"Does she have a husband?" she said.

"My sister's a widow."

A fine eyebrow went up. "A young widow."

"Blake died six years ago. They'd only been married a short time."

"Children?"

I nodded. "A daughter. She's six."

A sympathetic sound escaped from Nurse Kim. Sonia's tragic life could drag compassion out of a stone.

"You are close to your niece?" she said.

"Bethany? I haven't seen her in two years. She doesn't really know me."

I wanted her to go and take her questions and her charming little accent with her. I looked into my lap and noticed that my fingers were sooty. Something similar probably smeared my face as well.

"My husband went to get me some coffee," I said. "And I don't need anything else right now."

"Except a shower."

I blinked.

"We have facilities for family members. Many people come in covered in ash and do not even know it."

"I don't have clean clothes."

She stood up. "We have scrubs. You are no stranger to those."

What were the chances they'd have any in Size Tent? How humiliating would it be to have her scamper off promising a wardrobe, only to come back apologizing because they seemed to be running low?

Then I felt small hearted for even thinking about that while my sister—

"You stay. I will fix you up." Nurse Kim pointed a small finger at me from the door. "You have not heard the last of me, Missy. I am here for you, want me or not."

With the room quiet again, I looked around for my pocketbook so I could at least drag a Kleenex across my face. Oh, wait. I'd run off and left my handbag in the terminal.

Heaven only knew what had happened to my car by this time. I had a strange vision of coconut truffles folding over the backseat like the watches in the Salvador Dali painting.

I was about to heave myself out of the chair when Chip sailed in, napkins plastered to his sleeve by the breeze he stirred up. His hands were full of cardboard drink trays and paper bags that oozed grease. Something normal. I could pretend to be normal.

"You'll be happy to know I've been offered a shower and clean clothes," I said as he unloaded the booty onto a veneered table.

"I'm happy to know you're almost smiling."

Chip pulled a plastic top from a cup and dumped the contents of a packet of sugar in. He took my hands and wrapped them around its Styrofoam warmth, leaving his own on top of mine.

"It's going to be all right, babe," he said, his voice bedside-manner kind. "I know it seems overwhelming, but it's never as bad as it seems at first blush."

He could do that for me, Chip could: come in with his big-bear chest and his soft, thick words and his blue-denim eyes and dissolve my demons into some silliness we could laugh away, even in the desperate moments that had tried to undo us. That was why I'd married him. Why I'd stayed with him when even my most anti-divorce acquaintances told me I shouldn't. Why I wanted right now to let go into his arms.

"Chip? Oh, my gosh, Chip—I am so glad to see you!"

Something brunette flew into the room and hurled itself at him. He barely had time to pull his hands from mine before she collapsed against him and wept.

"Otto's dead," she sobbed into him.

"Okay, Marnie—shhh."

"What happened?"

She pulled away to look up at him, and something real crashed through my hope. I'd seen them have this kind of exchange already, and that obviously hadn't been the first time. Her eyes knew him, and they were trusting as a puppy's.

"We're not sure yet," Chip half-whispered to her. "Thank God you're okay." He gave her the crooked smile. "How many stitches, champ?"

"Six on my forehead. Seven here."

She leaned over to display her leg, and her eyes caught mine for the first time. Her face crumpled again.

"Thank you so much," she said, and flung herself at me.

The coffee overturned and dribbled off the table, onto my sandaled foot. I barely felt it. The girl in love with my husband curled into my lap, sobbing anew into my neck.

"I knew you two would connect," Chip said.

Was he kidding? I gave Marnie a push and grabbed the stack of napkins.

"Oh, I am so sorry!" she said. "Let me do that."

"I've got it, thanks."

"No, seriously."

"Marnie. Leave it."

I heard the laughter hiding in Chip's voice. Laughter that ripped through my stomach like a serrated blade.

"Come on," he said to her. "Let me tell you about Sonia."

Marnie abandoned me and the coffee and climbed into the chair Nurse Kim had just vacated, while Chip sat across from her, holding both her hands while he spoke to her like a doctor, giving her information layer by layer, waiting between for them to set. He'd once told me he broke bad news to families the way I built a torte.

I watched her shoulders settle and her face ease as he talked. I unwrapped a soggy hoagie and rewrapped it, creasing the paper and tucking in the ends until I, too, was safely packaged once more.

"I bet God's going to do a major healing on her," Marnie said when Chip finished soothing her. "Yeah, I can feel it, can't you?"

It took a full fifteen seconds for me to realize she'd asked *me*.

"She's in a great hospital."

"I mean fully recovered. This is going to be a God-thing. I'm sure ya'll have been praying. I have ever since the minute we crashed."

I got up and went for the door. Nurse Kim met me there with a pile of purple.

"I hope this is your color," she said.

She deposited a set of scrubs and a Ziploc full of toiletries into my arms and didn't acknowledge Chip or Marnie. I wished I could have dispensed with them so easily.

"Down the hall and to your right," she said.

I escaped.

In the shower, I scrubbed at the smoke smell on my skin until it was raw and the pain in my chest had resettled into an insensate lump somewhere behind my sternum. I had to keep it there, all of it, because somebody had to speak for Sonia until her people arrived. Then I could become invisible. Until then, I'd shove it all down until I only felt my stinging flesh, and relief that the purple scrubs went on my body and around my circumference.

I didn't look in the mirror. I had no doubt that I looked like an oversized eggplant. Surely a runway somewhere waited for this look.

I went to the nurses' station instead of back to the waiting room.

"I will show you where your sister will be," Kim said, and plodded just ahead of me.

She was petite, but I could envision her pushing a plow. Somehow that made me simply do what she said. She showed me their state-of-the-art everything, but I could feel my eyes glazing over. My legs were going heavy and losing all feeling, and I only wanted to lie down.

Uncannily, she looked at me and said, "Those chairs in the lounge—they recline so you can sleep."

My legs got even heavier as she led me back there.

"I wish we did not call it a 'lounge.' You are not there to relax and have cocktails, you know?"

Right. But what *was* I there to do?

Lounge A was empty when we arrived, and I was too nearly catatonic to worry about where Chip and Marnie had gone. Nurse Kim produced a blanket and coaxed me into the chair, where I dug my nails into the arms, suddenly sure I was going to explode and leave the thing in shards.

I closed my eyes and faked a yawn. "I'm exhausted," I said. "I'm going to try to catch a nap."

She grunted, but I felt her obligingly move away, and heard the door close behind her.

"Egan—man, I'm glad you're here."

I opened my eyes to see Chip embracing a fortyish man whose white hair belied a young face and whose arms muscled from the rolled-up sleeves of an Oxford shirt with Sonia's ALM logo on its pocket. My husband had never been a hugger of men.

When they finally let go of each other, Chip filled him in on Sonia's condition while the man listened, staring at the floor and tugging at his upper lip.

"Egan, this is my wife, Sonia's sister. I don't think you've ever met Egan Ladd, Lucia—general manager of ALM."

Egan gave me a startled look before he fumbled into, "I am so sorry."

I wasn't sure he was empathizing with my trauma or apologizing for mistaking me for one of the hospital staff.

"This is just—I can't get my mind around it. All the way here from Pittsburgh, I just kept praying, 'Lord, help me understand. What are You doing here?'"

I hadn't thought to ask that, but Chip nodded.

"I told the rest of the staff to stay in Pittsburgh," Egan said to him. "They can minister to people who've already shown up for the conference. They'll be upset. Have you called Roxanne?"

"Marnie did. She said Georgia and Francesca are already on their way, and she'll be right behind them as soon as she can."

There was no need to try to disappear into the woodwork now. I was already invisible behind this force of people I'd never even heard of.

When Egan said, "What can we do now?" I didn't answer. He and "the staff" would surely make it happen.

"We need to take this to the Lord, for starters." Egan rubbed his hands together before stretching out his arms to Chip and me.

I didn't know the meaning of that signal until Chip entwined his arm around Egan's and nodded at me.

We were going to pray, standing, arms around each other, heads bent like three myopic people searching for a lost contact lens. Aside from the fact that I didn't link arms with people I'd known for two minutes, my only prayer was one of thanksgiving that Kim chose that moment to stalk in with a steaming tray. By the time the introductions were made, the threat of the prayer circle had passed.

I have nothing against praying, bowing my head in some private place and pleading silently with God that if He would just let me have this one thing, I would give up anything else, do anything, be anything He wanted. I'd prayed such a prayer that morning when I'd hoped Chip and I could start over. I had been crying out *Dear God!* in my head ever since the plane hit the ground. I didn't want to head into the vortex that suggested that what I had to give up was my sister. Or my husband.

They gathered around the heap of turkey sandwiches and bowls of clam chowder—Chip and Egan and a made-over Marnie, who had apparently found the family facilities. She made a pair of turquoise scrubs look like they belonged in the pages of *Vogue*.

I took two bites of a sandwich that went down like wet cement and wandered out into the hallway to the glass doors that separated me from the ICU.

It must have been close to ten o'clock by then. The place had that eerie hush that falls when the lights are dimmed to a yellow blush and the patients enter the tunnel to battle the dark demons of doubt and despair. During the day and early evening, a hospital is filled with purposeful bustle and cheerful talk and the handle-hold of hope. The pain is tempered by smiles, the fear by the sense of things being done, healing things. Being sick is bearable when the sun beckons through the window and visitors talk of things to come beyond this temporary tangle with illness.

But at night, the life-giving machines taunt and the swish of shoes in the halls whisper what-ifs. The sleep we welcome at the end of a health-filled day eludes us when we're in pain. In its place comes the dark threat that there will never be health-filled days again. It is replaced by the specter of death.

I shivered, and Kim materialized with a blanket, folded lengthwise like a shawl, which she wrapped around my shoulders. I pretended to appreciate its warmth, but I didn't know if I was hot or cold, exhausted or merely so wired I'd blown all my circuits.

"Coffee?" she said.

"I'd kill for a Diet Coke," I said. "In a sixteen-ounce cup with crushed ice."

"No need to kill." Her voice smiled. "I can fix you up. The doctor is almost ready to give you an update."

It was all I could do to go back to the lounge, particularly when I saw that its population had nearly doubled.

Two women had joined the group, both in the constant motion of females who pride themselves on their stress levels. Sandals clacked, swing haircuts swung, hands raked through tresses. The atmosphere in the room had changed, the way it does with the arrival of the people who know how to take control of a situation.

The tall blonde dropped her phone into her bag when she saw me and said, "Can you tell us anythang?"

The "thang" overlapped the shorter woman's, "We're looking for her sister—they'll only tell us anything if we're family."

Kim looked at me sideways.

"Georgia," Egan said, "this is—"

"Evening, folks."

Dr. Abernathy appeared in the doorway, and Georgia and the other woman swarmed him like a cloud of honeybees. Marnie and Egan joined the hive, leaving Chip to return to his wall.

Dr. Abernathy looked over their heads at me. "This is all family?"

"Friends," one of the women said. "As good as family."

"This okay with you?"

I nodded.

He picked up the story where he'd left off, and I felt the facts calming me, brutal as they were. I could understand debriding and irrigating and applying topical agents. I could get through corneal desiccation and oral commissures and neck contracture in my brain. Just as long as I didn't have to feel them in my heart.

"Doctor."

We looked up at Georgia who, with everyone else except Chip, hovered behind me.

"Can you debrief your nurse later and use plain English with us?" she said, hands on narrow hips. "I have no idea what corneal decimation is, and I'm sure the rest of us don't either."

"Lucia's a nurse," Marnie piped up. "She can explain."

"Lucia, her sister?" Georgia said. "Well, where is she?"

"I'm so sorry!" Marnie thrust out her hands. "I thought you knew—"

"You're Lucia?" one of the women said.

"All right, look, just—what happens now?" the other one said.

They sounded exactly alike: imperious and entitled.

Dr. Abernathy waited for my nod before he addressed them. "We'll regulate her fluid intake, which is a delicate process. Keep an eye on her lungs—not much we can do but wait there."

"For how long?" Egan said.

"I'll be talking with Lucia about that, and I'm sure she'll keep you apprised. Meanwhile, Sonia's whole support group has access to her psychiatric nurse, Kim."

No one said anything until Marnie chimed in with, "And God."

"Most assuredly God," the doctor said. "That will be a huge factor in her recovery. She's lucky to have all of you."

"I don't think luck has anything to do with it." Egan gave his evangelical smile and opened his arms.

This time Chip didn't take him up on the offer.

"When can I see her?" I said to Dr. Abernathy.

"Right now, if you want. Then we want her to rest."

"We'll be able to see her tomorrow, then." Georgia nodded, willing Dr. Abernathy to nod with her.

"We'll see how her night goes. The staff will work through Lucia."

I could feel their eyes on me, disappointed, doubtful that I was the appropriate person for the job when better groomed, more technologically adept, thinner people were available. I watched the doctor slip out the door.

Kim replaced him, crooking her finger at me.

"I'll take you," she whispered to me.

I followed her through the doors without looking back at the stiffness we left behind. What possible difference could it make what they thought or said or assumed? I had to steel myself for what I was about to see—because once I saw it, there would be no erasing it. No matter how hard those people prayed.

CHAPTER FIVE

What I saw wasn't Sonia.

It was a slab of flesh on a bed. A bloated face smothered in tape and bandages, orifices trailing tubes like snakes on the head of Medusa. It was a scalp stripped of its proud mane and left yellowed and naked and seeping, with no connection to the sister always at the helm of life.

The vital functions blipping on a screen indicated she lived. The bracelet above the mitten of gauze on her hand and the name on her bed identified her as Sonia Cabot. Even with her ears swollen like red bell peppers, she had a dignified look, and admittedly only Sonia could pull that off. But the helplessness was foreign. The person before me was a fraud; Sonia Cabot would never allow this tangle of catheters and hanging bags of fluids to tether her to the bed. The real Sonia would return soon, and I would be there to once again resent her for being able to light up a room merely by breathing the air.

Now that air was bitter with the smell of her flesh, and I coned my hands to my nose behind the sterile mask. I thought she slept, but her eyes startled. Eyes that couldn't close, couldn't even blink, and couldn't hide from the horror that must be etched into my face.

"It's Lucia," I whispered. "I'm here, *sorella*."

She searched the ceiling for my voice.

"Here." Picking my way among the lines and catheters, I pulled myself as far onto the bed as I dared and got my face above hers. In the cap and the mask and the chalky complexion of my own fear, I was probably no more recognizable to her than she to me, but I attempted a smile. I hoped it reached my eyes and lied to her.

She examined my face like a small child trying to decide whether to return the smile or burst into tears. If there was something I should say to take the terror away, it escaped me, and as I grasped for it, I took hold of the first words that fled past.

"You cheated death again," I said.

It was the phrase our father had used in our childhood when we ran in whimpering over a skinned elbow or a case of injured pride.

"The good news is," he would say, "you cheated death again."

Our mother would shriek, as only an Italian mother can, "Anthony Brocacini, that is a horrible thing to say!"

"You baby them too much," Dad would shout back with equal ethnicity.

And Sonia or I would forget our wounds and run for cover as our parents volleyed insults and clattered pans and slammed doors.

I saw the memory now in Sonia's eyes, a glimmer of glee before it glazed.

"You're going to live," I said.

As she eased back into open-eyed sleep, I wondered if she'd want to.

What is the matter with you, Lucia Marie? that same Italian mother would have said. *You can't let your sister hear you thinking like that.*

Her voice was a tape that shouted down my thoughts from time to time. I hadn't heard it for a while, probably because the only time it played was when I dealt with her precious Sonia, whom our mother continued to protect, even from the grave. Usually I could bury her voice under busyness or a package of Oreos. Tonight, I could only sink under the weight of what I knew she expected of me.

You take care of her, do you hear me? No one else understands how sensitive she is. They think she's so strong, but you know her, Lucia Marie. You're the only one left who does.

When I went back to Lounge A after my shower the next morning, Georgia and the other half of the Designing Women—Francesca—had turned the place into the perfect setup for a Mary Kay party, complete with a pink tablecloth and a bouquet of tea roses. I couldn't imagine where a person got such things at that hour of the morning.

Marnie wafted an arm at the spread of bagels and fruit and every flavor of cream cheese and said, "We knew you'd be hungry."

Actually not. Seeing her took away what little appetite I had. The rest was swallowed up in her assumption that of course a woman of my weight was always ready to chow down. I just wanted a Diet Coke, and I wondered in some non sequitur way why we fat people always drank low-cal soda.

But I couldn't get away from the Southern hospitality.

"Ya'll eat," Georgia said. "Get you a plate, Lucy."

"Lucia." Francesca ran her eyes over the antacid-pink scrubs I'd just donned. "You haven't even been home yet, have you?"

All three of them were clad in versions of the same catalog-cover outfit; Marnie's was several sizes too big for her, having obviously come from someone else's suitcase, but she carried it off like a princess whose crown had dislodged only slightly. I was painfully aware that I bore a strong resemblance to a family-size bottle of Pepto-Bismol.

I cut a bagel in half and then took a quarter. They all watched as I pulled off a piece and let it dissolve in my mouth.

"Girl, you eat like a bird," Georgia said.

"Not me." Marnie loaded two blueberry muffins the size of small birthday cakes onto her plate. "Unless I'm a vulture."

I couldn't argue with that.

Georgia eschewed the buffet and brought her Starbucks cup over to sit beside me. "Can Sonia eat?" she said.

I shook my head. "They're feeding her through a nasogastric tube." I pointed to my nostril and felt only slightly guilty when Georgia went green.

"Marnie, honey, what is it?" Francesca said.

Marnie pushed her mini-banquet away and dropped her face into her hands. Her winged shoulder blades shook, and Francesca pulled her head against her collarbone.

"Bless your heart."

"She was so beautiful," Marnie said. "I never saw anybody so beautiful."

Francesca nodded, her own face now draining tears.

Georgia set her cup down decidedly and went to kneel in front of them. "Now, you listen to me, girl," she said. "Sonia is still gon' be beautiful. You know the Lord is with her, don't you?" She gave Marnie's shoulders a shake. "Don't you?"

"Uh-huh."

"And besides that, they can do wonders with plastic surgery these days."

Francesca nodded so hard I was certain her head would topple to the floor. "A little burn isn't going to change Sonia's inner beauty, Marnie, honey," she said.

Did Chip realize he would have to raise this girl he was smitten with? The nibble of bagel turned to rubber in my mouth, and I started to make an exit from the Mary Kay Lounge—off to my sister with the "little burn" that had singed all the way to her bone and formed a cave in the side of her face.

I stopped short at the door when Marnie said in her sob-voice, "I wish Chip was here."

"Didn't he go to the airport to pick up Ivey and Nanette?" Francesca dabbed at Marnie's eyes with a Kleenex. "We all gon' need waterproof mascara to get through this, aren't we?"

"I'm sure he didn't," Marnie said.

"Isn't that his job?" Francesca said.

Marnie shook her head. "He doesn't work for ALM anymore.

He quit. That's why we were stopping here in Philadelphia. To drop him off." Her face crumpled. "I'm so glad we did."

"You knew that, Frannie," Georgia said.

I didn't.

I fled. The wall down the hall rose up to meet me, and I stood with my forehead pressed to it, because the chaotic pieces were collecting so fast and so high, I couldn't move any further.

Chip . . . what the Sam Hill? He couldn't have told me he quit the only job that supported us? The job I'd never wanted him to take in the first place?

I squeezed my eyes shut and tried to file the pieces away, one by one, shove them into places I couldn't feel, but they wouldn't go. They kept accumulating—betrayals on top of lies on top of burned-up dreams.

Come on, Lucia Marie. Get out of this. Go back to ICU where you can hear the beeps and watch the blips.

If I didn't, the aches and the fears would burst me open.

I saw my baby sister as much as the nurses would let me. They let me assist in cleansing her face and hands in the hydrotherapy room, where in spite of their assurances that Ketamine kept her out of pain, I shrieked inwardly at every meticulous picking-off of dead skin, every pull at the good that came off with the bad and left her bleeding. A little blood couldn't make the puzzle of white ash and black char and gelatinous yellow look worse. Nothing could.

Nor could anything make it much better. We could clean and medicate, but Francesca was dead wrong. We were never going to return that face to its previous beauty. Those praying people in Lounge A didn't get that.

Egan and the Designing Women insisted they would see Sonia, and brushed aside my explanation that this wasn't the usual ICU where friends and family could visit for ten minutes every hour.

When I told them, teeth gritted, that Sonia had to be protected from infection at all costs, they vowed that they would dip themselves in disinfectant if they had to—because what I obviously didn't understand was that they would do whatever it took to be there to comfort their Sonia.

Really, I wanted to say to them. *Are you going to learn how to debride her wounds? Catch the drool when she can't close her mouth?*

I didn't say it. I actually wanted someone else to take care of Sonia in spite of my mother's insistence from the grave that I shoulder it all. The chances that one of these women would know what to say to Sonia the first time she looked in a mirror were far greater than they were for me.

I also tried to avoid the constant insistence that I eat something. *How can you eat so little?* they wanted to know.

Their eyes held the rest of that question—*and still look like Jabba the Hutt?*—which I'd seen on people's faces at dozens of lunch tables and barbecues and buffet lines. I would have gone on the Gandhi diet before eating in front of people who shopped in the petite section.

When I wasn't falling under their judgment, I kept moving, even to the point of volunteering to carry the greenhouse-sized collection of floral arrangements that arrived for Sonia into the Mary Kay Lounge, where the number of occupants continued to climb. The new arrivals—hurriedly introduced to me as members of the board of Abundant Living Ministries—shared the group's enthusiasm for the names on the cards. I didn't recognize any of them. As for the board members, five seconds after I was told they were Ivey Somebody and Nanette Somebody Else, I couldn't have identified which was which.

Every time I went into the lounge, everyone was in some phase of crying. Everyone except me. If I started, how would I be able to stop the flood that would express what I was trying not to feel?

The conversation in the lounge now centered on someone named Roxanne, who would be on her way as soon as she'd taped her show.

No, she would let the station do a rerun and be on the next plane. No, no, she'd come later with Bethany and Yvonne, the nanny.

That one slammed into me.

"Someone is bringing Bethany here?" I said.

The conversation muttered to a stop.

"Well, yeah," Egan said.

"Don't even think about bringing that child in here yet."

They stared. Some eyes shuttered, others blinked. I wondered who was making the decisions about my six-year-old niece's life.

"When do you think?" Egan said. "So I can let Yvonne know."

"When Sonia is able to talk, you should ask her," I said.

Egan folded his arms and crunched his forehead. "When is that going to be? I'm not clear on the timeline."

"Whenever they extubate her—take out the breathing tube. A week maybe."

"You think it's going to be a week?"

"Could be two."

Georgia stepped forward. "You're saying she won't be able to *talk* for two weeks?"

"Or breathe on her own or eat or be touched. This isn't a sunburn. Two layers of her face have been cooked away."

I could hear myself breathing as no one spoke.

I turned just enough to look at Georgia. "I don't think you get how serious this situation is."

"What we get," Egan said, "is how hard we have to pray and how large a work the Lord is going to do here."

The two new women sprang to action, as if Egan had just given them their cue. Their nods and amens brought the room back to nodding and Lord-praising and blessing people's hearts.

"I'd like to see her first," Egan said. "I want her to hear that from me."

"Fine," I said. "Excuse me." I didn't wait for them to step back, farther than they needed to, to let me through.

The silence behind me, I knew, was calculated to last until I was

out of earshot, but someone didn't do the math. I heard Francesca—
or was it Georgia?—say, "You know those medical people always
think the worst."

"Is she a believer?" Egan said.

At that point—or at some other time in the blur of hours that
ran one into the other—I asked the ubiquitous Nurse Kim if I
needed to tell them other people might want to use the lounge.

She angled her head at me. "I take care of those things," she said.
"You just take care of you."

That was the last responsibility I wanted.

CHAPTER SIX

Dr. Sullivan Crisp didn't know what he was doing. But then, that was his basic MO these days.

He gave the video camera his Serious Therapist Look, the one where his eyebrows twisted together and his mouth formed an in-half smile. In his best we're-in-this-together voice, he said, "As a result of my most recent study of dealing with your messed-up past and your burned-out present and your black-hole future, my best advice for making the Healing Choice I've become famous for is: fake it till you make it." He pulled his hands in a circle. "Fake it till you make it—uh-huh—uh-huh—forsake it, don't take it—uh-huh—uh-huh—fake it, make it—uh—forsake it."

That was enough to set Christian counseling back a hundred years.

Sully reached out to the tripod and turned off the camera.

An hour, and all he'd gotten on film was fifteen seconds of himself making faces and waxing sarcastic. He lifted his face to the squirrel that had been chittering from the top of a Georgia pine for the last hour.

"Do you have any suggestions, or are you just critiquing?"

A pinecone fell from the tree and popped off Sully's left foot. He was almost convinced the animal had pelted it at him.

"Cut me some slack," he said. "I'm a little off my game."

Actually, he wasn't sure he even had any game anymore.

"Dr. Crisp, have you taken to talking to your sweet self?"

Sully twisted to look at the tall, ebony figure emerging into the clearing. The sun dappled her face, but not enough to hide the all-knowing eyes.

"Talking to oneself is a common way to reduce anxiety, Dr. Ghent," Sully said.

"It's when you talk back that it becomes a problem."

"It's come to that."

"Do I need to call a mobile unit?"

"I'm not sure." Sully nodded up the tree. "I need a consult: if I think that squirrel is out to get me, does that qualify as paranoia?"

Porphyria shook her close-cropped head, frosted white like a cupcake. "No, I think it probably *is* out to get you. You're sitting under her nest talking to yourself. She doesn't want her young'uns exposed to that."

Sully grinned and stood up to give Porphyria the stump. She took it with the grace of a queen, letting the caftan puddle around her feet, mixing its brilliant shades of Africa with the woody greens of the forest. Porphyria was eighty, and he still thought she rivaled Halle Berry for beauty. The sight of her made him want to weep. But then, what didn't these days?

As he parked his lankiness on a nearby log, Porphyria nodded at the camera. "Any progress?"

"You don't want to know."

"Oh, but I do."

Sully gave a soft grunt. She already did. She knew everything about him, or she ought to. He'd crawled in here on his last emotional legs and spent the last sixty days—from May until now—doing a psychic dump with her. Her mind must be like a Sullivan Crisp landfill by now.

She closed her eyes in that way that made her face one smooth plane except for the two fine lines chiseled on either side of her mouth. Anyone who didn't know her would think she had drifted off into the doze common to octogenarians. He knew she was merely expecting, with an acuteness he could only dream of at forty-five. Clearly, what she waited for was the truth.

"I don't know about this idea of Rusty's," Sully said.

"Making a DVD."

"I don't know whether he actually wants Everything Sullivan Crisp Knows in Ninety Minutes, or he's just trying to 'build my confidence.'"

Porphyria watched him.

"Come on, Dr. Ghent," Sully said. "Where's that therapeutic response?"

"The part where I say, 'What do *you* think, Sullivan?'"

"That's the one."

Porphyria let her lips part in a smile. "I'm glad to hear that sideways humor again."

"Uh-huh. There's a *however* in there."

"However, I wonder if it's up to its old tricks."

"Tricks?" Sully made his eyes bulge. *"Moi?"*

"Oui, vous." Porphyria's java-colored fingers floated up, pointed at Sully, drifted back to her lap.

"I admit, sometimes it's a coping mechanism," he said.

"And what are we coping with at the moment?"

Sully let his grin collapse, and with it his bony shoulders and his bravado. "I know I need to get back to work, do something besides dwell on my stuff."

"Mm-mmm."

"Okay, completely on my stuff."

"I like that better."

"I just don't know what work I'm ready for."

"You've been working," Porphyria said.

"I've been recycling."

"There's nothing wrong with rerunning your shows. I like that young man who's doing the commentary on them."

"There's only about another month's worth left before they start having to run them for the second time." Sully gave his half grin. "It's going to be like *Law and Order* on TNT. People will be able to recite the words with me, if they're still listening."

"I don't think anybody has stopped. Your work bears repeating."

Sully got up and unscrewed the camera from the tripod. "Tell that to my agent," he said. "She says Thomas Nelson still wants another book proposal, but I can hear in her voice she doesn't know how much longer they're going to wait."

"That's the price you pay for being so perceptive."

Sully set the camera on a rock and propped his foot on the log. He stared down at a pad of moss, thick as his thoughts. "I don't know what I have to bring to the table at this point. I know I'm healing . . ." He glanced up at her.

Porphyria let her still-black eyebrows rise and fall. "Don't look at me. Look at you. You know what's going on in there."

"I do. But I'm afraid if I open it up as the next great Healing Choice . . ." Sully shrugged.

Porphyria lifted her own majestic shoulders toward her ears. "What is this?"

"It's plain ol' fear, Porphyria. I've cried and talked and prayed my way back together, but the way the pieces are fitting now—it's not the old Sullivan Crisp."

"Do you want it to be?"

"He worked for me. He built things—cars, ministries. He helped people reframe and reclaim. Find God."

The tissue paper skin around Porphyria's eyes crinkled. "Now who's hiding a however?"

"I did all of that to lose myself, and I can't anymore." Sully pulled his foot from the log and folded the tripod. "Anxiety's always lurking, Porphyria. And ripples of pain. The old poster child for a life well lived is gone. What—was I the quintessential fraud?"

"Do you think you were?"

Sully set the folded tripod next to the camera. "I wasn't consciously faking it. I did think I had it all under control."

Porphyria closed her eyes into a smile. "In a lopsided way, I suppose you did. That was your signature." She nodded, still looking into herself. "You were who you were then, Sully. A little wacky.

Definitely unconventional. But you were as authentic as you could be under the circumstances."

Sully scrubbed at his face with his hand. "But now the circumstances have changed, and I don't know what to do with that."

She nodded at the camera. "Are you making any progress?"

"I think I've found the right questions."

"Which are?"

"Can I actually tell people how to make godly choices after what I've discovered about myself? I'm not talking about whether I can write another book or record another radio show or make a DVD." Sully flung a hand toward the camera. "I'm questioning whether I can even sit down one-on-one with a client and do therapy. We both know I went into psychology to put off my own grief work. I mean, was that where God even wanted me in the first place?"

The woods went quiet. The air ceased its singing through the pines, and the squirrel seemed to wait in respectful silence for Porphyria Ghent to speak what waited on her lips.

"I heard some news today," she said. "On CNN."

The puddle jump to another topic didn't faze him. She'd find her way back to this one via some wily path.

"You're a news junkie," Sully said.

"I can't pray for the world if I don't know what's happening in it."

"So what's happening today?"

"Sonia Cabot was in a plane crash."

Sully felt his heart plunge. "Is she—"

"She survived. She was badly burned, though." Porphyria's eyes closed again. "That beautiful face."

"No."

"They didn't give much detail. Just an interview with her spokesman."

"Egan Ladd? Guy too young to have white hair?"

"That would be the one. He said her injuries were serious but not life-threatening. They cut him off before he got too far into Abundant Living's hopes for a miraculous healing."

Sully smeared his hand across his mouth. Sonia Cabot was a gorgeous woman, as gracious and generous as she was physically attractive. He and she could never agree theologically, and though she wanted to debate with him at every possible opportunity, he'd coaxed her into a pact to avoid doing battle over matters of faith. Still, their friendship was something of a mutual admiration society. Hers was a charisma as rare as the success she'd enjoyed in ministry. A success they'd both known.

And possibly both lost.

"She's based in Nashville, isn't she?" Porphyria said.

"She is."

"A place you know well."

"Too well."

"You think so?"

Sully felt a stab in the place already sore from the opening and reopening of the wound. "You think there's more I need to know, don't you?" Sully put a hand up. "I know we've been through this."

"And what did you tell me? You said in your soul God is saying there is still more that you don't *want* to know. Now, you can heap dirt on that again—but that's going to mean the death of the Sullivan Crisp you were made to be."

"I could keep digging it up here," Sully said. "You're the best gravedigger there is."

"Mm-hmm. And is that what you'd tell a client?"

Sully gave her the full grin. "I'd tell a client to get off his duff and hit the rapids. In my case, that would be the Cumberland River—and my Class 3 guilt." He straddled the log. "The answers are in Nashville, aren't they, Porphyria?"

She joined him on the log. "They're in here," she said. She pressed a hand to his chest.

It burned into him, the way her wisdom always did.

"You don't have to go to Nashville to find out the rest of what you need to know about what happened to your wife and your baby girl. But I don't think we can ignore an opportunity that God may be laying out right in front of you."

"You're not saying I should go try to counsel Sonia Cabot? She's a friend—I don't do therapy with friends."

"I didn't say you should do anything. But Sonia Cabot may *need* a friend in Nashville." Porphyria pressed the hand harder into his chest. "Only God knows whether Sullivan Crisp is ready to do therapy again. But Porphyria Ghent knows if she needed a friend, he'd be the one she'd want right there." She drew back her hand, but not her gaze. "Only someone who has been through hell can help someone else find their way through the smoke, Sullivan. You don't have to be a doctor to do that."

That was a good thing, he thought, as she gathered her caftan and her wisdom about her and moved soundlessly out of the clearing. Because a doctor of psychology was still the last thing he felt like. And Nashville was the last place he wanted to go.

CHAPTER SEVEN

Although the unit allowed only one visitor at a time, no one shooed me out when Egan came to see Sonia Monday morning. They probably hoped I'd be willing to catch him when he passed out.

His face went as pale as the prematurely white hair tucked under his required cap. For a long moment he stood eerily still, staring at Sonia above his mask as if he didn't want to see her but couldn't take his eyes away. In her ICU cubicle we were all somehow on a par with Sonia, faces covered, expressions muted.

"Does she know I'm here?" he whispered.

I leaned over the bed. "You awake, Sonia?"

Her eyes turned slowly to look at me.

"You have a visitor. You up for it?"

Without the wrinkling of a forehead or the pursing of a mouth, I couldn't tell what she meant when she widened her eyes. I took it as a yes and nodded to Egan.

He took an imperceptible step toward the bed.

"Hey, pretty lady," he said.

He looked as if he wanted to smack himself, though I would have gladly done it for him.

"Did she hear me?" he said.

I watched Sonia. Her eyes were darting, searching for the face to match the voice.

"You might want to come closer so she can see you," I said.

I might as well have asked him to throw himself from the fourth-story window. His hands twitched and clung to the gown, drawing its paper into his fists.

"We're praying for you," he whispered. "You know that. We pray without ceasing, right?"

His answer was the frantic beeping of an IV bag that needed to be changed out.

"I think I should go," he said, and did, gown swirling out behind him.

I wanted to grab him by the back of his Brooks Brothers belt and yank him back into that room Sonia couldn't escape and make him look at her, make him tell her to what face she had left that she was a living miracle. But I felt something nudge my hand.

Sonia poked me with her bandaged paw.

"What do you need?" I said. "Are you in pain? I can get you—"

I stopped, because what I saw in her eyes was not pain but confusion. I would have been befuddled, too, by what her staunch supporter had just done. Or hadn't done.

"He's not used to this look on you," I said. "It's different."

She gave me another nudge and drifted out again.

As much as I abhorred confrontation, I ripped off the sterile regalia and was on my way out to Lounge A to tell those people that unless they were ready to suck it up and talk to my sister like she was a human being, they weren't going to talk to her at all.

That ended when I heard Nurse Kim's voice raised on the other side of the glass doors. Did the woman never take a day off?

I stayed put until I heard her say, "We do not give out medical information to anyone except family members."

I went for the doors. Could those people be any more pushy?

But it wasn't the Designing Women or the Board of Directors that Nurse Kim held off in the hallway. I didn't recognize any of the three who faced her, apparently unfazed by her tiny firmness.

"We understand," said a woman who no doubt had applied Cover Girl with a spatula. "But can you just make a general statement about her condition?"

How many vultures did Sonia know, for Pete's sake?

"Are you with ALM?" I said. "Because they're all in Lounge A."

Heads swiveled to me.

"We'd like to hear from some medical personnel," the guy said. He pushed his glasses up his nose. "We're not trying to invade her privacy—we just want to be accurate."

"We're with the religion desk at the *Philadelphia Inquirer*," the woman said. "I'm not sure if you know this, but Sonia Cabot is well-known among—"

"I know," I said. "Go talk to her people. They're in Lounge A."

Nurse Kim gave me a small push back toward the doors and said over her shoulder, "We appreciate your sensitivity. Perhaps her manager will give you the statement."

The two chatty ones looked only slightly put off as they headed for the lounge. The other one, a square-faced woman, reached into the pocket of a periwinkle-blue blazer and pulled out what appeared to be her wallet.

"Are you Lucia Coffey?" she said. "Mrs. Cabot's sister?"

Honestly.

"Yes, I am," I said, "but like I told them, I'm not talking."

"I hope you will." She flipped open the wallet. "I'm Special Agent Deidre Schmacker with the FBI. I need to ask you a few questions."

I'd talked to a number of FBI agents in my recent past. They'd all worn black and gray and left no question that they could ruin my life. All of them had been men.

Special Agent Deidre Schmacker had fooled me with the periwinkle jacket and the heavy silver earrings and the understated manner.

Still, my mouth went dry as I followed her obediently to a lounge I didn't know about—Lounge C, the sign read. I barely waited until the door closed behind us to say, "I hadn't seen my husband in three months before yesterday. If he's in trouble again, I know nothing about it."

The agent gave me a long look, which, again, was nothing like the scrutinizing gazes I'd squirmed under three and a half years ago. Her eyes drooped at the outer corners and her mouth went toward a smile and stopped just short of it. She looked like a grandmother accepting an apology.

"Why don't we sit down?" she said.

As I edged onto a chair, I realized that she'd set up shop in Lounge C. A BlackBerry, a laptop, and a legal pad were arranged on the table. She opened a Thermos and drew her pale brows in. "Tea?"

"No, thank you."

She poured herself a cup, and the sound reverberated in the room. Already sucking in air, I wished she'd get on with it. I'd answer the questions and come apart later.

"Do you have a reason to think your husband is in trouble again?" she said finally.

"None at all."

She waited. When I didn't volunteer anything, she took a sip, waited some more, cupped her hands around the mug.

"I'm not here to talk about Halsey," she said. "Chip is what you call him, right?"

Of course right. You people know everything about us.

"You can relax. I just need to ask you a few questions about the plane crash."

She waited yet again. Something seeped into me like damp air.

"I thought the crash was an accident," I said.

"We have to look at all possibilities. The report from the NTSB—"

I shook my head.

"The National Transportation Safety Board. They're the investigative board that takes possession of the wreckage after a plane crash. Their findings indicate that we need to look more closely at the circumstances. Since 9/11 it's policy." She indicated the Thermos again. "You sure you won't have some tea?"

"Positive."

"All right, I just have a few questions for you. I know you want to get back to your sister, so I'll try not to take up too much of your time."

That had never been a consideration with the FBI before.

"You were there the day of the crash, yes?"

"Yes."

"And you saw your sister before the plane took off."

"Yes."

She paused after every answer, as if I might want to add more. I didn't.

"Where exactly did you see her?"

"On the plane."

"You were *on* the plane."

That was what I'd said, plainly.

"How would you describe Sonia's state of mind when you talked to her?"

I couldn't help the widening of my eyes.

"It's just a routine question," she said.

"She seemed like she always is. Upbeat. Anxious to get going."

"Anxious?"

"Eager."

"She didn't seem preoccupied at all, maybe distracted?"

"No." Sonia had been totally aware of what went on with everyone, inside and out.

"Who else was on the plane when you were on board?"

"My husband. Marnie, her assistant."

"Did she appear to have any issues with either of them?"

I scraped my palm with my nails. "I hadn't seen my sister in two years, and I'd never met her assistant before that day. I couldn't tell you if they had issues."

"Of course. I'm just asking for an observation." She took a long sip of her tea. "You seem like an observer to me. I just thought you might have noticed something."

I pretended to be considering that. One thing I'd learned about the FBI: if you didn't tell them something you knew, it came back to bite you later. You or someone you loved.

"Sonia wasn't happy with Marnie because she hadn't told me we weren't all going to my home—that they had to leave for Pittsburgh right away. That was evidently a last-minute change in plans that I wasn't notified about."

The agent scribbled something on the legal pad.

Good. A meaningless detail was now in writing.

"Do you know why the change in plans?" she said.

"No. I don't have anything to do with my sister's company."

She fingered her chin. "Even though your husband was employed by this"—she consulted the pad—"Abundant Living Ministries?"

"He lived in Nashville for the past three months. I stayed here. We didn't discuss it."

"So you and your sister are not close."

"No."

"How did the assistant react when Sonia called her on her mistake?"

I couldn't even remember, being too busy recovering from the sight of her making love to my husband with her eyes.

"I don't think it was any big deal," I said. "Sonia moved on to the next thing."

"Which was?"

"The pilot told her they needed to get going."

"So you saw the pilot."

"I got a glimpse of him."

"How did he seem to you? I know you're a nurse—did you notice anything about his color or his behavior that would indicate an illness?"

"I barely looked at him," I said.

And if I'd seen anything amiss, didn't she think I would have said something? He was about to take my sister to 15,000 feet.

"So he seemed fine to you."

"Yes." I was dying to say, *Why are you asking me that?* But it would only have prolonged what was becoming increasingly uncomfortable. I had already rubbed the skin raw in the palm of my hand.

"What did he say exactly? From what you can remember."

"I didn't hear him say anything. He must have given my sister a signal, because she said something like, 'Okay, Otto, I know we have to go,' and then my husband and I got off the plane."

"He didn't say anything to anyone else."

"Not that I heard."

"Did anyone react to him in any way?"

For Pete's sake, *no*. "My husband shook hands with him before we deplaned," I said. Maybe that would get her off this.

"You're doing great," she said. "I just have a few more questions." She consulted her pad, which gave me a chance to lick my lips. "How did your husband seem when you first saw him?"

"Fine."

Her brows pulled in. "You hadn't seen each other in three months, and he just seemed 'fine'?"

"I guess he might have been nervous," I said. I bit back the testiness in my voice. "Three months is a long time."

"What is his relationship with your sister like?"

My lips were so dry, they stuck together momentarily when I tried to open them.

"Would you like some water, Lucia?" she said.

"I'm okay. My sister was good enough to give Chip a job when he needed one. He was grateful for that. Like I said, we didn't discuss it much."

"So you didn't sense any animosity between them."

"No," I said. "Everything seemed fine to me." Could I use the word *fine* about twenty more times?

"Since the crash, has he said anything to you about their relationship or his relationship with anyone else on the plane?"

Had he said anything to me? No. Had he shown me exactly what one of those relationships was? In spades.

"Did you think of something?"

"We haven't talked about anything since the crash except my sister's injuries," I said.

"I can completely understand that. This must be difficult for you."

I wasn't sure whether she meant Sonia's condition or this interview. A yes to either one would have been an understatement.

"I just have one more question." She nodded at me, all concern. "I know this is probably the last thing you want to talk about, but I need for you to tell me exactly what you saw from where you were standing, from the time the plane's engines started up until the crash. Then I'll be out of your hair."

I wanted nothing more. I closed my eyes, saw and heard it all again, and described it to her. Terror tried to lick at me, but I talked it down with the best words I could choose to reproduce the experience, down to the heat that singed my eyebrows when I ran from the terminal. Then I prayed that when I opened my eyes at the end, she would be gone. Of course she wasn't.

In her grandmother voice she asked a few more questions, to clarify the color of the smoke and how long I estimated the time between the plane hitting the ground and bursting into flame.

I snapped my fingers.

"So you're saying instantly."

"That's what I'm saying."

She made a note on the pad. I saw that she hadn't added anything since the last time I looked. Nothing I'd said in my long harangue had been written down. Evidently she didn't need the ravings of a fat lady after all.

"I'm sorry," she said. "I lied—I do have one more question."

I wanted to stand up so she'd know I only had one answer left in me, but I stayed put.

"Did you notice the crew that serviced the airplane at all?"

"The crew?"

"Weren't there some people refueling the jet—"

"I know what a crew is." I closed my eyes again, but I only saw the scrawny kid with a wanna-be goatee who tried to hit on Marnie. "They were just kind of there," I said. "All I saw them do—"

"Them."

"Two guys. They put those blocks under the wheels. Other than that, I didn't pay attention."

"Neither of them went on board the plane."

"Not while I was on there."

"When you got off, did you notice them anywhere around the plane?"

How many ways did I have to say it?

And, more to the point, why? The FBI didn't come around unless they suspected somebody had committed a crime. It didn't sound like Chip's kind of crime this time, but I still wanted with every cell in my body to get out of there. Yet I couldn't leave with this piling on top of everything else I was hauling around inside. Even I could only expand so much to hold it.

"You said you weren't here to talk about my husband," I said. "Then why *are* you here?"

"That's a fair question." She added more tea to her cup. "We don't have a theory about the plane crash yet. At this point we're just gathering information. Would you like to hear what we know so far?" She gave a small shrug. "Who knows, maybe it will jog something in your memory."

Regret that I'd asked crept in, but I nodded.

"Air traffic control lost contact with the pilot within seconds of takeoff. Preliminary examination of his body by the medical examiner showed no smoke inhalation, which would indicate he died before the fire occurred. That jibes with the behavior of the plane described by the ground crew. Am I going too fast?"

It was too much to process at any speed.

"Mr. Underwood's medical records show he has no previous history of serious illness. The man was fifty-nine years old, though pronounced to be in good health at his last physical."

Her words were professional, but by her tone we could have been chatting on the back porch about our recently deceased uncle.

"The autopsy and full tox screen could reveal more. In any event, as the jet ascended, he apparently pulled the yoke too hard for some reason and caused a stall. The plane virtually fell out of the sky."

I nodded involuntarily. I'd described it that way to myself as I'd watched it.

"Now, here's the problem. The plane had gained no more than a few hundred feet in altitude before the crash. While the fact that it had been refueled literally moments before would account for its bursting into flame, NTSB is not sure the impact was enough to warrant the kind of explosion you saw." She gave me the grandmotherly look again. "I'm sorry, but we're looking for evidence of foul play."

"You think somebody did this deliberately?"

"We're just compiling the facts." She pulled out her badge case again and produced a business card, which she held out to me. "If anything occurs to you—even if you think it's insignificant—call me at this number."

I couldn't even reach out my hand to take the card. She set it on my knee.

"The idea that someone would want to hurt your sister, or anyone else on the plane, is probably difficult to fathom," she said. "Unless you can think of anyone who might."

"Everyone loves Sonia," I said before I even thought it. To meet Sonia was to drop to one's knees in awe, no matter how hard you fought it.

"There are people who hate the ones everyone else loves," the agent said. "It's sick, but it's the sick who perpetrate this kind of tragedy. And again, there may not be a perpetrator at all. We could be talking about a freak accident."

She put out her hand to shake, and I stuck mine in it, sure it had all the warmth of a branch.

"I'm so sorry for what you and your family must be going through. By the way," she added offhandedly, "we haven't been able to get in touch with your father. Any idea how we might locate him?"

"None," I said.

"He hasn't contacted you? This has been all over the national news." She glanced toward the door. "Those two reporters aren't the only ones looking for a story."

"I don't even know if my father has access to a TV," I said.

"If you hear from Mr. Brocacini, you'll let us know, yes? I think that's enough for now." The agent stood up.

Agent—

I couldn't remember her name.

I couldn't even remember my own.

CHAPTER EIGHT

The FBI agent vacated her domain in Lounge C later that afternoon, and I went in to close my eyes against everything, including a headache that threatened behind my brain. When I opened them, Chip was there.

"Hey, babe," he said. He put a bulging white trash bag in my lap. "I brought you some of your own clothes. Not that you don't look fabulous in those scrubs." He attempted a smile, which I didn't return. "See if those are okay."

I pulled the bag open and peered inside. Nothing in there went with anything else, and I hadn't been able to get into any of it in weeks.

"Thanks," I said.

"I found your purse and got the car to the house," he said. "And I watered your plants. You have enough to handle here. I thought I'd take care of things at home."

I couldn't help staring at him. When had Dr. Chip Coffey ever done a domestic chore in his life?

"You're scaring me, Lucia," he said. "Talk to me." He pulled the sack from my lap and pawed for my hand. "Tell me about Sonia."

"The FBI is going to question you," I said.

"Special Agent Deidre Schmacker. She got to you too."

"She already saw you?"

"They probably contacted me before anybody. She showed up at the house." He waved off my sudden tautness. "Relax, babe. Schmacker came alone. If I were a suspect she would have brought a partner." His smile was grim. "It was a refreshing change, actually. She didn't try to make me hang myself."

My insides shook. "Did you help her?"

"Probably not." He sat up again and took both of my hands. "Look, I don't know what Agent Schmuck told you, but nobody is out to get Sonia. All I've seen the last three months is complete idolatry. People worship her. It gets a little sickening, actually."

"Is that why you quit?"

It was out now, stirring Chip's faded-denim gaze. He didn't release my hands, though, and I didn't pull away. If I moved, it would all go.

"So you know," he said. "I was going to tell you. I never had the chance."

"Did you just decide on the plane on the way up here?" I said.

"No."

"Never mind." I floundered against the onslaught of openness. It was too much. "It doesn't matter right now."

Chip swore softly, around the edges of his sandpaper voice. "That FBI agent shook you up, didn't she? Lucia, listen to me. They have to do an investigation any time there's an explosion on an airplane, so they can rule out terrorism."

"Terrorism!"

He put his finger to my lips. "It's protocol. Nobody thinks the plane was sabotaged. They know there was structural damage, but they just aren't saying it. That combined with whatever happened with Otto—she told you that part, right?"

"He didn't have heart trouble or anything before."

"Not that anybody knew about."

"Did you?"

Chip stiffened. "I didn't practice medicine down at Sonia's, if that's what you mean. I didn't do much of anything except drive her around and run errands. That's why I quit. And because I missed you too much." His eyes softened. "I miss your cooking, babe. And your nagging—and the way you dance in the kitchen when you're making ravioli."

He lifted my chin—all my chins—with the tips of his fingers. It was a moment like so many I'd had with Chip, when I knew he didn't see my fatness and didn't care if he did.

Or at least I'd thought so.

I let the moment pass into one of the real ones, when I knew he couldn't stand the sight of this bloated version of his size 6 bride. When I knew the inevitable had happened, and I had been traded in for a size 2.

"I don't dance anymore," I said.

"I would guess not—you look exhausted. I wish you'd come home and get some decent rest."

"I can't."

"Why? Sonia's getting round-the-clock care right now. This is the perfect time for you to take care of yourself." He touched my chin again. "Or let me take care of you."

"Since when have you ever taken care of me?"

Dear God, why did You let me say that?

I groped to get the words back, saying, "Never mind, never mind," but the space they left gave me room to breathe. I got up and stood beneath a cooling vent and gulped in air.

"Since never," Chip said behind me. "I have never taken care of you. But I'm going to start now."

I felt him come to me, but he didn't touch me. "I said I didn't do much at Sonia's, but that's not completely true. I *thought*, babe, and I searched my soul, and I realized I could never have gotten through these last three years without you being who you are and standing by me. Now it's time for me to do that for you."

I felt his hands take my shoulders as if they were too hot to touch.

"Please come home with me and let me try."

I wanted to. I wanted to as much as I'd once wanted to believe he was innocent. And then later that he was at least remorseful. And then that he wanted a family as much as I did—children to focus on, a reason to start over. I always wanted to believe, and I had, over and over, because I somehow knew I was his only one. For once in my life, I was someone's only one.

Until now. Now he thought I was stupid enough not to know it. I was tired of being stupid.

"Babe, you're shaking."

"I'm fine," I said. But the bursting apart of pride and pain and panic was imminent if I didn't get it under control, here in the strange comfort of ICU where I knew what I was doing. Where I wasn't just a fat idiot. Maybe after that I could tell him what I knew. Maybe after that I could handle what he might say.

"I can't come home right now," I said. "Later, when Sonia's doing better."

He tried to turn me to face him, but I dug in. His hands slipped off my shoulders.

"You do what you have to do," he said. "I'll take care of things at home. I'll see about getting another job."

I nodded.

"I'm not giving up on us."

I let him get all the way to the door before I said, "I'm fine here by myself."

Chip put his hand on the doorjamb and squeezed until I could see his skin go white, but his face showed me nothing. There was a time, far back, when I could watch all his possible responses flip through his face like cards in a Rolodex before he landed on one. Now he could make his face as impassive as a tombstone. My only clue was the strained up-and-down bob of his Adam's apple.

"Call me when you need me," he said.

When he was gone, I went to the vending machines and filled the pockets of my pink smock. Later, in the lounge after everyone else had left, I had a supper of cheese crackers and Snickers and didn't think about Marnie perhaps slipping to my home to be with my husband, to whom I'd just given the perfect opportunity to have his affair.

Anything not to feel.

"No wonder we can't pry you out of here, Sully. This place is amazing."

Sully handed Rusty Huff a glass of iced tea and leaned with him on the railing of Porphyria's wraparound veranda. Below them a thick field of ragwort and bee balm tumbled toward the woods in happy abandon. Beyond, the Smokies seemed to drift in a blue-gray mist.

"Porphyria admits God doesn't live here," Sully said, "but she swears this is where He spends most of His time."

"It was the perfect place for you to heal." Rusty took a sip from the glass and looked at it reverently. "Did God make this too?"

"Close." Sully grinned. "Porphyria's trying to teach me, but I'm pretty much hopeless."

"Yeah, we all give anything you cook a wide margin."

Rusty furrowed his forehead, and Sully knew he was about to say something that made a huge amount of sense. It was the reason Sully had chosen him as acting head of Healing Choice Ministries in his absence.

"So—you planning to bring everybody up here for healing?" Rusty said.

"Who?"

"You haven't given me anything for the DVD. I thought maybe you were planning a retreat for all the hurting people who need what you've learned." Rusty looked into the glass as he swirled the ice. "I think you've got the lamp-under-a-bushel thing going on."

Sully left the railing and dropped into a padded wicker chair. "I don't think the DVD idea is going to work. I looked at what I've filmed so far, and I come across more like a prisoner of war than a spiritual-health guru."

"Yeah, you're pretty scrawny-looking right now, but we can doctor that up."

Sully shook his head. "I just can't get it all to come together yet."

"So maybe a full-blown DVD isn't what you need to do right now. Maybe it's more about the process. What about a series of podcasts?"

Sully picked up his glass. "You mean like for the HCM Web site?"

"Right. Like an audio magazine subscription. People can receive them however often you upload them and listen to them at their leisure—on their iPods or whatever. You can do one a week, more if you want."

"It's not a matter of *want*. It's a matter of *can*."

"Oh, come off it, Sully." Rusty narrowed his gold-flecked brown eyes. "So you're not the all-knowing Dr. Sullivan Crisp anymore. Personally, I like you better this way—a little more scarred, a little less I-got-it-all-under-control."

"You got that right."

"Then let people see that they don't have to be at the top of their form all the time—that you struggle too." He bounced his fist lightly off Sully's shoulder. "That's what you would tell anybody who came to a Healing Choice clinic."

"I hate it when you throw my own words up in my face."

"Yeah, it stinks."

"Podcasts," Sully said. "What else ya got?"

"Nothin'."

"Is that an ultimatum?"

"I wasn't going to call it that."

Sully turned at the weight in Rusty's voice. He studied his sweet tea. "What?" he said.

"KIHS in Burbank has taken you off the air. They said as soon as you have something fresh they'll be all over it. And they're not the only ones making noises."

Sully shook his head. "Then it's not an ultimatum, Rus. It's a perfectly reasonable request. It's definitely quiet enough up here to do it."

"We were thinking you might want to record them a little closer to Nashville."

Sully's chin snapped up. "Why there?"

Rusty refilled his glass from the pitcher on the table. "This isn't just your average iced tea."

"It's sweet tea," Sully said. "It's a Southern thing. Why Nashville?"

"You remember Dr. Ukwu?"

"Our psychiatrist from Nigeria."

"He wants to open a Healing Choice clinic in Franklin, just outside Nashville. We've got him all set to get started, but it wouldn't hurt if you were around to consult."

Sully grinned. "You're throwing me some bones here, Rusty."

Rusty didn't smile back. "All I'm trying to do is get you out there where you can do some good. People's suffering goes on, Sully. You're the only one who can get through to some of them."

"I'd just like to get to myself a little more first."

"For the love of the Lord." Rusty chunked his empty glass onto the table and brought his face close. "This isn't just about you, dude."

Sully blinked.

"You've never been anything but a vessel for God anyway—none of us is. You can keep wallowing in this if you want to, but in the meantime, at least let Him use you." Rusty pulled his car keys out of his pocket. "Call me tomorrow and let me know if you're going to shut up and get out of His way."

He backed away, hand up to stop Sully from following him.

"Dang," Sully said softly.

He was going to have to get out the shovel.

CHAPTER NINE

Chip didn't come to the hospital again for the next ten days. He called every night on my cell phone, said he was keeping things together—and that he worried about me. I went cold and told him I was fine. We repeated that scene nightly until it was letter-perfect.

I cocooned myself in the world of the burn unit, which wasn't difficult. The staff told me even they had to make an effort to keep the patients—and themselves—in touch with reality. Marnie provided enough pictures of Sonia pre–plane crash to fill a museum, and helped the nurses tack them to the walls and even the ceiling. She also suggested they play Sonia's CDs in her room during the day.

I'd forgotten how rich her singing voice was. I hadn't listened to her for two years; she turned a phrase differently now, with more passion than precision. The sound of her own voice praising the Lord did seem to soothe Sonia. I hated that Marnie was the one who'd thought of it.

An oversized calendar and a clock practically the size of Big Ben hung in her room, and the nurses said constantly, "It's Tuesday, Sonia," and, "What do you know? It's suppertime!" when they hooked her up to what they affectionately called "the feed bag." Dr. Abernathy warned me that if we didn't do that, she'd lapse into delirium.

Personally, I thought Sonia was far *too* aware of her surroundings. Her eyes expressed everything her face and voice couldn't, sometimes pleading for information, sometimes sparking with frustration. If she didn't get to call the shots pretty soon, she'd rip out that tube. I told her every night how many more days until she'd be able to talk.

"Remember how Grandma Brocacini used to tell us when Christmas was coming?" I said. "Three more wake-ups. Two more wake-ups."

I just wished it was Christmas morning we were waiting for. I wasn't sure I wanted to hear what Sonia had to say about all this.

The rest of her "people" could talk of nothing else. If she could just speak to them, they said. They couldn't seem to stand being in her presence without her reassurance that they were okay. God forbid they should look at her. Francesca and Georgia finally made their tearful exit back to Nashville, and Egan, Nanette, and Ivey departed soon after.

Only Marnie remained, and for ten minutes a day, at Nurse Kim's urging, she read Sonia the cards and e-mails she received not only from the supporters of her own ministry, but also from others whose names Marnie read with the kind of awe usually connected with Oscar winners. That and the outpouring of prayer reports and financial donations to Abundant Living Ministries brought a sheen to Sonia's eyes. Egan had obviously wasted no time.

Meanwhile, I tried to avoid being in any room alone with Marnie, but with only two of us left, that wasn't easy. At least as long as she was there, I knew she wasn't off with Chip. When she fled to her hotel in the evenings, I made myself a buffet from the vending machines and stuffed it on top of my fears.

On the morning of no more wake-ups, they extubated Sonia. I held my own breath as she tried to find hers. We all expected the rasp that comes with having a tube in your airway for two weeks, but her first words were as cream-filled as they had ever been, and the Southern accent was firmly in place, albeit at half its former speed.

"Thank You, Jesus," she said. And then, "Hey, ya'll."

Marnie clutched Sonia's mummified hand and literally giggled out, "I'm so glad you're back."

For an eerie moment, I couldn't share that sentiment. As long as Sonia couldn't speak, I could pretend this injured person wasn't really her. With her voice restored, and with it the first stirrings of her personality, I couldn't pretend. I knew the voice that made you feel like you were putting on lotion just listening to her, but it came out of the face of a deformed stranger.

I pulled away from the bed, but Sonia said, "Lucia, don't go. Marnie, leave us for a minute, would you?"

"I'm going to call Egan," Marnie said, and danced away as if Sonia's face were not still bandaged over scars that even then were making inroads in her skin like a mole. As if a nasogastric tube didn't still await her next feeding. As if Sonia was, indeed, miraculously healed and all was right with their world.

When Marnie had completed her waltz out of the room, Sonia said, "How's everybody else? Tell me."

I watched her tongue try to run itself over her lips. It must have felt like two grades of sandpaper rubbing together.

"I'll see what they're giving you for dry mouth," I said.

"No." Her voice caught for the first time. "Marnie seems to be okay."

"Marnie's fine. She just had some stitches, which she was pretty proud of." I didn't mention that she'd been eager to show them off to my husband.

"She's a godly girl," Sonia said. She groped for a moment. "What about Otto?"

I glanced over my shoulder, half hoping a nurse would be there, telling me that my time was up.

"Lucia." She pulled her head from side to side. "They're giving me too much dope."

"Quit your whinin'," I said. "Some people would give their right arm to have this many drugs."

"Otto's gone, isn't he?"

"Yeah," I said softly. "He is."

"Precious Otto. He's with God."

Her voice faded and, to my relief, it took her with it. Her breathing went even; her shoulders relaxed. I was momentarily envious.

Two days after the extubation, we moved Sonia out of ICU and into what they called the rehab unit. I thought of it more as her throne room. She loved being in the middle of everything, and as she emerged from the fog from time to time, everyone else seemed to enjoy having her there.

She prayed with each nurse, med tech, and member of the house-keeping staff who came through, and she doled out her plants and flowers to the other patients because she had too many to fit in her space. She laughed with Dr. Abernathy and assured him he would witness a career miracle.

She kept Marnie bustling, answering every one of those cards and e-mails and giving her a daily report of donations and hits on the Web site. Marnie had to keep her apprised on how God was working, as if He were an ALM employee too.

I helped the day nurses as much as they would let me. They were just as efficient as the ones in ICU and even more taken by Sonia's riveting personality. While Sonia's perfection made me want to consume carbohydrates by the bucketful, they were impressed that she wanted them to cut back on the pain meds and the sleep meds at night. They couldn't get over that she wanted Marnie to hold a press conference in Lounge A, to which Nurse Kim put her foot down. Sonia was convinced that was because she didn't avail herself of Kim's counseling services.

"She doesn't get that I don't need a psychiatrist," Sonia told Marnie one day while I tucked her back into a chair after a stroll down the hall. "I imagine she's a Buddhist, don't you?"

"Probably," Marnie said, though I was sure she didn't know Buddhism from sushi. "Yeah, I bet she's just not used to people as strong in their faith as you are."

Sonia smiled. "Bless her heart. We'll have to work on her."

I wondered what our Yankee mother would have thought, hearing

Sonia use phrases like "bless her heart," which all Sonia's people seemed to feel made any statement permissible.

I could only imagine Francesca and Georgia on the flight back to Nashville, whispering in sympathetic voices, "That Lucia is so heavy, bless her heart." But then again, they had more than likely forgotten about me the minute I was out of their sight.

As for my late mother, anything Sonia did would have been more than all right with her. She would probably have started saying "bless your heart" herself.

Not long after we moved to the rehab unit, I came into Sonia's room one morning to find her pawing at the sheets with her still-bandaged hands and rocking back and forth.

"What's going on?" I said.

"It hurts."

"What does?"

"Everything."

"Have you had your pain meds yet this morning?"

She put up her hand. "I'm not taking those."

"Then that's why you hurt."

She stopped rocking and glared at me. Her eyes were like two glittering pebbles.

"For Pete's sake, Sonia," I said. "Your whole body was traumatized. You've been through hell." I refilled her water glass to give myself time to craft my next sentence. "Look, I know you're expecting God to heal you, but—"

"It isn't just that."

I could feel my eyebrows lifting. "Then what is it?"

Sonia turned her face to the window where the sun teased between the slats of the blinds. She licked at her lips.

"I don't want to get hooked," she said. "You know how dangerous painkillers can be."

Yes, and thank you for your sensitivity on the matter. I rubbed my palms over the tops of my thighs and tried to recapture my numbness on this subject.

"All right," I said. "Yes, abuse of prescription pain medication is dangerous. But the operative word is *abuse*."

"Chip abused them," she said. "And he never would have if he hadn't had that back injury."

"Chip used them for nonmedicinal reasons. That's what abuse is." Even to myself, it sounded like a lecture, but how else was I supposed to keep Chip's past from slashing at me? "Most people who take pain meds as directed never become addicted, even during long-term use."

"Most people," she said. Her eyes studied me.

"I know you aren't 'most people' on just about every level I can think of," I said. "But in this case you are. They're not going to give you more than you need."

She drilled her unblinking eyes into me. "It isn't OxyContin, is it?"

I wasn't even aware she'd known what drug had destroyed Chip. But, then, he had spent three months with her, doing her program, whatever that meant.

"No," I said. "But it wouldn't matter. As long as you don't take it to relieve anxiety or deal with stress, you don't have to worry."

"What about our family history?" she said.

"Who abused drugs in our family?"

"You know I'm talking about Tony."

Tony. Our father—who had apparently lost his paternal title.

"Alcoholism is an addiction," she said, "and addiction can be hereditary."

"What about God?"

I didn't mean to sound sarcastic. Sonia's eyes took on a superior gleam.

"You don't put the Lord your God to the test, Lucia," she said. "You don't take a ridiculous risk and expect God to keep you out of trouble. That's secular thinking. I'm sure Chip thought the fact that he was a gifted doctor would keep him from being caught."

"You're not taking a risk. You're taking care of yourself."

I stuck a straw in her water glass and pushed it at her. She shook her head.

"I pray for Tony," she said. "I haven't seen him since Mother's funeral. Have you?"

As much as I didn't want to talk about Chip's issues, I wanted to discuss my father's even less. No, I hadn't seen him since shortly after that day, the same day Sonia had told me Chip looked worse than he had the last time she'd seen him, the same day she'd asked me when I was going to wake up to the fact that he was a drug addict and get him some help.

Really? I wondered at the time. *The same kind of help she'd gotten Dad, paying for expensive Christian rehab?* While he was in there, claiming to have found Jesus, Mother died from an aneurism. Sonia grieved publicly, while I handled the cleaning out of Mother's things and the sorry state of their financial affairs, and watched helplessly as my father relapsed.

"Where did you drift off to?" Sonia said. Even when she smiled in the only twisted way she was now capable of, she looked all-knowing.

"I'm going to tell the nurses you need more pain meds," I said, and left her there with her wisdom.

I'd barely delivered that message when Nurse Kim appeared with Special Agent Deidre Schmacker in tow. She wore a deep magenta jacket this time, though she had on the same heavy silver earrings and the same grandmotherly look of concern.

"I told her she could have ten minutes with Mrs. Cabot," Kim said pointedly to me, "if you will stay in the room."

"Are you prepared for what you're going to see?" I said as I led the agent from the lounge.

"Unfortunately, I've interviewed burn victims before," she said. "I'll be careful with her."

I wasn't worried about Sonia's reaction. I was worried about hers. Since the wounds had closed, they'd switched Sonia from bandages to a clear plastic pressurized mask that molded to her face. As masks went, it was fairly hideous—only the grotesqueness came from inside it. The first time Marnie saw her in it, I watched her turn the color of cream of wheat. I hated to admit that she recovered quickly. I'd have liked to have been able to tell Chip that his lover ran screaming from the room.

Sonia was in a chair, wrapped in a sage green silk robe Marnie had procured for her that made her look, from the neck down, like Marlene Dietrich in a film noir production. If Sonia's appearance from the neck up bothered Deidre Schmacker, she, too, covered well.

"This is Special Agent Schmacker," I said. "She's from the FBI, and she needs to ask you some questions about the crash. It's just routine."

"Oh," Sonia said. "Well, I feel like I'm on *Law and Order*. Or is it *Without a Trace*?"

"Hopefully neither," Agent Schmacker said. "We try not to be quite that dramatic."

Good. We had enough drama here. I was having trouble keeping my anxiety stuffed at the moment.

The agent accepted Sonia's outstretched, gauze-swaddled hand. "First of all, it's a pleasure to meet you, Mrs. Cabot."

"Please—it's Sonia. And what should I call you?"

The woman looked nonplussed. Obviously few of the people she interviewed cared to call her anything. Chip had referred to her as Agent Schmuck.

"Agent Schmacker is fine," she said. "Or just Deidre."

"I love that. Is it German?"

I rolled my eyes.

"It is." She opened a folder on the rolling tray. "I'm going to try not to take too much of your time. I know you need rest."

"I've had nothing but rest. This is a nice change." Sonia looked at me, her stare more disconcerting than ever from the poke holes of the mask. "Lucia, could you get Deidre something to drink?"

No, I wanted to say. *She travels with her own tea. Let's get this over with.*

"I'm good," Agent Schmacker said. "I need for you to tell me as best you remember exactly what happened the day of the crash, beginning from the time the plane left Nashville. You can stop and rest whenever you need to."

"I'm sure my sister will see to that," she said.

I felt like Nurse Ratched. I leaned into the corner, arms folded.

"So, you left Nashville International . . ."

"At one o'clock in the afternoon."

"Anything odd about the takeoff? Any noises that didn't seem familiar to you?"

Sonia tilted her head. "You think there was something wrong with the plane? They were supposed to service it."

"We just have to make sure we have all the bases covered."

"No funny noises," Sonia said. "Otto kept telling us all systems were go. He always liked to say that."

Her voice cut out, which didn't escape Schmacker. She let her eyes droop at the corners. "Did you know Mr. Underwood personally?"

"I kept him on retainer. He was forced to retire early from the airlines, which broke his heart because he loved to fly those commercial jets, but to me it was God's doing. He was the perfect pilot for my ministry. He would pray with us before every flight—except when we took off from Philadelphia. We were in a hurry."

Her voice broke again.

"You want to stop, Sonia?" I said.

"No." She sat up straighter, smoothed the sash on the robe. "I know Otto's with the Lord. He died doing His work."

"You may not remember much—people often don't," Schmacker said, "but what can you tell me about what happened from the time the engines started for your departure from Northeast?"

"You've done this before," Sonia said.

The agent almost smiled. "How can you tell?"

"Because you're right—I hardly remember anything. I said goodbye to Chip and Lucia. Otto told us to fasten our seat belts. Marnie was up in front and I was in the back, and I said something to her and she said she couldn't hear me, and the next thing I knew, my face . . ." Her hand went to the mask as if she'd just discovered it. "That's all I remember until Lucia was with me on the ground. I don't know how I got there."

She was as composed as I had ever seen her.

I, on the other hand, was shredding a tissue I didn't even recall picking up. I hadn't allowed myself to imagine what it must have been like for her. Now I had it in my mind, where it could attack me at any time. That had to be stuffed, too, onto the ever-growing compost pile in my chest.

"Nothing beyond that?" Deidre Schmacker said.

"That's it."

The agent tapped her pen on the pad. "Mrs. Cabot, as I'm sure you've gathered, we're not at all sure your crash was an accident. We're trying to rule out foul play."

"Let me save you the trouble," Sonia said. Her voice remained as warm and creamy as chocolate sauce, and her arms still hung, relaxed, over the arms of the chair. "No one wanted to hurt me, and if they did, they've failed."

"Have they?"

"This is about what God wants, and what He wants is for people to have a chance to see God's power at work. I'm going to be completely healed."

"I'm sure you are. You're in the best burn facility in the Northeast."

"But it's God who is going to do the healing, Deidre. The miracle is already taking place. No one expected me to be able to speak this clearly, and yet I'm having a fluent conversation with you."

Yes, unfortunately. I wiped my upper lip with the back of my hand.

"The wounds have closed. I've already graduated to this glamour mask. I'm going home in a matter of days, when people in my condition are normally here for months."

If Deidre Schmacker said anything, I didn't hear it. My own

thoughts were screaming in my head. She's going *home*? I didn't know which part of this monologue was the most ludicrous.

"It's God, Deidre. That's what we're seeing. I'm getting great care here—that's part of it. But this is about faith. I put my trust in the Lord. 'In your presence there is fullness of joy, and in your right hand are pleasures for evermore.'"

Deidre Schmacker didn't say anything. She definitely wasn't taking notes on what I assumed was a biblical quote.

"So no more questions about the crash," Sonia said. "In fact, just stop your investigation altogether, because it's pointless."

Sonia settled further into the chair as if she'd just succeeded in sending Special Agent Schmacker back to FBI headquarters with her marching orders.

Schmacker didn't move except to tilt her head back to look at Sonia. I hadn't noticed the color of her eyes before. They were a clear gray with a liquid quality. I couldn't read them, but I could feel them reading Sonia.

"I wish it were that easy, Sonia," she said.

"Isn't it?"

"Not under the circumstances. I am not quarreling with the possibility that you will have a miracle healing. I've seen stranger things happen. But as far as the investigation goes, I can't stop that. And in fact, I'm going to need your help."

Sonia shrugged gracefully. "I've told you everything."

"We've barely begun to scratch the surface. I need to know about your relationships with everyone on that plane and with everyone on your staff. I have to pick your brain about all of the events leading up to your trip. And I am asking you to think and think hard about anyone who might want to hurt you. Any hate letters you might have received."

"There is none of that," Sonia said. "I only have one more thing to say, and that is that I'll be praying for you. My whole ministry will. It has to be hard to hear all these stories and not become suspicious of everyone."

Deidre Schmacker's voice didn't change either. "I'm doing my job, which is to investigate a plane crash in which a pilot with no previous history of illness just happened to die from unknown causes and drop a plane that just happened to explode on impact for no apparent reason." She pressed her palms on the tray. "There were explosives on your plane, Mrs. Cabot. I need you to help me find out who put them there."

I wanted to hurl myself from the room and lose everything I'd packed inside myself, because I couldn't take this one more rotten piece of information. But I looked at Sonia instead, and saw as stubborn an expression in her body as she could ever have accomplished on her face.

"I'm so sorry," Sonia said. "It's a hideous job that you have to do, but I can't help you. I have to focus on what God's doing in this."

Deidre Schmacker closed her portfolio and tucked it neatly under her arm. "It's a lot to take in," she said. "I'll be back when you've had a chance to process it."

"It will be a waste of your time," Sonia said.

The liquid gray eyes went steely. "I'll be back," she said.

I barely waited for the door to close before I was on Sonia. If I didn't say this now, it was going to get crammed in with everything else.

"Sonia, I don't think you can—"

"I can do whatever God wills, Lucia." The cream in her voice curdled. "Would you please get Marnie? And tell her to get Egan on the line before she gets here—and find Dr. Abernathy for me."

"Why?" I said. "Why Dr. Abernathy?"

"Because I have to get back to Nashville before this thing gets out of control."

She was too late. It already was.

CHAPTER TEN

Sully lowered himself onto one of the red and gold chintz love seats in Porphyria's sitting room and pulled out his cell phone. Too bad he'd already keyed the number into his contacts. Also too bad he'd charged the battery and had good reception in the lodge for once. Too bad he'd run out of excuses not to call Sonia Cabot.

Holy crow. At one time confidence had shimmered out of his pores like sweat. Even three and four months ago, when he'd been fighting off freaking out, he could've still made a phone call to an old friend.

Besides, if Sonia still held on to her faith statement, she would just be eager to tell him how God was blessing her with a miracle. That would be the end of it.

He grunted to the empty room. The miracle would be if she wasn't shaking her fist at heaven and denouncing every praise-word she'd ever sung or spoken from a platform. Anger at God would be healthy, but it would also mean she'd need somebody to guide her through.

Sully flipped the phone open. Well, there you go. He'd tell her he knew how much she must hurt, and he'd offer to set her up with one of his best therapists. Or even Dr. Ukwu.

Feeling the kind of relief usually reserved for post dental work, he pulled up the number for Sonia's room at Crozer Medical Center and pressed Send. If every step back into the real world was this hard, he might not get there for years. Decades.

Though he wasn't sure Sonia would still have the luscious voice that reminded him of whipped cream, the one that said hello was flatter and colder than he expected. He felt his hopes wobble.

"Sonia," he said. "Sullivan Crisp."

"This isn't Sonia," the woman said. "Who did you say this was?"

"Sullivan Crisp."

"Oh." The voice gave in slightly. "She's talking to her doctor at the moment. I can have her call you back."

She bordered on brusque, which wasn't like anybody Sully knew on Sonia's staff. They were all so schooled in Southern hospitality they practically offered you a mint julep over the phone. He couldn't resist asking, "And who am I talking to?"

"Lucia Coffey," the woman said. "I can just give her a message—wait."

There was some murmuring and receiver shifting, and then fragrant oils were suddenly being poured on his head in the form of Sonia Cabot's voice.

"Sully Crisp," she said.

Sully felt himself grin. "When you produce an audition video for *Survivor*, you don't mess around, do you?"

Sonia laughed, a sound as delicious as her words. "When they create a show called *Thriver*, I *will* audition for that."

"I can tell this hasn't slowed you down much," Sully said. "You're still running everything."

"Why don't you come up here and tell that to everybody else? I can't convince these people I am ready to rock and roll." She laughed again. "No, don't. I'm coming back to Nashville anyway. Now, where are you? I haven't heard anything about you in forever."

"Taking a little hiatus," Sully said. "But I may be headed for Nashville myself."

"I love that! Come for lunch—no, dinner—no, spend a weekend. You know my guesthouse is always open."

She'd made that offer every time he'd seen her over the last five years. He could almost recite it word for word, and yet somehow it sounded different now—rehearsed. He'd never sensed that about

her before. Dang. He'd been just about to go with the miracle
theory that would let him off his own hook.

"I might take you up on that," he said. "Could you use a friend?"

She laughed softly again. "I know what you're doing, Sully, bless
your heart, but I'm good. God is going to use me in some amazing
way through this. I can't wait to get in front of my audience again
and share this."

Sully tried not to stumble over his tongue. He'd just read in an
e-mail from Rusty that her entire face, head, and neck were burned.
They must have made great strides in plastic surgery. Either that, or
Sonia Cabot was in some serious denial.

"You know what you can do, Sully," she said.

"What's that?"

"You can pray."

"I've already been on it."

"I want you to pray specifically. I want you to ask the Lord to
take the fear out of my staff's hearts so they'll stop trying to protect
me and get on with the work we've been given to do. Will you do
that for me?"

Sonia's propensity to turn a prayer into a homily was one of the
many ways her ministry differed from his, and Sully toyed with the
possible answers like a Rubik's cube. *No, Sonia, because they have
every reason to be afraid. No, Sonia, I'm not in the habit of giving God
instructions. No, Sonia, I think you* need *to be protected until you deal
with what's happened to you.*

"Tell you what," he said. "I'll talk that over with God and get
back to you."

"I can't wait to hear what He tells you." She sighed into the
phone. "Sully, I really appreciate your call. Will you promise to
come see me?"

"Absolutely."

One more item on the growing list of reasons to go to Nashville.
Take a list of possible therapists to Sonia. Be there for Dr. Ukwu.
Record some podcasts on God knew what.

Which was exactly the point. God did know what. And Sully knew where He might be willing to tell him.

A mere twenty-four hours after Agent Schmacker's visit, I was going to Sonia's room to take her to physical therapy and ran into Marnie—who was doing a stiff-legged fast walk down the hall with the I-have-to-get-this-done-for-Sonia lines carved between her eyebrows.

"I have to reschedule her appointment with PT," she said over her shoulder.

"What's wrong?"

"Nothing—she's having her board meeting in Lounge A."

"Her *what*?"

"I'm supposed to tell you to get in there—she wants you to talk to them."

Before I could tell her she was delusional, Marnie took off again, this time at a dead run. I yearned to escape with her. Just being in the same room with those people again was more than I could stomach. I would probably vomit if I had to actually talk to them.

I might have bypassed the meeting altogether if I hadn't heard Sonia's voice wending its way out of its usual creaminess and into a precipitously high place. I sucked in my gut and followed it.

Only because I had the worst luck possible did Sonia have her back to the door, while the board faced her—and me. I couldn't remember anyone's name except Egan's, but the other two members were there, as well as a redheaded woman I hadn't met before. Every face was ashen as Sonia sat before them in her silk robe and her now less-than-commanding posture. They had obviously realized that no miracle had yet occurred. I might have felt sorry for them if I hadn't warned them weeks ago.

"Come on in, Lucia," Sonia said. She must have smelled my presence.

As I edged inside, I saw Egan breathing so hard I could have driven a Buick into his nostrils.

"Tell my friends and supporters what kind of progress I'm making," Sonia said.

I didn't move. Didn't bring my dumpy self before this audience of slimness and righteousness. Bad enough they were all staring at me as I stood behind Sonia. I wouldn't give them a full frontal to judge.

Sonia waved her arm irritably. "Come on, Lucia. Tell them."

"You're making progress," I said to the floor.

"No, tell *them*."

The redhead nodded like a dashboard ornament. The rest still looked as if they'd just had electric shock therapy administered.

"Lucia." Sonia snagged at my sleeve.

If I didn't move forward, I would look even more conspicuous. I had on a black sweater Chip had brought me, and I crossed it over my chest as I stepped up to stand beside her.

"She's right on schedule," I said to the wall above their heads. "Everything is going the way it's supposed to."

"We get that." Egan leaned over the lid of his computer and looked at Sonia, yet not quite at her. "And Sonia, we're willing to hang in there with you until you're back . . . in shape."

"That's right." A woman in large hoop earrings poured out her words like molasses. "Honey, we aren't saying we're not behind you, but the idea of going out now and speaking—this way—that's not fair to you."

"Who ever promised fair? The only fair is where pigs win ribbons." Sonia poured molasses back at her, giving *fair* more than its share of syllables. "This is not about me—this is about what people need, and they need to participate in this miracle of healing with me."

"Amen," the redhead said.

No one else joined her. Nor did anyone else appear to have the intestinal fortitude, as Chip always called it, to say what they were all thinking.

Sonia drew herself up further. "So what you're saying is that you won't support me if I go out and speak like this." She pointed to her face.

"We're saying you should wait," Egan said.

"And I'm saying God doesn't want me to wait. I'm not afraid."

"Well, I'm afraid for you," a queenly middle-aged woman said. Her hands shook as she pulled a large jeweled ring on and off her finger. "People don't want to see you suffering, Sonia. They love you too much."

"And I'm here to tell you," Egan said, "the ones who do come will be curiosity seekers just wanting to rubberneck."

Sonia stood up abruptly and rocked on her feet. I reached out a hand to steady her, but she knocked me away. I swayed off kilter, and my hip collided with the table. For an instant the attention shifted, en masse, from Sonia to me. We cut such a pathetic pair that I would have laughed, if the Middle-aged Queen had not curled her lip and Earrings hadn't completely looked away.

Sonia seemed to miss the whole thing. "You all disappoint me," she said. "But I'm going to show some grace here."

She pulled her hands together at her chest, just inches beneath the chin that had slowly buried itself in scar tissue. "I will pray about this. We should all pray. And then we'll come back together when I get back to Nashville."

I saw relief in Egan's eyes. "Which will be in, what, two or three months?"

"I plan to leave here within the week," Sonia said.

I caught my mouth before it fell open.

Egan looked at me. "Do you agree?"

"Lucia will be right there with me," Sonia said.

I froze.

"You're not serious." Again Egan turned to me. "Do you think that's wise?"

"I think it's God," Sonia said. "In fact, I know it is." She twisted her torso around to look behind us and then leaned forward as if she were about to reveal a conspiracy. "They don't get it here—what we're about and what God is about. I can't stay here with the Holy Spirit of healing being thwarted at every turn."

"You absolutely cannot." That came from the redhead. She let a pair of too-green eyes fill with tears. "Let's get you home where you can heal. Your next event is scheduled for when?"

Egan gave her an exasperated look. "Roxanne, you're not even on the board."

"She does more to promote this ministry than anyone who is," Sonia said. "I want to hear what she has to say."

Roxanne dabbed at the corners of her eyes and shook her head. "No, I want to hear what Lucia has to say."

Egan let out a long, hissy breath. The Middle-aged Queen exchanged disgusted looks with Earrings. I jerked at the sweater, but it wouldn't close me off any further.

"Lucia is a medical professional," Roxanne said, "and she cares about Sonia. If she thinks she's ready to go home—if she thinks she's already making miraculous progress—then we have to pay attention to that."

There was my chance to stop this whole ridiculous plan, to tell these people I thought they were heinous hypocrites, to get out from under my sister's craziness and run back into myself.

But with their eyes on me, barely concealing their contempt, I could feel the fat rolling at their feet. I couldn't even open my mouth.

"This is not Lucia's decision," Sonia said. "It's mine—mine and God's." She swept the silk robe across the floor behind her as she turned to the door. "But Lucia will be with me. I hope I can count on the rest of you as well."

With one more awkward swish she made her exit, leaving behind mouths ready to share their horror as soon as she was out of ear-shot. I started after her, only to be blocked by the redhead.

"You are just an angel from heaven," she said in a voice intended only for us. "I'm Roxanne Clemm. It's going to be up to you and me and Marnie to hold fast until the rest of those people understand what God is doing here."

I just gaped into her green eyes. I didn't understand what God was doing, but I did understand what my sister was doing. She'd blindsided me. Made a decision for me in front of people who already thought I was inferior goods—where she knew I wouldn't stand a chance against myself.

"I think I better see about Sonia," I said.

"You are so devoted to her."

Devotion to my sister had nothing to do with it. I wasn't going to let her do what she'd done to me before, over and over. I was going to her room to tell her I absolutely would not travel away from what little life I had left, to put hers back together.

But I couldn't go yet. I was shaking inside like the proverbial bowlful of jelly, and that was no state to be in when I confronted my sister. My only hope lay in the vending machines, with their selection of comforters and courage boosters I'd been depending on for weeks.

I'd only purchased a Hershey bar when a scream penetrated straight through the walls. A scream that could only have come from a terrified six-year-old girl.

CHAPTER ELEVEN

Personnel I'd never seen before erupted from back halls and storage closets. I burst through all of them, shoved someone aside to get to Sonia's room, and plowed into Roxanne. She struggled, elbows flailing like an NBA forward, as she attempted to control the screaming mass in front of her.

"Bethany," she said between her teeth. "Listen to me. Honey, it's all right."

How could there have been anything "all right" about the scarlet face and the pumping fists and the crazed eyes that looked as if they had finally seen the monster they'd imagined—and found it worse than anything they'd conjured up?

"Bethany, stop!" Roxanne cried.

"Uh—you need to get this child out of here, now," someone else said.

Other voices poked in: "What is going on?" "Other patients are getting upset."

Sonia's voice rose from her chair above the others. "Lucia, can you do something?"

The room was reduced to silence. Even the screaming little girl fell into soundless sobbing, though she still tried to wrestle herself out of Roxanne's grasp. I felt all eyes on me as I leaned over and put my face close to hers.

"You're done here, aren't you?" I said.

She bobbed her head and looked up at me, although I knew she didn't see me. Amid the blotches on her chubby cheeks, the blue eyes peered out from an abject fear that would erupt again if she dared open that shivering little mouth.

I looked at Sonia, bent in the chair, hands outstretched but useless as she stared at her daughter. Real fear came through the holes in her mask.

"Do you want me to take her out?" I mouthed.

She barely nodded.

"Come on," I said to my niece. "Let's find a better place."

I didn't reach for the still rock-tight fist, but she followed me through the maze of bodies, still crying noiselessly except for the distressed huff of her breathing.

I kept making turns until I reached an exterior door and pushed through it, releasing us into a blast of heat and light. I hadn't seen the sun for days, and I blinked as I waited for Bethany to creep through the door and join me. We were in a fountain courtyard where cherubs splashed happily, as if the world on the other side of that door were not inhabited by suffering humanity and the people who strove against the odds to take care of them. This little girl certainly shouldn't be one of them.

"How 'bout that seat over there?" I said, pointing to a park bench just out of spitting reach of the cherubs.

She nodded, still hiccupping, and followed me once again. When I sat down, she hiked herself up, one bottom cheek at a time. She was something of a cherub herself. I hadn't seen my niece since age two, at an event Sonia had done in Philadelphia in 2005. I'd never experienced my sister on stage before, and I was so overwhelmed that I didn't connect with Bethany during the hour I did see her—an hour filled with offstage drama.

We had dinner that night after Sonia's evening address—my parents, Sonia, Bethany, Chip, and me. Sonia took one look at my newly expanded size and drew an immediate conclusion with her eyes.

When Chip excused himself to go to the restroom between the salad and the main course, Sonia announced that she could see Chip had a drug problem and that in my heart I probably knew it too, which accounted for my gaining "so much weight." Dad called her crazy, to which she replied that naturally he would defend Chip because he himself was an alcoholic. Dad vowed never to speak to her again. Mother fell into a black silence. I went home numb.

There hadn't been much opportunity to bond with my niece on that occasion.

I swept my gaze over Bethany now as she sat, motionless as the concrete figures in the water that she gazed at. She had the Brocacini thick, dark hair, which hung in limp ropes down her back. The bangs stuck out over her brows like a Yorkshire terrier's, as if someone had chopped them off when they noticed her round, blue eyes were being concealed.

She wore a baggy beige T-shirt over beige-and-beiger leggings, whose narrow stripes widened at her calves and knees and were mercifully hidden above that. Pudgy heels peeked from cream-colored Crocs, which now hung motionless from the bench.

We sat through a few more splashes from the fountain, and then she opened her little red bow of a mouth and said, "Can we stay for a while? I like it better here."

I forced myself not to smile at the Tennessee drawl, a miniature version of what I'd been hearing from the Southern contingent. *Kin* for *can. Heah* for *here.* Only she made it sound natural.

"We absolutely can," I said.

Her body language didn't change, and yet I felt some of the tension leave her. I reached into my pocket and pulled out a Hershey bar. I unwrapped it, broke it in two, and held out half.

"Wanna share?"

"Yes, ma'am," she said—and snatched the candy out of my hand. She devoured it before I even bit into mine.

"Chocolate makes things better," I said.

She didn't answer. We sat some more and watched the cherubs play in all their stillness for a long time.

Finally another thin woman, younger than everyone except Marnie, stepped out of the building. She had hair redder than

Roxanne's and skin so pale I could almost see the sun burning her as she came toward us.

"Hi I'm Yvonne I'm the nanny I'm taking Bethany back to the hotel."

She said it all without punctuation, and without a glance at Bethany. I thought the child stopped breathing.

I'm Lucia I'm the aunt and you aren't taking her anywhere, I wanted to say. But Bethany slid off the bench and stood stiffly.

"They said for me to take you to see the Liberty Bell or something," Yvonne said to her.

"It's a little hot for that," I said. "The lines will be long."

The nanny looked relieved. "Okay, then I guess it's TV in the hotel. I know you won't go in the pool."

Bethany's head jerked up.

"Okay, okay, forget I said that." Yvonne jerked her own head toward the door. "We'll go to McDonald's and get a Happy Meal. How's that?"

"And then we're going home?"

It was the first hopeful sound I'd heard chirp from her mouth, and even at that it was more like a plea.

"First thing tomorrow morning. You blew the surprise for your mom, so you'll have to wait till she gets home to talk to her."

I wanted to slap her. Bethany just let out a long sigh and dutifully trailed Yvonne to the door. Once there, she stopped and looked back at me.

"Are you ever coming to my house?" she said.

Before I could answer, she dropped her chin to her chest and disappeared through the doorway with Nightmare Nanny. It was as if I were watching myself go.

Bethany would not be absorbed into the compost heap in my chest. No amount of chocolate could erase the frightened cherub's face that tore at me from the top of the pile. As soon as every scrap of Abundant Living had blown out, I marched into my sister's room.

Sonia sat straight up on the bed, eyes on the door as if she'd summoned me. Before I got two steps in, she had the floor.

"They shouldn't have brought her here," she said.

"Ya think?"

She stretched up another inch. "I had no idea she was coming. I still don't know who's responsible, but I will see that—"

"What difference does it make whose fault it is?" I planted my hands on the footboard. "Bethany needs—"

"I know." The in-charge edge softened. "She didn't need to see this yet. But it's you I'm concerned about."

I blinked at her as she tried to crane her neck toward me.

"Will I, *sorella*?"

"Will you what?"

"Will I have you in Nashville?"

I let go of the bed and crossed my arms.

"Is that a no, you won't come?" she said.

"It's a 'gee, sis, you could have asked me first.'"

Sonia had the gall to look surprised. "I thought we talked about it."

"No, we didn't."

"Okay, that's it." She glared at the empty pill cup on the table. "No more pain medication. It's messing with my brain. I really thought I'd spoken to you about it." She let out a long breath. "Look, Lucia, you've held up better than anybody else, and they all went to a hotel at night. You haven't even left the hospital."

I opened my mouth, but she went on as if she were on one of her platforms.

"You can also tell me who I've talked to in the last twenty-four hours, in fifteen-minute increments—which my precious Marnie cannot do because she's completely stressed-out."

She stopped to lick her lips. I didn't go for the ice water.

"Besides all that, I know you and Chip have things to work out."

I got still. She slanted her body forward.

"Don't think I haven't noticed he's not around here, supporting you—and that isn't all because it's too hard for him to be in a medical environment anymore."

"I didn't come in here to talk about him," I said.

"He's benefited from our recovery program, Lucia, and I know the two of you would do great with our Recapture Your Marriage course. I'd give you plenty of time to work on that together."

She groped for my hand with her gauzy one. I let it hang between us.

"You're saying bring Chip with me?"

"Of course. I wouldn't ask you to leave your husband here." She pulled the hand away and folded it across her chest. "I wanted you to come to Nashville with him in the first place, if you'll recall."

"I thought he didn't work for you anymore," I said, voice stiff.

"That was his choice. He can come back if he wants. Same salary. I'll pay you both well."

Good. He could go back to working for Sonia and have his little thing with Marnie right under my nose.

I jammed my hands into my pockets. Why was I even thinking like this? No way I'd go.

"You can work on other things too," Sonia said. "I bet you haven't even looked at the materials I sent you on weight loss."

My neck jerked. *Faithless and Fat*, wasn't it? I'd gotten as far as the introduction that told me I needed to be delivered from the sin I literally wore on my body. The implication, barely buried between the lines: fat people don't go to heaven.

I'd forgotten which trash can I'd dropped it into.

Sonia leaned further toward me. Her eyes, even trapped as they were, took on the condescending sag that made my hackles stand up.

"You're not working right now anyway," she said, "and quite frankly, I think it's time you trusted God to heal your grief so you can serve again. You have a gift for taking care of people that comes straight from Him, and you have an obligation to use it."

My stomach wadded up. "I'm not grieving."

"But you can't bring yourself to go back into a hospital nursery, can you?"

I snatched up the water pitcher from her tray table and hurtled myself toward the bathroom.

"You obviously did something to calm Bethany down when you took her out of here."

I froze in the doorway.

"You always loved her. She needs you."

My fingers cramped around the handle.

"This is too much for a little girl," she said.

I turned back to the tray and slammed the pitcher onto it. "They brought her here to surprise you. Obviously nobody prepared her for the surprise *she* was in store for."

She caught my hand under hers this time. "This is exactly what I'm talking about. You really knew Bethany before I did. I think you're the only one who can walk her through this."

Don't. Don't you even use this on me.

"I know it's asking a lot," Sonia said, "but nobody can give her what she needs right now except you. This is God's will."

Curse you, Sonia Cabot.

"I've started a conversation with the admin office," said a too-cheerful voice in the doorway. "The social worker will be in tomorrow."

I had never before been happy to see Marnie. I half-ran to the restroom down the hall and hid in a stall. Not even bothering to sit down on the toilet, I pressed my forehead against the cold metal and imagined myself saying no to Sonia.

No, I can't pack up and leave my house for three months.

No, I can't take my husband back to Nashville where he can be with his lover.

No, I can't keep track of your meds and your appointments while some twenty-year-old fawns over him and I read about how faithless and fat I am.

No, I can't dump everything to do your bidding. Again. I can't. I won't.

But my imagination wasn't up for it. I only saw that little cherub face, heard that fragile voice saying, "Are you ever coming to my house?"

"Yeah, Bethany," I whispered. "I guess I am."

CHAPTER TWELVE

As the cab drove me home to Havertown on Sunday, I wondered how the life I'd left there could possibly have gone on. Why were cars still pulling into the drive-through grocery at the Swiss Farm just as they always had? Why were people still standing in line at Rita's Water Ice as they were on every sweltering summer day?

I let my head fall against the window. Why shouldn't they? Gut-wrenching things had happened to my family, but I hadn't changed at all. If I had, I wouldn't be dropping everything to keep Sonia's life afloat again.

Actually, my mother did the asking the first time. How, she'd wanted to know, could I *not* abandon my nurse practitioner studies at the University of Pennsylvania and move to Hershey and take care of that baby while Sonia kept a vigil beside her husband? I could always go back to it, Mother said. Blake could never go back to a normal life—think about that, she said.

Of course I thought about that. Sonia and Blake had been married only a few months when she called to tell me she was pregnant. That night I ate an entire package of Oreo cookies and threw them all up. I had never hated my sister in all the years I'd taken my place outside her spotlight, but I despised her then. She was starting the family I dreamed of.

I had given up my childhood so she could star in life, and now she was stealing the one thing I could do. I'd never known her to give a flip about kids, and I vowed I wasn't going to go to a half dozen baby showers or be her Lamaze coach or whatever else was asked of me. I dug into my nurse practitioner program and felt my mother's anger and my sister's disappointment and thought of myself for a change.

Just six weeks before Bethany was born, Blake suffered a spinal injury in a snow skiing accident in Vermont. While Sonia gave birth on January 1, 2003, Blake lay in a coma at a Montpelier hospital three hundred miles away.

To say that I almost suffocated in guilt was an understatement. On January 8, I left the NP program, put my career in obstetric nursing on hold, and moved to Hershey into the restored Victorian that Blake's parents had given them as a wedding present. That afternoon, before my mother and sister left to fly to Blake's bedside, Sonia put her newborn in my arms and said, "Take care of her, *sorella*. I don't trust anyone else."

Within a week I was completely in love with that baby girl. I lived for the contented murmurs she made during her feedings . . . for the warmth of her cheek next to mine when I rocked her back to sleep at 2:00 AM . . . for the tiny smiles, at first tentative, then purposeful, as if she, too, were living for smiles, my smiles.

Sonia was afraid to come home, afraid Blake would wake up in her absence. Mother was afraid to leave Sonia, who, she said, was like a piece of fragile glass at her husband's side. So it was just me caring for Bethany for the three months before Blake died, and for two more while my sister nearly suffocated in her grief and my mother became her air supply. I almost died of a broken heart myself when Sonia said she was finally ready to take over parenting the baby, the tiny girl I considered mine.

Sonia said Bethany cried a lot after I went back to Philadelphia. So did I.

The cabbie pulled into my driveway and looked over his shoulder at me. "This it?" he said.

One way or another, yes, this was it.

Chip's Saab wasn't there. The yard was mowed, the boxwoods trimmed, the mailbox empty. Chip had said he'd take care of things. My mind leapt to the conclusion that he'd done it all to get affairs in order before he left me for good . . .

Lucia Marie.

Okay. No. I wouldn't mention the Marnie thing.

In the dining room the mail was arranged in tidy piles on the table, and the morning sun splashed cheerily onto the Oriental rug. The fringe looked combed.

I finally made it to the kitchen and set my purse on the counter next to a pad filled with jottings in Chip's unreadable handwriting. He might not be a doctor anymore, but he still wrote like one.

On a piece of paper next to the pad, something was written in my cursive.

✓ paint bathroom
✓ put last layer on torte
✓ redo makeup
✓ call modeling agency—say NO
✓ shave legs
  tell Sonia I want my husband back

The list I'd made the day of the crash. It had been smoothed out and weighted down at each corner with a coaster, as if someone had tried to preserve the normal life I couldn't return to.

"What modeling agency?"

I jumped. Chip was suddenly beside me, smelling of musk and spearmint.

"I'm sorry, babe," Chip said. "I didn't mean to scare you."

I shook that away. "I didn't know you were home," I said.

"I didn't know you were *coming* home."

I picked up a sponge and went after the counter. "Where's your car?"

"Loaned it to a buddy of mine."

Since when did Chip have "buddies"?

He took the sponge from me and held my face in his hands. "Babe, why didn't you tell me? I would have come to get you."

"I didn't know myself."

"So how long are you here for?"

I felt color flood my face.

"I guess we're even," he said. "I didn't tell you I quit working for Sonia. You didn't tell me you were starting."

I folded my arms awkwardly. "How did you know?"

"Marnie told me. She thought you'd already said something to me, so I didn't act surprised. I didn't want to make her feel bad."

My chest began to tear. "You've been talking to Marnie?"

He shrugged. "I still care about those people, some of them. I wanted to keep up."

Don't go there. Don't get into this. But I said, "When did you see Marnie?"

My voice shook, and I hated it—hated everything about my fat, pathetic self at the moment, but I couldn't stop.

"Did she come here?" I said.

"Here? No. Babe, what are you talking about?"

"Don't play stupid with me!"

Dear God, don't let me do this.

I headed for the living room and tried to press it back down. When I threw myself into my overstuffed paisley chair, Chip was over me, face taut.

"It's not what you think with Marnie," he said. "And no, she didn't come here. I went there."

"To her hotel?"

"No! I met her in the cafeteria at the hospital when I brought your clothes. We talked on the phone until the day the board met. She was so upset, I went over there and bought her a cup of coffee."

"That sure sounds like what I think. When I see you with her, it looks like what I think. When you talk to her it sounds like what I think."

"It isn't."

"Then what is it?"

I didn't want to hear his answer. But the tiny rip in my container of rancid stuff let it spurt out. *Dear God, make me stop this.* I wanted my blessed numbness back.

"What? Lucia, *what?*" Chip said. "Talk to me."

I dug my fingernails into the arms of the chair.

"Can you even answer a yes-or-no question?" He leaned over and pressed his hands onto mine, penning me in. "Just tell me—do you want us to work out, or don't you?"

I turned my face away from him. "Do you?"

"That's what I came back here for. That's all I thought about the whole time in Nashville."

"Really?" I said. "What about Marnie?"

"Would you forget that!"

I tried to heave myself out of the chair, but he pushed me back. I looked up at him, stunned, heart slamming.

"I said it's not what you think with Marnie. It's not even worth going there. Let's talk about the real issue—which is that Sonia wants you to become her twenty-four-hour nurse because she's leaving here AMA."

"She doesn't trust anybody else."

He hissed. "She can't push anybody else around."

"Don't."

"You're going to end up like everybody else that works for her."

"I'm her sister."

"Is she going to pay you?"

"Yes."

Chip looked down at me as if I were pitiful.

"Let me up," I said.

I struggled to get to my feet and wrenched away when he went for my arm. He followed me into the kitchen, where I hurled open the refrigerator door and pulled out cheese and black olives.

"What are you doing?" he said.

"I'm cooking."

"You're cooking."

"Mexican casserole." I got the freezer open and snatched up a package of chicken breasts.

"Lucia, stop."

I slammed the chicken onto the counter and let my hand freeze to it.

"If you won't talk, then just listen."

"Fine," I said. "You talk."

He stuck his hands in his pockets, and with them went the anger and the hardness and the rest of what had become unrecognizable to me. I steeled myself against the old Chip that took its place.

"The one thing I did do for myself in Nashville was think," he said. "About us and how strong our relationship is."

Please. I dropped the package into the sink, but he put his hand over mine before I could turn the water on.

"Just hear me out. You waited for me when I was at Bradford. You understood when I took the job with Sonia because she was the only one who would hire me. You even sounded happy that I was coming home, when I hadn't called you for a month—like you knew I needed space. That's a strong bond, Lucia."

I went for the chicken again, but he grabbed my shoulders and jerked me to face him.

"Just take Sonia to Nashville, get her settled in, and come back. I'll be here."

I turned back to the sink, but I couldn't think of anything to do.

"Sonia wants you to come too," I said. "She says you can have your old job back. She said we can work on our relationship there."

Chip hissed through his teeth. "When you work for Sonia, you don't work on anything else, trust me."

"That's not what she said."

"She said what she wanted you to hear." Chip shrugged. "It's beside the point anyway. In the first place, if I move back in there,

I'm going to have the state medical board looking over my shoulder every minute, making sure I'm not practicing."

"Did they do that before?"

"They paid me one visit, but now she's turning the place into her own personal hospital. They'll be breathing down my neck." He jerked his head. "And what am I going to do for her, anyway? She can't think she's going to continue her ministry now."

"Yeah, she does." I rolled my eyes. "She's convinced there's going to be a miraculous healing, and she's going to look exactly like she did before—after all her followers have a chance to participate in her recovery. She wants to go back out on the road now, mask and all."

I suddenly wanted to laugh. I felt like I was telling a joke I'd been dying to have the right audience for.

But Chip didn't reward me with a guffaw. "That doesn't surprise me for a minute. Do you really know what it's all about down there?"

"You mean Bless Your Heart Ministries?"

He did snicker then, and let the tension fade from his face. "You've got that right. It's for All Ya'll Who Sin and Fall. Some of it makes sense, but most of it I can't buy into. That's why I quit, and that's why I can't go back down to Nashville and be her gopher." He shook his head. "Besides, I'm telling you, there isn't going to be a need for any of that. Her ministry is done. The first time two thousand people go into unanimous shock at the sight of her, she'll figure it out, if she gets that far."

"She thinks she's going to."

"I doubt Egan Ladd will even arrange an event for her. Two bits he has somebody in mind to take her place already." He pulled in air, audibly, through his nostrils. "It's all a moot point anyway. I have another job."

I stared.

"Friend of mine offered me a position in his firm, selling medical equipment. At least gets me close to my field."

"Okay." Suddenly we were in a different minefield, one I wasn't prepared for. I picked my way carefully. "Do I know this person?"

"His name's Kent Mussen." He tossed out a nonchalant hand. "You cross paths with a lot of people in medicine. I ran into him again the other day, and he said he'd give me a break."

I splashed the water over the package and watched the frost wash away. I didn't ask how long he thought it would be before he "ran into" some other doctor who didn't want him anywhere near his place of business.

I felt Chip's hands on my shoulders.

"We're on our way to starting over, Lucia," he said. "Just because Sonia's life has been shattered doesn't mean ours has to be."

I turned off the water and dried my hands, finger by finger, on a paper towel.

"What?" Chip leaned on the counter so I had to look at him. "I know you've got something to say. Just say it."

I took in a breath. "What about Bethany's life?" I said.

He winced. "I heard about that. I also heard you were wonderful with her."

I looked into the sink. "Sonia wants me to help Bethany get through this. You should have seen her."

"I have seen her."

"Then you know how much she needs—"

"She needs somebody, that's true."

"She needs me."

I kept my eyes on the stupid chicken and hated myself again. What the Sam Hill was I going to do if he just flat out said no? Could I see myself walking away from him, just when he was finally trying to put us back together?

Or could I see myself walking away from that little cherub face?

"All right, how about this?" Chip said. "You go to Nashville and take care of your family until Sonia finds a decent nanny and comes to her senses about this ministry thing." He nudged me. "How long would you say this 'miracle' is going to take?"

I looked up at him. His eyes were love-filled. Who was he, and what had he done with the Chip I'd known for the past three years?

"What do you say we give it a month?" he said. "I'll get adjusted to my new job, keep things going here. I haven't done so bad so far. The only thing I didn't do is shop for food."

Could it happen? Could we finally put the trash of our lives out on the curb and it would go away, and not come back smelling worse?

Should I fight it or believe it?

I realized I didn't have the strength to do either.

"I need onions," I said.

I heard him take in air again. "Can I take that as a yes?"

"You can take it as an I-guess-so."

"That'll work for now." He took another deep breath before he said, "Let me go to Swiss Farm for your onions."

"Get some tomatoes too," I said, "and sour cream."

He reached for the pad, then stopped, fingers on my old list.

"What modeling agency, Lucia?"

I ripped into the chicken package. "El Large."

"I'm serious."

"So am I. They say, 'We put more of our models in the picture.' They wanted me to model plus-size scrubs."

"No kidding. How did they get your name?"

"Evidently somebody contacted them and told them I had a 'really pretty face.'"

His arms, his big-bear arms, went around me from behind. "You do, babe. And about that last item." He squeezed tighter. "Sonia never had your husband. Neither did Marnie. I'm yours."

When he left, I crumpled the list and tossed it into the trash can and started a new one:

- make Mexican casserole
- tell Sonia she has me for one month
- hope for a miracle

Then I scratched out the last item and began to shred the cheese.

CHAPTER THIRTEEN

Sully pulled the Buick into what he was convinced was the last parking space in the city of Nashville. He didn't remember so much traffic here ten years ago. Driving down Broadway in Porphyria's land yacht was like trying to part the Red Sea. He'd turned off before he got to the blocks with the souvenir shops and the bars and the live music venues, but even Fifth Avenue and Demonbreun, formerly a nothing corner, was a clogged artery.

"Beggars can't be choosers," he commented to his reflection in the side window as he locked the doors and pawed in his pocket for an exorbitant ten to stuff into the slot, before he saw that the machine now took credit cards.

As he walked around the corner onto Demonbreun Street, the new version of the Country Music Hall of Fame overshadowed him on his right, just as the Sommet Center, which had only been a planned-for arena in his day, did on the left. Ahead, what looked like a condo building at least twenty stories high was going up—in a neighborhood where no one used to dare walk, much less live, after dark.

Sully turned onto Fourth Avenue and undid the three buttons on his polo shirt. Holy crow, it was hot down here. He was born and raised in Alabama, but he'd spent enough time out west and even in the Smokies to forget that summers in the South made him feel like he was walking through a pillow.

He shielded his eyes with his hand to read the stone lettering on the massive Greek classical building he passed on the right. The Schermerhorn Symphony Center. When he'd left Nashville, the music scene had been all about Garth Brooks and Vince Gill and Reba McEntire. Almost nothing he'd seen so far was the same Music City he'd known as a student. Even the Shelby Street Bridge he headed for was now only for pedestrians, Porphyria had told him. He could spend all the time he wanted on it.

Dang.

He slowed down before he got to the corner of Fourth and Shelby. The foreign feel of the city tempted him to pretend it had never been the way he remembered it. Maybe the bridge had never been a crumbling ninety-year-old piece of Nashville's history, and perhaps what had happened there had never gone down either.

Sully picked up his pace again. If it hadn't, he wouldn't have come back to dig through it like yesterday's trash, looking for pieces he shouldn't have thrown away.

He girded up his loins, as it were, and rounded the corner, onto what was left of the east side of Shelby Avenue. He steeled himself to feel the bridge like a slap in the face. He saw only a crowd.

The Shelby used to start here, but a happy mob carried him past the vast front of the symphony hall and across Third to the foot of the bridge, where the crowd climbed the steep incline as one. At the top, Sully could barely take in the new structure itself for the pockets of people standing in front of booths, and the lines of them circling what sounded like a jazz combo, and more of them moving across the long, straight stretch and disappearing down the other side for apparently more of the same.

"Welcome to Bridging the Gap." A tall African-American woman pressed a flier into his hand and flashed him a model-quality smile.

"Welcome to what?" Sully said. He almost had to yell over the crescendo of a saxophone solo happening yards away.

"We're bridging the gap between downtown Nashville"—she winked at him—"and uptown Jefferson Street."

"Really," Sully said.

The north Nashville Jefferson Street neighborhood, if he recalled, was another one of those places people used to avoid, unless they were interested in a drug deal. A chasm had definitely existed between it and the rest of the city, and most folks downtown ten years ago had preferred it that way.

"This is sponsored by JUMP—the Jefferson Street United Merchants Partnership," the woman said. "It's a prelude to the jazz festival up there tomorrow." She flashed the smile down the bridge. "We've got a great turnout."

Sully couldn't tell whether the sudden gelatinous feel of his insides came from relief or plain fear. A crowd might mean he was less likely to have a panic attack once he got there, to the spot. Or it could mean a couple of thousand people would witness it.

He rolled the flier diploma-style in his hand and stitched his way through the group gathered to drink in the sax. Sweaty fear turned the hair at his temples to strips of wet litmus. His stomach cramped badly; the smells of the Southern barbecue and fried pies that he loved were nauseating. But if he didn't do this, the brutal questions and the vicious guilt would do worse to him over time. He might not be practicing therapy, but he hadn't forgotten its fundamentals.

Sully stopped almost midway across the bridge, and so, for an instant, did his heart. For that surreal moment, he'd have sworn someone had erected a memorial, right at the place where his life had died.

Dude—it was just an overlook, curving from the main bridge like a balcony, suspended out over the river below. A circle of partiers occupied it, bright faced and trendy, leaving no room to get around them to the railing without asking someone to move. Sully couldn't trust his voice. If he opened his mouth he would betray himself as the coward he was.

A drum solo beyond them broke through the chatter, and the circle gave a unanimous delighted cry and hurried toward it. They left the space empty.

Dang.

There were two metal benches on the overlook, and Sully went to one and perched on its rounded edge. The area beneath the railing was metal, die-cut into waterfront images—steamboat wheels and dancing waves, playful yet somehow risky. They blocked his view of the water as he sat, and he was grateful. He wasn't ready to face the river yet.

He tilted his head back and looked up, beyond the silver steel girders to a cloudless, softening sky. This wasn't like that other night. It had rained then, in torrents. The police had determined that Lynn skidded on the wet pavement. That she was driving too fast in the Chevy Impala and lost control. They deemed it a tragic accident.

But it wasn't. He'd tried to bury that fact for thirteen years. Down where he thought it no longer mattered because he was serving the Lord. When he had finally let Porphyria help him drag it out, he had come to terms with the fact that his wife had purposely taken her own life, and their baby girl's, right here on the Shelby Street Bridge.

Behind him, the sax riff came to an end and the crowd hollered the way he remembered his people, his Southern people, did when they had the music and the fried things and the muggy night air that made them who they were. He used to be one of those people, but he'd been away from them—and himself—for a long time. It was time to come back.

He glanced up as a couple parked themselves at the corner of the railing and nuzzled each other.

Could God maybe cut him some slack here?

That could have been Lynn and him, back to visit Nashville, where they'd met when he was working on his master's in theological studies at Vanderbilt Divinity School, returned to celebrate the city where Hannah was born, there to join friends in a circle and remember how they'd all started out on the "real lives" they'd hoped they were working toward as grad students.

Sully looked away from the couple with plans in their eyes. His "real life" with Lynn had ended right here almost before it began. *What* happened was now in his consciousness where it belonged. But the *why* still refused to come to the surface. It would keep him forever on this bridge if he didn't dive all the way down and bring it up.

He peeled himself off the bench and went to the center of the railing, feeling each step across like the slow turns of a tire. As he pressed his palms on the round steel, flier still in hand, he half expected the metal to give way under him, just as it had for Lynn. When it didn't, he leaned and closed his eyes. He still couldn't look down into the river.

So he turned his head to the east end of the bridge. They'd lived beyond there in the house she'd left that night with the baby, Sully in pursuit. He tried now to see past the stands of silk-screened T-shirts and handmade baskets and the people bridging the gap, to the place where he'd been, in his pickup truck, following Lynn through the rain, thinking like an imbecile that he could stop her.

He'd only been able to watch as the Impala plunged through a railing that had once been here, right here. What was she thinking when the grille he'd shined and polished and put there himself had crashed through? He'd been over that with Porphyria until his throat closed from sobbing.

Lynn had suffered from postpartum depression. She wouldn't take the medication. She listened to a quack counselor named Belinda Cox who called herself a Christian, and the mental anguish pushed her over the edge and out of his life.

Those were the conclusions that had surfaced. If that were all of it, he might be healing by now. He couldn't change the fact that though he had tried, he couldn't help her. He'd grieved. He was grieving still.

But he couldn't get past the thought that grabbed at him every time he attempted to move forward—the relentless idea that there had been more to Lynn's hopelessness than hormones, more than the overwhelming responsibility of raising a child.

Behind him the couple's laughter lifted, and he sensed them moving away. Off to sway together, to nudge each other at the sight of some weirdly dressed teenager or an outlandish tattoo. Off to share a life.

If he just walked off, too, couldn't he live with this uncertainty? He'd coached enough hurting people through their pain to know a person could handle anxiety and be productive at the same time . . .

He'd tried that. Insanity, someone had said, was doing the same thing the same way, and expecting different results.

Still avoiding the sight of the water, Sully looked farther eastward. LP stadium filled the riverfront, the gigantic, red, twisted-metal piece of art in front of it the only reference to the eyesore industrial buildings that once tangled the view. To the west, the flat expanse of vintage buildings had been given a face-lift, and a tiny train depot had sprung up, housing a passenger train unheard-of when Sully and Lynn lived there. All the ugliness had been swept away, except what ran below him.

Sully forced his eyes open until he finally stared down into the river. The green-brown Cumberland was still littered with the detritus of nature. It still ate away at the shore and exposed the naked roots of its trees. No city redevelopment program could remove this ugliness. He loathed it with a hatred that grabbed him and shook him in a long spasm of grief that didn't end.

Maybe it never would. That was enough to push him over the railing himself, down to where her last living thoughts still dwelled at the bottom. It had swallowed up the people he loved—and he wanted them back.

Sully leaned both arms on the railing again, tilting himself over the water, feet on the concrete base. The flier floated away and down, and the bright letters printed across its top shouted at him. *JUMP.*

He could. He could hurl himself through the hundred feet of air to that heinous river and sink to where Lynn's thoughts lay at the bottom. JUMP and search through the junk and the silt that had piled on top of those thirteen years.

Sully sagged, head to the railing. Search and find nothing—because Lynn's thoughts were lost to him forever. She and she alone knew why she'd done it. She'd taken that secret with her. It must have been more than she could tell him.

Or perhaps more than he could hear.

Sully froze. Could that be what she'd left in the river—the part of it that had been his fault?

He stepped back from the railing, stumbling on the concrete. That was enough for now. Maybe enough for forever. Because if he himself had pushed Lynn off this bridge—that was a guilt he might never recover from.

Sully glanced at his watch. He could make it back to Porphyria by midnight, before too much darkness led him back to this place alone in his mind. He maneuvered around a knot of people and pointed himself toward the west end of the bridge.

"Excuse me. Aren't you Sullivan Crisp?"

Who around here still knew his name? He was tempted to pretend he didn't hear, but the insistence in the female voice and the turning of every head within three yards of him would have made that pretty conspicuous.

Sully turned to the voice, which oozed from behind a table at a booth. It belonged to a thirty-fiveish woman with hair a shade of red that didn't occur in nature, and eyes a green that didn't either. Everything about her looked enhanced, so that she seemed a hundred watts brighter than her natural self.

"You *are* Sullivan Crisp," she said, as if she were teasing at him to deny it.

She put out both hands, and Sully had to move toward her and put his hand between them.

"You caught me," he said.

"I have been wanting to meet you for so long," she said.

Sully tried to grin. "It should only take you about two minutes to get over that."

The woman laughed, not surprisingly louder and longer than his comment deserved. Make that a hundred and fifty watts.

"I'm Roxanne Clemm." She pointed to the banner above the

booth. "I'm with WTBG-TV in Mount Juliet. It's our local Christian station."

"Right. I'm familiar with it. You folks do some good work."

It was an excellent Christian cable station. They'd interviewed Sully eight years ago, when he first started out. A small tongue of anxiety licked at him. The next thing out of her mouth was probably going to be an invitation.

"Sonia said you were coming—she just didn't know when."

Sully stopped midway into withdrawing his hand. "Sonia Cabot?"

"Abundant Living has some of their offices at the station—but of course our friendship goes deeper than that." She squeezed his fingers. "From what she's said about you, it's just like you to be here for her homecoming."

Sully felt his left eyebrow go up. "She's coming back to Nashville already?"

"Tomorrow. You didn't know?"

"I had no idea." As much as he wanted to pry himself away, Sully leaned on the table with his palms. "I have to say I'm surprised."

"I'm not. Her faith is remarkable, but then, you know that. Did you want to fill out a card?"

She was talking to a bulky, faded man who'd wandered near Sully's elbow.

"If you have something you would like for us to pray for at WTBG," she purred to him, "you just fill it in here. Then check whether you want me to pray for you on the air—that way all our viewers can join us."

It would have been the perfect moment to make tracks for the car, but Sully waited. It wasn't completely out of the question that this Roxanne Clemm would know Sonia, but whether she had the inside scoop on her was something else. There was just no way Sonia could already be out of the hospital, unless everything he'd read about her injuries had been an exaggeration.

"You watch my show tomorrow morning, sir," Roxanne said to the older guy. "I promise you'll hear me praying for you."

Sully wondered if the man in the battered dress slacks owned a television, but he nodded soberly and moved off.

Roxanne turned back to Sully. "Well, it is just the work of the Holy Spirit that you're here in Nashville now, Dr. Crisp."

"What hospital will Sonia be in?"

The red head shook, as did a pair of gold fish with tiny diamond eyes that dangled from Roxanne's earlobes. "She's going home. They've set up a whole rehab situation for her there. I always think people recover faster in their own environment, don't you? And this way, she'll be able to get ready for her next appearance without all those interruptions."

"Appearance?"

"She was scheduled for a women's event in Indianapolis next month before this happened, and she's still going. Now, *that* is a God-thing." She pressed her hand on his. "I am loving watching the Lord at work in this. I just wish her board was more supportive."

She gave his hand a pat before she moved hers. Sully stuck his in his pocket.

"Sonia said you're praying about that," she said.

"Oh, I'm praying for her." Praying that she wouldn't lose her mind before he had a chance to talk to her.

"Will you let me tell our production manager you're here in town?" Roxanne said. "I don't want to presume, of course."

"What time did you say she gets in?"

"Noon. We're all meeting at her place." Her face lit up another fifty watts. "Won't you come on and be there? That would be a wonderful surprise for Sonia."

You are not responsible for every human being on the face of this earth, Dr. Crisp, Sully could hear Porphyria saying.

"What's her address?" he said.

"Bless your heart." Roxanne grabbed a pen.

No, he wasn't responsible for Sonia. But he did have an obligation to at least tell her she was making a mistake—the same one he'd made for thirteen years. What she did after that was up to God.

"Where are you staying?" Roxanne said. "I can give you directions."

"I'll look it up on MapQuest," Sully said. "Listen, thanks a lot."

He got away before she could manhandle his hand again. He hoped there were more hotel rooms in Nashville than there were parking places.

CHAPTER FOURTEEN

Early Saturday morning, while Marnie checked Sonia out, Nurse Kim plowed me into Lounge A.

It was empty again. The flowers and the pinkness and the heaps of fruit and bagels were gone, though I could almost hear the echoes of Southern female voices blessing each other's hearts.

Nurse Kim tucked a slip of paper into my hand. "The name of an excellent physical therapist in Nashville," she said.

And then she sank into the recliner, the first defeated thing I had ever seen her do.

"I do not like this," she said.

I sat gingerly on the edge of another chair. "Sonia leaving?"

"Sonia leaving when she has not even begun to deal with the emotional trauma. She will not look at herself in a mirror. She will not talk about her pain." Kim's almond-eyes narrowed even further. "She will not admit she has pain."

I nodded. Sonia wouldn't go to physical therapy. She'd barely eat. She'd been occupying herself with plans for her return to Nashville. And, watching Marnie skitter to and fro, phone in her ear, BlackBerry in her hand, two wrinkles resembling an eleven permanently etched between her eyebrows, I was at least glad I didn't have her job.

"And you will not either," Kim said.

"Excuse me?" I said.

"You will not look at your own pain."

"I'm fine."

"No, you are not. And now you will go far away to take care of her, away from any support you have here."

She looked around as if she were trying to find it, since it certainly hadn't manifested itself since I'd been there.

"You must find someone you can talk with about this."

And that would help how? Would whining to somebody change any of the circumstances that had me chasing myself around in a circle?

Nurse Kim gave a sigh that put my mother's legendary martyred breathing to shame. She put a tiny finger to my forehead and closed her eyes. "Take care," she said. "Take care of what is deep inside."

When she was gone, I was hit with a wave of homesickness I couldn't afford to feel.

The air-conditioning in Porphyria's Buick wasn't fully operational, and Sully was sweating like a prizefighter when he pulled up behind the line of TV station vans. Their occupants, and the clumps of people gathered on the street side of a line of police tape, were all in various states of heat prostration, as far as Sully could tell. Clothes clung to clammy backs, and perspiration flattened hair to foreheads. Nobody, not even the group holding up a banner that read WE ARE PRAYING FOR AN ABUNDANT MIRACLE, was without a water bottle.

But the lawn that stretched from the street to the circular driveway like endless galaxy-to-galaxy carpeting looked dewy and fresh, as if it didn't dare succumb to the humidity that threatened to suffocate Sully. The house, too, looked cool and oblivious to their suffering.

Sully took off his ball cap so he could see it more clearly. Holy crow. The place was enormous. It cascaded down a terrace in three stories that had to comprise ten thousand square feet. Screaming white in the sunlight, its even whiter shutters framed countless sparkling windows, and its flower boxes spilled over with vivid blossoms that should have been withering in the heat.

A covered breezeway led from one end of the house to another building, a long one with matching paint and shutters and individual balconies at each window that taunted Sully with their shade. That must be the "guesthouse" Sonia constantly invited him to. Sure beat the Motel 6 he'd tried to sleep in the night before.

He elbowed his way gently through a knot of reporters and camera people to get to a higher spot on the street. From there he could see the back lawn sweeping past a patio and tennis courts. Straight down to the river.

He turned abruptly. *Dang.* He'd forgotten that the Cumberland cropped up everywhere in this town.

"Here she comes!"

Sully shaded his eyes and watched a silver Cadillac Escalade make its way down the hill from the main road of what the dramatic entranceway had announced as Fairvue Plantation. It was so new, Sully hadn't been able to locate it on MapQuest. The original plantation house, if there had actually been one, couldn't compare to Sonia's mansionette.

Two annoyed-looking cops held back the spectators as the Escalade eased up the driveway and stopped in front of the house. Sully half-expected to see a SWAT team stationed on the balconies, or at the very least a muscled bodyguard emerging from the front seat. But besides the police officers, the only person who looked the least bit interested in security was a squarish-looking woman in a pearl gray suit, who stepped down from the veranda and surveyed the crowd from behind sensible sunglasses. She had to be somebody official. She didn't even appear to be sweating.

The driver finally opened the back door of the SUV, and a young woman, who virtually disappeared when she turned sideways, got out first. Sully didn't recognize her as part of Sonia's staff, but then, he hadn't seen Sonia in a year. This child was probably still in high school then. She had the ubiquitous Bluetooth in her ear and chattered away as she stood back to let somebody else out of the car. The crowd gave an audible mutter of disappointment when it turned out to be a plumpish, dark-haired woman in black who immediately turned her back to the cameras.

The woman leaned into the car as if she were pulling something out and then stepped abruptly aside, swaying unsteadily and grabbing for the side to keep from tumbling to the driveway. No one seemed too concerned about her as two long legs stretched from the vehicle and brought with them Sonia Cabot.

Or, at least, Sully thought it might be Sonia. The woman wore a large, floppy-brimmed hat that reminded him of something out of an old Katharine Hepburn movie. It covered most of her face, which had a decided tilt downward and didn't seem to move. That wasn't typical of the Sonia Cabot he knew.

But it was Sonia. The willowy figure, the flowing, gauzy-looking white thing she wore, the graceful way her hand floated up to greet the crowd even with her face pointed toward the ground.

One group behind the tape called out greetings: "Sonia, we love you!" "We're praying for you!" "Welcome home!"

But sharper voices prevailed: "Ms. Cabot! Ms. Cabot—will you answer a few questions?"

Sully looked down at those who were straining cameras and microphones past the police officers. Unlike her well-wishers, they wanted to see something they could broadcast on the six o'clock news with the warning, "The images we are about to show may be disturbing to some viewers."

Sonia stopped at the bottom of the front steps, and for a horrified moment, Sully thought she was going to give them that chance. *Sonia, don't do it. Don't let them have a field day with your pain, not before you even know it's there.*

She didn't go to the crowd that beckoned to her, however. She spoke to a man who'd come out of the house with the unmistakable Roxanne and pointed him toward the reporters. Sully recognized him as Egan Ladd, Sonia's manager. He couldn't mistake the prematurely white hair and the smooth get-up.

With obvious reluctance Ladd approached the crowd, while the dark-haired woman tried to get Sonia up the steps. Sonia didn't move.

It was so much like watching a made-for-TV movie, Sully would have been amused if he hadn't known the players.

The reporters jockeyed forward, and the police looked back over their shoulders.

"I can answer any questions you have," Egan called to them.

They had plenty.

"Does she plan to keep her commitment in Indianapolis?"

Not if Sully had anything to do with it.

"Has support for her ministry dwindled since the crash?"

Vultures.

"How does she feel . . ."

Why did they always go there?

". . . about the investigation being conducted by the FBI?"

Sully jerked his head toward the voice. What investigation?

"What can you tell us about that?"

So far Egan Ladd hadn't been able to get a complete sentence out. Sully craned his neck and heard him say, "That is a routine investigation required since 9/11," just as another voice, unprofessional in pitch, yelled, "Hey—what's under that mask?"

The other reporters whipped their heads in the direction of the shout, and Egan took a visible step back.

"Why don't you take it off and let us see the 'miracle'?"

The voice came from a guy in a ball cap and a sleeveless T-shirt. He probably weighed about a hundred and twenty, and most of that appeared to be tattoo ink. Sully hadn't seen a bona fide redneck in a long time.

The kid tried to push his way past one of the policemen, who grabbed him by both scrawny shoulders.

"You're a fraud, Cabot!" he shouted in a raucous voice that grated across Sully's eardrum. "My mama died 'cause of you. You're a fraud—and now you're a freak! Serves you right!"

Most of the cameras were now on him, their microphones

picking up the guy's swearing. Sully heard Sonia's voice coming from the porch, rich even in a shout of, "We'll pray for you." No microphones turned her way.

Egan marched away from the police line and the reporters. The dark-haired woman and the young Miss Thing turned Sonia toward the house. Her head came around awkwardly, and the floppy hat toppled off. The crowd gasped as, in the instant before the dark-haired woman retrieved it and stuck it back on, a half-bald head, puzzled in raw-red pieces, was revealed. The formerly proud-maned Sonia Cabot looked as if she'd been scalped, and a hundred people had just seen it.

And not only them.

"Who is that?" someone in the crowd yelled. "Is that her daughter?"

Sully squinted at the open front door. A child stood there, a round little girl of about six, with hair the fudgy brown Sonia's had been. She appeared to be frozen, as was Sully himself, until a scream came out of her that silenced even the worst of the stalkers below.

Sonia's entourage swept her and the child through the front doorway. Below Sully, reporters scrambled, and the handful of people who had called out their support searched each other's faces in horror. Redneck Boy spit out one more projectile expletive and was pushed by the two officers straight into the path of the woman in the gray suit. She flashed a badge.

Sully stood still. *That's only a taste of it, Sonia, my friend. Don't bite off any more. You have enough to deal with inside your own house.*

He let the crowd begin to disperse before he ventured down the street. He'd come back in an hour or two, give her a chance to settle in and calm down.

He was halfway to the car, mind reeling, heart breaking for Sonia, when someone touched his elbow. He looked down at a red head.

"I think Sonia could use a friend right now," Roxanne said. "Come on with me."

CHAPTER FIFTEEN

When the door slammed behind us, I didn't know what to do first. Evidently, nobody else did either.

Bethany still screamed, chubby hands over her face as she backed across a marble floor and into an ornate floor-to-ceiling mirror.

Sonia shouted over her, "Who let her out there? Where is Yvonne?"

Marnie still tried to straighten the hat I'd smashed onto Sonia's head after I knocked it off in front of what seemed like five thousand people. Egan just stood there, a blotch of red high on each cheek of an otherwise pasty face. Roxanne was nowhere to be seen.

I would have given a lot to have Special Agent Deidre Schmacker step in and break the whole thing up, but she'd marched off the porch before we even got to the door. I grasped for some of her calm and found a thread of it.

Shoving past the ineffectual Egan, I got to Bethany and squatted in front of her, afraid that if I touched her she'd become even more hysterical.

"Bethany—remember me from the hospital? Can you look at me?"

She spread her pudgy fingers beneath the dark fringe of bangs and peeked between them with streaming blue eyes. She hiccuped silent sobs.

"It's okay," I said. "That's your mom, see?"

"Hey, darlin'," Sonia said. "It's all right, it's Mama. Come here and give me some love."

Bethany screamed anew, and I looked at Sonia, waiting for her to come to her little girl.

"She's too upset, Lucia," Sonia said. She herself was tending toward a fetal position. "Please, just help her."

I turned back to the little person who shook before me. She had stopped screaming, at least on the outside.

"Do you want to come with me, Bethany?" I said.

She didn't answer, but she didn't shrink away. As Chip would have said, I took that as a yes. Standing up, I looked for an escape route, but I had no idea where to go. I felt like I was in a hotel lobby.

"Marnie," I said, "take Sonia someplace quiet where she can lie down and have some water." I stabbed a glare at Egan. "Could you tell me where Bethany's room is?"

Before he could answer, Sonia said, "Egan, tell them I'll talk to one reporter from each network on the back deck in thirty minutes. We have to do some damage control."

I bit my lip, my tongue, the inside of my cheek to keep myself from saying, *You are seriously nuts.* As baked and churned up as I was, I might have, if Deidre Schmacker hadn't opened the front door, momentarily letting in the din from outside.

"Sonia," she said, "I have first dibs on that interview."

"I have nothing to say to you."

Sonia's voice was even, but her shoulders sagged. If she didn't lie down, there would be no amount of control for the damage.

"I have plenty to say to you," the agent said. "And I'm happy to wait."

The foyer we stood in went silent, except for a thin whimper from my niece.

"Can *anybody* tell me where Bethany's room is?" I said.

"I can," Bethany herself said.

She half ran to a wide, polished staircase, and I followed, leaving Sonia's insane mess behind me.

When we reached the first landing, Bethany looked up at me and said, "Are you the new nanny? 'Vonne isn't here."

"No," I said. "I'm just Aunt Lucia."

Her red bow of a mouth drew up, as if that weren't in her small storehouse of information. "Do you have any more candy?" she said.

I shook my head and felt one damp string of hair stick to my cheek. "No," I said, "but we'll see if we can find some."

We'd barely resumed our climb when a woman appeared from somewhere and said, "I'm DiDi I'm the housekeeper I'll take her you go get settled."

I determined that if you were part of Sonia's labor force you weren't allowed to use commas and periods.

"I don't want to leave her," I said.

"She's fine aren't you Baby Girl you go."

Bethany went dutifully after her.

By then the sweat that had traveled between my breasts in rivulets and puddled in my belly button had all chilled to my skin in the air-conditioning. I could have used a shower and about twelve hours to put some of the insanity into slots somewhere. But I'd made a promise, and if I wasn't mistaken, most promises made to little Bethany Cabot weren't kept. I was getting her some candy.

I was about to descend the stairs again in search of the kitchen, when Sonia's driver met me with my bags. He'd changed into green fatigue shorts and working boots. The gardening gloves made me want to say, *Let me guess you're John Doe you're the gardener you're pruning the roses.*

"These go in your suite?" he said.

"I guess so," I said.

He seemed to know its location. I trailed him to a set of rooms on the second level and thanked him only vaguely—because I found myself before a wall of windows and French doors, where sunlight shimmered in from a large, sparkling body of water. I stepped around my suitcases and went to a windowsill so I could lean and look.

The river was magnificent, wide and strong and bordered with gray and white layered rock stacked straight down in some places, sloped and giving way gently to the shore in others.

For a magical, liquid moment I could breathe, deep and full.

The only truly happy times of my childhood had been spent on the water, and Grandma Brocacini had been solely responsible for those. Whether we were feeding ducks on a pond in a Philly park or catching minnows in a stream in the Poconos or digging tiny holes to get to the sand crabs on the Jersey shore, I was laughing. Giggling, chortling, chuckling from some deep place in my young soul. It was probably the way most little girls carried on every day, but for me those times were brief, and even then, at five or seven or ten years old, I knew they were fleeting.

I decided not to unpack my suitcase. My small collection of clothes would have looked pathetic hanging in the walk-in closet the size of our master bedroom at home. Everything in the room—the multiple layers of queen-sized bedding, the wide chair, the window seat, and the chaise longue—was some shade of white. I didn't want to touch anything for fear of leaving a sweat mark on it.

I went off on my quest for treats for Bethany.

On the same level was a home theater—which had neither a candy counter nor a popcorn machine. Another room was full of what appeared to be untouched toys and a TV only a few inches smaller than the theater screen. That area, too, sadly lacked snacks. I found four bedroom suites, two of which appeared to be unoccupied. One was apparently Bethany's, because I heard Didi-the-housekeeper talking in a too-loud, I'm-speaking-to-a-kid voice.

I didn't want to show up without the goods, so I took a back set of steps to the lower level, an area with a ping-pong table, a jukebox loaded up with Sonia's own CDs, and a full kitchen. Hope soaring, I went through all the cabinets and the refrigerator, but found only bottled water and energy bars, which I knew from experience tasted like someone's flip-flop.

Further inspection of the lower level led to another suite, which did appear to have someone staying in it, since a quick peek revealed clothes strewn across the bed and a towel on the floor. The only other room down there was a mini Gold's Gym, complete with shower, dressing rooms, and sauna.

From there I went out onto the lower veranda. I'd already forgotten how Hades-hot it was. The sun threatened to blister my skin right through my black sleeves. Above me, on probably another porch, I could hear Sonia talking silkily.

"I've told you, I don't get hate mail. Why would I?"

The next voice was unmistakably Agent Deidre Schmacker's. "You've never heard anything from a Clay Burwell?"

"Who would that be?"

"Your heckler out there."

"That poor sad thing."

"He says your program kept his mother from seeking proper medical treatment. You don't know anything about that?"

"It sounds to me like either his mama misunderstood what Abundant Living teaches, or poor Clay hasn't been delivered from his grief. I suspect it's the latter."

"So he has never threatened you?"

"No one has ever threatened me. No one is out to hurt me, Agent Schmacker."

I could imagine Sonia sitting up straight like a queen. If she even could at this point, from the way she was fading. I needed her lying down and hydrated. I looked around for a way to reach the upper deck.

I stopped when Schmacker said, "It may not be you they were trying to hurt. Otto Underwood could have been the target."

"My precious Otto? That is even more ridiculous."

I heard papers rustle.

"We've received his autopsy report as well as a full tox screen," Agent Schmacker said. "They show that Mr. Underwood had cyanide salts in his system."

In spite of the heat, I froze.

Cyanide?

"Poison. The ME initially found 70 percent of Mr. Underwood's blood hemoglobin to be methemoglobin."

I flipped through my mental textbook. It had been years since I'd studied anything related to hematology, but I remembered methemoglobin as a form of hemoglobin that couldn't carry oxygen. Two percent was normal.

"That wouldn't be surprising with smoke inhalation," Schmacker said, "but as you'll recall, I told you Otto Underwood never inhaled any smoke. He died before the plane ever hit the ground. He ingested cyanide."

"There is absolutely no way Otto poisoned himself," Sonia said. Her voice was tissue thin.

"People seldom do. More than likely, someone else did it for him. Someone who had access to him or something he ingested. Unfortunately, any food you had on the plane was destroyed in the fire."

More rustling paper.

"I have a warrant to search the premises for any household products containing cyanide—rat poison, for instance, or a pesticide you would use to kill ants."

"We don't have anything like that here."

"I don't imagine you do a lot of pest control, Ms. Cabot, so I'm not sure you'd know that."

"Are you accusing my gardener?"

"We're not accusing anyone."

I could imagine Agent Schmacker's eyes dropping at the corners.

"Then what are you saying?"

"I'm saying what I've *been* saying to you, Ms. Cabot. Your plane crash was not accidental, and we need to find out why. I don't think I can do that without your help."

Sonia didn't answer.

"Ms. Cabot, are you all right?"

I could hear Schmacker's alarm.

"What's going on?" I called up to her. I looked around wildly for a way to get to the upper deck and again found none.

"It's okay, Lucia," Sonia said, though she was clearly less than okay. "I think it's just too hot out here."

Ya think? Burn patients can't handle heat.

"Get her inside," I barked at Agent Schmacker. "Now."

I bolted for the inside door, tore up another set of stairs, and found myself in a kitchen. Francesca, Georgia, and three other women in various stages of anorexia looked up from counters covered in casseroles.

"Well, hey, Lucia," somebody said.

"How do I get to the deck?" I said, and then ignored the answer as I careened across the floor toward the sound of voices—Deidre Schmacker's and Sonia's and more.

When I reached them, a tall, long-limbed man was carrying Sonia across a palatial living room, with Roxanne on one side and Marnie on the other. Deidre Schmacker led the way, cell phone in hand.

"Should I call 911?" she said to me.

"No!" Sonia said from the tall man's arms. "Sully, you can put me down."

"So you can fall on your face?"

The man winced briefly at his own faux pas and hitched Sonia up tighter. "Are you in charge here?" he said to me.

"Yes, she is," Marnie said.

"Then where do you want this?"

The man—Sully, Sonia had called him—smiled a wide, almost sloppy grin. Brown eyes seemed to be trying to sparkle at me.

"In her bedroom," I said, "wherever that is."

"Does this place have a navigation system?" he said.

Marnie giggled, and Roxanne laughed—louder than she needed to, in my opinion—and Sonia pointed a weak arm to the left.

"You don't need an ambulance, then?" Deidre Schmacker said to me.

I shook my head as I followed the mob. "And if you don't need Sonia any more today   "

"No, but we will be searching—"

"I heard," I said.

She nodded. "I'll call her. We're not done."

I was about to be. I left Agent Schmacker to find her own way to the cyanide and bolted after Sonia.

CHAPTER SIXTEEN

Sully carried a protesting Sonia to a hospital bed that looked grossly out of place amid the heavy gold décor of the suite little Miss Thing led them to.

The girl, whom Sonia referred to as Marnie, looked so exhausted, she probably talked incessantly just to keep herself awake. Dark circles under her eyes and two vertical lines that dug into the skin between her brows made her look, up close, like a stressed-out thirty-year-old, though she couldn't have been more than twenty-two.

In spite of her nonstop directions, however, he was sure the woman in black he'd seen on their arrival was the one heading up this operation.

Sully stopped beside the bed. "This where you want it?" he said to her.

Woman in Black nodded.

"Just put me on the chaise longue," Sonia said.

Sully grinned and deposited her on the bed. "I'm not arguing with the Boss Lady." He put out his hand to the woman. "Sullivan Crisp," he said.

The palm she put into his, with obvious reluctance, was damp, and she pulled it away as quickly as manners would allow. Blue, very blue, eyes failed to meet his as she said in a low, husky voice, "I'm Lucia Coffey."

"You've never met my sister, Sully?" Sonia said.

Sister? He'd heard Sonia talk about recovering from the grief of her mother's death and the pain of being estranged from her father, all of which she claimed God had healed her from in abundant ways, but he'd never heard her mention a sibling. Evidently the sister had caused Sonia no suffering worth mentioning.

"We have to get you cooled down," the mysterious sister said in a clipped Mid-Atlantic accent decidedly different from Sonia's Southern drawl. "Marnie, could you get some water, please?"

"I absolutely can. Do you want ice in it?"

"No."

"You want a whole pitcher, or just a glass?"

"Marnie, you're about to get on my last nerve," Sonia said.

"I'll get it, darlin'." Roxanne smiled knowingly at Sully and brushed her hand across his arm in passing, as if they were old friends who shared inside information.

"Hat off, shoes off," Lucia said as she relieved Sonia of both.

"If you're going to start disrobing I'd better leave," Sully said.

"No, Sully, don't be silly." Sonia beckoned to him with the same arm Lucia tried to pull from a filmy sleeve. "You have to at least stay for supper."

Sully grinned. "That's up to Lucia."

The woman-named-Lucia glanced at him, and Sully saw a flicker of surprise in her eyes. Just as quickly, she went back to pulling Sonia out of extraneous clothes and administering the fluids Roxanne finally showed up with and directing Marnie to the bag that held the medications.

"I don't need any pain meds," Sonia said. "I'm fine. Sully, tell them I'm fine."

Marnie and Roxanne looked at him as if he were about to deliver a medical verdict. He caught Lucia pursing a bee-stung mouth as she took a pill container from Marnie and dumped two tablets into a paper cup.

"Is she fine, Lucia?" Sully said.

She met his eyes for the first time, and Sully caught his breath. Holy crow. She looked right into him, gaze bright with an intelligence she couldn't hide, though she obviously tried to. A rose flush spread over her round face as she surveyed him. He wasn't sure he avoided blushing himself. Sonia Cabot's sister was even more beautiful than she was.

"No," Lucia said, "she isn't *fine*. And if I don't get some of this into her and get that face bathed . . ."

"There'll be no living with her," Sully finished for her.

"Now, I haven't heard Sonia complain one time," Roxanne said. "Bless her heart."

Sully sure would have been complaining. With the hat off, he could see the tangle of scars on Sonia's nearly hairless scalp and the painful distortions of her face through the mask. Most disconcerting of all were her eyes. Though they moved constantly, they never blinked, and when she wasn't talking or actively listening, they took on a glazed, blank stare, the way eyes must look when they were safely tucked behind eyelids. Sully fought back a nauseous rise of anxiety.

Lucia put the pill cup in Sonia's lap and said to Roxanne, "There are some straws in the bag."

"Marnie." Sonia felt for what remained of her hair with her hands, which were a tender-looking pink.

The girl turned from the window where she'd been peeking out from behind the heavy drapes. "There are two guys going into your garage, Sonia," she said. "Do you want reporters in there?"

"They aren't reporters." Lucia gave Marnie a shut-up look.

"Where I want reporters is in the Gathering Room," Sonia said. "Go make sure it looks decent. Have Didi help you."

Roxanne said, "The living room would be bet—"

"Stop. Just stop." Lucia put up a hand, which brought the room to silence.

Sully folded his arms and tried not to grin. He was really starting to like this woman.

"Are you actually planning to talk to reporters right now?" Lucia said to her sister.

"I'm going to hold a little press conference, yes." Sonia's voice took a sharp turn. "You don't understand, *sorella*. I can't let them go off with just footage of that young man yelling obscenities."

Or, Sully suspected, film of her without her protective hat and a child screaming in holy terror at the sight of her. The urge to grin faded.

"I want to set the record straight."

"You're in no shape to do that," Lucia said.

Sully looked around the room.

Marnie looked dumbfounded.

Roxanne bordered on disgust.

Sonia herself paused only for an instant before she said, "You take care of me physically, *sorella*. God's taking care of the rest. Now, Roxanne, what do you think about dimming the lights, and I'll sit this way."

She positioned herself at an angle away from them.

Sully bit back the words that would tell her that no matter how she sat, the television audience would see that Sonia Cabot was a frightening distortion of her former self.

Lucia picked up the untouched pill cup. "Then you have to take these."

"After the interview. They make me weird. And don't say it, *sorella*." Sonia gave her a disfigured smile. "I know you think I've always been weird."

Her attempt at sisterly camaraderie appeared to be wasted on Lucia. She set the cup on the table beside the bed, and Sully watched as she visibly accomplished a self-conscious stillness.

Roxanne and Marnie and Sonia continued their planning as if Lucia had disappeared.

"Is there anything I can do to help you?" Sully said to her.

"Talk her out of this," Lucia said, and then looked astonished that she'd answered him.

They both watched Roxanne and Marnie scurry from the room like first graders, each wanting to be first in line.

"What are you two whispering about over there?" Sonia said. She tried the smile and gave it up. "Have you seen Egan, Lucia? I want him to make sure those reporters don't see the FBI people poking around." She looked at Sully. "Forget anything you may have heard about that."

He hadn't heard anything but vague allusions.

"Could *you* go find Egan for me?" she said. "And you *are* staying for supper. Are you in a hotel right now?" She glanced at her watch. "How much time do we have?"

Sully felt an instinctive stirring of unease. Lucia was right: Sonia was fraying at the edges. He didn't care how "delivered" she was from physical pain; one small tug on the wrong string by a reporter could unravel her emotionally.

"We have to at least bathe your face," Lucia said. She glanced over her shoulder at Sully.

"I'll go find Egan, give him the 411," Sully said.

"What about—"

"Yes, I'll stay for supper."

"And check out of your hotel. I'll tell DiDi to make sure the guesthouse is in order."

"Will it get you to hush up for seven seconds?" Sully said.

"It just might."

"Good luck," he heard Lucia mutter.

Sully gave her a grim nod. It was going to take far more than luck to deal with Sonia Cabot.

But he didn't have to be the one to deal with her. He told himself that as he found the front door and headed through the breezeway toward the detached garage. Still, he couldn't in good conscience leave without at least putting a few recommendations for therapists into Lucia's hands, and impressing on her that her sister could use some professional help.

Sully grunted under his breath as he strode across the driveway. Lucia wouldn't need convincing. She obviously had a medical background and a degree of influence on Sonia, but even she was probably no match for the famous Cabot stubbornness.

He might have to stay a couple of days, if Porphyria could live without the Buick for that long.

Sully had almost reached the garage when the woman in the gray suit appeared, hand up. It took him a second to see she palmed a badge.

"Special Agent Deidre Schmacker," she said. "And you are?"

He identified himself, while attempting a peek behind her. She stepped out into the sunlight, made Sully take a step back, and slid on her sunglasses, all in one smooth move.

"You don't work for Mrs. Cabot, do you, Mr. Crisp?"

"Just a friend."

"Close friend?"

Sully was fascinated. This woman was interrogating him with a look on her face she could have worn to ask after his health. Not only that, but the silver earrings weighing down her lobes were clearly the faces of Chinese pugs. He wanted to ask to see that badge again.

"Sonia and I are friends, yes," he said. "We both work in ministry, but mine isn't connected with hers."

"Have you visited her here recently?"

"This is my first time." Sully fished his own sunglasses out of his polo pocket and stuck them on, as much to hide the mirth in his eyes as to shield himself from the blinding light.

"Do you know anyone on her staff?"

"I just met her assistant today. I've met Egan Ladd, but I don't know him personally."

"Then you don't know her gardener. Bryson Porter."

Sully shook his head.

"Agent Schmacker." A guy beckoned to her from the doorway.

To Sully he looked more like a country singer than someone with the FBI. Boots. Pressed jeans. A wry expression.

Of course, Agent Schmacker didn't fit the stereotype either. Not with the sympathetic smile and the canine jewelry.

"If you'll excuse me," she said to Sullivan, and made it clear with a nod that he was dismissed and should take advantage of that.

Sully wandered back toward the house and pretended a sudden

interest in the rosebushes bordering the driveway. What was this all about? Not that it was any of his business, but . . .

"Am I under arrest?"

Sully looked over his shoulder. The question was asked by a man about forty with a sunburned face turned redder with what Sully guessed was humiliation. Agent Schmacker and Agent Country Singer flanked him as they came out of the garage, followed by another guy carrying a bag.

"We're just taking you in to ask you some questions," Agent Schmacker said soothingly.

"What's going on?"

Sully swiveled his head back toward the house. Several of the people he'd seen earlier with microphones and cameras ran down the front steps with a stress-sweaty Egan Ladd in pursuit.

"Excuse me, ma'am?" one of the reporters said. "Are you with the FBI?"

"I told you—it's a routine investigation," Egan called out.

The group disregarded him and followed the agents and the now scarlet-faced man, who Sully assumed was Sonia's gardener. He still had a wad of peat moss hanging from his left work boot as they ushered him into the backseat of a car with government plates.

"Is there a criminal investigation into Sonia Cabot's plane crash?" someone called out.

"Mr. Ladd can give you an official statement." Agent Schmacker closed the back door and opened the front. Agent Country Singer already had the engine running.

"Who's that you just arrested?" someone else said.

"Stand back, please," the agent said out the window.

The tires crackled over pebbles the gardener hadn't had a chance to sweep off and left Sully behind with the reporters. They were immediately back on Egan.

"Who did they take away?"

"Is he a suspect?"

"Yes."

Heads turned to Sully, who put out his hands and beckoned them closer with his fingers. They moved in with their microphones.

"He's suspected of illegal use of coffee grounds on bareroot rose-bushes. It's a felony offense in some garden circles."

"Cute," someone said.

They turned back to Egan Ladd, who Sully hoped had taken the opportunity to compose himself. He still looked as if he were about to be hit by a train.

"They're questioning everyone on Ms. Cabot's staff," he said lamely. "As I explained, it's protocol since 9/11 whenever there's a plane crash."

"Who was that they took in?"

"Sonia is waiting to give all of you an interview," Egan spoke over them. "But we would appreciate you limiting your questions to matters of her ministry. She doesn't know any more about this investigation than I've already told you."

"I think I have everything I need," one of them said.

"Yeah, thanks for your time, Mr. Ladd."

The crowd thinned, leaving one young woman and a sweaty cameraman.

"Come on in," Egan said. "She's waiting for you inside."

They shrugged at each other and followed Egan through the door. Sully felt a pang of hurt for Sonia. This was going to be a blow to that eroding ego. Maybe one blow too many.

He sighed and went in after them.

CHAPTER SEVENTEEN

I stood in Sonia's dining room and witnessed the famed Southern hospitality with bulging eyes.

Francesca, Georgia, and a bevy of their clones brought in platter after casserole after Crock-Pot full of sour cream–soaked, white sauce–based, cheese-encrusted dishes that overflowed the Queen Anne table onto the matching buffet. As imaginative as I prided myself in being when it came to cooking, I had to admit I had never dreamed that certain things could be fried—olives, okra, pickles. Asparagus. Apparently nothing was sacred.

It was almost five o'clock, and my stomach was so empty it was consuming itself, but once again I was confronted with a banquet and a whole cast of supermodels to watch me eat it. I turned to go in search of Sonia, ostensibly to make sure she ate something, and literally ran into Sullivan Crisp.

"I'm sorry, Lucia," he said.

He'd said my name several times, but I was still startled that he remembered it. Guys like him usually forgot me with ease.

"It's okay," I said.

"No, I'm a bull in a china shop. Here." He handed me a heavy stoneware plate from the stack at the end of the buffet and took one for himself. "Would you look at this spread?"

I wanted to dive under the table. It was bad enough having to eat under the scrutiny of Georgia et al. Throw in a famous, nice-looking man that everyone fell over each other to be noticed by, and I was headed for starvation.

"You're not from the South, are you, Lucia?" he said.

"No. Pennsylvania," I said.

"Then I bet you've never had hush puppies." He paused with a pair of tongs around a small breaded item that shone with grease. "Try one?"

"What is it?" I said. Good. Now I sounded rude.

"It's actually a fried hunk of dough. Unhealthiest thing you can put in your body, which is probably why it's so delicious."

He dropped one on my plate and moved us along to the next platter. "Tell me that isn't fried shrimp."

"*Fresh* fried shrimp." Georgia put out her hand, forcing Sullivan Crisp to juggle his plate to grasp it. "Georgia Jansen, Dr. Crisp," she said. "It is a pleasure."

I skirted the shrimp and the casseroles and dumped a tong full of salad on my plate next to the lone hush puppy. Then I gave that up, too, set the whole thing on a tea cart, and looked around for Bethany.

Was anybody feeding her? I'd had to abandon my quest for candy, though while Georgia and her group were setting up the table I had ventured into a pantry that rivaled Swiss Farm in inventory—but contained nothing remotely resembling a Hershey bar.

At that point I had gotten a look around the kitchen, a grand affair with appliances hidden by oak panels and a black-granite-topped island in the middle. It matched the curved snack bar that formed a half circle and could seat four in black iron chairs padded in white. My hands begged to be washed in that pristine sink below the snack bar and go to work at the range, the double oven, the broad cutting board that smelled of linseed oil and garlic.

"It's on after this commercial," Marnie said from somewhere. "Sonia says let's watch in the Gathering Room."

I held back as the rest moved through the sunny breakfast nook I could see beyond the kitchen and disappeared. I might be able to get something down while they were watching the news coverage of Sonia's arrival.

"Are you coming, Lucia?"

Sullivan Crisp startled me from the dining room doorway. I felt like he'd caught me with my mouth full of hush puppies.

"I thought I'd fix Sonia a plate," I said.

It was a lie on a number of levels, which I regretted the minute I said it. Sonia had told me this guy was a therapist. He was probably reading my mind that very minute.

"It might be a good idea for you to be there when she sees this," he said. "A really good idea."

His tone made me look harder at him. For all his boyish charm, something deeper hid in his voice. Or maybe that was just magical thinking on my part. Everything around here was so nuts right now, I half-wished Nurse Kim would appear.

"I was there when she did her interview," he said, "and let's just say she might be a little disappointed at what she sees."

"Sonia doesn't do disappointed," I said. "I don't think it's in her rule book."

Good. Now I'd said something sarcastic to this icon of godliness, or whatever he was. I opened my mouth to mangle an apology, but he grinned. I couldn't describe it any other way. This thing that went up slowly on one side and then the other wasn't a smile. It was a grin that begged to be grinned back at. Too bad I wasn't the grinning kind.

"I'd love to hear your take on all this," he said. "But let's go in. Seriously, she might need you."

Unless Sonia went into cardiac arrest, I couldn't imagine her needing me. She was ensconced in a chair-and-a-half in a golden-yellow sitting room with a stone fireplace and computer terminals and more chairs that begged to be collapsed into, though no one had taken them up on their offer. Roxanne, Marnie, Francesca, Georgia, and a raft of other people I hadn't been introduced to stood like sentinels around Sonia. Only Egan stood apart with a remote control pointed at a flat screen mounted above the fireplace. His face was pinched. He'd lost the *GQ* look.

"Are we TiVo-ing the other stations?" Sonia said.

"Yes," he said wearily.

Marnie squealed. "Here it is!"

Roxanne shushed the room unnecessarily. Next to me against the wall, I thought I felt Sullivan tighten up. I didn't think therapists got uptight. That alone would have made me anxious if fear hadn't already been grabbing at my insides.

"Christian celebrity Sonia Cabot returned to her hometown of Nashville today," said a woman on the screen, who could have passed for half the women in the Gathering Room. ". . . after a plane crash that tragically disfigured her face. It was not a completely joyous homecoming."

There was a long shot of Sonia on the steps, the sunglasses and the Katharine Hepburn hat making her look like a washed-up actress coming out of the Betty Ford Clinic.

"While supporters cheered her on—"

The camera panned a crowd with a banner I hadn't been aware of at the time.

"—one man was less than happy to see her back."

The entire sequence of the kid yelling about his mother played across the screen, complete with me, looking like a pig in a herd of svelte cats, knocking off Sonia's hat, and the camera zooming in foggily on her head. Bethany's screams pulled the footage to her sobbing on the porch and our entire entourage scrambling to get through the front door.

We were flipped back to Reporter Girl, holding a microphone, with Sonia's estate behind her. "That isn't all Sonia Cabot has to deal with. The FBI is investigating the plane crash that took place on July tenth. While sources close to her say this investigation is, quote, 'routine' . . ."

We got a flash of an overwrought-looking Egan Ladd before we were reeled back to her.

"—we are still looking into the identity of a man taken in for questioning."

The camera gave us a full view of Agent Deidre Schmacker and another guy escorting Sonia's driver-gardener to a car and tucking him in. The screen split, showing the anchor people in the newsroom. They could have been Egan and Roxanne—before they were stricken with what they'd just seen.

"One has to wonder how all of this will affect Sonia Cabot in the long run," said the woman on the set.

"I talked with her personally, Susan," Reporter Girl said, "and while she shows remarkable strength right now, I think you're right. This is bound to take its toll."

We got no glimpse of Sonia in her living room, holding her press conference.

"Who was the child on the porch?" Anchor Woman said.

"That would be her six-year-old daughter, I believe, Susan."

Susan shook her head with practiced sympathy.

"Thank you, Nicki." Anchor Man turned to his colleague. "It's a shame. Sonia Cabot has been a valuable member of the Nashville community."

"Yes, she has, and—"

"She's not dead!" Georgia waved her arm at the TV. "Could that have been any more biased?"

"What do you expect?" Roxanne said. "They aren't believers."

"Do you want to watch what they did on the other channels?" Marnie said to Sonia.

"I think we've seen enough." Egan turned off the television and tossed the remote onto a nearby chair. "Sonia, I need to talk to you. Alone."

"Whatever you have to say to me you can say in front of these people. We're all in this together."

Sonia had to look around the room before heads nodded, some of them less eagerly than others.

Sullivan Crisp folded his arms and pressed further into the wall.

He couldn't hope to push as hard as I did. *Please, God, let me disappear. I so don't want to hear this.*

Egan spaded his hands into his pockets. "I don't know what this

whole day has said to you, Sonia, but to me it couldn't be clearer."
He looked at the women crowded behind Sonia, and then, oddly,
at Sullivan Crisp before he turned back to Sonia. "Are you sure you
want me to go on—here?"

"Say whatever you have to say, Egan." Sonia shook away the
hand Marnie put on her arm.

Egan nodded at the plasma screen. "This isn't God at work. This
to me is evidence that you can't represent Abundant Living right
now."

I jerked my head toward Sonia. I had no idea how my sister
would react to rejection. To my knowledge, she'd never had to.

She twisted the smile at him. "Because some poor sad child
attacked me verbally?" she said. "Or because the news media blew
everything out of proportion? Egan, we have dealt with that
before."

"No, Sonia." Egan shoved his already-rolled sleeves farther up
his arms. "ALM is about being healed in the faith. You can't represent healing until you're healed yourself."

"In your opinion," Sonia said. Her creamy voice chilled.

"In the board's opinion. We had a conference call this afternoon,
and we've agreed to ask you to step down—just until you can be an
example of the kind of healing we stand for."

"You can't *fire* me. Abundant Living is my creation."

Egan tilted his head at her. "You always said it was God's creation,
Sonia. And let me remind you that when ALM became a not-for-
profit organization, you turned your power over to the board,
which—"

"All right, all right." Sonia put up both hands. "I will concede
that the public is not ready to see me. So I will confine myself to
answering mail and promoting the books and DVDs through the
Web site."

But Egan Ladd shook his head. "You need to be out of it completely, Sonia. This isn't just about what the public can handle. This
is about faith."

"You mean *my* faith. You're saying if it were strong enough, I would be further along in my healing."

"I'm saying we can't plunge the people who embrace the abundant living of Christ into doubting it because you have been attacked and mutilated and—"

"Hey, Egan—man, you want to lighten up a little?"

I stared up at Sullivan Crisp, who peeled himself from the wall to face Egan.

"It's all right, Sully," Sonia said. "I'm hearing what I've been suspecting I'd hear since the day Egan saw me in ICU." She turned to Egan. "This isn't about my faith, Egan; it's about your revulsion."

"Mine and everybody else's."

More than one person gasped.

Egan was white-faced, but he went on. "You have always said— and I believe it—that a person's life will be abundantly blessed if her faith is strong enough. 'If you keep the commands of the Lord your God and walk in His ways . . . the Lord will grant you abundant prosperity.' We give all the credit to God for that, and the abundance flows. 'You will always be at the top, never at the bottom.'"

"You're preaching to the choir," Sonia said.

"Am I? I learned from *you* that when misfortune comes our way, it is either God getting ready to show His glory—or it's a sign of a deep lack of faith that has to be dealt with." He craned his neck toward her, tendons straining. "I don't think we have any choice but to pull you back and wait to see which it is—not let it play out in front of the thousands of people whose belief is still fragile, whose whole walk is still tentative."

Sonia poked her gaze at him through the holes in her mask. "You're wrong, Egan. We're on the verge of a miracle of global proportions."

Egan pulled his shoulders up to his ears and folded his arms across his chest. "I hope it is, Sonia. I pray that it is. If so, we'll share it with the world."

"No." Sonia stood up and pushed away the hands that reached

out to steady her. "No, *I* will share it with the world. On my own."

"Then I'll be praying for you." He unfolded his arms and looked around the room, which held its collective breath. "If you'll excuse me, ladies," he said.

When he was gone, hands went to mouths. Eyes sought out each other.

"What just happened?" Marnie said, but Sonia waved her off.

"Girl, I am so sorry," Georgia said.

Sonia shook her head. "For what? This just means the burden now falls completely on us—and we have some work to do to educate people in faith."

"Starting tomorrow." Roxanne stood up, arm flashing a diamond tennis bracelet. "Ya'll watch my show in the morning. We'll take care of this."

Right. But who would take care of Sonia? The squaring of the queenly shoulders and the resolution in those unblinking eyes might be convincing them, but I knew my sister's voice. It had risen from its creamy depths and was headed for a thready pitch I'd only heard once before: the day she called to tell me her husband was in a coma. Pre-salvation. Pre-Abundant Living Ministries. Pre-Sonia Who Can Handle Anything and Who Can Tell You How to Handle It Too.

"Let's get her out of here," someone said close to my ear.

I nodded at Sullivan Crisp without looking at him.

"Sonia," I said, "it's time for you to get some rest."

"I wouldn't argue with the Boss Lady," Sullivan said.

He scooped Sonia into his arms for the second time that day, and I followed him gratefully through the door. Behind us, silence fell.

CHAPTER EIGHTEEN

The guesthouse was larger than any *main* house Sully had ever lived in, including Porphyria's lodge, though thankfully it wasn't furnished with the same kind of grandeur as Sonia's own living quarters. Brocade made him itch, and gold tassels on drapes brought out his Alabama-country-boy urge to use them for fishing lures. Even that elaborate cross hanging over her bed made him think of a sword about to fall.

He was grateful for the leather couches and the enormous made-for-a-man chair, which he sank into. He peeled off each shoe with the other foot before he turned on his cell phone.

Porphyria answered on the second ring and listened with her usual intensity while he filled her in.

"Where do you think she's headed?" she said when he'd finished.

"If she doesn't start facing what's happened to her instead of burying her head in work nobody wants her to do, I'd say she's headed for trouble."

"Mm-mm-mm."

"I know what you're thinking," Sully said.

"Do you, now?"

"She's doing exactly what I did. Only she's getting there a lot faster. I can't counsel her, obviously, but I am going to talk to her sister about a therapist tomorrow, if you don't need the car back sooner."

"She's the nurse you mentioned."

"Sonia listens to her more than she does anyone else, although

Lucia doesn't have the confidence to push her, as far as I can tell. Too bad, too, because she's got a lot going for her."

"Such as?"

"Beautiful face—something out of a Pre-Raphaelite painting. Bright. Sensible." Sully grunted. "Hasn't bought into the toxic aspects of Sonia's belief system."

"But she doesn't stand up to her sister."

"There's a lot going on there. She definitely has some issues."

"Have you already done an assessment session with her, Dr. Crisp?"

Sully heard the smile in her voice.

"I think anybody could pick up on it," he said. "She's fairly over-weight, for one thing. Not obese, but I think she's a closet stress eater. She takes about enough food to feed a flea and then doesn't eat it. The only way she's keeping that much weight on her is to eat in secret, and my guess is that's due to some unresolved stuff of her own."

"Sexual abuse, you think? That's often the case with weight issues."

"I don't think so," Sully said. "If they'd been molested as kids, don't you think Sonia would have told the world by now? No, I think it's something else."

"Mm-hmm."

"What 'mm-hmm'?"

"You might not be able to counsel Sonia Cabot, but you'd sure like to get your therapeutic hands on her sister."

"She's just interesting."

"So it would seem."

Sully scrubbed at his cheek. "I'm not ready, Porphyria. I found that out on the bridge last night."

"What you found on the bridge is that there's more you need to find out."

Sully had to grin. "Now there's comfort."

"Tell me something."

"Do I have a choice?"

"Always."

Sully scratched at the back of his head with his fingernails. "Okay—what do you want me to tell you?"

"If you *were* going to advise Sonia, what would you say?"

He didn't even have to think about it. He'd been seeing it all day.

"I'd tell her to take Egan Ladd up on his offer to let somebody else handle the big ministering for a while and concentrate on what she needs to do emotionally to deal with what's happened to her. But I'd advise her not to—to use Rusty's psychological term— wallow in it. I'd say she needs something she can do that keeps her in touch with God and her relationships with other people, something that moves her in a healing direction."

"Excellent advice, Dr. Crisp."

"Out of your mouth into my ears."

"And so far you've taken most of it, much to my surprise."

"I had to hit rock bottom."

"Sonia hasn't yet?"

"I'd like to see her start healing without having to go that far down."

"So what would you tell her to do to stay in touch, as you said?"

"I don't know yet. Her daughter might be one avenue, for both their sakes. Sonia's not taking care of her physical needs either— there's probably something there that needs to be happening. She's running everybody around her into the ground. I'm not sure how long sister Lucia is going to last."

"All good, all good," Porphyria said. "So isn't that what you're doing right now?"

"Am I?" Sully unfolded himself from the chair and padded barefoot into the adjoining bedroom, where a king-sized bed invited him to flop down. He ignored it and went to the bookcase. He rubbed at the title on a spine. *Delivered from Grief.* One of Sonia's.

"I'm going to have to do the podcasts Rusty wants if I'm going to have any future in this ministry at all."

"And?"

Sully laughed out loud. "Ticks me off when you pull that therapy stuff on me, Porphyria."

"Anger is good in therapy," she said.

He could imagine her eyes closing, her marvelous mouth spreading. Waiting.

"I think I can get Sonia pointed in the right direction," Sully said. "I'd like to try anyway. As her friend."

"Good. And her sister?"

Sully put up his hand as if Porphyria were sitting across from him. "I'm not going there."

"That may not be your destination. But don't be afraid to drive by."

"Speaking of driving, I need to get your car back to you."

"I've got my pick-em-up truck," she said. "You know my hind parts fit better in it than they do in that silly Buick. Just don't be tinkering with the engine."

He hung up and looked at the laptop he'd set on the desk—solid cherry, if he knew wood at all. He'd already downloaded the software the Healing Choice tech guy had sent him for the podcasts. Audacity, the program was called. How ironic was that?

He did have one thing he wanted to say, which had occurred to him when Egan outlined the credo of Abundant Living. What a prince, that Egan. With friends like that, who needed a personal assassin?

Sully ambled over to the computer, set it up, did a test for mic volume, and dropped into one of the swivel chairs.

"Sullivan Crisp here," he said into the microphone. "If you ask me—and no one has in quite some time—through no fault of theirs—I just haven't been available for asking." He clicked Stop.

"Thank you for playing, Dr. Crisp. Better luck on your next round."

Maybe not so self-deprecating this time.

"Crispy Critters of Wisdom, Take Two," he said, and clicked Record.

"As you may have noticed, I've been out of the scene for a few months."

Stop again. It was pretty arrogant to assume anybody had missed him. Make that Take Three.

"I've spent the past few months giving serious thought—well, not so much thought as experience . . ."

How lame was this?

"That is to say that I've taken some time to consider this thing called faith. I've had some opportunities to observe different kinds of faith up close and personal, and I've discovered that for an inordinate number of Christians, faith is equated with belief. If you don't believe certain things, you don't have faith." Sully swallowed.

"The only thing I believe about that is: faith has far less to do with what you say when you recite the creed or chide your neighbor with chapter and verse than it does with what you simply come to know to be true. That's what I'm about here in these podcasts . . ."

He stared at the microphone for longer than what could be considered a dramatic pause, and once again turned himself off. At least he'd made a start. At least he had a direction.

Where it would take him was anybody's guess. Except God's.

I got Sonia into the bathtub and was headed to the kitchen for some tea, and hopefully a snack for myself, when Didi-the-housekeeper flagged me down at the bottom of the stairs. She still wore the perpetual smile, but it seemed to be on overtime.

"Bethany's been fed and had her bath," she said. "I've got her watching TV, but I really have to go home."

It surprised me that anyone who worked for Sonia actually had a home. And that Didi was now actually using commas and periods.

"Who usually takes over from here?" I said.

"Well, Yvonne. Before she quit."

"She quit? When?"

Didi averted her eyes. "She gave Egan her notice when she and Bethany came home from Philadelphia. He said he'd take care of getting another nanny, but . . ."

"Okay." I closed my eyes and thought, with a brain so over-loaded I was surprised it didn't spill out onto the marble floor. "If you'll just do one more thing and make Sonia a cup of tea, I'll go up and see about Bethany."

The way she snatched up a tote bag from the bottom step and backed toward the front door, I might as well have said, *If you'll just take that side of beef into the lion's cage for me . . .*

"Bethany will be fine while you get Sonia's tea," she said. "She's used to watching videos until she falls asleep. I have to get home."

Then—and I could put it no other way—she flew out the door. I so wanted to fly with her.

I continued on to the kitchen, thinking, *Okay—first, tea for Sonia, and then a tuck-in for Bethany,* who for all I knew was view-ing an R-rated movie.

Marnie looked up, unguiltily, from the sit-down counter where she noshed alone on a fried chicken leg. The plate in front of her was heaped with mashed potatoes and gravy and green beans that, from the smell of them, had been cooking in bacon drippings for days. She could surely hear my stomach growling.

"This is so gross, Lucia," she said. "But I'm starved. You want some?"

Did I breathe air? Yes, I wanted some, but I would rather have dined with Godzilla than break bread with the girl who'd done more than that with my husband. I hadn't thought about that all day.

"I wish Sonia would hire Hudson back to cook," Marnie said. "I don't know why he left. He made amazing chicken cordon bleu." She bit off another hunk of the drumstick. The girl ate like a truck driver and had a body like Kate Moss.

"I need to make Sonia some tea," I said.

She looked at me blankly. "I am absolutely no help there. Coffee I can do. The closest I can come to tea is picking up some chai at Starbucks."

I desperately wanted to forage through the cabinets for tea bags, but I was afraid I would come upon a box of crackers and devour the whole thing in front of her. Opting for warm milk, I found a quart of 2 percent in the refrigerator and stuck a cup of it in the microwave.

"Do you know where I might find some nutmeg?" I said.

"Are you serious?" Marnie said. "Lucia, I'm not even sure what that is."

I wondered if Chip knew his cute little trick didn't cook.

"It's a spice," I said.

"Oh."

"Never mind." I willed the time on the microwave to flip by faster. I wanted to get away from this child, off to the one who deeply needed somebody.

"Do you know if Egan was interviewing nannies for Bethany?" I said.

Marnie spewed mashed potatoes back onto the plate. "Are you *serious*? *Egan*?" She dabbed at her mouth with the back of her hand. "Why would he? What's wrong with Yvonne—besides the fact that she basically hates kids?"

"She quit," I said.

"No, she did not. Seriously?"

"Didi just told me. She said Egan was handling it."

"Yeah, don't tell Sonia." Her shiny blue eyes met mine and darted away. "Sorry," she said. "I'm not trying to tell you what to do, but *I'm* not going to give her that news."

The microwave dinged, and I took my time getting the cup out—time enough to decide whether to keep talking to the little vixen, even if it meant finding out what I needed to know—but didn't want to know.

Good. I was officially losing it.

"Why don't you want to tell her?" I said finally, and with as little warmth as I could without suffering from frostbite.

She poked at the green beans with her fork. "I don't know if I can say this to you—I mean, since you're her sister—but I used to talk to Chip about it, and he totally understood, so yeah, you probably would too."

Was this girl, as she herself would put it, *serious*?

"We totally used to talk all the time, just like this, when everybody else was in bed, and we'd come in here and eat leftovers—Hudson's leftovers, which were to die for. Okay, I'm babbling, but you're so easy to talk to. Just like Chip."

And you're so hard to listen to. I picked up Sonia's warm milk.

"I'll deal with Sonia," I said. "Good night."

Her sheer cluelessness followed me across the foyer to Sonia's suite. *Dear God, please don't let me lose control and strangle that girl. I have enough to deal with.*

Sonia's room was quiet when I got there. She lay in bed, even though the sky was barely dark, and from the even sound of her breathing, I surmised she was asleep. Her eyes stared, sightless, at the ceiling. So much for the warm milk.

I downed it myself and thought of Grandma Brocacini and the way she always gave us a cup when we wailed that we didn't want to go to bed, that we would never, ever fall asleep.

"This will take away all the ooja-oojas," she would say. She made it taste like dessert, with nutmeg and cinnamon and the sweetness of her soul. It always put Sonia right out. I would fight to stay awake for a few minutes alone with Grandma Broc, when I could just be Lucia on her lap, and not Sonia's big sister.

"How's Bethany?" Sonia said.

I almost dropped the cup. "I was about to go check on her," I said.

"You're her angel, Lucia. I can feel it."

She breathed deeply again. I put off telling her Bethany had no nanny, because tomorrow she also had no job. Perhaps she could once again take on the task of being her child's mother—if we could get poor Bethany to look at her without becoming hysterical.

I climbed the stairs to her room and grunted to myself. If I were Bethany's angel, I would never get off the ground at this rate. I was famished, and too exhausted to drag myself back to the kitchen.

The only light in Bethany's room flickered from the small flat-screen television on the wall opposite her bed. Something called *Hannah Montana* had lulled her to sleep. I switched it off and crept to the edge of a bed big enough for a set of triplets. The cherub was curled in a pink-pajama ball amid pillows clad in tailored cream cases. Whatever she had around her neck was jarringly dingy amid all the cleanness. What was it doing around her neck anyway?

I tugged gently and held up a ragged strip of fabric that had long ago lost its color and consistency. The smell made me pull it to my nose, and when I breathed it in, something caught in my throat. A memory trying to work its way up.

It was her smell, Bethany's special baby aroma. I had discovered it in her warm neck and her soft blankets on wide-awake nights when I rocked her colic away. I'd smelled it on my own clothes for months after I left her with Sonia to go back home. I never did wash my bathrobe. It still hung in the back of my closet.

Bethany stirred in her sleep and pawed at her neck and drew her frail, dark eyebrows together.

"Here, Bethie," I whispered. I tucked the rag into her hand.

She pulled it up to her face and relaxed again, into dreams I hoped were better than what I'd seen her live in the daytime.

"You and me both, Bethie," I whispered to her. "You and me both."

CHAPTER NINETEEN

First thing the next morning, I slipped out onto the deck for a look at the river. A pink mist hung just over the water like the opening to a fairy tale. I lingered until the sun burned through the fairy-veil and brought the day's first breaths of heat, because what I had to face inside the house was more like reality TV.

Once in the kitchen, however, I made a positive discovery: the Cabot household loved its coffee and had every accoutrement imaginable. Some marvelous French blend was already brewed when I got to the kitchen at seven thirty, and I gazed in appreciation at the display of syrups and sugars on the counter and the milks of every fat content in the refrigerator.

I reached for the half-and-half. And then I remembered that I was now an angel.

I rolled my eyes there in the kitchen all alone, but I selected the skim milk and poured it and a single packet of Splenda into my coffee. Then I went in search of Bethany. The nearest TV was probably my best bet.

I sipped from my cup as I passed through the empty breakfast nook and tried to convince myself it tasted good. I could do this. I might even lose a little weight while I stayed here. Go home to Chip all sleek and lovely.

I'd checked my cell phone before I went to sleep the night before; a text message from him said simply: *29 days.*

Bethany was curled up in one of the comfy chairs with the tattered piece of cloth around her neck. A bowl of granola sogged on the table beside her, and a video featuring dancing vegetables flickered across the big TV screen.

"Hi," I said.

She just looked at me.

Okay. Not a morning person. I could relate.

"Whatcha watching?"

"*Veggie Tales*," she said into the neck rag. She sat up straighter. "I want to watch the Disney Channel, but I can't find it."

"I think we can make that happen," I said, and silently hoped I'd do better at that than I had with the candy search. Any other kid would have brought that up by now, but I had the strong sense that Bethany was used to disappointment.

I picked up a remote that had more buttons than a professional sound board and punched a few. Roxanne's red head appeared on the screen.

"Oh, look who it is," I said.

"I know," Bethany said. "She's on every day."

"She's going to talk about your mom today. Do you mind if we watch for a minute?"

Bethany shrugged. I wasn't sure why I wanted to see it either. Maybe it would help me decipher the code everyone around there seemed to talk in.

Roxanne was heavily made up, even for television, and sat in a sleek set with a plain cross hanging behind her and a logo that read *Power Praying with Roxanne Clemm*. A tape along the bottom of the screen indicated how a person could call in with prayer requests, but today Roxanne was already at the end of what sounded like a tirade against all those who said Sonia Cabot wouldn't overcome this latest tragedy.

"They'll see, won't they?" she said, gazing intently at her television audience. "Sonia Cabot will emerge from this more beautiful than ever. The Lord will remove the scars and restore her to the woman you have come to love, the one whose beauty shows us a glimpse of the face of God."

I aimed the remote at the TV and jabbed buttons until an animated fish appeared.

"I like *Finding Nemo*," Bethany said.

It was definitely better than *Power Praying*. And I was going to need something stronger than skim milk.

I dumped my mug in the sink and foraged in the refrigerator for that half-and-half. I opted for the whipped cream instead.

When I got to Sonia's room, Marnie was frantically poking at her BlackBerry while Sonia paced. I busied myself making the bed.

"And I want some kind of worship service this morning," Sonia said to her. "It's Sunday, isn't it? I lose track of time."

Marnie looked at her warily.

"What?" Sonia said. "Darlin', just say it."

"There isn't anybody here to do a worship service. Everybody left."

"They'll be back." Sonia stopped by the window, hand on the brocade drape. "After that I want to go down to the exercise room."

Good. And work up a sweat and get dehydrated.

I gave the sheet a yank. "Physical therapy is going to burn plenty of calories."

"Physical therapy."

"I called that therapist they recommended at Crozer yesterday. She's coming Monday." I chewed momentarily on my lip. "I'm not sure your insurance is going to cover someone coming to the house, since there's rehab available locally. I don't know who handles the financials for you—"

"What insurance?"

"Excuse me?"

Sonia reached back to undo her mask. "They dropped me because I left the hospital against Dr. Abernathy's advice."

Just when I thought the situation couldn't get any more complicated.

"This way I can choose whoever I want," she said cheerfully. "And I want a Christian."

No doubt the person in question would have to sign an affidavit to that effect.

I punched a pillow into place. "Let's get your face done so I can see about Bethany."

"Yvonne can—"

Marnie jerked her face up from her current text message. "Bethany's going to Sunday school. Francesca's picking her up."

"Good," Sonia said. "That will make her happy."

It would be the first thing I'd see bring a smile to that child's face. Besides a Hershey bar. Just how I was going to acquire one was still a question.

A phone rang, and Sonia ignored it.

Marnie looked momentarily puzzled, and then laughed. "Oh my gosh, that's the landline. Nobody calls on that."

She reached for the telephone tucked onto a tiny table behind a chair, but Sonia shook her head impatiently.

"Let Lucia get that," she said. "I want you to start calling people about a service this afternoon."

So now I was the receptionist too. I made a mental note to add

- disconnect the landline

to my growing list, and snapped a hello into the phone.

"Is this—egad, is this Lucia Marie?"

I closed my eyes and turned toward the window. "Dad?" I whispered.

"It's you, all right. Your sister never calls me anything but Tony."

My father coughed juicily and gave me a moment to corral all my responses inside one pen. I hadn't spoken to him for six months, since my forty-first birthday, when he'd called to tell me that I was officially over-the-hill and that he hoped my downhill slide would be more of a joyride than his had been.

He hadn't contacted Sonia at the hospital as far as I knew, to Agent Schmacker's surprise but not to mine. Sonia herself had said she'd not seen him since he relapsed from the rehab she'd paid for. Tony Brocacini might have been a drunk, and maybe he still was, but his strongest suit had always been his pride. I couldn't imagine him crawling to Sonia's bedside, begging for forgiveness out of fatherly guilt.

The coughing subsided, and he apologized in the same gruff voice he'd always used with me, whether to ask me to get him a beer or to say he loved me.

"Are you sick?" I said.

"Aaaah—the doctors want me to quit smoking—and don't go gettin' all nursey on me. I know those cancer sticks are gonna kill me eventually."

If the booze didn't first. Although he didn't seem drunk. I knew the sounds of under-the-influence well.

"Listen, Lucia Marie, I'm glad I got you."

I glanced over my shoulder, but Sonia was engrossed in giving Marnie instructions. Still, I kept my voice low.

"Really?" I said. "When I picked up you sounded surprised to hear my voice."

"That's because last time I tried to get in touch with your sister I had to go through fifteen levels of that operation she has going there. What the Sam Hill do all those people do, anyway?"

"Ya got me there, Dad. I'm still trying to figure that out myself."

"I should have left well enough alone, because when I did talk to her, she preached me a sermon and hung up." He coughed again. "She hasn't given you religion yet, has she?"

I almost laughed. "You make it sound like a disease."

"It's more hazardous to your health than my cigarettes, evidently. Tell me the truth, now, Lucia Marie—how is she?"

I tried to look nonchalant as I passed Sonia and Marnie and slipped into the bathroom so I could close the door. I turned on the exhaust fan before I gave him a synopsis of Sonia's condition.

"I got a glimpse of her on the TV," he said when I'd wrapped it up. "I was surprised to see her walking around, to tell you the truth. You looked good, by the way."

I let that go without comment.

"I'm glad you're there with her. That's what I called to say. I don't trust that crowd she's got working for her. She needs family with her."

I scrubbed at a dried blob of toothpaste on the counter with my fingernail. "What about you?" I said.

"What about me?"

"You're her family too."

"Not according to her." His gruffness went to a coarser grit. "She told me she only had to answer to her heavenly Father, not me, so I should stop trying to make her feel guilty." My father emitted a hard laugh that didn't convince me he was amused. "All I called for was to wish her a happy birthday."

I wanted to reach through the line with a large piece of cheesecake, my traditional means of comforting the man who at this point made more sense than anybody else I had to talk to.

"That was before, Dad," I said. "And I could use some help."

"You think I could help out?"

"For openers, the FBI carted the gardener off."

"It's bad, isn't it?"

"I'll talk to her," I said. "Just hold on."

I pressed the phone to my breastbone before he could protest and stepped out of the bathroom as Marnie hurried from the room.

"Who's on the phone?" Sonia said. "If it's the press, you need to refer them to Marnie."

"It's Dad," I said.

Sonia's gaze bulleted through the holes in her mask. "He's been drinking," she said.

"I don't think so. He wants to come and help, and I think we should let him."

"Absolutely not. You can make me take pain medication, but you cannot make me take him."

"He can—"

"Is he still on the line?"

"Yeah."

"Give me the phone." She was close enough to grab it from me and jammed it to her ear.

"Hello, Tony," she said. "No—I'm fabulous, I'm sure Lucia told you. Now let *me* tell you."

I pressed my fingertips to my now throbbing forehead and went for the door.

"No, *sorella,* you stay. I want you to hear this too."

She missed the glare I delivered as she lifted her eyes to the ceiling. My father had been telling the truth: a sermonette was in our future.

"Have you come to the Lord since the last time we spoke?" she said. "There is no need to swear. A simple no will do . . . My stand is no different now than it was before. If anything, I am more firm than ever when I say to you that I will open my home and my heart to anyone who repents and is willing to go to the foot of the cross with me." She put up a hand. "I know you've heard this from me before, but it apparently hasn't sunk in. I will not have you under my roof if you refuse to give your sin to Jesus Christ and let Him heal you."

I didn't have to hear my father to get the gist of what he said. Sonia held the phone away from her ear before she spoke into it again.

"Do not come here, Tony," she said. "Or I will have you removed. I cannot be surrounded by unrepented sin when I am being healed by the Holy Spirit."

I heard the click. Sonia pressed the receiver to her chest and then handed it to me.

"Bless his heart," she said. "He could be healed so easily."

I let the phone drop into its cradle and headed for the door, determined to get out this time before I imploded.

"You understand why I had to do that, don't you, *sorella?*" she said.

"I'm going to go get your saline," I said. "It's time to do your face."

By the time I got through Sonia's morning routine, Francesca pulled into the driveway with Bethany, and I still hadn't had an opportunity to inform Sonia that Yvonne had ridden off into the sunset and nobody was taking care of her child.

The one moment when I was about to broach the subject, she'd barked at Marnie, "So, were you able to get hold of anyone to come worship with us today?"

The eleven between Marnie's eyebrows went to an all-time depth.

"What?" Sonia said. "Why are you acting like you're afraid of me?"

Because you're acting like Meryl Streep in The Devil Wears Prada, I wanted to say.

"I had conversations with several of the volunteers." Marnie avoided Sonia's eyes. "And, uh, they all basically told me the same thing."

"Which was?"

"They're going with what Egan said and giving you some space."

Sonia turned toward the bedroom window, and the face that couldn't move took on a paralyzed anger.

"Get my laptop," she said. "We are going to blog."

She was talking to Marnie, but I escaped to the kitchen just in case. I was taking inventory of the pantry when the door from the breezeway opened, and Francesca and Georgia swept in. Boys were suddenly everywhere. There were at least enough for a platoon, but in reality I could count only four. Bethany was the only stationary being in the room.

"We thought Bethany might enjoy a little play date," Georgia said, as the small males opened the refrigerator and hoisted one in their party up to view the top shelf.

Bethany stared at the floor like she would enjoy nothing less.

"Shall we go up to the playroom?" Francesca said.

She put her hand on the back of Bethany's head and guided her toward the back staircase while the boys, ranging in age from six to eight, abandoned the open fridge and swarmed ahead of them.

"We heard about Yvonne," Georgia said, sotto voce, to me as we brought up the rear. "I never thought she was that good anyway. We can help out a bit till you find somebody else." At the top of the steps she stopped and looked down at me, shaking back her blonde bangs. "This is all Sonia needs right now."

The boys had already assembled in the playroom and, apparently, ransacked it by the time we got there.

"This is all girlie stuff," was the verdict.

Ya think?

I wanted to ask Georgia and Francesca if they had ever actually met Bethany. Even I knew you didn't bring in four trainees for WWE to play with a little girl who didn't even ask for a glass of water.

Bethany shrank against the doorway and watched with round eyes as Francesca's twins, who I gathered were Isaac and Jacob, used a Barbie doll for a missile and launched it at the back of the head of Caden, one of Georgia's. They were both assaulted by the fourth kid, also one of Georgia's, judging from his blondness and command of the situation. His name sounded like a partner in a prestigious law firm.

I went to Bethany and squatted beside her. "So what do you and your friends want to do?" I said.

She looked at me, blue eyes somber, and said, "They aren't my friends."

"Bethany, honey, of course they are," Francesca said.

To prove it, Isaac—or Jacob—yelled, "Here—catch!" and hurled Barbie in her direction.

Bethany covered her eyes, but she didn't hightail it down the hall the way I would have. The way I wanted to.

Georgia looked down at me, running the fingers of one hand

over the pristinely manicured nails of the other. "We brought a picnic. What do you say we take this party outside?"

"Sweet!"

"Dude, I'm goin' swimmin'!"

"I'm there!"

As they bowled past us, I wondered why they all sounded like half-grown men instead of little boys.

"Get your swimsuit on, girl," Georgia said to Bethany before she went after her boys, who were clattering down the stairs, throwing dares at each other.

I personally hadn't been swimming in years for various reasons, the first one being the swimwear situation. But at least it might be fun for Bethany. I hadn't seen anybody take her down to the river since I'd been there. At her age I would have at least been catching minnows, bathing suit riding up over my then-small bun cheeks.

I looked down at Bethany. Her buns were anything but small, though that didn't usually bother your average six-year-old. But something bothered her. The cherub face went as white as anything in my room, and she kneaded her hands like wads of dough.

"You okay?" I said.

"Yes."

"You sure?"

She took in a big breath and held it as she nodded.

"I found your suit, Bethany," Francesca sang out from the hallway. "It's precious."

"I'll put it on her," said Didi, who had also appeared—even on a Sunday. "Ya'll go on. I set up your picnic in the gazebo. I'll bring her down."

Bethany followed her dutifully, and Francesca looked at me.

"Are you coming, honey?" she said. "You probably need to stay with Sonia, don't you?"

She nodded in that way that practically commanded me to nod with her. And I wanted to. She wore a stark white sarong that no doubt hid a figure-hugging thing designed to show off her tan. Georgia had just exited in a red ensemble that could only be pulled off by someone with legs like the unfortunate Barbie doll. I would rather have peeled skin from my sister's face any day of the week than subject myself to that.

And then Bethany emerged from her room, wearing two pieces of pink fluff that left her white puffy belly exposed for all the world to point at. She looked like nothing but the Pillsbury Doughboy in a bikini.

"Honey, you're going to need a little top to put over that," Francesca said. She concealed her horror with less success than she had the first time she saw Sonia in her mask.

"Right," I said. "You don't want to get sunburned."

"I'll get one," Didi said.

"And I'll take her down with me," I said.

"You don't have to."

I looked at both her and Francesca and said, "Oh, yeah, I do."

Bethany didn't speak as we waddled our way down to the river. A repast covered the table in the gazebo, complete with balloons, but it remained untouched so far. The boys were already in the water and on the covered dock that jutted out into it and on the large inner tube. They did enough splashing and shrieking and cannon-balling for an entire Olympic swim team.

"Doesn't that look like fun, girl?" Georgia said to Bethany.

Clearly, it didn't. I saw Bethany swallow.

"You can just play by the edge if you want," I said.

I felt Francesca and Georgia look at each other, sunglasses hiding their obvious disdain.

"It's not deep, honey, you know that," Francesca said.

"Can I have lunch first?" Bethany said.

"Absolutely," I said.

"You can't go in the water right after you eat."

That came from the dripping future attorney who now stood next to us. His skinniness showed every rib.

"I know." Bethany folded her arms. "You're not the boss of me."

"Whatever," Skinny Boy said.

"Judson Taylor Jansen, come here," Georgia said to him.

"Aw, man."

Georgia went to deal with that. I looked down at Bethany, who gazed longingly toward the gazebo.

"Why don't I bring you a plate down here?" I said.

"Okay," she said.

I headed for the food, passing a whispered conversation between Georgia and young Judson Taylor Jansen. His side was actually in a sotto voce similar to his mother's and consisted mainly of "No way!"

The fare was, of course, abundant, but low cal. I put some carrot sticks, a little string cheese, and a handful of reduced-fat Wheat Thins on Bethany's plate and vowed absolutely to take that child out for a pizza the first chance I got. No wonder Georgia and Francesca's kids looked just short of malnourished. I was pawing through the Williams-Sonoma picnic basket for something a little more filling when I heard the scream.

I don't know what I did with the plate. I just hauled myself toward the water, heart up in my lymph glands. It was the same scream I'd heard from Bethany in the hospital and on the front porch the day before—a cry of sheer terror.

As well it should be. Bethany was in the water, out past the posse of boys, flailing and splashing and screeching in a voice that lost volume and gained water.

"Can't she swim?" I heard one of the women call out.

I didn't wait to find out. Not even bothering to kick off my sandals, I plunged in and past the boys. Far beyond me, Bethany went under and didn't come up. I pushed on until the bottom disappeared beneath me. I had to swim. Dear God. *Dear God.*

Slapping one arm and then the other ahead of me, I made my way out to her. The water was murky, and my heart threatened to come all the way up into my mouth as I called out.

Her head came up, three feet away, and was swallowed up again. She wasn't screaming anymore.

I tried to kick myself forward, still reaching with arms already turned to lead. One hand hit on something soft, and I grabbed. At once Bethany grabbed back, hands on my arms, my shoulders, the top of my head. I went down with her and took in a mouthful of water. Thoughts spun—*she'll drown us both we're going to die Dear God*—until I snagged onto one that made sense. *Let her go. Let her go.*

I shoved Bethany away from me and surfaced, gasping. She thrashed again, but I got behind her. Wrapping both arms across her chest, I pressed her to me and shouted, "Stop! Stop fighting! I've got you!"

Out of exhaustion she ceased struggling and sagged against me. I churned my legs, trying to tread water, but we were both sinking fast. I didn't have enough energy left to keep us both afloat. With the last of it, I screamed, "Help!"

"Are you okay?" someone called.

"No! Help me!"

I scissored once more and got up high enough to see Georgia and Francesca at the end of the dock, peering at me, hands shading their sunglasses.

"Are they in trouble?" I heard a male voice shout.

Georgia's and Francesca's voices were lost in a splash. In approximately half a lifetime, Sullivan Crisp was on us.

"You want me to take her?" he said.

"Please. Go with Mr. Crisp, Bethany. It's all right."

Bethany had gone limp by now, but her eyes were wild. She nodded and let Sullivan wrap an arm around her and sidestroke toward shore. Which left me gasping and heaving to keep my head above the water. My legs were like diving weights. There was no way I could make it back.

And no way I could ask anyone to pull me out.

With a final heave I got myself on top of the water and lay back in a float. I was certain that from the riverbank I resembled a whale separated from its pod, but for once I didn't care. Bethany was alive.

Above me, the sun sizzled from a sky so seamless it didn't look real. Beyond me, birds twittered and called and carried on like the boys in their droopy swimsuits. Around me the water was like a womb. I could just sink into it and escape back to nothingness. That sounded far too inviting.

I rolled over and surveyed the shore, where Sullivan Crisp handed Bethany over to Didi, and Georgia and Francesca gathered their boys and their picnic baskets and their beach wraps. The party was over. If I never made it to shore, nobody would notice. But I wanted Bethany to notice. God love her, I wanted her to know somebody gave a rip.

Somehow I got back to the low place at the shore and tried not to breathe like a freight train as I dragged my body out of the water. My gray pants and tunic hung heavily, reminiscent of elephant skin, clinging only in the places I always hid so carefully. I gave Sullivan Crisp that vision as he stepped down to hold a hand out to me.

"I'm fine," I said. "But I could use a towel."

He pulled one, miraculously, from around his neck. It was approximately big enough to cover my face. I pretended to dry my cheeks and let it hang in front of my chest, and to his credit, he looked discreetly past me into the water.

"You sure you're okay?" he said.

"Yeah."

"Good, because I'm not."

I pulled the towel down to get a better look at him. His hair stuck up in frightened spikes, and his face was the color of porridge.

"Why?" I said. "Is Bethany—did she get hurt?"

"Just her pride, I think. That scared the heck out of me. You've got to be pretty shaken up."

"I'll live," I said. "I need to find her."

I turned to go, only to see Francesca and Georgia hurrying toward me from the gazebo, where the four terrorists sat on benches with their legs swinging. If I could have run, I would have.

"You all right, honey?" Francesca reached out as if to touch my arm and then didn't.

If she had, I would have bitten her hand off.

"Girl, you just went right in after her." Georgia bobbed her head at Sullivan. "I was impressed."

"Me too," he said, without warmth.

I squeezed the water out of a handful of my tunic.

"You sure you're all right?" Georgia said.

"I'm fine," I said firmly, though I still gasped for air and felt my legs giving out. Those legs had to at least carry me away from the two of them, because despite the brilliant smiles and the nodding heads and the assurances that I was brave and selfless, the unspoken message was clear: *If you weren't such a fat pig, you could have saved her yourself.*

Then something struck me.

"Why was Bethany out that far?"

The smiles suddenly looked starched.

"She went down to the end of the dock," Francesca said. "And I guess she slipped and fell in."

"But why did she go out there?" I said. "She acted like she didn't even want to go near the water."

"Look." Georgia sighed and adjusted her sunglasses and pressed her palms together and looked at Sullivan as if she wished he would just handle this for her, him being the strong male and all that.

"I told Judson to encourage her to come in the water with them," Georgia said. "Just to be nice."

Francesca pressed her hand to her chest. "I didn't know she couldn't swim. My kids have been in the water since they were six months old."

"Whatever," I said. Judson Taylor Jansen Esq. had done more than "encourage" her, and I couldn't go there. I had to get to Bethany before she did drown, in her own shame.

Again I started up the bank, and there was Sonia, standing above us, mask askew, minus her hat, chin nearly attached to her chest.

"What is going on?" she said. "I heard screaming."

"It's all right, honey," Francesca oozed. "Bethany just went for a little unplanned swim. She's okay."

"No, I don't think she is okay," I said. "She could have drowned."

"She *what?*"

"Lucia, honey, I think you're exaggerating just a little bit."

"Not from where I was standing," Sullivan said.

Sonia looked at him. "What happened, Sully? You tell me."

Whatever he would have said was lost beneath Francesca's gasp.

I followed her gaze to the gazebo. All four boys were on their knees on the bench, gaping at us. It didn't take a therapist to determine from the terrified expressions on their faces that they had gotten their first look at the new Sonia.

"Mo-om," said one of the small twins.

His brother burst into tears. The rest of the mini macho platoon backed away, bravado dissolving as they reached for the mothers who ran to them.

"Sonia, what's going on?" Sullivan said.

I looked at my sister. She took two staggering steps toward the house.

"It's the heat," she said.

"Will you take her?" I said to Sullivan. "I have to see about Bethany."

I had to get to the little girl who would never be able to go home and forget the hideous lady she'd seen on the riverbank. She had to live with her forever. And nobody was showing her how.

I found Bethany parked, predictably, in front of a video in the Gathering Room, dressed in a dry outfit and eating a peanut butter sandwich. She couldn't possibly be tasting it. She didn't look up when I came in.

"I'm sorry," I said.

She took another bite and stared at the screen. I found the remote and clicked it off. Her fine, black eyebrows came together in a frown.

"We'll turn it back on in a minute," I said. "I just want to say I'm sorry I made you play with those boys. It wasn't your fault you fell in the water. I know that."

She looked at me with her round, blue eyes, and her lips drew up as if she were about to say something. She was so precious at that moment, and I wanted to hug her.

But she went back to the sandwich, downing it in bites far too big for a little-girl mouth. Cheeks stuffed, she gazed at the remote.

"Okay," I said. "The Disney Channel."

I clicked the TV on and rose to go. She looked up, swallowing hard.

"Are Judson and them coming back?" she said.

"Do you want them to come back?"

"Not ever," she said.

"Then they never will, not ever," I said.

She sighed from somewhere deep in her young soul and turned back to the screen.

Sonia wasn't the only one who needed help. I went in search of Sullivan Crisp.

# CHAPTER TWENTY

Sully stood in the shower for thirty minutes. It took that long to get the stench of the river out of his pores. But he could have stayed there the rest of the day and not gotten rid of the angst that throbbed under his skin. He still shook when he got out and put on fresh clothes.

Although the heat was at its midday worst, he stepped onto the balcony that opened out of his suite and stood in the sun. The water beyond taunted him.

Gotcha. Sucked you right in, right where you didn't want to go.

Sully sat on the edge of a wrought-iron table and stared it down. It had gotten him, because he couldn't stand there and let it swallow up another little girl into its insatiable gut. He'd saved this one. He should be thanking God for that.

But it only mocked him, only shoved a picture in his face of the tiny girl he didn't rescue.

Hannah had just learned to smile, just started to search his face with her new brown-eyes-like-his until a grin appeared, first one small side, then the other. She had only begun to sense that he could be trusted.

Had she been wrong?

Dear God, hold me fast. Hold me fast until I can know if I failed.

And then what?

"Marnie!"

The urgency in the voice made Sully twist to look toward the house. Marnie ran down the steps from the dock, and Lucia was hard after her, calling out her name.

"I can't do it!" Marnie cried over her shoulder. "I just can't."

Sully moved to the railing. This could be just a female squabble,

which wouldn't surprise him, with the tension building up a head
of steam around here. Or it could be another situation gone mad.
That wouldn't surprise him either.

Marnie had stopped by now, only a few yards from his balcony,
and Lucia joined her. Marnie hugged herself against Lucia's hands-
on-hips stance.

"Why is her door locked?" Lucia said.

Marnie curled into her own chest and flung her head back.
"Because she kicked me out."

"What happened?" Lucia said.

"I didn't mean to upset her, I swear."

"I didn't say you did. What happened?"

The steadiness of Lucia's voice impressed him.

"She wanted me to write this blog, and I couldn't do it."

"What blog?"

"Against Egan and the whole board—saying they weren't really
Christians because they were trying to take her down. It's wrong. I
think she's losing it, Lucia—even if she is your sister—and it doesn't
matter because I'm quitting anyway."

Lucia took a step toward her. "Okay—what was Sonia doing
when you left the room?"

"She grabbed the laptop from me and said she'd write it herself.
I didn't see how she could, so I didn't try to stop her, but then she
started typing. And I said she was going to hurt her hands, and
that's when she told me to get out." Marnie started to cry. "I'm
sorry to leave you with everything, Lucia, but I just can't do this
anymore. I have to get out of here."

Lucia was already halfway back up the steps. "Do what you have
to do," she said, not unkindly, and headed inside.

Sully wasn't far behind her.

I couldn't get Sonia to open the door, and neither could Sullivan.
She assured us she was fine, in a smooth voice that sounded nothing

like a woman who had just thrown out her assistant and was writing some scathing blog on MySpace. That in itself was disturbing.

Sullivan motioned for me to follow him out into the foyer, which I did, gladly.

"We might want to leave her alone for now," he said. "I don't think we're getting anywhere, and if we push too hard, we'll just make things worse."

"How much worse?" I said.

He gave me a long look, eyes a sad brown. "Let's talk," he said.

We went to the kitchen, where he nodded for me to sit.

"You want something to drink?" he said.

"I can get it."

He peered into the refrigerator. "What we need is some sweet tea." He pronounced it as if it were all one word. "What do you say we talk while I make some?"

I wanted to get back to Bethany. I wanted to hunt down Marnie and find out if she was actually quitting. I wanted to break down my sister's door and tell her to come out and stop being an idiot. But I watched him fill a pan with water and put it on the stove and disappear into the pantry and come out with a canister of sugar and a box of tea bags—all with a methodical rhythm that made me stay there. Something about it made sense. I wanted above all for something to make sense.

"Your sister needs therapy," he said as he turned on the burner.

"There's a physical therapist coming tomorrow," I said, and then felt like I'd just said *I painted the bathroom.* I shook my head. "I know you meant a psychotherapist."

"The other kind will help, too, I'm sure. But, yeah, she needs professional help dealing with all this."

"She refused all counseling at Crozer."

He dumped two cups of sugar into the pan before he turned back to me. "Was she behaving like this in the hospital?"

"You mean being irrational and ticking everybody off?"

"Yeah."

"That didn't start happening until the board made noises about her not doing public appearances, about a week ago. I thought she was nuts then, even thinking about that. This is worse."

Good. I'd just used the word *nuts* with a doctor of psychology.

But he nodded as if I'd just said something clinically profound. "It's definitely not sane thinking, and quite frankly, she's headed for trouble if we can't talk her into seeing somebody. I have a couple of people in mind."

"We?" I said.

He looked up from stirring, and to my amazement, his face went red.

"I'm sorry," he said, "was I overstepping my boundaries?"

"No," I said. On the contrary. The idea of having someone sane in this with me was the first hopeful thought I'd had since I'd arrived.

"I'm speaking purely as a concerned friend," he said, "but a friend with a little expertise."

"Can you try to convince her, then?" I said. "She listens to you."

He grinned. "Only because I haven't crossed her yet. First we have to get her to unlock the door."

We. I never thought I could love a pronoun so much. My life had been *I* for so long, I wasn't even sure I could handle anything plural. But he said it with such ease.

"I'm going to let that boil," he said. "You hungry? I haven't eaten anything all day. We might be able to lure Sonia out with a home-cooked meal."

He cocked an eyebrow and shook his head as I shook mine.

"She won't eat," I said, "and I'm not hungry. Thanks for offering."

"Talk to me while I try to concoct something," he said.

"There's something else I want to ask you."

"Ask away."

He came around the counter and folded himself into the chair next to me, which swiveled to face me. I waited to feel uncomfortable—and didn't.

"I want to hire you to counsel me about Bethany," I said.

He tilted his head at me. "I see."

"That poor little girl has been so ignored it borders on abusive neglect as far as I'm concerned." My words were coming out with too much emotion. I needed to be more professional about this.

"I was hoping somebody would see it. It doesn't surprise me that it was you." He rubbed at his chin with his thumb. "Now would be the perfect time for someone to start working with her. I haven't actually done much work with kids, but I could probably recommend someone."

"No," I said. "Not Bethany. Me. I don't want her to know anything about this. I just want some help so I can help her."

He looked at me with a sadness I didn't expect. Must be the expression that came before *I'm sorry, ma'am, but you are beyond help.*

"I have to give you a two-part answer," he said.

"Yes or no would be fine."

He gave me half of the grin. "I wish it were ever that easy. Here's the deal. I'm not sure how ethical it would be for me to counsel you about Bethany without her mother's permission."

"And here's my deal," I said. "If it weren't for her mother, I wouldn't be asking you this."

I was dumbfounded by my own moxie, but things were just coming out of my mouth. If they offended Sullivan Crisp, he was a great actor. He leaned an elbow on the counter and nodded at me as if we were colleagues.

"It's a gray area," he said.

"That sounds like a *no* to me."

"Not entirely. Let's look at this and see what we can come up with."

A gleam formed in his sad eyes. We were apparently entering territory he found fascinating.

"If we limit ourselves to just discussing your relationship with Bethany and what you can do for her in that capacity, I think we'd be within the limits of therapeutic propriety."

"And not discuss Sonia's role in her life."

"Could be difficult, couldn't it? And here's something else to think about: you might make tremendous progress with Bethany, but when you leave, she's still going to be living here with the same mother."

As if I hadn't been hearing *my* mother saying that in my head all day, just like she'd reminded me every time I had ever touched anything that belonged to Sonia: *Lucia Marie, don't get attached to that. You know you're going to have to give it back to her.*

Sullivan waited. He looked as if he were going to listen to me.

"I'm working on that too," I said. "That's why I want you to keep trying to get her to see somebody. I want them both in some kind of good place before I leave."

"How much time are we talking about?"

"Twenty-eight days."

He gave me the whole grin. "Sounds like a jail sentence."

"I thought it sounded more like a stint in rehab."

"There you go."

It wasn't a taunt. In fact, his voice was like an arm that drew me into some inner circle of decision.

"Look, I'll do anything to help them," I said.

"All right. Then let's give this a shot."

I hated to break the ease that had crept into me, but I said, "How much do you charge?"

He shook his head. "I'm here as a guest, and I don't know how long Sonia is going to put up with me, especially if I push her too hard on getting psychiatric help. I can't in good conscience charge you if I can't commit to working with you long-term." It wasn't the grin he delivered this time, but a soft smile. "I'd be honored to do this as a gift—to Sonia's family."

I didn't know what to say then. It had been so long since I'd talked with anyone who treated me like an intellectual equal, and more than that, a person capable of making wise decisions. I didn't want the conversation to be over.

"Two things we need to agree on," he said.

"One?"

"Although our circumstances are pretty unconventional for a

therapeutic setting, we need to observe certain boundaries, for your sake more than mine. You don't want me observing you 24/7, ready to jump in with a suggestion."

"What does that mean, exactly?" I said.

"That once we start—counseling—we should limit our conversations to that—not that we can't chat it up on the lawn when we pass, that kind of thing, but don't you agree that we wouldn't be comfortable barbecuing steaks together on the back deck after a session?"

Okay, so there went that comfort zone.

"And number two?" I said.

He leaned back and shoved his hands into the pockets of his baggy shorts. "If we're going to figure out your relationship with Bethany, we may have to talk some about you, personally."

I stiffened. "Like what?"

"Maybe some things about your childhood that remind you of Bethany's—that's just an example." He shrugged. "We may not have to go there."

But that same gleam in his eye indicated that he sincerely hoped we would.

He could hope all he wanted. I wasn't about to revisit the childhood I didn't like the first time I was there.

"You may want to think that over before you decide," Sullivan said.

"No," I said. "I'm in."

For Bethany. For her childhood, not mine.

Sullivan didn't make any progress with Sonia that evening. When I came downstairs after tucking Bethany into bed, he was waiting in the foyer, his back to the mirror, which meant I had to see myself as I faced him. I'd showered after my dip in the river, but I hadn't dried my hair or put on makeup, and I was the picture of loveliness. I looked instead at the marble floor.

"The door's still locked," he said. "She says she's turning in for the night."

"She needs her meds," I said.

"She told me she took them already. Do you think she'd take too many? Because if you think she would—"

"She'd throw herself into the river before she'd do that."

I looked up to see him wince visibly.

"I'm being sarcastic," I said. "I'll sleep down here tonight."

"Please call me if you get concerned about her. I left my cell number on the kitchen counter." He gave me the half grin. "And some sweet tea in the fridge. You should try it—especially if you want to stay awake. There's enough sugar in there to give you ADD."

I tried to decide that he was just another man who assumed that since I was fat, I'd love to consume large amounts of refined cane. But I couldn't quite get there, not with the way he tilted his head at me and said, "Rest well, Lucia."

I sat up at the kitchen counter for a while, afraid to eat because I could hear Marnie in her room downstairs, probably packing. I found a piece of paper and tried making a list of things I could do to draw Bethany out.

- turn off the TV
- inventory toys with her; find out what she likes to play with
- set up play date with some GIRLS
- find Hershey bars
- for Bethany
- and me

I was about to crumple it up when I thought I heard Sonia call to me. But when I got there, her door was still locked, and a quiet call to her elicited nothing but a sleepy moan. After that I attempted to sleep on a suede love seat in the office just outside her bedroom, but between my backside hanging halfway off and the stuff wrestling in my head and the muttering that came from my sister's direction, I gave up around five and went for the kitchen. Muttering meant she was alive. But I wouldn't be if I didn't eat something.

The empty kitchen met me with its arms open. Arms that beckoned with promises of comfort, and in spite of the hope that Sullivan Crisp could help me with Bethany and Sonia, I still had such an empty place to fill.

But the kitchen's arms were jealous ones, I knew. Once I let them take hold of me, they weren't going to let go. At five in the morning, though, who was going to find me there, giving in to them?

I walked resolutely to the pantry. I didn't have to give in completely. I needed to eat or I wouldn't get through a day that promised to be more draining than the day before. Just eat a bowl of cereal. And a banana. A little milk.

I saw a bag of potato chips first. Somebody had gone grocery shopping. Must have been Marnie.

I licked the salt off of the first chip, softening it to dissolve like a Communion wafer in my mouth. As it turned soggy, I added another one and another one, until I had to gulp to swallow them. A few more and the pain would disappear and I could stop. I ate the next twenty without ritual, faster, with the fear that they wouldn't fill me up. As I dug deep into the bottom, my cell rang in my pocket.

I dropped the bag like a thief and rummaged for the phone. I didn't take the time to see who it was before I whispered a hoarse, "Hello."

"You didn't call me yesterday," Chip said.

"Hi," I said. "I'm sorry."

"You didn't have time."

It wasn't a question, but I said no anyway. With one hand over the phone, I shoved the chip bag to the back of the pantry shelf.

"Lucia."

"What?"

"It's pure chaos, isn't it?"

"It's—yeah."

"I know. That's why I'm calling you at this hour. It's the only time you're free, am I right?"

His voice didn't hold an I-told-you-so. It was somehow understanding, and I wanted to cling to it, let it hold me for a minute.

"I called to tell you I'm going on the road today," he said.

"Where?"

"Up Boston way. We're demonstrating a new MRI."

"Okay," I said. I wondered vaguely where Marnie planned to go from here. The urge to cling passed.

"Lucia."

"Yeah?"

"Can you do this for twenty-seven more days?"

Dread descended on me.

"You don't have to answer," he said. "I miss you, babe."

He didn't wait for me to answer that one either.

The faint call of "Lucia?" from Sonia's suite made me stuff the phone back into my pocket and hurry to her. She stood in the open doorway, mask off, head bare, eyes unnaturally bright.

"I'm glad you're up," she said. "I'm ready to start the day. Does Marnie have the coffee ready?"

"I thought Marnie quit," I said carefully.

Sonia gave me the twisted smile. "So did Marnie. Get her, would you? I'm going to pray with her. I've been praying all night, in fact, and I know what has to be done. Oh, and while I'm talking to her, would you mind calling Roxanne?"

I would mind incredibly.

"She and I are going to start a whole new ministry. I can't wait to get started." She stared at me. "So—go get Marnie."

I did not get Marnie. I went to the kitchen and found the card Sullivan Crisp had left on the counter.

CHAPTER TWENTY-ONE

Part Two of What I Know to Be True," Sully said into the microphone. "God is a divine loving presence. I couldn't have gotten out of bed this morning if I didn't know that. And if it sounds like I just did, you're right."

He'd considered gargling to get rid of the morning croak before he started this, but since he'd awakened with the first thought he could possibly use, he'd decided to capture it before the day tangled it up.

"But I can't be out of bed for more than about five minutes before I'm keenly aware of another presence, and that is human suffering. It's a presence so real I can feel it in my empty gut, taste it with the morning bad breath. This is what I do not know, and what I hope I can explore with you in these podcasts: how can we reconcile the stinking, groaning, biting fact of human suffering with the undeniable existence of a God who loves us?"

The cell phone rang, and he could have kissed it. He was too close to tears to go on with this right now. When he heard the concern in Lucia's voice, he was out the door before she even asked him to come.

Sonia was enthroned in what she called the Gathering Room, minus mask and hat and any semblance of normality. While Sonia Cabot was never what he considered "normal" by most standards, she'd always been uniquely within the bounds of sanity. One look at the wild gleam in her already disconcerting eyes, and he was ready to call 911.

"Sully!" she said. The rich voice was in threads, and she didn't seem to be aware that it had come undone. "I didn't know you were an early riser. Lucia—where is Marnie? Sully needs coffee."

Sully exchanged glances with Lucia, who shook her head almost imperceptibly. She made an obvious attempt to keep the fear out of her eyes.

"I haven't seen her yet," Lucia said.

"I thought I told you to go get her. You know what—never mind. I'm done—I'm firing her. Lucia, you can be my assistant. I should have hired you a long time ago."

Sully studied the rambling as it went on. Sonia was flirting on the edge of reality. He needed to see if she could focus on demand, or if she was about to start looking for Marnie under the wallpaper.

"Lucia," he said. "I think I *could* use a cup of coffee." He widened his eyes at her.

She nodded and left the room.

"I should hire you too," Sonia said.

She gave him the smile he had to force himself to return. He sat down across from her and watched her twist her fingers together like a dishcloth.

"How are those?" he said, nodding at her hands.

"Wonderful. I've almost forgotten they were ever burned. Isn't God good, Sully?"

"He is. It's amazing the number of different ways He works."

"I love that too." She picked up the remote control. "Do you mind if I turn on Roxanne's show? I want to know the minute she's done so I can call her."

"Roxanne's been a good friend to you."

Sonia nodded as she switched on the TV. "The best. We're starting an entirely new ministry together. Abundant Living has turned completely away from what it started out to be."

Roxanne's unmistakable red hair appeared on the screen.

"That has to be a disappointment," Sully said.

"No—it's an enlightenment. It's God showing me that if I'm going to keep my ministry pure, I have to steer it myself."

"You and Roxanne."

Sonia nodded and turned up the volume. "Listen to her. She has such a heart for faith healing."

"We reject the suffering of Paula and Roger, in your name, Lord," Roxanne said. "And we embrace your power to take away their grief and bring them to the understanding that you have new and abundant life for them. Amen."

Sonia knotted her fingers and nodded vehemently and muttered amens.

Sully couldn't quite squeeze one out for this God-as-a-cosmic-fairy-godmother approach.

On the screen, Roxanne opened her green eyes and looked into the camera. "Today is both a happy and a sad day for me," she said. "Sad because this is my last appearance on *Power Praying*, which ends a period in my life that has blessed me and I hope has blessed you too."

Huh. Roxanne hadn't wasted any time heeding Sonia's call. Sully wondered if she had any idea of her friend's mental state.

"But it's a happy day as well. You know, they say that when God closes a door He opens a window, and He certainly has for me. Abundant Living Ministries has honored me with the position of spokesperson."

Sully stopped breathing.

"You know that our dear Sonia Cabot has had to step down due to her recent injuries, and we are all praying for her physical and spiritual recovery. I have been asked to take her place, and I have accepted that call."

"Excuse me, Sully."

Sonia rose from her chair and stood unsteadily, reddened hands searching the air for support.

He reached for her, but she stiffened her arms.

"If you'll excuse me, I'm going to my room. I prayed all night, you know."

"Sonia," Sully said. "You have to be hurting. We can talk, just friend to friend."

The eyes she turned on him were blank. "I'm not hurting. Roxanne is hurting. People hurt because they have no faith, Sully."

"That's certainly part of it. Let's get that coffee we were talking about."

"That's all of it. You don't know. That's all of it." She darted suddenly from the room. "That's all of it," she said—again and again until he heard a door slam.

Sully met Lucia coming out of the kitchen.

"Did you get all that?" he said.

She didn't have to answer. He saw it in the knot she made with her mouth.

"Do you have any suggestions?" she said.

Sully folded his arms. "We could call a mobile unit or try to get her to the emergency room, but unless she's a danger to herself or someone else, they're not going to do much."

"Next," she said.

Sully nodded. "Yeah, I'm not too crazy about that option myself. Look, she just suffered another huge blow. Why don't you try to keep things as normal for her as possible, and that might give me a chance to talk to her, get her to see somebody willingly."

"Normal?" she said. "What the Sam Hill is that?"

"I hear you," he said. "I'd also suggest that you find someplace else for Bethany to go today. Just in case something does—"

"I could have Didi take her out for the day." Lucia gave him a near-grateful look. "Coffee's ready. Help yourself."

He let her escape and wandered into the kitchen, where even in the midst of her sister teetering on the edge of madness, Lucia had set out a cup, a spoon, a napkin, a bagel.

Sully doctored a mug of coffee with sugar and cream and took it to the sit-down counter and blew into the steam. He started to move a piece of paper out of the way. Looked like a list, possibly something Lucia meant to take with her.

Okay, God, forgive me . . .

He read it:

For Bethany —

- turn off the TV
- inventory toys with her; find out what she likes to play with
- set up play date with some GIRLS
- find Hershey bars
- for Bethany
- and me

An ache formed in Sully's chest. What could make a beautiful person hide that kind of goodness? He wasn't confident of finding that out, not if she kept insisting it was Bethany she wanted to help. And Sonia. What he wouldn't give to get her to dig into her own . . .

He stopped and stared into the swirl of cream in his coffee. How many months had it been since he'd felt that pull to help someone embrace her pain? That he felt it again after two long months was a miracle. Whether he could ever pull it off again was the question.

I got Didi to take Bethany out. *Do something fun,* I told her. She looked doubtful, but she agreed.

Then I took a deep breath and approached Sonia's room. To my utter amazement, the door was unlocked and she sat placidly at the window, still without her mask but dressed in slacks and a tunic that swallowed her diminishing frame. Even her frail tail of hair was neatly tucked into place at the nape of her neck.

"Are you okay?" I said.

"I am more than okay," she said. "As each person I depended on betrays me, I just become more aware that God and I are in this alone." She looked up at me, eyes bird-bright. "Except for you. You're with us."

"I'm here to take care of you," I said. Was that the right thing to say? Should I play along with her—let her think I would be her assistant?

"I want you to answer some e-mails with me. I'll show you how I like it done." Her eyes darted. "Did Marnie leave yet? I want her gone. I'll pray with her before she goes, but she has to know that I won't tolerate—"

With a knock on the door, Sullivan stuck his head in.

"There's a Wesley Kane here to see you."

"Right," I said and got out the door before Sonia could batter me with questions. I took Sullivan with me.

"That's the physical therapist," I said. "Should I bring her in?"

"Talk to her. See if you think Sonia will be receptive."

I pressed the heels of my hands to my forehead.

"Do you want some help with this?" he said.

"Is it within the limits or the boundaries or whatever they are?"

He tilted his head at me. "It's within the realm of common sense."

We found Wesley Kane, an African-American in her late thirties, looking out the breakfast nook window toward the river. A low breeze made the water dance lightly in the sun, and I couldn't blame her for gazing at it.

"This is one beautiful view," she said. "Look at that heron."

I followed the point of a sturdy finger, which, I noted, bore no rings or nail polish. The rest of her was the same way—smooth and clean and without unnecessary ornamentation except for gold hoop earrings, and those, too, seemed part of her. Even her licorice-colored hair, contoured to her head, said there was nothing about her that didn't matter.

"He's a gorgeous thing," she said, and finally turned to us. Her dark eyes, shadowed beneath, were large and rich as oil.

"You're the physical therapist?" I said.

She gave me a sardonic smile. "Well, I'm not the cleaning lady."

"Oh, no, I didn't mean—"

Good. She hadn't been here a full minute and I'd already insulted her. I abandoned the idea of making it better and simply shook her warm hand.

"Lucia Coffey," I said. "You've met Dr. Crisp?"

The bright eyes went to Sully, who grinned and shook his head. "Not that kind of doctor," he said. "I'm a psychologist, just here as a friend. I'm not treating Sonia."

"Does she need treating?"

I felt my eyes widen. Okay, this woman cut right to the chase.

In the long pause that followed, I realized Sully was waiting for me to answer.

"Maybe you should fill her in," I said.

Sully began the story while I went to the kitchen for coffee and made a mental Wesley Kane list.

- *full of confidence*

Not the kind that came from owning a Louis Vuitton bag.

- *direct*

I wouldn't lie to those eyes.

- *not one to be told how it is*

My heart sank. Sonia wouldn't have taken to this woman even in her right mind. Armed with the expectation of disappointment and a tray of steaming coffee mugs, I rejoined them.

"So, what I'm hearing," Wesley said, eyes on Sullivan, "is that her mental state is precarious, and you aren't sure she's going to respond to physical therapy at this time."

"That's it," Sullivan said.

Wesley turned to me. "Is that what I've been smelling?"

I nodded and put a cup in front of her. "What do you take?"

"I'm going to need it black and strong for what we have ahead of us."

Sullivan looked at me.

"So you'd like to give this a try?" I said.

"I'm not going to walk out of here without seeing her, if that's what you mean."

Yeah, I guessed that was what I meant. I wasn't going to argue with her.

Sullivan picked up a Splenda packet, frowned at it, and got up. "We do need to tell you a little about Sonia's spiritual background," he said as he exited for the kitchen.

"I looked at a couple of her books before I came," Wesley said. "Watched one of her videos."

I tended to forget that Sonia's persona was an item you could pick up in any Christian bookstore.

Wesley sipped her coffee in a deliberate manner, the way she seemed to do everything so far. "I think I know what we're dealing with here. I can't make any promises, because the outcome of physical therapy depends as much on the patient as it does on the therapist." She looked at Sullivan, who returned to the table with the canister of sugar. "I'm sure it's the same in your line of work."

"Absolutely," he said.

She paused again, and her eyes went back to the window. I found myself holding my breath and hoping she'd say yes. I liked something about this woman. Maybe the fact that she had actual flesh on her bones, though I had her beat by at least thirty pounds. Or maybe the absence of the praise the Lords and bless your hearts I'd been drowning in. Which brought to mind—

"I do have one more question for you," I said. "And I guess legally I can't even ask it, but Sonia is going to want to know . . ."

"If I'm a believer."

Wesley folded her smooth brown hands around the coffee mug and leaned in. Her eyes wouldn't let me go.

"Am I a Christian the way Sonia Cabot thinks of herself as a Christian? No, I am not. Do I take myself before the Lord Jesus Christ every day and ask Him to show me how to live that day?" She smiled, an elegant, velvet thing that spread magnificent lips and brought her cheeks up to her eyes. "Yes, ma'am, I do."

Sully stopped stirring his coffee. I thought I heard him whisper, "Amen."

What Sonia would say, I had no idea, but I nodded at Wesley.

"Let's go meet our patient, then," she said.

Sully watched Wesley as they passed through the house toward Sonia's suite. She looked around, but her gaze remained clinical rather than awestruck, and her lips moved slightly as if she were making a note to self. He'd be interested to see how this turned out.

Still, he hesitated outside Sonia's door. Lucia's bow mouth wasn't knotted quite so tight now, but he'd already learned that if he edged in on her too far, she closed down like a winter boardwalk.

Wesley strode right into the room.

Lucia stopped behind her and looked over her shoulder at Sully. "You're coming, aren't you?" she said.

"I wouldn't miss it."

Sonia was posed on the chaise longue, with a Bible in her lap. Though she still twisted her fingers, she seemed relatively calm otherwise.

Wesley nodded to her. "Ms. Cabot, I'm Wesley Kane."

"You're the physical therapist." Sonia's voice was tight.

"Yes, ma'am, I am." Wesley pulled an ottoman close to the chaise longue and sat on it. She looked every bit as queenly as Sonia. "I understand you don't think you need my services."

Sully saw Lucia hedge slightly toward the bathroom door. He wanted to tell her not to bother escaping. This wouldn't take long, one way or the other.

"I don't want to offend you," Sonia said. "But, no, I don't think I need what you have to offer."

"And why would that be?"

"Two reasons. One, I am going to be healed by God. It's that simple. And two, because my healing is going to take place according to His timing. In the meantime I am giving people an opportunity to accept me as I am—just like this."

Sonia swept her hands past her face. The sun streaming in through the opening in the drapes brought her scars into bas-relief. Sully hadn't noticed them being that pronounced even the day before, and he wasn't sure what it meant.

Wesley frowned deeply. "Wouldn't it be nice if people could do that?"

"They will."

"Ms. Cabot, have you looked in a mirror without that mask?"

"I've had a glimpse, yes," Sonia said. "But what I see is only temporary."

"But what you're asking people to accept *now* is not a pretty sight." Wesley nodded toward Sonia's face. "In fact, I'd say it scares most people half to death."

Sully watched Sonia carefully. Her hands went still on top of the open Bible as she stared hard at Wesley. He wasn't sure how far Wesley could push this.

"Did you know that it's hard for a person with facial burn scars to even get a job taking orders at McDonald's?" Wesley said. "It's not because they can't do the work. They're the same people inside that they were before they got burned." She leaned in. "It's because customers won't look at them. Makes them uncomfortable. They'll go on down to Wendy's rather than face that."

"I'm not selling hamburgers, Miss—Kane, is it?"

Sully could tell Sonia was groping for her charm. She wasn't finding it.

"I know what you're selling," Wesley said, "and I want to be clear before we go any further that I'm not buying it."

Her voice was low and firm, and it held Sonia in place for the moment.

"Miracles do happen, I know that," Wesley said. "But I don't work with patients who sit around waiting because they think God would never let them down. I don't care how much faith you have, God doesn't heal everyone who believes."

Sully bit back an amen.

"Now, I am talking about physical healing. I know the good Lord heals everyone emotionally if they stay connected. But if you aren't going to work at this because you think God's going to make it all right without you doing a thing about it, then you're right—PT is not for you."

Sonia gave her a condescending laugh. "Wesley—may I call you Wesley?"

"You can call me anything you want, and you'll be calling me some pretty ugly things if we do work together. I'm going to be your best friend and your worst enemy."

"Do you believe in the power of deep prayer?" Sonia said.

"I do. I also believe you need more than prayer to heal. People are always waiting for God to do what God is waiting for *them* to do."

"Jesus said, 'Apart from me you can do nothing . . . if you remain in me . . . ask whatever you wish and it will be given you.'"

"I didn't say you can't pray while you work. I'll be praying right along with you. And the minute that healing starts to happen, we'll give all the glory to God together."

Wesley's voice didn't change. Sonia's was climbing up the scale one disturbing note at a time.

"It takes courage to get up and do that work," Wesley said, "and some of the things I'm going to ask you to do, I promise will bring you to your knees."

She stopped. Sonia became an impervious wall.

"Lucia," she said without looking at her sister. "Would you please escort Miss Kane out? I won't be needing her."

Wesley appeared unscathed as she stood up. "I'm sorry we couldn't reach an understanding on this," she said. "I would like to be part of your healing."

"Then pray and believe," Sonia said. "Lucia, could you—"

"No," Lucia said.

Sully let himself stare. Lucia pulled away from the wall, cheeks aflame.

"Don't go anywhere yet," she said to Wesley. "Sonia, you are making a big mistake. This lady can help you."

Sonia's eyes glittered. "You're going to betray me too?"

"Take it however you want, but I'll tell you this. If you refuse to let her help you, then I'm out of here. Permanently. I'm going home."

Sonia let out a hard laugh. "You wouldn't leave me."

"Try me. And if I go, Sonia, I am taking Bethany with me."

Sully tried to keep his face expressionless. *Holy crow.*

"They wouldn't let you," Sonia said.

"You mean the people I'm going to tell that you have grossly neglected your child?" Lucia marched across the room and put her face close to Sonia's. "God's not taking care of her either, Sonia. Somebody has to, and that person is me, wherever I am."

Silence ate up the air in the room. Sully watched Sonia try to achieve her power posture, but her face was drawn forward and held against her neck by a stiffened thickness of skin. It left her spine a question mark before her sister. He glanced at Wesley, who merely waited with unmistakable admiration in her eyes.

"On my terms, Miss Kane," Sonia said.

"Depends on what they are," Wesley said. "I have terms too."

"I would want to do this 'therapy' in the late afternoon, when my other work is done. I'm starting an entirely new ministry that is going to take a great deal of time."

"That doesn't work for me. I have to pick up my son at preschool at two."

"Bring him with you. We would love to have him."

Sonia tried the twisted smile, and the attempt to save her pride stabbed at Sully's heart.

Wesley's face was incredulous. "I can't have him with me when I'm working, Ms. Cabot."

"Lucia can take care of him."

Wesley turned the scandalized eyes on Lucia.

"I'm fine with that," Lucia said. "Whatever it takes."

She appeared to have spent all the fortitude she'd stored up.

"And," Sonia said, "do not think that this means I have given up my faith that God will do what you cannot."

"I have no problem with that." Wesley pressed her lips together, then said, "I will let you know."

She nodded at Sonia and Sully—and gave Lucia a look loaded with things she intended to say when they were out of the room.

They barely made it that far before Wesley was, quite literally, in Lucia's face. "Before I bring my baby here—"

"I will take care of him like he was my own," Lucia said.

"You going to let him bully you like you just let your sister do?"

Sully crossed one arm over his chest and covered his mouth with his other hand. It was hard to hide a satisfied grin.

"James-Lawson is the light of my life." Wesley pulled her eyes into slits. "I can't let you take care of my son unless you are doing it of your own volition. He deserves that."

"I am doing this for my niece," Lucia said.

"How old is she?"

"She's a precious six years old," Lucia said.

Wesley gave her a slow series of nods. "I guess that's a reason to back down with her." She nodded toward the door. "But just so you know, I won't be doing that."

"I hope not," Lucia said.

The blue eyes Sully had seen turn to the floor so that she could remain invisible appraised Wesley Kane right back. With that kind of devotion to a child, he knew she'd throw herself in front of a train if she thought it would make a difference.

He just hoped he could get her to have even half that much love for herself.

CHAPTER TWENTY-TWO

By the time Wesley's car pulled into the driveway the next afternoon, the last thing I wanted was to babysit. I'd spent the last thirty-six hours feeling like the only waitress in Sonia's personal restaurant. She barely spoke to me except to place her order.

Miss, could you treat my face at 6:00 AM so I can be ready to work by 7:00?

Would you do a load of laundry and tidy up my office? Didi doesn't seem to have shown up today. Or Bryson either, for that matter. I don't want the yard to go to seed.

Oh, and when you have a chance—I know you're busy—could you call my accountant and have him transfer funds? I'm going to need some accessible cash for this new venture.

I suspected she was punishing me for blackmailing her into working with Wesley, but I could deal with that—for Bethany.

And at least Sonia had reconsidered her decision to fire Marnie and replace her with me. After a two-hour, behind-closed-doors "conversation," the girl emerged, eyes tear-swollen, and said she would give it one more chance.

"She's been so good to me," she told me as she polished off the bag of chips I'd broken into. "I just don't want to abandon her."

She gestured toward me with a chip between her fingers. "But I wouldn't be staying if it wasn't for you. I wish Chip was still here too. The two of you could whip this place into shape."

She'd had me until then. When Chip called me an hour later, I let my voice mail pick it up. He simply said, "Twenty-five more days."

Even without having to run around with a BlackBerry, I was exhausted when Bethany and I crossed the foyer to answer the door. She pressed against the mirror, face pensive. When I'd told her someone was coming to play, her only response had been, "It isn't Judson and them, is it?"

If it was, she and I were both going for the potato chips. And the graham crackers. And whatever else we could find.

But when I opened the door, I was greeted by a chocolate drop of a four-year-old with enormous eyes and a mouth just like his mother's. He put out a small hand and said, "I'm James-Lawson Kane. It's nice to meet you."

I melted all over the front porch.

"It's nice to meet you, too, James-Lawson." I squatted and gave him my hand. "I'm Lucia."

"That will be Miss Lucia to you."

I looked up at Wesley. Her "mother look" was firm, with a side of twinkle.

"Yes, ma'am," James-Lawson said. He peered behind me. "Hi, I'm James-Lawson Kane. It's nice to meet you."

I turned around to find Bethany extending her own chubby hand to reach his. They shook solemnly.

James-Lawson looked up at his mother, who nodded. "Good job, son," she said.

He went back to Bethany. "Are you her kid?" he said, pointing at me.

My precious niece blinked her blue eyes at him and then at me, and my heart split. She didn't even know whose kid she was.

"They belong together, son," Wesley said.

"Do you have a daddy?" James-Lawson said to Bethany.

She shook her head.

"Me neither. You wanna play?"

Bethany nodded, and he shrugged.

"Then let's go," he said.

And they were suddenly off—the boy-child tearing across the

lawn, the girl-child running after him with an energy I didn't know she possessed in her quiet pink chubbiness.

Wesley looked at me with her rich-oil eyes. "Now that they know everything that's important to know about each other, I think they're going to be just fine."

When I got to the duo, they were standing midway between the house and the river. James-Lawson had his hands on his almost nonexistent hips.

"Miss Lucia," he said, "I want to go down there."

He pointed to the water. Beside him, Bethany folded her arms so tightly across her chest, her hands were in her armpits.

"What do you want to do down there, James-Lawson?" I said.

"Well," he said, hands still firmly planted, "I can't go swimming, because you know what?"

"No, what?"

"I don't have my swimming suit with me."

"Oh well, there's that."

"And I just ate. You can't go swimming if you just ate."

"Right."

He gave an elaborate sigh. "The only thing left is to go down there and find stuff, I guess."

"What kind of stuff?" Bethany said.

"I don't know," he said. "I ain't seen it yet. Oh, wait." He frowned at himself. "I haven't seen it yet."

His eyes went to me. "I'm not 'posed to say *ain't*."

Back to Bethany. "You wanna go find stuff with me?"

By the water? James-Lawson, my friend, you are about to be sorely disappointed.

But Bethany's face did something I had never seen it do. The somber cheeks dimpled, and the red bow of a mouth untied into a smile that went all the way to her eyes.

"Yes," she said.

"Then why are we just standing here?" he said.

He took off at a dead run, but before I could get my mouth open to stop him, he did an about-face and put up his hand so I could see his cream-colored palm.

"Don't worry, Miss Lucia," he said. "I won't go near the water till you get there."

"I appreciate that, James-Lawson," I said.

He bolted again.

Bethany whispered to me, "Isn't he cute?" and took off after him at a delighted trot.

James-Lawson was indeed cute, as was she as they spent the next two hours "finding stuff." The discoveries included enough small limestone rocks to rebuild the pyramids; a family of Canada geese that talked back as James-Lawson, and eventually a giggling Bethany, honked at them; and an entire flotilla of magnolia blossoms. Though James-Lawson informed her how much fun it was to stand in the water and make boats out of them, she wouldn't go quite that far.

I suggested we have a snack.

"Do we have to go inside to get it?" James-Lawson said.

"We don't have to go inside," Bethany said. "I have these." She pulled a bag of Gummi Bears from her shorts pocket.

"Where did you get those?" I said.

"Didi got me 'em yesterday. At the movies."

So imaginative, that Didi.

Bethany put the bag into my hand and dropped her chin to her chest. "I'm not supposed to have them."

"Why not?" I said.

"My mom said I couldn't have candy."

"She told you that?" I said, hopefully.

"No. Yvonne said she wouldn't want me to have it."

James-Lawson raised his hand.

"Yes?" I said.

"You know what? My mama says I can have candy on special occasions. Is this a special occasion?"

"I don't know what that is," Bethany said.

My heart broke cleanly in half.

"It most definitely is," I said. "And before I eat Gummi Bears, I like to divide them by colors."

They watched, gaping, as I selected one of each from the bag and lined them up on a rock. I made the yellow one dance.

"Why did you do that?" Bethany said.

"Because it's more fun to play with them before you eat them."

James-Lawson snatched up a red, and then cast his enormous eyes on me. "May I please have this one?"

"You may," I said.

He put it between two fingers and wove it in the air, his mouth making a noise that sounded for all the world like a helicopter. Bethany watched, a puzzled look on her face, and then daintily picked out a green one. I could feel her stiffening.

"Mine dances," I said. "James-Lawson's flies. What do you want yours to do?"

"I don't know how to dance."

"What would you do if you were a bear?"

She gazed at the green candy until I thought the thing would dissolve in her hand. Then she said, "I think it wants to stand on its head."

"You've got the power," I said.

She turned the tiny bear upside down and looked at me. "Now what do we do?"

"Now we eat," I said, and popped the yellow bear into my mouth.

She and James-Lawson followed suit.

"Let's make a whole circus!" James-Lawson said.

I held my breath, but it seemed that Bethany had at least been to a circus, though she still needed some tutoring in how to bring gummified bears to life. We were in the middle of constructing a tightrope with a piece of string James-Lawson miraculously produced from his pocket when Wesley found us.

"Looks like we've got it going on down here," she said.

"We're having a special occasion," James-Lawson told her. "Do I *have* to leave now?"

His mother squatted beside him and observed the three rings they had painstakingly formed with pebbles. "You do, but if you want, we can come back tomorrow for another special occasion." She looked at me. "How would that be?"

With a pang that lasted no longer than two seconds, I realized I hadn't thought about my sister for two hours.

"It went well, then," I said.

"It did on my end. How about yours?"

"Our end was great," James-Lawson said.

"Did I ask you, boy?"

"What do you think, Bethie?" I said. "How did we do?"

She looked up from the green bear, who was currently crossing the tightrope with the greatest of ease. "This was the best day of my life," she said.

Wesley put her hand on my arm, a warm hand that didn't make me want to wrench away. "That about says it, doesn't it?" she said. She put her lips close to my ear. "We'll talk about Her Highness tomorrow. I don't want to break this magic spell."

She stood and reached for James-Lawson, but Bethany scrambled up and got to her first. She put her hand shyly in Wesley's and said, "I'm Bethany Cabot. It's nice to meet you."

Wesley pulled Bethany's hand to her lips and kissed it. "It is nice to meet you, too, Miss Bethany. You are one special lady."

When Wesley turned to go, I saw tears in the rich-oil eyes.

As Bethany and I sat with our circus and watched them leave, the very air seemed to empty.

"Shall we save our tightrope and our bears for tomorrow?" I said.

"You aren't going away, are you?"

I drew in a breath. She searched my face with her eyes, just the way she had done as an infant, when she first realized I was another being and not just the bearer of bottles.

No, Bethany, never, I longed to say to her. *I'm going to stay with you until you know that you are worth more than what you're getting.*

But I didn't even need the mother voice to shout that down and tell me she wasn't mine, that I couldn't be with her forever.

"No, Bethie," I said. "I'm not going away yet."

And I would make sure that when I went, I didn't leave behind a little girl who would turn out just like me. I prayed that Sullivan Crisp could help me with that. *Dear God, please.*

CHAPTER TWENTY-THREE

Sully always prayed before a session. He pressed his palms to his forehead, elbows resting on his knees, and breathed in.

This time, for an agonizing minute, nothing came.

Well, to borrow Lucia's expression, what the Sam Hill did he expect? He was sitting in an Adirondack chair three yards from the Cumberland River.

The praying had always been easy—opening up and letting the light pour in, asking God to channel it through him and into the sad and painful depths of his client. It was hard enough to begin with, now that he knew for himself the agony that could arise from shining that light in there. It seemed almost sadistic to ask someone else to take that risk.

But to have to do this mere feet from the river? He couldn't get away from the thing. The water smelling of slimy green algae and boat fuel. The crickets setting up their taunting racket. The moon cutting a swath straight into his memory.

When he asked Lucia where she would be comfortable meeting with him, she'd said here, as far from the house as possible without leaving, because of Bethany. Which was also why she asked if they could get together at night, after the little one had gone to bed. He'd thought she'd take about five minutes of the mosquito population and want to escape inside, but when he'd arrived for his alone time, there were already two lighted tiki torches stuck in the ground. It was like being on *Survivor*.

He just wasn't sure if either or both of them could see this thing through. Lucia was sure to balk when he tried to get her to talk about *her* issues, as opposed to Bethany's. And what about himself? This was his first session in two months. Did he even know how to do this anymore? Did he even have the right to try—when he'd obviously failed miserably with his own wife? Podcasts and some friendly advice to Sonia were one thing, but—dang.

He felt the tikis' light flicker over his face. Maybe he ought to just vote himself off the island right now and be done with it.

Except that he could hear Porphyria saying the words self-doubt couldn't argue with: *Dr. Crisp, until you're dead, you're not done.*

So he let his hands cup his face, and he breathed and he found the only thing there.

Use me, Father. Use me as you will.

"Should I wait?" someone whispered.

Sully jolted in the chair. Lucia was there, looking so firmly packed up, Sully wondered if she was even allowing herself a pulse.

He stood up and slung a hand toward the other Adirondack. "No, no, I was just talking to God."

She frowned at the chair.

"These were the only ones down here," Sully said. "It's not as uncomfortable as it looks."

He half-hoped she'd suggest they go inside, where every surface was padded in something opulent, although he didn't think he could do therapy in that living room without black tie and tails. But she sat down tentatively at the chair's edge and slid slowly back.

Scared to death. And her fear had to trump his.

"Were you done?" she said.

"Done?"

"Talking to God."

"Oh. No, never. It goes on pretty much all the time. I figure the squeaky wheel gets the grease."

It was meant to put her at ease, but her frown went deeper.

"I brought us some sweet tea," he said, nodding toward the pitcher and glasses he'd set next to the Kleenex on the small table between them.

"Do you think I'm going to cry?"

"I'm sorry?"

"The tissues. Does that mean you think I'm going to cry?"

"I don't know," Sully said. "But *I* might. We're going to be talking about Bethany, and that is one sad little girl."

She seemed to breathe into that.

"Just so you know," she said, "I don't cry. Is that the kind of thing I'm supposed to tell you?"

Sully gave a soft buzz and waited. If his shtick didn't work, he really would flounder.

"What was that?"

"Do you watch many game shows, Lucia?"

Her eyebrows went together. "Are you serious?"

"I am."

"No. I'd rather be shot."

"That's a shame," he said. "Because I like to think of therapy as something like being on a game show."

She stared at him.

"If we find an answer that takes us somewhere, we ding ourselves."

"Ding?"

He let his voice go up to bell level. "Ding-ding-ding. And if we hit a dead end, it's a buzz. The best part of this game show is that nobody loses. Our goal is for you to win."

"For Bethany to win," she said.

She did like that category.

"So, me asking you what I was supposed to tell you got a buzz?"

"Only because there are no 'supposed tos' here," he said. "I don't know if you've ever worked with a counselor or anything before . . ."

She shook her head.

"It's like playing *Jeopardy*. The answers are all there—we just have to ask the right questions, and we'll do that together."

"May I go first?" she said.

He was surprised, pleasantly.

"Absolutely."

She folded her hands in her lap and composed her face, looking every bit as if she were about to deliver a prepared speech.

"I didn't think of this when I asked you to work with me," she said. "And I apologize if this makes a huge difference and I've wasted your time—"

He stifled a buzz.

"It's just that I don't know anything about your work, as a minister, and I don't want to offend you, but, I mean . . ." She gave herself an exasperated sigh. "I'm not one of Sonia's 'followers.' Do I have to be for us to do this?"

Now he smothered a ding-ding-ding.

"Not at all," he said. "In fact, quite the opposite. And I can say this to you because I have always been honest about it with Sonia. Your sister and I are on different sides of that fence."

"What does that mean?"

"To be blunt, I think parts of her belief system are toxic. There's a lot of taking Scripture out of context, viewing suffering as punishment, that kind of thing. But you heard what Wesley said to Sonia yesterday?"

"Yes."

"That's where I'm coming from too." He leaned forward, forearms on his thighs. "It's a pity you don't watch game shows. Just about everything I needed to know I learned from the Game Show Network."

She gave him a wry look. When she did allow herself a facial expression, it spoke volumes.

"All right, so that's an exaggeration," Sully said. "I actually think of it as Game Show *Theology.*"

"Like a religion?" Wry morphed into incredulous.

"No, no—more like a way of expressing religion, though I'd rather call it faith."

"Ding-ding and buzz-buzz is faith."

She seemed to be increasingly surprised at her own chutzpah. Sully liked it.

"Take *Wheel of Fortune*, for example," he said.

"My father watched that. I know the premise."

She rolled her eyes, and Sully grinned.

"Just humor me for a minute," he said. "The Gospel According to Pat Sajak: when we set out to seek our fortune in life, whatever that is, we don't know what the turn of the wheel is going to bring. We just have to keep spinning, even when it makes us lose a turn or bankrupts us, because if we don't, we're out of the game."

She watched him with less skeptical eyes.

"To me that's like taking what God sends and working with it. We do have some choices—we can decide what consonant to guess, when to buy a vowel, whether to try to solve the puzzle. We know how to do that by listening to God, reading what He's already said in the Word, experiencing the love of Christ." He sat back in the chair. "You don't have to share my faith for us to work together, but I would love to know where you're coming from, if you feel comfortable telling me."

She clearly didn't see how this would get her where she wanted to go, but she said, "I believe in God."

"Did you go to church as a kid?"

"My grandmother took us. My father's mother. She lived next door and she always made sure Sonia and I went to Catholic Sunday school, until she died."

"How old were you then?"

"Ten. Sonia was five."

Interesting how she included Sonia in every fiber of her story. Interesting, but not surprising. He wasn't sure how many more questions she'd answer before she realized what she'd revealed, but he risked another nudge.

"What about your parents? They weren't churchgoers?"

Lucia gave him a deadpan look. "The extent of my mother's

religious teaching was to explain to me that God didn't like little girls who weren't nice to their baby sisters."

Ouch.

"I always was, but she seemed to feel that I needed frequent reminders."

Sully pulled one foot up onto the chair. This part he hadn't lost: his love for the unfolding of a client's story.

"So after Grandma died . . ." he said.

"Grandma Brocacini. We called her Grandma Broc." Lucia rolled her eyes again. "I guess you don't need all the details."

"Actually, I love them. I think God is in the details. So after Grandma Broc died, did you continue on some kind of path with God?"

"I kept talking to Him. I still do. He doesn't ever answer, but I keep talking. Mostly when I'm desperate. I don't know—maybe I just hope He'll love me a little more if I do. So far I don't think that's panned out."

She blinked, as if she'd just discovered she was telling this near stranger a thing she hadn't uttered before.

Sully eased into the space. "I hear that," he said. "Prayer can seem futile sometimes."

"Not according to my sister," she said drily.

Sonia again. Sully might as well pull up another Adirondack and get her down there to join them. But it did give him a way to keep Lucia adding brushstrokes to the picture she was painting for him.

"Tell me about that," he said. "About your experience with Sonia's belief system."

"I didn't even know she had one," Lucia said, "until one night when Bethany was nine months old." She scowled into the past for a moment. "Blake—her husband—had died."

"Right. I know about that."

"And she had been telling me about having this 'salvation experience.'" Lucia put the term in quotation marks with her fingers. "This one night she talked me into going with her to the church she said had pulled her out of the pit of despair and saved her life."

She was still quoting, heavy on the irony.

"She told me I was going to see Jesus for the first time—not the pretty, Sunday morning Jesus who Grandma Broc had been content with, but the living, breathing, personal Savior who could heal me."

She gave Sully the blank look again.

"I take it you didn't think you had anything to be healed from," Sully said.

"No. But I sat through the sermon, and I tried to sing along with the music. I didn't wave my hands in the air, though. I didn't get that." She peered at him. "I hope that doesn't offend you."

"Buzz," Sully said.

"What buzz? What did I say?"

"You don't have to worry about what offends me. I want you to feel free to say whatever you want here."

Lucia looked doubtful, but she went on. "I didn't see Jesus, but I was convinced they all did, and I didn't want Sonia to be embarrassed by me. So when the pastor smiled right at me and said anyone who wanted to be saved should come forward, I did. Sonia went with me and sobbed and prayed, and when someone asked me a string of questions, I nodded my head to all of them." She gave a soft grunt. "I was thirty-seven years old, but they said I'd been born again."

Sully hiked the other foot onto his chair and rested his wrists on his knees. "Did Sonia follow up on that in any way?"

Lucia shook her head. "She never even asked me about it after that night—thank heaven. I didn't want to make her feel bad, but I did not have a 'salvation experience.'"

At any later point in therapy he would have called her on *I didn't want to make her feel bad,* but if he did, she might shut down. He was amazed she'd said this much.

"Why do you think she never talked to you about it?" Sully said.

"She got completely enmeshed in that church, and then right after that she wrote her first book and did the promotion tour, where everybody found out about her singing voice and what a charismatic speaker she was." Lucia gave him the most ironic look yet. "The rest is Abundant Living history."

"And what was going on with you at that time?"

"I met Chip that year and we got married." She smiled sheepishly. "I guess I thought that was my salvation."

Every therapeutic cell in his brain pulled Sully to take that train, but from the way she resituated herself in the chair, he knew he couldn't even keep her on this one for much longer before she asked "what the Sam Hill" this had to do with Bethany. If he could just take her one more inch . . .

"How do you feel about God's love?" he said.

"You mean, like He loves us all?"

"So you think that's true?"

She gave him a real smile. She was such a pretty woman when she smiled.

"That's what Grandma Broc taught us, so I've always believed it. She never told me anything that didn't turn out to be true. However . . ."

Sully waited. That part came back to him too: the fact that about half of being a therapist was knowing when to shut up.

"What she didn't tell me, that I do believe, is that He loves some of us more than others. I guess part of my 'theology' is that Sonia is one of those God loves more deeply than other people."

Holy crow. "Why is that?" he said.

"Because. She's the one with the singing voice and the magnetic personality and the way with the written word. She inspires everybody with her charm, gets people to move. She's beautiful, she's stylish." Lucia frowned. "She's slender."

Sully spoke with care. "And look where she is now. And where she's been."

"Oh, I'm not saying she hasn't had tragedy. Are you kidding? But it's never been anything she's brought on herself, and God always seems to fix things somehow."

"How about now?"

She pursed her lips for a moment. "Isn't that why ALM fired her, because God isn't fixing it, so she must have done something wrong?"

"What do you think?"

"I hope they're full of crap."

"So you don't think Sonia has ticked God off somehow and now she's being punished."

"I don't see how she could have. I might not believe in what she's doing, but I know she's trying to help people, and she has. Thousands of them."

"In some ways, yes. She's a good woman. And what about you? You've had hard things happen in your life, I'm sure."

"Which," she said, "we are not going to talk about."

When she closed down, she closed down. He could almost hear the shutters on her soul being nailed shut.

"No offense—" She cringed. "Oh, please. Don't buzz me."

Sully grinned. He had to say one thing about her: she caught on fast.

"You're the professional psychologist," she said, "but I don't see what any of this stuff about what I do or don't believe has to do with Bethany and what I can do for her."

"I think it has everything to do with it. Even people who call themselves atheists make their decisions based on what they do or don't believe."

"Example, please," she said.

Sully steepled his fingers under his nose to give himself a chance to think. He had to be so careful here.

"If you do believe that God loves some people more than others, where does Bethany fall on the love scale?" he said. "Will you base that on the things that have happened to her? She lost her father before she ever knew him. She's apparently been raised by nannies. Now her mother's been so disfigured, Bethany's afraid to look at her. Does that mean God doesn't love her as deeply as He does, say, Wesley's little boy?"

Sully brought his feet to the ground and leaned forward, hands working with the words. "I'm not trying to offend *you*, Lucia. I'm just trying to show you that if you do believe that, it's going to affect Bethany in some major ways. Quite frankly, I don't think you do believe it."

"Why do you say that?"

"I have an advantage in this situation that I seldom have with clients. I got to know you a little before you came to see me, and I've seen you interact with Bethany. What you're giving her in terms of love and acceptance doesn't match what I'm hearing you say."

He saw her swallow hard. This was as far as they were going to go tonight, which was farther than he'd expected. But he didn't think she was satisfied with where they were.

"So what do I do with that?" she said.

"You want a goal," he said.

For an answer, she pulled a small pad and a gel pen out of her pocket. She was nothing if not motivated.

"Okay," Sully said. "What would you like to see happening for Bethany before we meet next time—say, three days from now—since, as you said, we may not have a lot of time."

"In three days? I want to see her start having a childhood. Until Wesley brought James-Lawson this afternoon, all she did was follow me around, carrying things for me and handing me stuff." She shook her head. "I just don't understand why she hasn't been taught how to be a little girl."

"Sweet tea?" Sully said. His throat was parched.

"Excuse me? Oh, sure."

He poured them each a glass while he tried to decide whether to chance what poked impishly at his brain. She took a sip and widened her eyes at him.

"You made this?"

"You watched me."

"It's amazing," she said, and then clicked the pen expectantly.

It was worth a shot.

"From what I can see," he said, "you're doing a great job providing Bethany with some childhood experiences, as much as you have time for."

"Do you think I should tell Sonia I'm not going to clean the house and handle her banking, so I'll have more time to spend with Bethany?"

"Do you?"

Lucia wrote on the pad and looked up. "What else?"

"I also recommend that *you* play a game—with yourself."

"You're not going to make me play *Wheel of Fortune*, are you?"

"I'm not going to make you do anything, but what I have in mind is *Family Feud.*"

She groaned. "Is that the one where that Australian guy kisses all the women?"

Sully let out a guffaw. "You mean Richard Dawson?"

"I don't know. I told you I don't watch that stuff."

"On *Family Feud* they give a category, like Things You Can Use a Toothpick For. And the family of contestants has to come up with the top five answers the audience gave."

"There's a lot of buzzing on that show, too, if I remember," Lucia said. She didn't write that down.

"I want you to be the audience for your family and make a list of the first five significant things you can remember in your life with them."

"About my childhood." She narrowed her eyes at him. "I knew you'd get back to that. Go ahead."

"These don't have to be major events—not your family won the lottery, or you vacationed in Europe."

"As if."

"Just five things that come straight into your mind when you think back as far as you can go."

She did write that, and tucked the pad and pen back into her pocket. "Can I ask you a question that doesn't have anything to do with any of this? It's about Sonia—you know, about what's going on with her right now."

Sully took a long drag from his sweet tea glass. This required some shifting of gears.

"How do you think she did with physical therapy today?" he said.

"Wesley didn't tell me much, but she's coming back tomorrow. I guess that's positive."

"It is if she can get Sonia involved in her healing, but she still needs to talk to a therapist, I think. She's fragile right now."

"So what do we do?" Lucia said. "I mean, what do *I* do?"

Sully caught the pronoun switch and filed it away for later.

"I'd like to call a psychiatrist I know," he said. "I think he'd come out as a favor to me. She may need medication to get her to a place where he or someone else can even start to help her work this through."

"I can barely get her to take her pain meds."

"If this goes on much longer, she may have no choice."

Lucia gave a grim nod and stood up. "Three days from now, then? That would make it Friday."

Sully stood up too. "Same time, same station," he said.

She almost smiled at him. "Same game," she said.

Sully left her putting out the tiki torches and tried not to flat-out run to the guesthouse so he wouldn't be left alone with the river. It had kept to itself while he talked to Lucia—he had to give it credit for that. But any minute now it would mock him, tell him that no matter how well he'd been able to lose himself in the session, how easily things had come back to him, how good he felt about the start they'd made—he hadn't gotten close to the pain he suspected hid under all her control.

What then, Dr. Crisp? the river seemed to ask him. What if Lucia, too, succumbs to my waters? What if Sonia throws herself into my arms because yours weren't strong enough?

What then, Dr. Crisp?

Sully took the guesthouse suite in two strides and closed the vertical blinds to shut out the river. But the only way to stop the taunting was to know why he couldn't help his wife. That was what he had come here to do, and he couldn't make the same mistake he'd made for thirteen years.

No matter where this went with Lucia and Sonia, he couldn't let it suffice for where Sullivan Crisp had to go.

CHAPTER TWENTY-FOUR

I had just about decided life didn't get any better than an afternoon with James-Lawson and Bethany. Fresh–squeezed lemonade, James-Lawson's small feet hanging off the dock next to mine, Bethany's tucked up under her like a shy kitten's—and a concerto of squeals and giggles as they watched a line of turtles sun themselves on a log and take turns sliding in and out of the water. I was as close to happy as I'd been in forever.

Until a nondescript sedan pulled into the driveway, and a squarish woman emerged from the driver's seat, in a turquoise pantsuit this time.

Bethany pointed as Special Agent Deidre Schmacker opened the car's back door and reached in.

"Is that a stranger?" she said.

Well, she's strange, I wanted to say. But I shook my head. "No, I know her. We can talk to her."

As if I had a choice. But I did have a choice for Bethany.

"You two can play in the gazebo while *I* talk to her," I said. "It's going to be boring."

"Oh." James-Lawson nodded sagely. "Big people stuff."

"Definitely," I said.

I put out both hands for them each to take one and started for the gazebo. Agent Schmacker came toward us, carrying something in her arms. Something that moved.

"Hey, Miss Lucia," James-Lawson said. "She gots a dog."

She did indeed. A pug, to be exact, who I could hear sniffing and snorting from its almost nonexistent nose even from yards away.

Just when I'd been sure she couldn't have been any less like any FBI agent I'd ever met.

Dropping the kids off at the gazebo wasn't an option at that point. Bethany matched the irrepressible James-Lawson on the enthusiasm scale.

"I see that you're being well taken care of, Mrs. Coffey," Agent Schmacker said when she reached us, a squirming canine in her arms.

James-Lawson took his eyes off the dog long enough to inform her that *I* was taking care of *them.*

"Sonia is in physical therapy right now," I said.

"That's all right. I actually came to talk to you, and perhaps Bethany."

I could feel my eyes going cold.

She leaned over. "Do you like dogs, Bethany?"

Bethany bobbed her head.

James-Lawson stuck out his hand. "I do, too, and my name is James-Lawson and it's nice to meet you."

"It's nice to meet you, too, both of you. This is J. Edgar."

In spite of my rising annoyance, I had to choke back a laugh.

"Would you like to pet him?" she said.

James-Lawson pulled back his hand. "Does he bite?"

"Oh no. And he loves kids. He's just waiting for you to say something to him."

Bethany put her hands on her chubby knees. "Hi, doggy," she said.

The pug leapt out of his "mother's" arms and into Bethany's. He licked and snorted until I thought she'd giggle herself to death. I felt a smile sneak across my face.

Agent Schmacker clasped her hands behind her and looked on as if she were Bethany's grandmother, there to enjoy the moment.

"Can I hold him next?" James-Lawson said.

Bethany handed J. Edgar right over and dug into her pocket, producing half a Pop-Tart. When had she stowed that?

"May I give him some of this?" she said.

Schmacker shook her head. "I don't give J. Edgar refined sugar. It would decay his teeth and make his bones weak, and I love him too much to let that happen."

"Oh," Bethany said.

The agent's voice was kid-kind, I had to admit, but Bethany wilted as if she'd just been scolded.

"Here." Schmacker reached into her own pocket and pulled out a bone-shaped something. "You can give him this. It has all kinds of nutrients in it. Make him sit, though."

James-Lawson set the dog on the ground, and the delight returned to Bethany's face as she chirped for J. Edgar to sit and deposited the bone into his grinning mouth. He took off across the lawn and looked back over one of his too-big shoulders at her.

"May I go out there with him?" Bethany said to me.

"Me too?" James-Lawson said.

"Absolutely."

They bounded off, squealing anew and calling "Doggy! J. Edgar!"

I put my hand to my throat to force down a lump. Deidre Schmacker, too, watched appreciatively before she pulled a piece of paper from her other pocket.

"Mrs. Coffey," she said, "this is a list of everyone who has worked for Sonia. I'll be going over it with your sister at some point, but I also thought—" She gazed across the yard where J. Edgar and the children were cavorting like Shakespearean nymphs. "I'm wondering if Bethany might be able to tell us anything."

"No," I said.

"Mrs. Coffey, I'm not going to interrogate her."

"No, you're not. So far Bethany has not been told that her mother's plane crash wasn't an accident, and I want to keep it that way."

"You're her legal guardian, then, now that her mother is incapacitated?"

I struggled to swallow. This was why I despised these people so much, no matter how warm and fuzzy this one tried to be.

"No, I'm not," I said. "But as her aunt, I am not—"

Schmacker put her hand up. "Don't worry. I'm not going to try to usurp your authority. How about a compromise?"

How about no?

But I said, "What would that be?"

She held up the paper. "I will leave this list with you, and sometime, when you and Bethany are just chatting, you might ask her about some of the people on it. Who was nice, who wasn't. Who liked Mommy, who didn't. Make it a game."

I shook my head. "I can already tell you that Bethany will be no help whatsoever. They sheltered her from everything that went on."

Agent Schmacker gave me a long look before, still holding the paper, she put her fingers in the corners of her mouth and produced a high-pitched whistle. J. Edgar twisted in midair and made a beeline for her, with Bethany and James-Lawson behind him.

"Children are aware of a lot more than we think," she said to me. "I'd appreciate anything you can find out."

Which would be nada.

J. Edgar jumped into her arms and snuffled at her face.

"Does he have to go now?" Bethany said.

"He does. We have work to do."

"Oh." Bethany twisted the bottom of her shirt in her fingers. "Will you ever bring him back?"

"Would you like for me to bring him back?"

She nodded hungrily. James-Lawson chimed in with his "Me too."

I glared at Schmacker. *Oh, I'll get you, my pretty. And your little dog too.*

"Then he'll be back to visit," she said.

She touched Bethany and James-Lawson each lightly on the head, pressed the list into my hand, and went toward her car with the panting J. Edgar pug.

Bethany ran to the driveway and waved until they were out of sight, and it shook me to the core of all the stuff I had crammed inside myself.

She truly was afraid to take a step without asking somebody's permission. She was defeated by the slightest hint that she'd said something wrong. It took small beings like a four-year-old boy and a homely animal to make her at ease enough to smile, beings who wouldn't tell her to go away, be quiet, eat a cookie and be happy with that. J. Edgar and James-Lawson had achieved what no one else in her little life had: they had made her believe that there wasn't always someone else more important than she was.

When Agent Schmaker's car disappeared around the corner, Bethany trudged back to James-Lawson and me. The glow left her face, and I couldn't let it go.

"You know," I said, "we have other animal friends right here."

James-Lawson took a survey of the lawn. "Where?"

"Right there," I said.

I pointed to a blue heron that stood skinny-knee deep near the bank. I had actually taken an immediate dislike to the bird the first time I saw him, since he was thin and graceful, but he might serve me well at the moment. If he did, I would thank him later.

"What's his name?" James-Lawson said.

"He hasn't told me," I said. "We've only just met. Why don't you two give him one?"

"We can do that?" Bethany said.

"Of course."

"May we name him J. Edgar?"

I hated to squelch this burst of creativity, but I wanted to keep Agent Schmacker off her radar.

"Do you think J. Edgar would want to share his name?" I said.

Bethany shook her head and looked faintly frustrated.

"Okay," I said. "What about Harry? Harry the Heron?"

It wasn't terribly inspired, but the dimples returned, and James-Lawson ran toward the river, hand already outstretched. I could have predicted that he'd say, "Nice to meet you, Harry the Heron," which he did.

Harry beat his wings against the air and lifted himself easily out of reach of the small boy who would have shaken his claw if he'd allowed it.

"Hey, Mama—that's Harry the Heron."

I turned to see James-Lawson jumping into Wesley's arms. Bethany looked on as if she were watching a display she'd never been privy to before. I wanted to hold her, but so far I'd felt the invisible shield that said, *I don't want anybody touching me. It hurts when they let go.*

James-Lawson finished informing his mother of everything we had said, done, and eaten in her absence—punctuating himself with 'You know whats?' and then grabbing Bethany's hand and pulling her to the stack of rocks they'd collected.

"You're good with him," Wesley said to me.

"He's good with *me,*" I said. "He pretty much tells me what needs to happen, and I'm happy to oblige."

"That's what you do, isn't it?" Her eyes were pouring their oil into mine. "Let's sit for a minute."

I followed her to the chairs Sullivan and I had left on the lawn. I didn't hesitate to sit in one now that I knew I would fit into it without a shoehorn. Besides, once again I knew I couldn't argue with this woman, even if she was about to call me on something. I could see it in her lips.

"I'm not letting James-Lawson do anything he shouldn't," I said.

"Oh, I know that. But you're letting your sister get away with everything."

"Excuse me?"

"This is probably going to make you mad, but it's got to be said. You are at that woman's beck and call. I'm talking about 'Lucia, take care of me while I refuse to take care of myself.'" Her voice rose in pitch. "'Lucia, take care of my baby, because I won't do that either.'

'Oh, and Lucia, honey, could you do everything Marnie can't do because I'm drivin' her to drink?'"

To my own utter surprise I laughed out loud.

"I'm not trying to be funny."

"No," I said. "It's just that I thought that same thing not a day ago. I feel like a waitress for Sonia's life."

"Girl, from what I can see, you are a waitress for everybody's life." She waved her hand. "But that is not my business. Sonia is my business, and if you keep doing everything for her, she is never going to recover."

Lucia Marie—don't you listen to this.

But I did, because Wesley Kane's voice spoke with more power than my mother's tape, and that was a first.

"I know you are crazy in love with that child." Wesley nodded toward Bethany. "But you catering to Sonia's every whim is not helping either one of them. Now I am not going to tell you how to run the rest of your life . . ."

Though she clearly would have been glad to, and I might have let her.

". . . But I will tell you that you have to stop doing the hydrotherapy on Sonia's face. She can do that herself now. The same goes for the medication, taking care of her mask, and her mouth prosthesis."

"Which I can't convince her she has to wear."

Wesley pulled her chin in. "Do you hear yourself? *You* have to convince her to wear the thing that is going to keep her mouth from turning into this?"

She pulled her lips sideways and looked like the figure in the *Scream* painting. I wanted to laugh again. I also wanted to cry.

"I've left her a list of the things she has to do for her self-care," she said, "and if you want to help your sister—and that precious baby girl—you won't do any of the things that are on it."

I could feel the slats of the chair pressing into my back. "I won't know what to do with myself," I said.

"If I were you, staying in this beautiful place"—Wesley pointed her chin toward the river the children were tossing their stones into—"I'd be in there swimming every day."

"I love to swim, and I would if I owned a bathing suit—and there were no neighbors—and I didn't have stick women all over the place."

Had I actually just said that? Out loud?

Apparently so, because Wesley's face contorted. "Whatchoo talkin' 'bout, girl?"

The professional voice was gone. I got the feeling we were suddenly two sisters in the 'hood or something.

"I'm talking about this body," I said.

"What about it?"

I just looked at her.

"It's not like you have your own zip code," she said. "You got some junk in the trunk, but—"

"Junk in the trunk?"

She leaned forward and patted her backside. "I have some too. That wouldn't keep me out of that water. You white women kill me, all wanting to look like death on a cracker."

I could only laugh until tears stung my eyes.

"That's it," she said. "Tomorrow I am bringing you a swimming suit."

I opened my mouth to protest, but she put her hand practically in it.

"I don't want to hear about what size you wear and don't wear or any of that. You just going to put it on and go in the water with those children and have a ball."

"Only if you'll bring one for yourself and get in with us," I said.

I waited for the *That would be unprofessional,* but she smiled her magnificent smile.

"I thought you were never going to ask," she said.

CHAPTER TWENTY-FIVE

Sully experienced some serious déjà vu when he walked into the San Antonio Taco Company, known in his divinity school days as SATCO. The customer still had to walk down a narrow corridor and check off his choice of future heartburn on a printed form to be handed to the cashier. Sully picked the bottled water and leaned against a post, more to stem the tide of memories than to look for a table.

They used to come here a lot, he and Lynn and their divinity school friends, not for the food or the atmosphere, but for the price. How many late nights and Saturday afternoons had they spent here, feeding themselves soggy tacos and unspeakable guacamole and debating things like free will vs. the sovereignty of God?

There were three tracks in the divinity school—for ministers, academics, and seekers—and all three had been represented in the group. Sully bristled at the memory that he had been the academic.

He found a corner table and sank into a red plastic chair. His eyes went to an object hanging from the ceiling over the cash register, a replica of a handgun with a sign that read, WE DON'T CALL 911 . . . A whole chunk of conversation dropped into his mind.

"I don't get that," Lynn had said the first night they went in there after the thing went up.

"That's because you're the kind of person who doesn't need to get it."

Who had said that? Anna—or that guy she ended up marrying? What was his name? He'd called himself a recovering Catholic.

"Why don't I need to get it?" Lynn said.

"Because, darlin'," he himself said, "you're not going to come in here and try to hold the place up or take out somebody eating an enchilada."

Everyone else chimed in.

"They're saying you don't get a chance at a trial."

"Or an ambulance."

"They just shoot you."

Sully recalled Lynn blushing up to the roots of her hair. "Oh," she'd said. "Du-uh."

"What duh?" He was sure Anna had said it. "The fact that you don't get it is what I love about you. You're so innocent."

Lynn laughed then—the bell of a laugh he'd loved so much. "Good," she'd said. "I thought I was just being stupid. As usual."

Sully scraped at the wrapper on his water bottle. He couldn't remember what he'd said then. He hoped he'd taken her in his arms and assured her she was far from stupid. He truly hoped so.

"No—no bucket today," a familiar voice said.

Sully looked toward the counter, and there she was. The San Antonio Taco Company had changed less than Anna Thatcher-Dickinson had. The only thing he recognized about her was the signature out-of-control hair, thick and poodle curly and barely kept in line by several devices that looked to Sully like chopsticks. Some gray shot through the dark brown now.

Her face, however, made her look as if she'd exchanged her former self for a new one. She used to travel everywhere on a ten-speed bike and eat only food that had never had a face, all of which had left her as bright eyed as the Energizer Bunny. Either the diet or the mode of transportation had evidently gone by the wayside over the last thirteen years, because her eyes sagged as she navigated the tables to get to him, and her mouth had settled into a discontented line.

"Sully," she said when she finally reached him. "I would have known you anywhere. Why have I aged and you haven't? There's no justice."

Sully grinned as he accepted her hug. That was why he and Lynn had liked her so much. She always saved people the trouble of being diplomatic.

"Have you ordered?"

At the shake of his head, she waved him off.

"That's okay, I probably got enough for both of us and a small third world country."

She then gave a thumbnail sketch of the last decade of her life, which revealed that whatever she'd been looking for as a "seeker" at Vanderbilt Divinity School still had not been found. She was interrupted by the announcement that her order was ready. She started right in on the chalupas without missing a beat in her monologue.

"What about you? You said over the phone you wanted to talk about Lynn." She dabbed sour cream from her chin. "Are you writing your memoirs or something? I've read some of your books, by the way. Not bad."

"Thanks."

She pointed to the Spanish rice, but he shook his head.

"I just have a couple of questions," he said. "Just to button some things up."

How cheesy did that sound? Why didn't he at least pretend to want to give her a personal update? He was really bad at this.

"So, like what?" she said.

"Like—did Lynn seem happy to you? Did she ever say anything to you about—not being—"

"You're not writing your memoirs."

"No."

Anna set the chalupa down in the paper dish it hadn't touched since she took the first bite. "Look," she said, "if it were me, I'd want to put that whole period of my life behind me and move on."

"This is part of my moving on," Sully said.

She scratched at her chest, revealing a tattoo of a Celtic cross. "Okay—all I know is Lynn was nuts over you, like, over-the-top nuts. You know why she never got her degree. She majored in you. You were all she wanted."

Sully felt the thickening in his throat again. Why had he even started this?

"I told her she was an idiot, of course." Anna stabbed the corner of a tortilla into the guacamole. "You don't build your whole life around somebody else. If I'd done that with Tom Dickinson, I'd be a basket case right now. You knew we were divorced."

"No, I didn't. I'm sorry."

"Don't be. We're both better off. We were never like you and Lynn were at first."

Sully felt something stir. "At first?"

"You know, before the shine became patina. How poetic is that?" She laughed. "Look, you two were good together, Sully. Just go with that. You know how to love, so take that into another relationship. Have you even dated since Lynn died?"

"Uh, no."

"Then there's your trouble. What are you doing Saturday night?"

Before Sully could get his tongue untangled, she laughed again. "Just kidding. I always thought you were a remarkable person, but you and I, I don't think so."

Sully tried to smile. "Do I even want to know why?"

"Oh, it's nothing against you. I always told Lynn she got the last good one. I just need a guy who can take care of himself so I can do my thing."

He couldn't even begin to sort that out.

"You know what?" she said. "Lynn and I weren't that close after—gosh, when was it? Sometime after that retreat up at Fall Creek Falls. You remember that? It was you, Lynn, Tom, me, and that Ukrainian couple. What were their names?"

Sully shook his head.

"It's probably not important. Right after that, Tom and I got married, and it was hard enough keeping up with him and going to school, much less devoting time to friends." For a moment she looked sad. "Lynn always managed, though. I wish in some ways I could have been more like her." She tossed her head back and laughed once more. "If I were, we'd be going out Saturday night."

Sully stayed long enough to be polite, but in the end it was Anna who took off, after getting his phone number out of him and saying they ought to get the old gang together.

"I'll arrange it if you want," she said.

"I'll call you," he said.

"Ten bucks says you won't."

And with a kiss on his cheek, she left Sully to wonder if the meeting had been a complete fiasco. All he'd gotten out of it was Anna's impression that he was a man who needed to be taken care of, which had at least let him out of a duty date. He looked dismally at the Spanish rice she'd left for him.

She was the only person he'd been able to get in touch with.

Lynn might have taken all her secrets to the bottom of the Cumberland after all.

Wesley appeared with a bag of swimsuit choices the next day, but the sky dumped rain and treated us to a lightning-and-thunder show. Bethany, James-Lawson, and I took shelter in the playroom, where they set up a fort with blankets and chairs, and I attempted my *Family Feud* list for Sullivan.

It wasn't the kind I usually made. Mine were usually about things like:

- find out when school starts for Bethany
- figure out who pays the bills so the power company doesn't turn off the electricity
- call Didi—see if she actually quit or if she's just on an unscheduled sabbatical

The biggest difference between that and the thing Sullivan wanted me to do was that when I wrote down the first five significant events of my childhood, I wouldn't be able to check them off. Those pieces of my life were always going to be there, and I couldn't do anything about them.

I clicked my pen aimlessly. My childhood memories were less like a game show than MTV. They came out in disconnected flashes I couldn't even focus on before the next one flickered in and out.

Flash: my mother wailing in the hallway in the middle of the night that it was too early, and my only later realizing that she meant too early for the baby to be born.

Flash: Grandma Broc taking me to my first dance class, probably to distract me while my parents anguished over the premature baby struggling for her very young life. That was probably the only time in my life when I danced through the days aware only in some narrow place that something was amiss.

Flash: my mother bringing home the ugliest little being I'd ever seen. Another "only": the only time I was ever prettier than my sister.

I put down the pen. I still wasn't convinced that exhuming my past would help the present—or Bethany's future. So I looked back at the list I *had* made. The results of that one had been depressing too.

A call to Trinity Christian Academy revealed not only that classes started next week, but that Bethany was enrolled in first grade, when she'd never been to kindergarten. Or, for that matter, preschool.

No arrangements had been made for her to be picked up by their bus program—though they were sure they could fit her in—and since no one had attended the parents' orientation event, they would be happy to e-mail me the particulars about uniforms, supplies—oh, and the process for paying tuition.

From what I was able to get out of Marnie, who was now so stressed she could barely put two sentences together, Sonia's accountant paid her personal bills. That would have been a relief, except that she seemed to think I should be in touch with this Patrick person.

"If he's already dealing with her finances," I said, "I don't see why."

"I just don't know how much longer he's going to stay on," she'd said, eyes shifting. "He and Sonia aren't on the best of terms."

"What does that mean?" I said.

"I have no idea." She'd already been halfway out of the room by then, heeding Sonia's bark from the office. "You should call him. I'll get you the number."

Didi-the-housekeeper had been more difficult to locate. I wrote out a message and read it over the phone so I wouldn't tell her she was a complete flake for terminating her employment by just not showing up anymore.

"Didi, we have no problem with your missing work," I read through gritted teeth. "With all that's been going on around here, and all the long hours you've put in, you obviously needed a break. But could you give me a call and tell me when you might be returning?"

I didn't add, "Or if," but I realized now that her silence was my answer. The dust collected on tabletops and baseboards, and the bathrooms exuded an unpleasant aroma. I couldn't keep up with the laundry or do more than spray a little Lysol in the toilets, and I could find neither the vacuum cleaner nor the time to use it.

And that was just the inside of the house. Bryson Porter didn't come back, either, after his encounter with the FBI. I assumed from Deidre Schmacker's visit that he wasn't their guy, in spite of whatever they had found in the garage, but he must have decided this was no longer the place for him. The lawn was ankle high, and the weeds brazenly encroached on the flower beds. I toyed with the idea of doing the yard work myself until I remembered what Wesley had said to me, and what I'd promised Sullivan Crisp I would do.

So I crossed Didi off the list and added:

- tell Sonia I'm hiring a lawn service
- and a once-a-week maid
- eat more chocolate

The doorbell rang, and despite my assurance that I would be right back, both James-Lawson and Bethany tailed me down the stairs, chattering about how they hoped it was J. Edgar. I of course hoped it was not—or that he at least had come alone. Deidre Schmacker's was another list I was avoiding.

I peeked out through the glass in the front door. "Sorry, kids," I said. "It's the mailman."

Bethany shrank against the foyer mirror.

"It's okay," James-Lawson said to her. "The mailman's not a stranger."

Bethany just shook her head.

When the carrier had handed me more mail than would fit in the box and left, I turned to her.

"Were you afraid of him?" I said.

"I'm not allowed to talk to strangers," she said.

"That's true." I squatted in front of her, arms full of envelopes. "But it's okay if I tell you the person is safe. Just like yesterday."

She looked extremely doubtful.

"I would never let anyone hurt you," I said.

"You might not be able to stop them."

I could feel my eyes springing open.

"If someone wanted to take me, they just would," she said.

I didn't even ask where that had come from. The child watched entirely too much television.

"Come on, you two," I said. "Snack time."

We were pulling a sheet of chocolate chip cookies out of the oven when I heard Wesley come into the kitchen behind me.

"You're just in time," I said, "as long as you don't mind a little kid-spit in your dough."

"I think we'll be all right with that," Wesley said.

We.

I turned, pot holder still in hand. Sonia was with her.

Immediately something brushed past my leg: Bethany, sliding around me and retreating into the pantry. At least she wasn't screaming.

James-Lawson, on the other hand, walked up to Sonia and offered a hand still gooey with butter. "I'm James-Lawson Kane," he said. "It's nice to meet you."

Sonia still stood above him, so he couldn't possibly have seen her face yet. What the Sam Hill was Wesley thinking?

Or Sonia, for that matter? Could she possibly still believe that any new person who laid eyes on her wouldn't recoil in some small way? And a child—for Pete's sake.

"Aren't you just about half-cute?" Sonia said.

She bent over to James-Lawson, who shook his head.

"No, ma'am," he said. "I'm all the way cute."

Sonia smiled, a grisly affair with the prosthesis firmly lodged in her mouth.

James-Lawson leaned his woolly head to the side. "You got a boo-boo, huh?"

"Just a little one," Sonia said.

"You know what? No. It's a really big one."

Sonia stood back up. "Don't worry," she said. "It's going to go away."

"I know, 'cause my mama's helping you."

Dear God, please don't let her start preaching at this child.

God seemed to answer for once. Sonia nodded, as best she could, and patted his head.

"I have work to do, boys and girls," she said, and turned to go.

"The kids and I baked cookies," I said again. "Maybe Bethany would like to give you one."

Sonia looked around as if she'd just discovered her child's absence. "I don't want to push her," she said. "Let's just wait until I'm better."

Wesley gave her a look hard enough to pound her into the ground, but Sonia simply drifted out of the kitchen.

"You know what, Miss Lucia?" James-Lawson said.

"What?" I said.

"*I* want a cookie."

"And *a* cookie is all you're going to get, boy," Wesley said.

"But this is a special occasion!"

"You think every time you see Miss Lucia it's a special occasion."

"It is!" he said. Only because he was a very smart child did he not add, "Du-uh."

"Two," his mother said. "And that's all."

"Bethany!" he hollered. "We each get two cookies."

She appeared from the pantry, peering around the corner until she apparently decided that the coast was clear.

I heard Wesley sigh, and our eyes met in a tacit agreement that it didn't get any sadder than this.

"You going to find out what that's about?" she whispered to me.

"Oh, heck yeah," I whispered back.

I put a plate of four cookies on the sit-down counter and helped James-Lawson onto his stool while Wesley went to the fridge for the milk. Bethany took one and eyed it suspiciously.

"What's wrong?" I said.

"Was that white stuff we put in this refined sugar?" she said.

"Yeah," I said.

"Then we shouldn't give one to James-Lawson."

He looked at her as if she'd just suggested we take away his birthday.

"Why not?" I said.

"Because it will decay his teeth and make his bones weak. I love him too much to do that to him."

Recitation complete, she moved the plate out of his reach, to an indignant "Huh?!" and took a cookie for herself.

"Hey! Miss Lucia!"

"Thank you for your love, Miss Bethany," Wesley said, "but two cookies are not going to rot James-Lawson's teeth, I promise you that."

She bulged her eyes at me.

"Ms. Schmacker was talking about her dog, Bethie," I said. "He can't brush his teeth like you can." As her gaze went for the floor, I added hastily, "That was wonderful of you to think of James-Lawson, though."

"But I have to ask you," Wesley said, as she placed a cookie firmly into Bethany's hand. "If you thought he shouldn't have one, why was it okay for you to have one?"

Bethany stared down at the cookie. "Because I love James-Lawson," she said.

"And you don't love you?"

She looked up at her, blue eyes startled.

"Well, I do," Wesley said. "And James-Lawson does and Miss Lucia does, so if you don't want to be left out of this party, you better love you too."

Bethany nodded and took an obedient bite. She, too, had discovered you didn't argue with Wesley Kane.

But, oh, dear God, please let her believe it.

Once they'd gone, I let Bethany help me put the rest of the cookies in a bag for the freezer, lest Marnie should polish them off. I did consider briefly encouraging Marnie to eat all she wanted, so her teeth would fall out and she would no longer be attractive to my husband, but I shoved that back in with the Chip trash and looked at Bethany.

The tip of her tongue had crept to the corner of her mouth as she positioned the goodies just so in the bag.

"James-Lawson saw your mom," I said.

"I know."

"He wasn't scared."

"I know."

"Of course, she's not his mom, so that's different, but—"

"I'm not allowed to," Bethany said. She tried to press the top of the Ziploc bag together, tongue still working.

"You're not allowed to what?" I said.

"I'm not allowed to see her without her face."

I didn't know which thing to scream first. I had to chomp down on my lip to keep from letting them all spew out.

"Did someone tell you that?" I said.

"Yeah—yes, ma'am."

"Who?"

She got the bag zipped and showed it to me proudly.

"Great," I said. I set it on the counter and closed her hands between mine. "Bethie, who told you that you weren't allowed to see your mom without her face?"

The blue eyes blinked at me. "She did," she said. "May I go play in the fort now?"

"Absolutely," I think I said. It was hard to know, with everything else that shrieked in my head. I pressed my fingers to my temples. *Dear God.*

Just—*Dear God.*

CHAPTER TWENTY-SIX

Sully took off his ball cap to mop his forehead with it. Four o'clock in the afternoon wasn't the smartest time of day to be out using a weed eater, but if he'd stayed inside the guesthouse with that microphone much longer, he would have flushed the thing down the toilet. He'd spent the hour before he came out here looking up Ukrainian names on the Internet. When they all started sounding like characters from *Fiddler on the Roof*, he'd opted for edging Sonia's walkways.

It helped some, he decided—his head, not necessarily the yard. Lawn maintenance had never been his strong suit. Lynn had always taken care of that.

And of him, according to Anna. He released the trigger on the weed eater. That could have merely been Anna's take on it, but the more weeds he ate up, the less he thought so. When he was in divinity school, even before they were married, Lynn did everything—the chili making, the window washing, the bill paying, the mailing of birthday cards to relatives.

He headed to the garage with the contraption hanging awkwardly over his shoulder. Lynn had even made weekly trips to Birmingham during Mom's illness when Sully couldn't, and had begged her to come to their house for hospice care. Mom refused, only days before she passed away, and left Lynn crying with him while she made the funeral arrangements.

Sully sat on the fender of Sonia's Escalade. Lynn had cared for every detail of their lives so he could devote all his time to his doctorate. But she seemed to love it. She swore to him she was made to do that.

But had there been some hidden resentment because she never got her degree? He stood up and shook the sweat out of his hair before he put his ball cap back on. If there had been, he must have been blind, because Lynn wore her feelings everywhere: in her eyes, in the way her hands moved, in the way she flipped the pancakes. Until the night she died, he'd thought he knew every emotion that passed through her heart.

A car pulled into the circular drive, and Sully was grateful for the interruption.

Special Agent Deidre Schmacker got out of the passenger side of the white sedan as he emerged, blinking, from the garage. Agent Country Singer stretched his long legs from the driver's seat and adjusted his sunglasses as he looked at Sully.

Sully braced himself.

"Dr. Crisp, isn't it?" Agent Schmacker said. "Are you working for Ms. Cabot now?"

Sully shook his head as he extended his hand, noticing too late that it was striped with dandelion stems. Schmacker looked amused. Agent Country Singer did not.

"I'm Special Agent Ingram," he said, still taking a veritable CT scan of Sully with his eyes.

Sully didn't think it was a good time to ask what made them all "special" agents. They were obviously here on serious business. Even Deidre Schmacker's benevolent fairy godmother demeanor was less evident today.

"I'm just staying in the guesthouse as a family friend," Sully said.

"You're a psychologist, aren't you, Dr. Crisp?" Agent Schmacker said.

"That's right."

"Have you ever worked professionally with Sonia Cabot?"

"You mean as her therapist?" Sully said.

"That's what we mean." Agent Ingram's voice snapped, making him sound more like a junkyard dog than a country singer.

Sully felt vaguely uncomfortable. "No," he said. "I haven't. We're colleagues. Friends."

Agent Schmacker's eyes dropped at the corners, though with less empathy than he'd seen there before. "Then there is no client-patient privilege in effect, so you could tell us from a purely observational standpoint whether you think Sonia Cabot was stable before the plane crash. In your professional opinion."

Where was this coming from?

"I didn't spend a great deal of time with her," Sully said.

"You're telling us she's letting you stay in her house," Ingram said, "but you don't really know her."

"Not enough to have had deep insights into her psyche. But, no, I never saw anything that would indicate that she was unstable." Sully tried a grin. "Not any more than any of the rest of us."

Ingram looked unamused. "Would you consider Sonia Cabot's religion to be a cult?"

Sully felt his jaw drop. "A cult? No."

"Don't her followers basically worship her?"

"What? No—the people Sonia ministers to are Christians. They have some ideas that are different from the mainstream, but—"

"So you'd say she's a radical."

"I wouldn't put her in any category." Sully shoved his hands into his pockets. He'd never been called as an expert witness in a trial, but he'd heard horror stories about cross-examinations that could turn the most single-minded psychologist into a double-talking idiot. He'd always thought his colleagues were exaggerating—until now.

"I'm not comfortable with this conversation," he said.

Ingram snarled something, but Agent Schmacker put up her index finger. If Sully had known that was all it took to shut him up, he'd have had all of his digits going several minutes ago.

"Dr. Crisp," she said, "we're just trying to determine who had a motive for wanting Sonia Cabot dead. As I'm sure you know, sometimes leaders of less, as you called it, 'mainstream' religious organizations can become somewhat careless with the power they have over their followers, and that can cause a great deal of anger."

"That's true," Sully said. "But to my knowledge, Abundant Living Ministries did not fall into that category."

"Nevertheless, we have to explore the possibility, particularly since Ms. Cabot has been less than helpful in this investigation."

"She here?" Ingram said.

Agent Schmacker glanced at her watch. "She should be finished with her physical therapy by now."

Sully had seen Wesley and James-Lawson leave, as, he now suspected, these two had also. Uneasiness crept up his spine as they started for the front door.

"Look," Sully said, "I will say that Ms. Cabot's emotional state since the crash has become somewhat fragile. You might want to tread carefully with her."

"Then perhaps you should join us," Schmacker said.

Agent Ingram gave him a look that said it was not merely a request.

"Purely as an observer," Sully said.

"Of course," she said.

Of course.

Bethany and I were on our way to the kitchen to discuss whether to have macaroni and cheese for the third night in a row or try my ravioli, when they came in the front door—Sullivan and Agent Schmacker and a man who flashed his badge at me.

Bethany ran up to her, round face dimpled in expectation.

"Did you bring J. Edgar?" she said.

Agent Schmacker went to her knees. "Not this time, sweetheart," she said.

"Oh," Bethany said. "Big people talk."

"Yes," I said, just in case Agent Schmacker had any ideas about going over the list with Bethany herself.

"That's right," she said. "J. Edgar doesn't like big-people talk, and I bet you don't either."

Bethany shook her head.

"Then perhaps your Aunt Lucia can find something fun for you to do so she can talk big-people talk with us and your mom."

"I can watch TV," Bethany said.

I cringed, but I didn't have a whole lot of choice.

The male agent scrutinized the foyer as if he were about to start a full-out search of the premises.

When Marnie appeared, more than likely on Sonia's order to find out what was going on out here, I said, "Take Bethany up to the home theater to watch a movie, would you?"

"We can just go in the Gathering Room," she said.

"No. I want her up there—away from here."

Her eyes rounded. The girl truly was not the sharpest knife in the drawer.

"I'll take you to Sonia," I said when they were gone.

To my relief, Sullivan came with us.

Sonia sat at the desk in her office, shuffling through the mountain of mail I'd deposited there. None of it appeared to have been opened.

"What is it *now*?" she said. "I don't mean to be inhospitable, Agent Schmacker, but I am far too busy—"

"This is Special Agent Ingram," Schmacker said. "And I have to warn you, he does not care how busy you are. He has some questions to ask you, and he and I will stay here until you answer them."

My stomach seized. This was the FBI I remembered.

"I've asked your sister and Dr. Crisp to join us, but if you would rather do this alone . . ."

"I'd rather not do it at all."

"That's not an option." Agent Ingram pointed to a brocade wing chair in front of her desk. "Have a seat."

Sonia moved from behind the desk to the chair with an attempt at dignity, but she mangled her hands, and her eyes took on their wild stare.

Agent Schmacker stood behind the desk at the window. Ingram

pulled the other chair to face Sonia, close enough for her to detect what he'd had for lunch. This was what they did. I felt like I was seeing Sonia's skin removed all over again.

Ingram pulled a piece of paper out of a file folder and smacked it onto the desk.

"I am going to give you some names," he said, "and you are going to tell me anything these people may have against you. Anything, and everything."

She shook her head.

"Then we have no choice but to take you in to *our* office and ask you the same thing, and I guarantee you, you won't like the accommodations there."

"Are you threatening me?" Sonia said.

"Oh yeah," he said.

"Sonia." I took a step forward from the wall I hugged next to Sullivan. "Just tell them what they need to know, or it's going to get worse. Trust me on that."

I could feel Sullivan looking at me curiously, but I didn't care. Sonia's look was the only one that mattered at the moment. She cast it angrily on me, but she finally nodded.

"Good," Ingram said. "Now, let's start with Bryson Porter, your gardener-driver type."

"Bryson is my brother in Christ."

"You've never had even so much as an argument with him?"

"No. We always prayed together before we went out in the car. He made my yard so beautiful."

"Were you aware that he used pesticides containing cyanide?"

"Doesn't everyone?" She tried a smile.

Don't do that, Sonia. Don't try to charm them.

"Diana Gables."

"Didi. She's completely committed to my ministry."

"Then why did she quit?"

Her back straightened. "She quit?"

"That's what she told Agent Schmacker."

Sonia looked at me. "Lucia, did she?"

"We haven't seen her in several days," I said.

"She said she was overworked," Agent Schmacker put in from the window seat. "Can you think of any other reason why she might have quit? Did you have an argument with her? Shortchange her on her pay? Cut down on her hours?"

"None of that, no."

For a face that couldn't show expression, Sonia came across quite clearly as obstinate. Beside me, Sullivan recrossed his arms.

"Halsey Coffey," Ingram said.

"Chip," Agent Schmacker put in.

I closed my eyes.

"He is my brother-in-law," Sonia said. "And he worked for me for three months."

"We know all that. Why did he quit?"

"He wanted to go home to his wife—my sister."

"You were aware that he had done prison time for drug trafficking, racketeering, and money laundering, but you still had him working for you." Ingram's voice lowered to a growl. "You're a pretty trusting soul, aren't you, Ms. Cabot?"

"Chip was completely repentant," Sonia said. She raised her voice for the first time, all trace of cream gone. "He did wonderful work here with God and was delivered totally from his former sin."

"And you were responsible for that."

"God was, Agent Ingram. And Chip was grateful. He sobbed right here in this office."

I forced myself to open my eyes, if for no other reason than to make sure Sonia was actually saying this. Sullivan caught my eye and looked discreetly away. At least I wouldn't have to spill my guts about this part in therapy.

"Then let's move on to Yvonne."

"She was my daughter's nanny."

"And she came after these others—Holly—"

"They had no reason to want me dead! They took care of my

child, and I paid them well and allowed them free access to all ALM services."

I looked nervously at Sullivan, who rubbed his chin. I wondered if that meant he, too, heard the brittle breaks between words.

"And Hudson Fargason?"

Sonia didn't answer. Hudson. Hadn't Marnie said he was the cook at one time?

"He was a wonderful chef," she said finally. "I wish he hadn't left."

Ingram leaned back in his chair. "You seem to have a hard time keeping staff, Ms. Cabot. Why did Hudson Fargason leave?"

"I don't know."

"I think you do." Ingram angled himself forward again. "Isn't it true that you fired him?"

"All right, I let him go."

"Then you just lied to us."

"What happens here in my home is my private business. It has nothing to do with this."

"Why did you fire him?"

She said nothing.

"Why, Ms. Cabot? We can go downtown and do this—"

"Because I got food poisoning twice. I thought he was being careless, and I had to let him go—but I didn't even tell him why. I just said I didn't need his services any longer."

"Why would you do that?"

"Because I had no proof. I still don't." She tried to jerk her head away and failed against her gnarled skin. "Hudson has a sweet spirit. He would never hurt anyone."

"He tried to poison you!"

"That was a mistake! He had no reason to do it on purpose. I accepted him when no one else would."

I wanted to stop this. So, I could tell, did Sullivan. He opened and closed his fists and shifted against the wall.

Schmacker looked at him. "Just two more names," she said.

Ingram pulled his face from the hand he leaned on. "You think you can be honest about these?" He didn't wait for an answer. "Tell us about Roxanne Clemm."

"Roxanne didn't work for me," Sonia said. "She was my best friend."

An eyebrow shot up. "Was?"

"Until she moved into my place at Abundant Living after I stepped down. I took that as a betrayal. But isn't that me having an issue with her, and not the reverse?"

That was my sister. Even backed into a torturous corner and ready to snap, she still tried to get herself in command of the conversation.

"Did it ever occur to you that she wanted your position all along?" Ingram said. "That she might have wanted you out of the way so she could take over?"

I never thought I would want to hear Deidre Schmacker's grandmotherly voice instead of anyone else's, but I was just short of begging her to take over now. This bordered on cruel, and Sonia couldn't take much more.

She bore down on Ingram with her eyes. "That is a slanderous, evil thing to say. Roxanne is an opportunist, not a murderer."

"Then that leaves us with only one more name on our list," he said.

"And who is that?"

He looked at Deidre Schmacker and nodded. She came around to the front of the desk and leaned against it, arms folded.

"You, Ms. Cabot," she said.

I plastered myself to the wall so I wouldn't lunge forward. Sonia did. Agent Ingram went to his feet, hands out as if he were going to wrestle her to the floor. Sullivan Crisp was halfway to them when Sonia fell back into her chair. Her chest rose and fell as she struggled to breathe.

Ingram gave Sullivan a hard look that sent him back.

"Are you suggesting that I planned my own death?" Sonia said.

"Not your death," Ingram said. "Maybe a near-death experience that went awry. If it had gone as planned, it would have bolstered your ministry. You could write your next book about it. You could claim that God saved you because you've been His loyal servant. Isn't that what you propound, Ms. Cabot?"

Sonia drew herself up on the thread that held her together.

"That is Satan talking through you," she said. "And I will not have Satan in my home. I want you both to leave."

I shoved my fist against my mouth. This was the part where they would put my sister in handcuffs and push her head down into their car and take her away. This was the part I couldn't handle.

But Agent Ingram stood up and put his list back into his file, and Agent Schmacker picked up her bag.

"It isn't Satan, Ms. Cabot," she said. "It is merely two frustrated investigators who do not understand why you won't help them find out who did this thing to you."

"You know something," Ingram said. "And we will find out what it is."

I let Sullivan show them out, but I couldn't leave Sonia alone to suffer a humiliation I knew only too well. My soul ached for her.

"I'm sorry you had to go through that, *sorella*," I said.

"Don't call me that."

Her voice froze me.

"If you are going to turn on me and God like everyone else, you are not my sister."

"What are you talking about?"

"You let them come in here with their evil—"

"They're the FBI, Sonia. You don't tell them where they can and can't go."

"You okay, Sonia?" Sullivan said from the doorway.

She rose from the chair, eyes menacing and unstable. "Get out," she said to me. "Get out and leave me with my God."

"Sonia," Sully said.

"You get out too!"

"Hey, okay—we'll give you some space."

He nodded to me, and I moved robotically to the door.

"How about if one of us stays with you?" he said.

"I want you out. I want you out now—"

"All right, we're going."

"Close the door behind you."

"I'll do that," Sully said. "But there's no need to lock it. We're going to respect your privacy."

She sank back into the chair and knotted her hands until she had them where she wanted them, tied into her lap. "Just go, please."

We did, Sully closing the door behind us. The lock didn't click, but I heard her prison doors slam.

CHAPTER TWENTY-SEVEN

When Lucia lowered herself into the Adirondack, Sully could see the strain on her face, but he didn't need the light of the torches to know it was there. He could feel the tension come off of her like radio static.

"You need a minute?" he said. "Just to take a few deep breaths, maybe?"

She shook her head. Her dark ponytail barely moved, as if it, too, were weighed down by too much everything.

"I'm okay," she said.

"You have to be exhausted after that scene. I know I am."

"Well, as you now know, I've been through something like that before." She tilted her head to the back of the chair. "Thank you, FBI."

"That's why it's not fair to you that I'm privy to things about your life that you don't choose to tell me," Sully said.

She shrugged.

"I'd buzz you for that," he said, "but I don't think you're in the mood."

She moved only her eyes toward him. "Why would I get a buzz?"

"Because a shrug doesn't take us anywhere. If you're upset that they spilled the proverbial beans about your husband in front of me, that's okay. You have a right to be."

Lucia lowered her forehead into her hands. "Nothing is sacred with those people. They just tear your life apart until they find what they want, and then they leave you with the mess to clean up." She looked at him, eyes as close to frightened as he'd seen them, even at times when she should have been terrified. "Do they really think Sonia staged the plane crash herself?"

"I don't think so. I think they just did that to scare her into helping them come up with somebody who had a motive. Answering their questions about other people might seem safer after that."

"It didn't work, did it?"

Sully looked over his shoulder at the house. "Did you check in on her again?"

Lucia nodded. "I knocked on her bedroom door, and she said she was praying and to leave her alone. I heard one of her DVDs going in there, so I guess she's watching herself. Is that healthy?" She put up her hand. "I'm sorry—we're not supposed to be talking about Sonia."

He did buzz her then, and she let her face collapse into a smile she seemed too tired to hold back.

"Let's just go where we need to go with this," Sully said. "Whatever helps you get a handle on it."

He watched her assemble a question.

"I feel bad even asking this," she said, "but you don't think Sonia would do something to hurt herself, do you?"

"Are you talking about the plane crash?"

"It's stupid, isn't it? Those people have me so paranoid."

"It's not stupid. They put it out there, and you have to process it somehow. Personally, no, I don't think the thought ever entered Sonia's mind. She looks for ways to show God's power in her life, but I seriously doubt she'd manufacture something."

Lucia let out a long breath. "I didn't think so either."

"Would she hurt herself now?" Sully propped one foot across the other knee. "That we don't know."

"Marnie's in the Gathering Room. Sonia won't let her in either, but I asked her to keep an ear open and let us know if she heard anything . . . strange."

"Good plan."

Sully waited, hoping she'd go farther down the path she was obviously glancing at. When she didn't, he said, "Do you have a relationship with Marnie?"

"No, and I don't want to talk about her if it's all the same to you."

For somebody who let half the world walk on her, Lucia Coffey knew when to put her own boots on.

"Do you want to see my list?" she said.

"That's why I came out here tonight," he said. "You did it?"

In answer, she pulled a piece of paper out of the folder she'd brought and handed it to him. It was a list all right, typed, complete with bullets. And he'd expected her to show up telling him to forget it, that he was full of soup.

He grinned. "So, how was it for you, making this?"

She looked slightly annoyed.

"Seriously. I'm as interested in the process as I was in what you wrote down. Was it as easy as falling off a log? Or more like pulling out your own molars?"

"I procrastinated," she said. "And then once I started—" She looked straight at him. "It was like pulling out my nose hairs, one by one, with red-hot tweezers."

"Holy crow!" Sully said.

"You asked," she said.

"I did. I'm sorry it was that painful."

She gave him a squinty look. "I don't think you're that sorry."

"Therapy does seem a little sadistic sometimes."

"I told you, I'll do whatever I have to for Bethany. The more I'm with her, the more I find out that just rips my heart out."

"I *am* sorry about that," Sully said. "So tell me about what you wrote here."

She pointed in the general direction of the first item.

- my first dance lesson

"How old were you?" Sully said.

"Five. My grandmother took me."

"She was important to you, your grandmother."

He watched her swallow.

"The most important person in my life."

"What about your parents?" He glanced at the list. "I don't see them on here."

"They were parents. You know. My mother was a stay-at-home mom. My father was an iron worker."

That much Sully knew. Sonia had made their father's loss of career due to alcohol public knowledge, part of her rising up from a bad start in life. He just wanted to hear Lucia's take on it.

She didn't give him one.

"So you liked the dance lessons," Sully said.

"Loved them. I was good—so they told me." She frowned down at herself. "Hard to believe now, right?"

"Why would it be? I can see you as a dancer."

"I'm ready to move on to number two," she said.

Sully looked back at the list, where she'd written:

- Sonia's singing voice was discovered
- Grandma Brocacini died
- Sonia went on the audition tour

Holy crow.

"So—what do I do with this?" she said.

"I'll tell you what I see." Sully pulled his feet up to sit cross-legged, knees sticking out like cricket legs over the arms of the chair. "I think Sonia would win at *Family Feud*. She would probably say most of these same things about *her* childhood."

Lucia gave a soft grunt. "Sonia's childhood was my childhood. When they discovered how well she could sing, everything sort of revolved around that."

No bitterness bit at her voice. That bothered Sully.

"How old was Sonia then?"

"Five."

"And you were how old?"

"Ten." Lucia looked upward, fingers on her chin. "I was playing a record in my room, practicing pirouettes, and Sonia was watching me. I had a solo in the recital coming up. Grandma Broc was making my costume." She knotted her mouth. "You said you wanted details."

"I love it."

"I was thinking about the tutu I got to wear, and Sonia started singing with the record, making up words, which she'd never done before. It wasn't this sweet little kindergarten chirp. She just belted it out like she was trying out for Broadway. I was, like, 'Could you hold it down? I'm trying to dance here'—but my mother tore into my room, and I remember she had a potato and a peeler."

She stopped and looked at Sully. "You really want to hear all this?"

"I'll let you know if I get bored."

"It couldn't have been more than a few days later that they started her in voice lessons."

Sully studied the list. "Where in this timeline did your grandmother die?"

"About two days after the big discovery."

"So Grandma Broc didn't get to see you in the recital."

"I wasn't in the recital."

"Why?"

"The funeral, and nobody could finish the costume." Lucia churned slightly in the chair. "It didn't matter, because when she died, so did the lessons, because she always paid for them."

"Who paid for Sonia's voice lessons?"

"My mother got a part-time job at a needlepoint shop. Crewel work was big back then, and she taught classes, that kind of thing."

"But she didn't make enough to pay for your dancing lessons."

"I know where you're going with this," Lucia said. "I recognized a long time ago that Sonia got more than I did, but she was the one with the talent."

"People said you were a good dancer. Did your parents think you were, by the way?"

She gave him the wry smile. "When I made the dance team in fifth grade, my mother told me she was proud of me—and surprised."

"Oh?"

"She said I was the only one with meat on my bones—all the other girls were such skinny little things—and yet I could still keep up with them."

Sully felt his heart turn over.

She shrugged. "Anyway, I wasn't going to make a career out of it. Sonia was."

"They knew that then?"

"My mother did. She got Sonia all these auditions for shows and commercials, and when she finally got a part in a regional production of *Annie* and the review was all over what a powerhouse voice she had and how the world would be hearing from her in the big time, that was it. Mother homeschooled her so they could go on the road anytime an opportunity came up."

"She was a real stage mom, huh?"

Lucia rolled her eyes. "She was insufferable."

He was glad to see at least that much resentment. Something about all this resignation nagged at him.

"What about your father?" he said. "Was he on board with all that?"

Lucia almost smiled then. "My dad was—well, it wasn't like he had a whole lot of choice. My mother just always did exactly what she wanted to do when it came to Sonia."

"And what happened for you while Sonia and your mother were off chasing stardom?"

"I stayed home with my dad," she said. "We ate a lot of pizza. In fact, we became experts on which pizza place made the best sauce, the thickest crust. Until I got sick of it and started cooking."

"At what age?"

"Probably twelve. I found some of Grandma Broc's recipes, and I figured if I could read, I could cook, so . . ."

"How did you feel about that?" He cringed inwardly. He sounded like a shrink.

But Lucia looked up with a flash of realization in her eyes. "I think I was relieved."

"Really. How so?"

"With my mother gone, I didn't have to listen to her and my father scream at each other. They were both Italian, so they were emotional anyway, and they fought about everything. There wasn't any syrup for my father's pancakes, there wasn't enough money for Sonia's dance lessons . . ."

"*Sonia's* dance lessons?"

"You don't get on Broadway just because you can sing. You have to be able to dance, act, walk on water. But at least when Mother was away they didn't fight."

Sully waited for some indignation to spark. When it didn't, he said, "You and your father got along."

"When Mother wasn't there. When she was, we just didn't talk to each other that much. He went to work, and then he went to the bar, and then he came home soused and fought with my mother and went to bed."

"Did he go to the bar when she was out of town?"

Lucia shook her head. "No, he came home with the groceries, and I cooked and we watched *Different Strokes* and *Facts of Life* while I did my homework. Oh, and the Olympics. I remember we watched the whole Olympics together, especially the ice skating. It was like dance to me."

"Did you miss dancing?"

"I danced when they were gone—just in my room to my tapes."

Her voice grew thin, and Sully wondered if she had ever opened up even this much to anyone since Grandma Broc died thirty years ago. What he wouldn't give for the luxury of spending six months just sifting through all this . . .

"You did great with your list, Lucia," he said.

"All it tells me is that I had to give up my childhood for Sonia, which I basically already knew. How does that help me with Bethany?"

Her eyes locked with his.

"That's it, isn't it?" she said. "Bethany has had to give up her childhood for Sonia too." She sat up in the chair, and her face came alive under the torch flicker. "Then what I'm doing is right—I'm giving her a childhood." She held up both palms. "That's why I'm here—so you can help me not mess it up."

Sully closed his eyes. Dang. This was the part he didn't like—where he had to burst that first bubble.

"What?" she said. "No ding-ding-ding?"

"How about a ding and a half?" Sully said. "You're absolutely right that both you and Bethany had to give up too much for Sonia. And you're halfway there when you say you need to provide whatever you can to make sure Bethany gets to be a happy little girl."

"I know it's only until Sonia is well enough to be a mother to her again. I know that." Lucia shook her head. "But isn't it going to be awhile before she's emotionally ready?"

"Could be, yes." He wondered what had happened to the twenty-three-day countdown. "But that's not exactly what I'm talking about."

"Then what the Sam Hill *are* you talking about?"

He didn't stop to savor the anger. "I'm talking about the fact that if you replace giving yourself up for Sonia with giving yourself up for Bethany, she's going to end up just like her mother."

Lucia searched his face so hard, Sully could almost feel her yearning digging through him. He'd never seen a client try so hard to understand.

"I'm sorry," she said. "You're going to have to explain that to me."

"Here's the deal," he said. "I haven't heard your whole story, but from what little I know, I'm convinced you have lived your life for 'them.' Your mother. Your father. Your sister. Now for Bethany." He gave her half a grin. "I recall from a conversation we had one evening that you are into pronouns."

"Pronouns?" she said. But her face colored. She remembered.

"You liked the sound of *we*, and so far we—you and I—have been a pretty good team dealing with Sonia. But I sense that you aren't used to *we*. You've always lived for *them*, and it's hard to be part of *we* without caring a whole lot more about *I*."

"What game show is this?" she said.

"This would be *Extreme Makeover: Home Edition*, where we set you up with a whole different life." Sully grinned all the way. "Only it's not a house, it's a new way of looking at yourself—as *I*, a valuable, significant person created by God—not just as someone who can do a whole lot for *them*."

Before she even seemed able to begin to absorb that, Sully heard the door to the deck open and slam into the side of the house. Right on cue.

He looked up in disgust and saw Marnie hanging halfway over the deck railing.

"Lucia!" she screamed. "It's Sonia—you have to come here!"

Sully would have turned to Lucia and named it Exhibit A—if he hadn't heard the glass shatter.

CHAPTER TWENTY-EIGHT

We both tore to the deck at full tilt, where Sullivan pushed past me and disappeared inside the house through the French door. I didn't even get to it before I heard the shattering again, closer and more alarming. By the time I crossed the living room, crashes were cascading like an avalanche.

Everything turned surreal as I took the last corner into the foyer and plowed into Sullivan's arm held out as a barrier. My sister stood in the center of the entryway in a gold silk dress that hung haphazardly off one shoulder, with the copper cross from over her bed clutched like a sword in her raw hands. All around her lay shards of the mammoth mirror, their shattered edges pointing accusingly at her walls and her treasures and herself.

Behind me, Marnie screamed.

Sonia didn't look up, but she said to the wreckage around her, "Yes, I'm hideous, aren't I? I'm hideous."

Sullivan leaned his head down until his lips were next to my ear.

"Dr. Ukwu's number is in my cell phone. Text him and tell him to meet me at Vanderbilt emergency. Then I might need you to call 911. We'll see."

He pressed his phone into my hand and took a small step toward her. Glass crackled under his sandal.

"Sonia," Sullivan said. "Honey, it's Sully."

He used a Southern accent I'd never detected in his voice before.

"I want you to let me carry you out of there before you cut your feet, okay?"

"It doesn't matter, Sully," she said. Her accent was gone.

"It matters to me," he said. "It matters to God."

"I hate God!"

She swung the cross, barely missing the side of Sully's head. He caught it in one hand as she tried to swing it back, and he grabbed her wrists with the other.

"Lucia!" he shouted over her screams. "Make that call!"

As he lifted my thrashing, cursing sister out of her ruins, I dialed 911.

Sully remembered why he hadn't gone into inpatient psychiatric care. He hated hospitals.

He crossed and uncrossed his legs, checked seven times to make sure he'd turned off his cell phone, picked slivers of mirror out of the soles of his sandals. It would have to be this ER. They'd expanded Vanderbilt Medical Center in recent years, but it was still the same place he'd brought Lynn to one night with chest pains, before she got pregnant with Hannah. Was there nothing in this town that didn't have some memory of her lurking in it?

He turned to Lucia next to him, still as a fear-paralyzed rabbit. Actually, she'd remained supernaturally calm through the entire ordeal so far. She'd kept her voice low and flat as she gave Marnie instructions to make sure Bethany didn't come downstairs and see the broken glass in the foyer and the bedroom and bathroom. Sonia had been systematically smashing every mirror in the house.

On the way to the hospital behind the ambulance in Porphyria's Buick, Lucia had been on the phone to a cleaning business, getting them to come in and remove the debris. Here at the hospital, she'd gone straight to the business office to tell them Sonia had no insurance, but that she'd pay with Sonia's American Express card, which Lucia had remembered to bring.

Twice he'd heard her leave messages for Chip, who, he recalled from the FBI's visit, was her husband. Both times when she hung up, she withdrew deeper into the folds of her flesh. It was hard to hold back the urge to counsel her right here in the waiting room.

"Isn't that your guy?" Lucia said.

Dr. Ukwu crossed the waiting room and motioned for them to follow him to a small room off the waiting area. Sully heard Lucia suck in air as they trailed him in.

"You sure you want me here?" he said.

She gave him the full-on blue-eyed look. "Just try to leave and see what happens," she said.

Ukwu was elegant but straightforward as he explained what Sully had guessed: that Sonia's defenses for dealing with the horror of her disfigurement had been overwhelmed, and the floodgates of her held-back rage had opened. Because she had lost her grip on reality, at least temporarily, and couldn't guarantee her own safety, he would have to admit her for at least seventy-two hours, probably longer.

Sully was as relieved as he knew how to be.

While Ukwu ran through a list of medications and possible therapies, Sully watched Lucia take notes in perfect cursive, practically sucking Dr. Ukwu's brain out with her eyes. When the doctor reached for her hand to say good-bye, she shook his with the poise of a diplomat, and then tripped over Sully's feet as she lunged for the door.

He found her outside the ER entrance, biting into a Snickers bar. When she saw him, she shrank as if he'd caught her ripping off a homeless person.

"I'll pay you to give me half of that," he said. "Better yet, let's go to the cafeteria and grab a bite while you're waiting to see Sonia. My treat."

"Isn't that against the rules?" she said.

"Let's just call it a bonus round," he said.

He almost got a smile out of her, almost had her turning toward the door with him, when her phone rang. When she looked at it, she handed him the candy bar.

"Sorry, I need to take this," she said, and walked several paces away.

As Sully watched her, he knew something new about Lucia. She was ripe with some kind of grief ready to burst through her skin. Seeing Sonia border on psychosis, even watching her suffer physically wasn't everything that Lucia had buried inside her. A trip to the ER with her sister was a trigger, but the pain he saw was all hers. And it lay at the bottom of everything.

There was a lot of that going around. His gaze went to the ER sign above his head. He'd carried Lynn under it the night he'd brought her here gasping for air. He'd carried her through the door right there, reassuring her that she wouldn't die, while he told himself she had some rare lung disease that would take her away from him.

Sully swallowed. The first doctor they saw put that to rest when he diagnosed an anxiety attack. Was she under a great deal of stress? Would she like to talk to someone from psych?

They'd both rejected that idea. They were newly married, happy as a pair of otters, Lynn always said. She'd promised to cut back on her work hours, get more rest. Sully silently vowed to spend more "quality time" with her. How easy it had all been to solve.

The thought rankled like a chain. It must have been easy. He couldn't even remember doing it. Lynn had never said another word about it. They'd just gone on from there.

On to an end that didn't have to happen, that still tore him apart because he didn't know why it did. And if he ever hoped to get himself back together, he had to find out. He had to keep trying.

CHAPTER TWENTY-NINE

I went straight to Bethany's room when we got back to the house.

She was sprawled across the cream print sheets, head hanging over one side, feet pudgy as biscuits poking out from the other. She breathed with effort, as if a dream were making her work very hard. In the pale moonlight that illuminated the room from the rounded, curtainless part of her window, I could see her red bow of a mouth forming words. I longed to know what they were.

The usual rag was wrapped around her neck. How it stayed on with all the flailing around she did in her sleep, I hadn't figured out. I loosened it with careful hands and moved it next to her cheek. She turned to it and sighed.

"God love you," I whispered.

For a magic second I sounded like Grandma Brocacini. How many times had she said that to us when she tucked us in?

"God love you, Lucia."

I wondered now if she had been assuring me that He did, or asking Him if He would. Sullivan Crisp would have a field day with that.

Back in my room, I climbed into the too-white bed, under the 400-thread-count sheets and the down comforter that could have been the bedclothes for angels, but I couldn't sleep. All the nights I'd spent in that recliner in Lounge A, and the ones I'd passed here with one ear cocked in case Sonia called for me, I'd been able to succumb to slumber, sometimes even lapsing into a veritable coma of exhaustion. Now that I had no patient to worry about, the prospect of an uninterrupted night on a decent mattress stretched before me, and I couldn't even keep my eyes closed.

Part of that, I knew, was because of my conversation with Chip on the phone outside the emergency room.

"Sonia's right where she's supposed to be, babe," he'd said to me. "She should have stayed in the hospital in the first place, and this never would have happened."

I tried not to sound defensive with my "I know."

"The good news is, twenty-two more days just got cut down to one."

"Excuse me?"

"You can come home now."

So far that thought hadn't crossed my mind, and I tripped on it.

"Sonia's being taken care of. You said the doc told you she shouldn't have visitors until he gets her stabilized." Chip offered his sandpaper laugh. "You're mine again. Let's get you on a flight tomorrow."

I flung the covers back now and padded to the window. The water was dark and thick as maple syrup except for the silver path the moon made, straight at me.

"You know I can't leave Bethany," I'd said to him. "She doesn't even have a nanny, for one thing."

"A nanny isn't what she needs. What she needs is a new mother."

His voice took a sharp turn. I'd only heard it sound that way when he denounced the judicial system or the medical profession or the unknown snitch who had turned him in and ruined his life. Hearing it tonight, and cringing before it again now in my memory, I felt every bit as nauseated as I had in any courtroom or U.S. attorney's office or prison visitors' room.

"If you're going to make arrangements for Bethany," he said, "don't get her a nanny. Get her into foster care."

"You know I'm not going to do that."

"All right—forget I said that." His pause had been chilly. "I'm being selfish. Do what you have to do. A lot can happen in twenty-three days, right?"

Dear God, I prayed now, *I sure hope so.*

An attempt at sleep was pointless, and hunger gnawed at me. I wrapped up in a robe that hung on the back of the bathroom door and went down to the kitchen. White terry cloth was not a good look for me, but Bethany was asleep and Didi was long gone and Sullivan had left for the guesthouse.

The one person I hadn't accounted for was Marnie. She sat at the counter, polishing off a glass of iced tea. Could this day get any worse? The only saving grace: she was dressed to go out, and her purse was perched on the seat next to her.

"Who made the sweet tea?" she said.

"Sullivan," I said.

"He makes it like my grandma. Get you a glass, and I'll pour you some."

Heaven knew I wanted some. It couldn't hurt to drink something in front of her, and I was almost past caring. Almost.

"My grammy always put in an extra half a scoop of sugar before she boiled it with the water," Marnie said.

"So it makes a syrup," I said, more to myself than to her.

"Well, yeah. That's how you make real sweet tea."

No wonder it tasted so doggone good. Most things that fattening *were* delicious.

Marnie giggled as she filled my glass.

"What?" I said.

"That look you just got on your face. Most of the time you look so serious and then you'll—I don't know, you're so hilarious sometimes, and you don't even have to say anything."

So glad I've been a source of amusement for you.

She slid the glass toward me and went back to a piece of carrot cake she was working on. "I'm leaving tomorrow. I was ready to quit anyway—I tried once, remember? And Lucia, that thing tonight was so . . ."

She closed her eyes and pressed her fork into the cake. "I'm just confused. I'm going to go to my parents' and spend time with the Lord so I'll know what to do next."

I nodded. That actually did make some sense.

"Will you be going home now?" she said.

"I can't leave Bethany."

"That poor kid." Her voice was genuinely sad. "You know what—I don't have to be careful about what I say anymore, so I'm going to be totally honest with you."

In that case, there were a number of things I wanted to ask her, but I pushed them aside.

"Here's the deal with Sonia," she said. "She actually feels like because the Lord's given her such a big thing to do for Him, He'll see that Bethany is taken care of."

I didn't care what kind of look I got on my face. "You're not serious," I said.

"Yeah, only . . ." She drew her hand to her chest. "I don't think the Lord did take care of her. Do you know that nobody has ever spent as much time with her as you do? Yeah, Yvonne made her meals. Got her dressed. Stuck her in front of the TV. She had the easiest job in the whole house. There were days I wanted to sit around and watch videos all the time too." She pointed to the half cake on its pedestal. "You want some?"

"No," I lied, and watched her cut herself another piece. "Bethany watched that much TV when she had a nanny?"

"Except when Chip wasn't busy doing stuff for Sonia or working with Bryson in the yard."

As much as it galled me, I said, "Chip?"

Marnie took another bite of cake and pulled her long legs up under her on the counter stool. "He did more to entertain Bethany than Yvonne ever did. He was so good with her." Marnie smiled as she eased the fork out of her mouth. "He was good with me too."

She did not just say that.

"Yeah, I could talk to him about anything. He'd be a great father—which is probably why I hung around him so much. I have so been missing my dad. I can't wait to get home." She looked at me as if she'd suddenly remembered something. "Are you and Chip ever gonna have kids? I mean, ya'll are such a great couple."

Only because there is a God in heaven did her phone jingle. She looked at her text message, smiled at it, and slipped out of the chair.

"My friends are out front," she said. "I'm so glad we finally got to talk. Too bad we waited until right when I'm leaving."

Before I could stop her, she flung her arms around my neck.

"Thank you so, so much for being here. I would have ended up in a bed right next to Sonia on the psych ward if you hadn't been." She pulled away and looked at me tearfully. "Give Daddy Chip a big ol' hug for me."

When she was gone, I stood motionless in the middle of the kitchen, wrapped in unbecoming white terry and the realization that Marnie and Chip had not had an affair.

It should have been a marvelous moment that lifted at least that one layer of torment from my soul. I should have snatched up my cell phone and called Chip to apologize for doubting him.

I would have, if she hadn't asked me that question.

Just when I thought I was on a path, when I thought I could take the next thing and the next and the next until I got through it all and left it behind me, why did someone always have to hurl a firebrand across it? Something to burn in the truth. My one dream was gone, and I could never get away from the loss. It would always be there, eating me empty, creating caverns I had to work so hard to fill up.

I went to the refrigerator and leaned my forehead against it. The firebrand was never anything I could throw back, screaming, "How dare you say that to me? How dare you remind me?" It was always an innocent comment, a harmless question. Like, *Are you two ever gonna have kids?* Harmless to anyone else, but it seared a hole in me, and the emptiness it left gaped like huge, aching jaws.

Dear God. Take away the pain. The awful, gnawing, insatiable pain.

God didn't. He never did. It just stayed there, chewing me up inside, and I couldn't stand it.

I stumbled to the pantry and didn't turn on the light. I knew where everything was, and I grabbed it blindly and tore open packages. I stuffed the cashews on top of the dreams. I chewed up the chocolate chips and the anger. I swallowed the ice cream and the cake and the chicken cordon bleu, and with it the pain. I bit and tore and gulped until my mother and Sonia and Chip and hope were hidden once more in my gut.

Heart thudding hard and fast inside my chest, I took stock of the casualties. An entire can of mixed nuts. A half-pint of Blue Bell peach. Two cold slabs of Marnie's favorite chicken. The rest of the carrot cake.

I punched my forearm across my mouth and tried not to vomit. I was fighting back the heaving when a voice spoke softly from the shadows.

"Lucia?"

I turned from the counter and looked up at Sullivan Crisp.

Blimpish and gluttonous and ashamed, I stared at him and waited for the disgust and the contempt. He only pressed his hands to the countertop and tilted his head at me. His eyes shimmered.

"Lucia," he said, "I can help you with this."

CHAPTER THIRTY

Sully took a sip of the worst coffee he'd tasted since the last time he'd lost his head and bought a cup at a gas station. It was instant, the only thing he could find in the guesthouse, minus his usual three sugars and two creams. Before this day was over, he was finding a Starbucks.

He picked up the microphone. He couldn't risk going over to the main house for a cup. Last night's foray for sweet tea had resulted in finding poor Lucia surrounded by the remains of her binge. The biggest difference between that scene and the earlier one with Sonia was the debris that lay around her. The smallest difference was the pain. Sonia he couldn't help now. Lucia he might.

Although whether she would continue to work with him was still up in the air. He'd tried to lessen her humiliation, offering to help her look at this thing when she was ready, keeping judgment out of his voice, leaving before she had to meet his eyes for too long. But no amount of tactful sensitivity could have lessened the shame he saw. It would be hard for her face him again.

Which led him here.

Sully clicked Record and propped his feet on the desk.

"What I Know to Be True: Part Three," he said. "I've posed the question: 'Why, God, if You are such a loving being and You care about every bit of toe jam and belly button lint that affects us'—I think the Bible says that much more poetically—'why, then, do You allow suffering?' It's a question most of us have asked, especially in our own personal moments of misery. I don't have the answer yet, because I think that I, at least, have been directing my query to the wrong place. Rather than asking God, why not put the question to Suffering itself?"

Sully got to his feet and paced along the low bookcase under the window. What he had discovered to be a collection of Sonia's books and CDs and DVDs seemed to watch him accusingly as he continued on.

"When Suffering grabs me by the heart, as long as we're that close, why not take the opportunity to say, 'What's your deal? What's this about?' Since we're spending so much time together, can't I ask, 'Look, what do you want from me? What can I do to get you to leave me alone?' Or better yet, 'What do I have to stop doing so you can heal me?'"

Sully ran his hand across Sonia's titles. He was surprised they didn't leap out and drag him to his knees so he could repent and be delivered before God.

"Some of you may think this is blasphemous, but I'm not going for the shock factor. I know this to be true: since we cannot eliminate suffering in this world, we must have a relationship with it, because God apparently does. Rather than merely hate it—which we have every reason to do at times—or try to eliminate it completely, which we can't do—we have to get to know it, as it so intimately knows us. That is truth. Where that takes us, we have yet to find out."

Sully clicked Stop and pressed the mic to his forehead. "And, Father," he whispered, "please, please, let me."

"What should I draw next?"

I looked from the sorted mail on the desk to the floor of Sonia's office, which I could barely see for the pictures of pigs and puppies and flowers Bethany had been making all afternoon. It was as if she had discovered a new land she could romp in at will. Only the shimmer across the pert bridge of her nose kept me from sinking into despair that she had never been brought to this land before. I was neck-deep in despair already; any further and I would smother in its muck.

"Draw a tree," I said.

"Is it okay if I don't? I already drew two trees."

"Bethie," I said, "you can draw absolutely anything you want."

"May I draw you?"

I stopped, mouth already wrapped around an "absolutely." What would she come up with? I had visions of a large ball with hair and arms and legs, food spurting from its greedy mouth.

I forced a smile. "I would love for you to draw me," I said.

She pulled her tiny lips into their pink knot and bent over a clean sheet of paper, concentration etched between her fine, black eyebrows. I was so envious. Although I'd spent the last thirty minutes sorting the days', perhaps weeks' worth of mail heaped in a basket beside Sonia's desk, I hadn't been able to focus. At least not on what I was doing. The ability to concentrate on what I didn't want to think about was painfully keen: Sullivan Crisp had caught me in the aftermath of gorging myself on every piece of food that, as Grandma Broc would have said, wasn't nailed down.

Beneath the bills I hoped to be passing on to that Patrick person, if he was still with us, was the disappointment that I couldn't go back to Sullivan now, not after he'd seen how out of control I was. He had offered, but I couldn't survive one more person telling me that I just needed to use some willpower, that I just had to want to be thin, that I just didn't have enough faith, because if I did, I wouldn't be fat.

Until last night, I had believed that when Sully looked at me, he didn't see an obese slob. Now that I had shown him to what depths I would sink to remain that way, how could he see anything else?

I studied several of the envelopes addressed to Sonia personally, most in hesitant handwriting. Both Sullivan and Wesley had said I needed to stop living Sonia's life and start living my own. But what life was that? The one where I stuffed myself numb?

Could I even go there?

I found a silver letter opener with an ornate cross at the end, and slit open a letter.

I miss your voice on the radio, it said. *It has always guided me out of my pain into the arms of Jesus. I try to go there by myself, but it's hard without your encouragement.*

I smoothed it out and stapled the envelope to it and cut open another one.

You got me through my son going to prison and my daughter being addicted to drugs—but, Sonia, my grandson has been diagnosed with leukemia, and I just don't know if I can go on. What could God be doing in this? You always seem to know.

I did the same with that one, and the next, and the next. They were all alike, all crying out to Sonia for relief from the agony of their lives as if she alone were the guru who could lead them to salvation. By the time I had twenty-five of them in a neat stack, I could feel the pain vibrating from the pages, up into my throat, but I kept reading.

You are so full of it, Sonia Cabot, the next one said. *If what you say is true, that God deals with those who refuse to do His will, then you're being dealt with, aren't you?*

I plastered my hand to my mouth so I wouldn't gasp out loud and flipped the envelope over. No return address. The postmark was only half there.

This isn't the end of what you've got coming to you, the letter continued. *I can guarantee you that.*

I dropped the paper on the desk and shrank back from it. The air in the room went dead. *Dear God—what am I supposed to do with this? Dear—*

The phone rang, and I thought I'd been shot. It had to ring a second time before I trusted myself to pick it up.

"Is this Lucia Coffey?"

"Yes," I said, guardedly.

"This is Dr. Ukwu's nurse."

I pressed my hand to my forehead and melted into it.

"Oh," I said, "I'm sorry—can I help you? How is Sonia? Is she all right?"

"She's holdin' her own. We takin' good care of her."

"Does she need me?"

"No, no, she would just like to have some of her things."

"Look what I drew."

"If you have a pencil, you could write these down."

"I drew this for you."

"Just a minute." I unearthed a pen from under the pile of mail. "Go ahead."

"See—I drew it."

I put up a wait-a-minute finger to Bethany and pressed the phone tighter to my ear.

"Maybe some of her own clothes, you know, something a little more stylish than the pj's we hand out."

A small cry went up from my elbow. Bethany turned and waddled like a frightened duck from the room. I could hear her whimpers down the hall.

"And her pillow. And she would like for you to talk to—"

"Excuse me," I said. "Can I call you back?"

I didn't wait for her answer. I was down the hall, calling out Bethany's name, probably before the good nurse hung up. My heart throbbed in my throat.

I found Bethany up in her room, curled into the round cream chair in the corner. With the rag around her neck, she no longer whimpered, but tears filmed her eyes.

I pulled the matching chair close to, but not touching, hers and sat gingerly. By some miracle, my rear fit into it.

"What's wrong?" I said.

"I'm sorry," she said, and then she pulled the rag over her mouth.

"Sorry for what? You didn't do anything wrong."

"I interrupted you. Please don't send me away."

I wanted to shriek, *What?* "I don't understand," I said instead. "Where would I send you?"

She scrambled from the chair, careful to keep the neck rag in place, and got down on all fours beside the bed. I watched as she pulled out a box with a picture of Cinderella, Disney version, on it. With heartbreaking precision, and the familiar tip of a pink tongue sticking out of the corner of her mouth, Bethany opened it and took out what appeared to be a brochure.

"Here," she said, and put it in my hand.

NEW CREATION CHRISTIAN ACADEMY was printed above photographs of girls barely older than Bethany in gray uniforms, heads bowed in a chapel, hands raised demurely in a classroom, legs kicking at a ball on a soccer field. *We educate body, mind, and spirit,* the text proclaimed, *in a full-time residence program.*

A boarding school.

"Where did you get this?" I tried to keep the anger out of my voice.

"My mom."

"She gave this to you?"

Bethany nodded. "She said when I got old enough I would get to go there. Only . . ."

She pulled the rag over her mouth again.

"Only what?" I said.

"Only I don't want to," she said through it, "because I don't know how to do any of that stuff."

She poked a finger at the photographs, and the film of tears spilled silently over.

"Did she say you had to go there?" I said.

"No. Holly did."

"Who is Holly?"

"The nanny before Yvonne." Bethany frowned. "Or before Katie. I don't remember."

"It doesn't matter. Holly isn't the boss of you, and neither is Katie."

"Are you?"

I didn't even hesitate. "I am now, until your mom gets better."

She shook her head. "My mom is never the boss of me. I have to leave her alone so she can work, and Holly said if I get in her way, she will send me there." With one more stab at the brochure, she burst into tears.

I no longer cared whether she wanted to be touched or not. I took her in my arms and rocked her sobbing self against my chest.

"Nobody is sending you anywhere as long as I'm here," I said. "And you can interrupt me any time you need to. You come first."

She stopped crying, and for a moment I credited myself with comforting her. But when she sat up, she almost literally sucked the tears back in and said, "I'm all better now."

She wanted this conversation to be over, but I couldn't leave it at that.

"Bethany," I said, "I don't think your mom would ever send you away if you didn't want to go. Those nannies weren't telling you the truth."

"Yes, she would." Bethany repositioned the rag. "She always sends people away when they're bad."

"Are you sure about that? Sometimes people just quit, you know."

"She sent Hudson away. He baked cookies for me, and then she got mad at him and he went away."

"Not because he baked you cookies," I said.

"No, he did something else bad, I think. And Holly was bad. She stole stuff from my mom. I heard Marnie say it. And I guess Uncle Chip was bad because he never came back." Her face began to crumple. "Will you please promise to be good so my mom doesn't send you away too?"

She fought hard to keep the tears back. I wanted to tell her to let them go until there were none left to torment her, but she seemed determined to get them under control. I knew the feeling.

"Do you see this thing about the place you don't want to go?" I said, waving the brochure.

She nodded.

"You're not the one going away. It is."

I tore the paper into as many pieces as I could until I'd reduced it to a pile of rubbish in my hand.

"Follow me," I said.

She trailed me into the bathroom, where I opened the lid to the toilet.

"Would you like to do the honors?" I said.

"What does that mean?"

"That means flush this awful place down the potty."

The round moon lit up, and with the same painstaking exactness with which she did everything else, she scooped up a handful of pieces and poured them ceremoniously into the toilet. I let her push the handle, and we watched as the thing she feared circled and disappeared.

"Now then," I said, "do you think there is room for me to bring another bed into your room?"

"Why?" she said.

"Because I would like to room with you from now on, if that's okay with you. It's lonely where I'm staying."

"My room is ugly," she said.

"That's not a problem," I said. "What color shall we paint it?"

The smile she gave me seared into my heart.

God, please let it mean she no longer thinks I would send her away because she interrupted me when I was doing . . . what? Listening to Sonia's request for lounging pajamas?

"Could we make it look like a princess lives here?" Bethany said.

"We'll go buy the paint right now," I said.

And Sonia could find somebody else to fetch her personal pillow.

CHAPTER THIRTY-ONE

Sully watched from the front window of the guesthouse as the Escalade pulled out of the driveway with Lucia at the wheel and Bethany in the backseat. He liked seeing them get out of the house. Maybe it would help Lucia decide to keep working with him.

He let the curtain fall and nursed a pang. If she didn't, he'd have to find another place to stay, possibly even go back to Porphyria's and regroup. He couldn't justify continuing to hang out here if he wasn't doing therapy with Lucia, no matter how much yard work he did.

He glared at his laptop. He'd tried all day looking up more distant divinity school acquaintances and discovered he couldn't remember most of their names. Partials like "Ulea Somebody" and "Something Harrison" didn't help much. He considered calling Anna for help, but discarded that idea as well as her suggestion that the "old gang" get together. He couldn't see doing this by committee.

He actually didn't envision anything, except drinking another cold Frappuccino from the six-pack he'd picked up when he went out for Starbucks. He pried the cap from his second one and stared at the computer screen again.

Anna had said something about Fall Creek Falls. It probably had more to do with her than with Lynn—most things did—but maybe a picture would tease something else out.

Fall Creek Falls State Park came up right away, with a photograph of water tumbling from the top of the Cumberland Plateau to the base of the Cane Creek Gorge. *The highest plunge waterfall east of the Mississippi River*, the caption said. How could he have forgotten something that impressive?

He hadn't, he remembered as he cruised through the Web site. A small group of them went that last year he was working on his master's. Right—the three couples had scraped together enough to rent a cabin for two or three days of spring break.

He couldn't shake loose the names of the couple from Ukraine, but he did remember them all in front of a fireplace. Tom stoked the fire, and Lynn whispered to Sully that he was making it too hot. If he could remember that detail, come on, there had to be more.

Sully got up from the computer and paced the room that became too small. There was something . . .

Lynn talking. Lynn saying . . .

"I'm the only one here without a college degree."

It was like picking one tiny hole in a water balloon. That was all it took for the whole thing to burst out.

"And your point is?" Anna had said.

Everyone else followed suit. Nobody cared. But Lynn wouldn't let it go. It came up in every conversation after that.

When it was time to eat, she wouldn't let anyone else cook. Shooed Anna and—what was that woman's name? Ursula? Chased them out of the kitchen like a hen. Said smart women shouldn't waste time at the stove.

When they sat down to eat, she talked about what novels were selling at Davis-Kidd, the bookstore she managed, while the rest of them discussed Paul Tillich. She was the first one to point out how much more sophisticated their reading material was.

They had all hiked the short trail from the top of the plateau down to the base of the gorge to get access to the waterfall's plunge pool, and they'd watched in awe as the water shook a boulder loose and sent it tumbling like a small toy.

"I can't believe I ever wasted a moment wondering whether the resurrection actually happened," Sully could hear himself saying.

"If God can move that rock, why couldn't He move the stone away from the tomb?"

"You have wondered that, Sully?" his Ukrainian friend said.

Clyde, was it? His accent had sharpened with somewhat judgmental surprise, Sully remembered now. The guy was in the ministry track, and he and Sully had several friendly debates about what should be questioned and what should be left alone.

"Of course he has," Tom said. "He wonders if Mary was actually a virgin. Why shouldn't he wonder that?"

A discussion had ensued, during which Lynn insisted on giving him a neck rub. Later, when they were alone, she asked Sully if he was upset because his friends had given him a hard time. No, he was upset because she fawned over him in front of his fellow scholars. He didn't tell her that, did he?

Sully stopped in front of the computer and stared at the picture. They'd been standing on the plateau during that conversation, watching a raccoon fish below in a patch of moonlight. It was a romantic venue where he should have taken her up on that neck rub, told her he didn't care if she read Danielle Steele instead of systematic theology. Did he do that?

He scratched his hand through his hair. It stabbed at him that he couldn't remember *what* he did. Was she that inconsequential to him at that point? Was that why she didn't want to live? Anna said he was all she had cared about.

"Come on, man," he said out loud. "You're going to drive yourself crazy."

When he knocked the laptop sideways at the tap on the door, he was convinced he was losing his grip.

He tried not to look too terribly insane as he opened the door.

"I hope I'm not interrupting," Lucia said, making an obvious effort to look him in the eye. "It sounded like you were on the phone."

"You're fine," he said.

"I don't know about that," she said. "But I want to be."

He watched her throat work, and he knew he was seeing a woman swallow her pride.

"Will you please help me?" she said.

Sully nodded, enough times to get control of his voice. Still, it was thick when he said, "I'll meet you tonight."

Sullivan was out by the river early, face in his hands. I knew he was praying, but it always looked so desperate to me somehow. Maybe that was how you were supposed to do it—like you actually believed you'd get an answer.

Bethany had been asleep for an hour. I had worn her out, not only buying everything that even remotely suggested a princess, but by making her try on school uniforms and pick out supplies and listen to me trying to convince her that this thing called school was special. When I tucked her in, I told her there were only three more wake-ups before she got to go be a big first grader—and come home every day.

I had a few minutes before I was supposed to meet with Sullivan, and I had to get through them without changing my mind.

I went resolutely into Sonia's office to get my Sullivan Crisp folder, still next to three envelopes I'd separated from the rest, now staring at me accusingly. They were the hate mail, the kind of letters Sonia told Deidre Schmacker she never received. Either she had never gotten anything like them before the plane crash or she had out-and-out lied, and frankly I didn't know which to believe. At least I only had two options to choose from: tell Special Agent Schmacker, or don't.

At the corner of the desk, I'd left a nest of things people had sent Sonia—coupons for the Christian bookstore, a vial of water from the Jordan River, a jar of burn ointment. They were at once touching and absurd, and I decided I could throw them away without feeling guilty. Just as I was about to dump them into the wastebasket, I saw a crayoned drawing at the bottom. Interesting.

All the rest of Bethany's artwork hung on the refrigerator, the deep freeze, the washer, and any other large appliance I could attach a magnet to.

I lifted it out and studied it. It was one of Bethany's better efforts, embellished with detail I could imagine going on while her pink tongue worked at the corner of her mouth.

The figure drawn in peach crayon was obviously female, with a mass of black curls and eyelash-fringed blue eyes that took up half the face's circle. She wore black, but she didn't look funereal. The bright red lips were drawn as a heart-shaped smile.

I held it out to get the long view. Sonia? No. Sonia's hair wasn't curly. And the only person around here who wore black was me.

"Can I draw you?" Bethany had said to me.

I eased the wrinkles out of the paper and pawed through the drawer for a thumbtack. I was still hunting when the doorbell rang. I picked up the drawing and my Sullivan folder and glanced at my watch as I made my way to the foyer. Who the Sam Hill was dropping in at eight PM?

You shouldn't talk to strangers, Bethany had told me, and the man on the doorstep definitely fell into that category. He was stocky and pockmarked, with skin the color of a Florida sunburn. He all but breathed fire.

"I need to talk to Lucia Coffey," he said, "like, now."

Sullivan chose that moment to lope up onto the porch. He gave the man, whose fists were now doubled, a long survey and eased his way between us.

"What's this about? You look a little worked up, my friend."

The guy shoved his fists into the pockets of a pair of dress slacks that rode below his protruding belly.

"Look, I'm fired up," he said, "but I'm not here to make trouble. I just need to talk to Lucia Coffey." He looked past Sullivan at me. "I'm Patrick Fargason."

"Are you Sonia's accountant?" I said.

"Yeah. And I got something to say."

Although he looked more like WWE in a necktie than a CPA, I nodded at Sullivan, who stepped aside and let the man pass, but his eyes never left him.

"This is private," the man said.

"I'd rather he stayed," I said.

Sullivan, to my relief, didn't look like he was going anywhere anyway.

"Is there something wrong with Sonia's finances?" I said.

"Yeah, and I've already turned that over to her lawyer. There's money missing—and don't start in on me. I had nothing to do with it. If I had, I wouldn't have pointed it out to him, now, would I?" His face went a deeper red, if that was possible.

"I wasn't accusing you of anything," I said.

"No, you people are too busy focusing on my brother."

"Your brother?" I felt my face knot up. "Who's your brother?"

"What, are you new?"

"As a matter of fact, I am. I had nothing to do with my sister's business until her accident."

He jerked his neck. "Oh. Then maybe you don't know." Some of the redness slid from his face. "Hudson Fargason," he said. "He was Sonia's chef."

I exchanged glances with Sullivan.

"The FBI's at my brother's door, accusing him of having something to do with her 'accident.'" Patrick made quotation marks with his fingers. "The biggest explosion he ever made was lighting a baked Alaska, but they won't leave him alone. He got fired from Fleming's because they harassed him on the job. Lost the best gig in town, all because of that—"

"Lucia, do you mind?" Sullivan said.

"Go for it," I said.

He folded his arms as if he and Patrick were about to discuss the upcoming NFL season. "Exactly what do you want Lucia to do? It's not like she has a whole lot of influence with the FBI."

"She has influence with her sister, doesn't she?" Patrick bulleted his eyes into me. "I want you to tell her to back off on the accusations."

"O-oh. I see where you're coming from. But Lucia can tell you that's not what's going on."

I shook my head. "Sonia told them Hudson had no reason to hurt her. She said she—" I pawed through my memory. "She said she accepted him when no one else did."

Patrick hissed. "Accepted him my backside. She fired him because he was gay."

I blinked at him.

"She hates homosexuals. She says it on her CDs. No, wait, she doesn't hate them, she hates their 'sin.'" The quotation mark fingers came out again. "You'll never convince me she didn't find out and fire him because of it. How would that make her look, having a chef who was a sinner?"

Patrick jabbed a finger toward me, and Sullivan edged forward.

"She ruined my brother's life," he said. "He lives to cook, and now, because of this whole investigation thing, he can't get a job flipping burgers at Hardee's in this town." He drove his index finger through the air again. "She'll pay for this. Everything she ever preached about is gonna come right back in her face." He gave the hard laugh again. "What's left of it."

"You need to leave," I said.

"Going. Like I said, I got everything up-to-date, all the bills paid and the accounts balanced." He laughed harshly. "Except for the $350,000 that's missing. As of today, I quit. I've turned everything over to her lawyer—if you want to know more, contact him."

"No," I said. "I want nothing to do with it."

But as he made his bristly way out the door, I felt deeper into it than ever.

CHAPTER THIRTY-TWO

D o you need a minute?" Sully said. "That was pretty disturbing."

Lucia gripped the arms of the Adirondack like it was about to take flight with her in it. "It's just so surreal. It's like something you see on CNN."

"It *is* something you see on CNN. But I know what you mean. I'm starting to feel like Cato Kaelin."

"Who? Oh—you mean O. J. Simpson's houseguest?" She shook her head. "I don't know what that makes me."

"It makes you somebody who has a right to be pretty shaken up by this whole thing. You want to process it a little?"

"No." Lucia pressed the ever-present folder to her chest. "I want to talk about what you saw last night, in the kitchen, before I chicken out."

A lump for her formed in Sully's throat.

"What you saw . . ." she said. "I go for weeks without doing it, and then something happens, and I have to eat until I don't feel anything but sick and gross and disgusting. Which is why I look the way I do, but I don't care about that—what I care about is that when I look at Bethany, I see me, and I don't want her to live this way."

Lucia breathed hard, and Sully let her catch up to herself while he assembled his next words like the precise instruments they had to be. She was so close to getting it, but the part she didn't want to see could cut her open if he weren't careful.

"Do you want *you* to live this way?" he said.

She didn't look at him. "I said I didn't care about the way I look."

"It's not about how you look; it's about how you live. Do you want to live this way, Lucia?"

He waited, chest aching. It was up to her, and to watch her decide was excruciating. If she couldn't go there, they were done.

"I hate it," she said.

"You hate what?"

"I hate my life."

Sully hardly dared to breathe. "Ding-ding-ding, Lucia," he whispered.

She looked at him, blue eyes startled.

"Now we can begin."

Lucia gave a tiny, frightened nod. She'd taken a huge step into a land where she couldn't yet trust the ground, Sully knew. He had to make it safe for her.

"Usually I try to let a person I'm working with find all the answers for herself," he said, "but I'm going to tell you one thing that I think is true, and you can tell me if you agree."

"Okay," she said. She looked away.

"You have buried some things, some very hard things, deep inside you where you won't have to feel them. How am I doing so far?"

She nodded again.

"But they aren't dead things. They're still alive, and because you've buried them alive, you have to feed them."

"Because if I don't, they come out and scream at me."

"Ding-ding again," Sully said softly. "That screaming, what does it feel like for you?"

"Like I'm going to explode. Like if I don't get myself numb, I'm going to burst open and land like confetti all over the place."

"And how do you get numb?"

She finally looked at him. "I eat," she said.

Sully let himself grin. "If I ding you any more, I'm going to wear out my bell."

"I don't feel like much of a winner."

"Why not? These are great insights. You're wonderful at this."

"Because I know you're going to tell me I need to dig up what's buried in there, and I don't want to do that."

"Nobody *wants* to do it, any more than they *want* to have an appendectomy. It's painful."

"That's comforting."

"But I'll promise you something." Sully put his hand on his chest. "I will try my hardest to keep it from hurting any more than it has to. We're not going to just dig things up and let them scream at you. We're going to find out what they have to say, and then we'll know what to do with them so you don't have to keep stuffing them down and feeding them."

Sully leaned back and let her sit with that. She didn't sit for long.

"Okay," she said. "Let's get started."

She had the first flicker of hope in her eyes, and Sully hated to chance snuffing it out. But one more thing had to be said.

He tilted forward again. "I want *you* to promise yourself something, too, Lucia."

"What?" she said.

"I want you to promise yourself that you will do this for yourself—not just for Bethany, but for Lucia. Whatever you do for the *I* we talked about last time will become part of the *we*—you and Bethany and whoever else you love in your life. Can you promise yourself that?"

She didn't answer. Instead she opened the folder she hadn't let go of since she sat down and pulled out a wrinkled sheet of paper, which she looked at with the kind of tenderness reserved for precious objects.

"This is a drawing Bethany did of me," she said.

"Can I have a look?"

She handed it to him, and Sully grinned at it.

"It looks just like you. Really."

"It took me five minutes to figure out it was me."

"Why?" Sully said.

"Because . . ." She sucked in air. "This person isn't fat."

"I think I know why that is."

"Why?"

"Because when Bethany looks at you, she doesn't see fat. She sees beauty."

"I need to have her eyes checked."

"Aw—your first *buzzzzz* of the session!" Sully said.

She put her hand up. "Okay—if that's what she sees, it must be in there somewhere. So I'll *try* to do this for me. I'll try—that's all I can promise myself."

"Ding-ding," he said.

"So how do I start digging?"

"We'll do that in our next session. Before then I want you to explore a little Game Show Theology."

She groaned. "I knew it. More *Family Feud*."

"No," he said. "*Dancing with the Stars*."

She stopped digging in her pocket for her pen.

"How long has it been since you really danced?" Sully said.

"High school."

He was surprised it had been that recently. "What did it feel like? Do you remember?"

"I was the only freshman to make the dance team. Of course, I went on a Tab diet that summer—do you remember Tab?"

"Wasn't that a diet soda? A gross one?"

"Yeah, and I practiced blisters onto my feet, but I made it. Rehearsals and performances kept me out of the house, except when I was doing my housework."

"Were your mother and Sonia still on the road?"

"No. My mother had to have Sonia tested because she home-schooled her, and they found out she was two grade levels behind. That was the one time my father put his foot down and made her enroll Sonia in school." Lucia rolled her eyes. "Of course, Mother became the most involved parent in PTA history, so she barely noticed I wasn't around that much."

"And since it was a school activity, nobody had to pay for lessons."

"Oh, it was expensive." She looked a little sheepish.

"What?" Sully said.

"Well—I figured out that whenever I needed money for costumes or a field trip or something, I could get it out of my dad if I went down to Shenanigans Bar when he was only two beers in."

Sully only let her stew in that for a moment. "So why didn't you continue dance after high school?"

Her face clouded. "At the end of my junior year, I made dance captain for senior year." She looked at him. "This all sounds so high school."

"It was high school! Besides, it's amazing how often the rest of life looks like it."

She glared mildly and went on. "The coach offered to give me free private lessons over the summer if I would help her with her junior dance camps. And then my father got fired for being drunk on the job, right before junior year ended, and my mother had to go to work full-time, which meant I had to stay home with Sonia all summer because she was only twelve."

Lucia shrugged as if that explained everything. Sully shook his head.

"Nothing could be worked out?"

"My dance coach said Sonia could come to dance camp for free, but my mother said no. It would interfere with her voice lessons and her piano lessons and her drama classes, which I had to drive her to."

Sully curled toward her. "Weren't you angry?"

"Sure—but what was I supposed to do about it?" Lucia smiled without mirth. "I'll tell you what I did about it. I ate. All summer. I couldn't even fit into my uniform in the fall, so I just quit the dance team." She dropped her hands into her lap. "I don't want to keep whining about this. It was what it was."

"Then let's go back to our original question: when you were dancing, how did it feel to you?"

She pulled in her chin again. "How did it feel?"

He nodded.

"I don't know. I can't even remember."

"Then before we meet again, Lucia," he said, "I want you to dance."

I couldn't sleep again that night.

I could have attributed it to the futon I'd dragged down from the garret above the playroom to put next to Bethany's bed. It was like sleeping on a cement slab. Or to the fact that my niece had an adenoidal snore that was loud enough to wake my mother from her grave.

Not that Mother was really that dead. And if she were, Sullivan and I had done plenty to rouse her that evening. She yelled in my head, the way only an Italian mother can. Something along the lines of: *Lucia Marie, I cannot believe you aired our family laundry to that stranger. And now you're going to tell him more?*

Actually, I probably hadn't told him enough. I'd lied when I said I didn't remember what it felt like to dance. I did, but how ridiculous would it sound to say, "When I danced, I never felt like Clifford the Big Red Dog, which I did all the rest of the time. I was a fawn, prancing through the forest with my tail up, able to leave the ground and land without disturbing a leaf."

Sullivan Crisp would do more than grin if I came out with that.

I gave up on the futon and went to the window seat Bethany and I had peopled with stuffed bears and rag dolls in princess costumes of our own creation. It was a motley crew, but she loved it.

Even at this hour I could hear a boat out on the water. They busied the Cumberland all the time—wakeboard boats in the late afternoons, sending out tsunamis with their speakers blaring hip-hop—pontoons traveling at sipping speed in the early evening—the occasional houseboat at night, still bursting with laughter. This one sounded like one of the fishing boats I'd spotted near our bank just after dawn, deceptively quiet until the fishermen decided there were better prospects elsewhere and took off like some kind of marine NASCAR, hulls barely cutting the surface.

I peered through the glass and tried to see it, but the light of the waning moon was fragile, only enough for me to see the layered rock wall. I decided oddly that I was glad it was shades of gray—like maybe there was strength in things that weren't clearly black or white. Any minute now the mother tape would tell me how much she hated it when people blamed every issue they had and every mistake they made on their childhood sexual abuse or their parental neglect. Nothing that bad had happened to me. Something obviously had just gone wrong with my personality, something I did. Some punishment from God.

Or not, Mother.

Bethany stirred in her sleep, and I went over to make sure she wasn't strangling on that rag thing. When I came back to the window, I saw more light on the lawn. It took me a minute to realize it came from the motion-sensitive fixture out on the deck a floor below me. What was moving down there?

A chill rippled through me, and I backed involuntarily away from the window.

The author of a hate letter, looking to express his hatred in person.

Patrick Fargason, coming to avenge his gay brother.

Hudson himself, armed with his sharpened chef's knife.

Holly, the cruel, thieving nanny, ready to break in and take the rest of the valuables.

Accompanied by Bryson and his supply of cyanide.

I pulled a pink throw around me. The lights had probably been bumped on by a deer family or maybe even Harry the Heron. Or Sullivan out for a midnight stroll. There was no need to call 911.

But it didn't escape me that the people I'd just conjured up—Patrick, Hudson, Holly, Bryson—were all on the list Agent

Schmacker had gone over with Sonia, and left for me to discuss with Bethany. She'd been right on one count: Bethany did know more about what went on around here than I'd given her credit for.

My mouth went dry. I ought to call Agent Schmacker and at least tell her about the hate letters. What she did with them was up to her.

Which was exactly what held me back.

Patrick Fargason didn't have to tell me his brother was ruined because the FBI had come to his workplace. I knew only too well how that happened, all in the name of justice.

Another light came on, this one at the other end of the deck. My fear zone gained another five thousand square feet. Bethany and I were here alone. The doors were locked and dead bolted, but the alarm wasn't turned on. Everyone had abandoned ship without telling me how to operate it.

Stop. Just stop.

I lay resolutely down on the futon and pulled the covers up to my chin and tried to do what Grandma Brocacini always said to do: pretend you're asleep until you are. But my mind slid into the forming of an escape route for Bethany and me.

The process had almost put me out when I heard a shout down in the yard. Under our window.

I sat up, heart like a battering ram in my chest.

The shout came again—an urgent male voice, calling, "Stop right there!"

Sully shouted again as he tore across the lawn. "I said stop!"

The figure didn't. The man—it moved like a man—took an abrupt right turn and headed down the slope for the river. Sully kicked his heels out behind him, taking the terrace in strides that strained his hamstrings.

Ahead of him the figure seemed to go airborne and thudded to the ground with a curse.

Sully dodged the rock he'd tripped on and made a dive for the body that struggled to get back on its feet. Sully's arms took in nothing but air until one hand hit cloth. He clawed it into his fingers and held on as the man tried to kick free. In the same instant that Sully realized he was clutching a pant leg, a heel slammed into his mouth and sent him rolling sideways.

Footsteps pounded the turf toward the river, and Sully tried to get up to go after him, hands plastered to his lower face. But Kick Boxer had too much of a head start. The sound of a motor bit into the night before Sully could even make out that the guy had climbed into a boat. It growled its way down river, leaving Sully panting on the dock.

He put his fingers to his mouth and drew back blood. What just happened? One minute he was talking about theodicy into a microphone, and the next minute he was auditioning for *SmackDown* on Sonia's lawn. He looked down into the river and shivered, even in the night heat. Dang, this thing was cursed.

"Sullivan?"

He jumped a foot and wasn't altogether sure he didn't wet his pants as well. Lucia stood on the rock ledge, wrapped like a burrito in that white bathrobe that was about six sizes too big for her. She held a lamp, complete with shade.

"I didn't mean to scare you," she said.

"That's okay. I was already scared."

"Are you all right?"

"Did you come down to rescue me?" He tried to grin, but his lip screamed in protest.

She looked at the lamp. "It was the first weapon I could find."

"You probably would have done more good than I did. What is that, Snow White?"

"Yeah, Bethany's into princesses. Sullivan—what was that about?"

Sully wiped at his mouth again and walked unsteadily up the dock walkway to the bank. His legs were like cooked pasta.

She met him there, eyes squinted. "Ouch," she said.

"Yeah, well, you oughta see the other guy."

"Should we call the police?"

Sully reached for his phone. "No," he said. "Do you have Deidre Schmacker's number?"

"The FBI? For a prowler?"

Sully took the lamp and nodded for her to follow him toward the house. "I don't think it was just any prowler. He had on a hood and a mask, Lucia. He made his getaway in a boat with at least 250 horsepower—and I know it was a four-cycle from the sound of it. That's a high-end motor. It doesn't look like an attempted burglary to me."

"Then what? Are they still after Sonia?"

"The press hasn't gotten wind that she's back in the hospital," Sully said. "The point is, the FBI should be notified of anything unusual." He dabbed at his lip again. "I think this qualifies. Look, I probably shouldn't stick my nose into something that isn't any of my business . . ."

She stopped at the bottom of the steps that led up to the dock and frowned at his lip. Her face was ghostly white in the light.

"I think you've stuck more than your nose into it," she said. "And I can't handle the FBI alone."

It would have been a perfect segue if they'd been in a session. Sully just nodded.

"I'll get the number," she said.

CHAPTER THIRTY-THREE

Deidre Schmacker arrived in yellow sweats, stripped of makeup but as brisk and awake as if it were noon. She brought an entire platoon of people in blue vests that ever-so-subtly announced they were the FBI in large yellow letters on the back. Armed with flash-lights, they combed the lawn and fingerprinted the dock and the deck posts and all but dragged the river, while Deidre questioned Sullivan in the kitchen and I made her tea. I hoped they'd be gone before Bethany woke up, though I wasn't sure how she was sleeping through any of it.

Sullivan was polite and cooperative, patiently going over and over the details until I wanted to ask if Grandma Schmacker needed to get a hearing aid.

"Can you think of anything at all that might help us identify him?" she said for what must have been the twelfth time.

"From what I could tell, I think he was shorter than me," Sully said *again*. "Didn't have much heft. Wiry." He nodded at the ice bag I'd given him. "He was strong enough to take me out."

"And you're sure he didn't say anything?"

I ground my teeth and plunked the teapot in front of her. Did she want it in blood?

"Just that one four-letter utterance I told you about, when he tripped and fell. If he hadn't, I never would have gotten hold of him."

When Schmacker launched into a review of what the cloth *felt* like, I was ready to head for the pantry and devour its contents.

"Dr. Crisp, you've been very helpful," Agent Schmacker said

finally. "Now if you'll excuse us, I'd like to speak with Mrs. Coffey privately."

I froze, fingers around the teapot handle. "I would rather he stayed."

"This will just take a few minutes." Her eyes did their grandmother droop. "If you don't mind, Dr. Crisp."

He gave me a reassuring look, but I felt less than bolstered as I went mechanically to the counter stool she nodded to. I was reenacting a scene that had happened to me before.

What now? I was about to be implicated in the continued threats on my sister's life?

"This is a nice tea," she said. "Won't you join me in a cup?"

"No, thank you," I said. I would rather drink hemlock.

"You don't care much for me, do you, Mrs. Coffey?"

As hard as I tried to remain expressionless, I knew my eyebrows shot up.

"I'm an observer, just like you are," she said. "I see these things."

I shrugged. "Does it make any difference whether I like you?"

"It makes a difference that you trust me. I know this must be hard for you. I looked into it—you had a rough go with the FBI when your husband was arrested. That can leave a bitter taste in your mouth."

She obviously wouldn't leave me alone if I didn't give her something.

"Okay," I said. "I did come across some hate mail for Sonia, just yesterday, that I was going to call you about."

"I'm not accusing you of holding anything back, Mrs. Coffey, although I would like to see those."

"I'll go get them."

She put an unwelcome hand on my arm. "That can wait. My concern right now is not for Sonia. She's in a safe place—unlike Bethany."

The air in the room went dead. I was surprised I could breathe in it.

"Bethany," I said. "You think whoever came on the property was after *Bethany*?"

"I think we have to consider the possibility. Someone obviously isn't done with Sonia yet, and anyone who would go to the kind of professional lengths that this person did would also know that she is not here."

Everything on me shook. I gripped my hair, my knees, the counter.

"Put this on," she said. She hung her sweat jacket around my shoulders and filled the teacup, which she slid toward me. "Drink that."

"You can't mean that somebody would try to hurt Bethany to get at Sonia," I said.

"We don't know. No direct threats have been made, but we'll have the house watched. And you'll let us know if you see or hear anything the least bit suspicious."

"Of course I will." My hands went to my temples, and I pressed until my thoughts began to line up. "The list—Bethany said Holly, one of the nannies, was fired because she stole from Sonia."

"Good. We'll look into that."

"And Patrick Fargason." My teeth jittered against each other. *Dear God, please don't let me throw up.* "He came here about eight o'clock tonight."

I somehow managed to describe the visit, eyes closed, words pinning the details like tacks on a board. His ruined brother. The missing money. Their hatred for Sonia.

"You say he was stocky," Deidre said.

I nodded.

"Dr. Crisp described tonight's intruder as being thin." She paused. "That is incredibly helpful, Lucia. I know you would do anything to protect that child. It's obvious that you love her."

I could feel my eyes narrowing. "You aren't just suggesting she's in danger so I'll give you information."

"I wouldn't do that to you."

"You did it to Sonia." I shoved my forehead into my hands. "I'm sorry—I'm just upset."

"Of course you are. If you're referring to our posing the possibility that Sonia might have arranged her own near-death experience, it was a theory we worked with. We've had more than one celebrity beat himself up and claim to be mugged, just for the publicity. In Sonia's case, we've now discarded that. Which brings us back to Bethany. And yourself. You are part of Sonia's family too. We have spoken to your father, by the way."

I brought my head up. "Is he a suspect?"

Agent Schmacker smiled. "No. And you don't have to regard everyone as suspicious. You can leave that to me."

I detected a twinkle in the liquid gray eyes.

"I do it so well. But I hate having to alarm you," she said.

"I needed to know. I have to take care of Bethany."

"Then keep things as normal for her as possible."

"She starts school Monday. Should I not send her?"

"No. Just don't put her on a bus. Drive her yourself. We can talk about precautions." She slid the tea toward me again. "You have to take care of yourself, Mrs. Coffey. This is a stressful time, and you need to be in the best possible condition to help us."

. I took a sip from the cup and made an involuntary face.

"You don't like it?" she said.

"It's not my favorite," I said.

"That's a shame. Tea is so good at taking the edge off the uglies." She looked at me with grandmother sadness. "And I'm afraid we will still have more of those to deal with."

Monday I drove Bethany to school myself, as Agent Schmacker suggested. If she'd told me to dress her in a suit of armor, I would have. *Normal, normal,* she'd drilled into me. Warn her about strangers, of course. I'd told her there was no need. Bethany already had a suspicion of unknown people that made her a good candidate for the FBI.

By the time I walked Bethany inside the school, the sweat matted my hair to my forehead and soaked through my top. Why did these Southerners send their children to school when it was still ninety degrees? The anxiety alone emptied my sweat glands.

When I saw Bethany's teacher, Miss Richardson, in the classroom doorway, it occurred to me only briefly to hate her. She was a rail-thin blonde in her late twenties, wearing horizontal stripes that would have made me look like Tweedledee or Tweedledum. Or both. But she squatted down to greet Bethany and asked her name in a voice that made me want to stay and be in first grade.

Bethany looked up at me.

"This is Bethany Cabot," I said.

"Can you introduce me to your mom?" Miss Richardson said.

Bethany nodded, bouncing her curls. "This is my mom, Aunt Lucia."

"How lucky are you?" the teacher said. She stood up and smiled at me. "We're going to be just fine, Aunt Lucia Mom."

To be certain of that, I went to the headmaster's office to inform her that Bethany would need to be watched closely on the playground—that no one else but me was authorized to pick her up—that Miss Richardson and I were to make contact before Bethany got into the car with me when I collected her in the afternoon—that I was to be notified if anyone from the UPS man on up took an unusual interest in her.

"A Deidre Schmacker from the FBI was here first thing this morning," the headmaster told me. "Your Bethany is safe with us."

If I could have cried, I would have, all the way out to the car, just like any other mother who took her baby to her first day of school—her baby who was in danger of giving up more than just her childhood for her mother.

And fear wasn't the only thing that nagged at me. By the time I walked into the empty kitchen that still smelled like the blueberry waffles and sausage patties I'd fixed Bethany for breakfast, loneliness had descended on me.

I hadn't felt lonely in that pointed a way for a long time. Maybe, I decided as I threw myself into doing the dishes, because lonely had become a way of being.

"Your life may be a pile of crap," my father had said when he got out of rehab, "but if it's a familiar pile of crap, you'll live with it before you'll risk exchanging it for something else that might be worse."

Sonia had instructed him to turn the pile of filth—she would never utter the word *crap*—over to the Lord, and He would transform it.

That had always been about as helpful to me as "Don't worry. Be happy." All I knew was that loneliness dulled the longer you just lived with it. Now that Bethany had filled my hours with her rare giggle and her emerging chatter and her enchantment with every ordinary childhood thing I introduced her to, I had gotten a taste of living without that loneliness. Her absence now was painful.

Made all the more so by the additional ragging from my mother's voice as I nearly scrubbed the Teflon off the waffle grill.

Don't get attached to her like you did before, Lucia Marie. I know you have a tender heart, but Bethany doesn't belong to you. She's Sonia's. You're the strong one. You'll go back and fix your own life sooner or later.

My own life.

What the Sam Hill was that anymore? Right now I was suspended in a strange place, hauled out of Sonia's healing, but only beginning to poke my toe into my own. I didn't know whether to plunge in or run. I wanted a Hershey bar.

I went to the pantry and unearthed one and pulled the wrapper half off. There was no one there to stop me.

But there was also no one there to make me want to consume it so I could get through the next hour with him or her. Or without them.

I buried the bar back in the stash and escaped from the kitchen, out onto the deck. Harry the Heron looked up from his distant stance in the river as if he, too, were missing Bethany and James-Lawson and Wesley—who, I remembered, I needed to call to tell her we wouldn't be needing her, at least not for a while. That made me feel worse.

I looked back at the serene Harry. He just stood. His stillness wasn't the kind I always tried to accomplish. He seemed so sure of his place there in the shallows at the bank. He didn't try to make himself invisible. He didn't hate his life. Not like I hated what mine had become before I came here. That's what I'd told Sullivan.

Dear God, do I really feel that?

This time, I was sure God answered me, because my soul cried out a resounding yes. It burned and it scraped and it clawed and it wouldn't be pushed down. It was too real.

When I heard a car pull in, I jerked out of my reverie, heart slamming. Sullivan was still at the guesthouse.

I got myself back inside the house and locked the French door behind me. Someone was already knocking at the front door, and only by sheer force of will did I go to it, fingers curled in my pocket around the phone I'd keyed Deidre Schmacker's number into.

"Who's there?" I said.

"The cleaning lady," a familiar voice said. "Lucia, it's Wesley."

I was a puddle of pure relief when I got the door open.

She greeted me with her magnificent smile and a handled shopping bag.

"Swimming suits," she said. "You and me and the children, this afternoon."

My heart took a dive. "Come on in," I said. "But Sonia isn't here."

"She isn't here?" Wesley stepped in and scanned the foyer as if Sonia might be hiding in the umbrella stand. The search stopped at the blank wall.

"She got you to take down the mirrors," she said.

"No, she did it herself," I said. "The hard way. You want some coffee?"

"Try and stop me."

While I brewed another pot and brought out the banana nut muffins Bethany and I had made the day before—with raw instead of refined sugar—I brought her up to date. Even as I told the weekend's story, including a rendition of me fending off a few local reporters who'd gotten wind of the FBI's presence, I had a hard time believing all of that had happened in just three days.

Wesley listened with her warm-oil eyes, giving the occasional nod and stirring her coffee in a meditative fashion. I sank onto a stool beside her when I was finished, spent but somehow calm, as if merely saying it all took some of its bite away.

I hesitated to say it, but I had to. "I'm glad you came by," I said.

Wesley pulled in her chin in that way she had. "I didn't just come by. Sonia told me Friday she wanted to work with me twice a day. I'm here for my morning shift."

"She said that?" I shook my head. "That was before the FBI showed up and triggered the whole mirror-smashing thing, I guess."

"Miss Sonia was ready to smash things long before that. She's right where she needs to be."

"Absolutely."

"And where does that leave you?"

I shrugged. "Here with Bethany. I'm definitely not leaving her now, with all this going on . . ."

I let that trail off. Wesley lowered her head to look at me.

"What?" she said.

What was the thing Sullivan and I talked about—how I needed to become *I*. Why that came to me at that moment I didn't have a clue, but I reached for the wisp and pulled it in.

"I know what I'm doing for Bethany," I said. "But I don't know what I'm doing for me."

A smile rose on Wesley's face. "Well, I know a good place to start. Pick you a bathing suit, girl. We are goin' swimmin'."

CHAPTER THIRTY-FOUR

Well, ho-lee crow.

Sully clicked Stop and put the microphone down so he could move closer to the glass door. His eyes hadn't lied—Wesley and Lucia were in the river, upper bodies propped side by side on a raft, feet kicking out behind them. As he watched, grinning, Wesley scooped a handful of water onto Lucia's shoulders.

When his cell phone rang, Sully answered without checking caller ID. "Sullivan Crisp," he said.

"Cyril and Una Eremenko."

"Anna?"

"Yeah, and by the way, you sound way too professional when you answer the phone. It makes me feel inept. Cyril and Una—that was the other couple with us at Fall Creek Falls. I don't know why I couldn't remember before. I'm blaming menopause."

Sully looked at the ceiling. "That's way more than I need to know, Anna."

"You know you can always count on me for that. Anyway, I thought I'd call and tell you, since you're on a quest."

"You don't happen to have any contact information for them?"

"You underestimate me, which is another reason we wouldn't be good together. Got a pencil?"

He unearthed one. "Go," he said.

"You won't believe this. They ended up in Lebanon."

Sully's heart sank. "Are they doing mission work?"

"Not Lebanon the country. Lebanon, Tennessee. You know, *Leb*-nun."

"You mean, out east of Nashville?"

"Yeah, which I think is even weirder than if they'd gone to the Middle East, but, hey, none of us wound up where we thought we'd be, right?"

Not by a long shot.

She said, "If you really want to know anything about Lynn that you didn't already know, Una's your girl. She was the pastoral type, unlike me. I know Lynn talked to her a lot, even after Hannah was born. I didn't know from babies, but Una was freakin' Mother Earth. She's probably got six of her own by now—"

"Listen, thanks a lot, Anna. I owe you."

"No, you don't. But what I'd love to see is you getting this out of your system and moving on. Some woman out there is looking for a guy like you that she can pamper."

He heard the gravel-laugh.

"She's nuts, but she's out there."

When he said good-bye and hung up, she was still talking.

Just when he'd been about to resign himself to being forever ignorant, here was a chance, a mere twenty-five miles away, to finally know. It was a little like being flung back and forth on an amusement park ride. With none of the amusement.

He flipped his cell phone open and closed it again on his chin. First he had to get his mind around the fact that Una Eremenko had been Lynn's confidante. He thought Lynn only talked to that quack Belinda Cox—the so-called Christian counselor—after Hannah came. But this was all about what he didn't know. What perhaps he'd never paid enough attention to find out when he could have done something about it.

Sully jammed the cell phone into his pocket and picked up the microphone. What would he be able to do about it now, anyway, except suffer more guilt? He tapped the touch pad and meant to click Record. His finger slid to Play.

"What I Know to Be True: Part Four," his own voice said.

Sully closed his eyes. He sounded older than he did in his head.

"When I look Suffering in the face, trying to see what it wants me to know, I find that it's like confronting a felon who's done hard time and asking him to tell me about his feelings. He spits in my face. Kicks me in the gut. Grabs me by the neck and shoves my head against the wall. Call me slow, but I'm getting the impression that he doesn't want to tell me what it would take to change him. He's miserable, but his misery is familiar and in some twisted way, comfortable. It isn't easy to push him. What's easy, at least on the face of it, is to refuse to accept that he has power, and walk away. I brush the dirt from my feet and say, 'I think I'll just avoid him in the future.'"

Sully heard his voice shift. "But it can't be done. And so I nudge and coax and plead with the felon until he breaks. Because even the hardest of criminals has a soft-belly place where, when palpated, he will cry out, 'I'll tell you what I am! I'll show you how we can live together!' What he tells me may be different from what he confesses to you. The truth is in the asking."

Sully clicked Stop and fished for his phone.

"Baby girl," Wesley said, "when are you going to get in the water with us?"

It was our fourth afternoon of hide-and-seek on the lawn and watermelon-seed-spitting in the gazebo and—at least for Wesley, James-Lawson, and me—splash contests in the river. After our first dip together, followed by lunch at Swett's, Wesley said there was no reason why she and James-Lawson couldn't come for a visit in the afternoons until she acquired another patient to fill Sonia's opening. I suspected she wasn't trying all that hard.

Bethany, of course, loved coming home from school to find Wesley and James-Lawson waiting with their swimsuits on. She kept hers in a downstairs bathroom so she didn't have to waste time going upstairs to change. But once she got to the bank, she always skidded to a halt on her bottom, and while the rest of us bobbed and shrieked in the water, she patted it with her feet and watched us with undisguised envy.

Today, as usual, I paddled around for a few minutes, then headed for the shore to join her.

"You don't have to know how to swim," Wesley said to her. "James-Lawson didn't know how the first time I put him in the water."

"You know what? It's easy," James-Lawson said, and proved it by wriggling under the water and bobbing to the surface, spitting and grinning.

Bethany giggled, but she shook her head. "I'm fine," she said.

I leaned my arms on the rock she sat on and let my legs float out behind me like a frog's. Bethany patted my hand.

"Your swimsuit is pretty," she said.

"It's Miss Wesley's. She's letting me wear it."

"That's because she's your BFF."

"My what?" My Aunt Lucia Mom antennae went up. Was this some elementary-school profanity I needed to be brought up to speed on?

"Best Friend Forever," she said.

"Oh," I said. "Where did you learn that?"

"At school. I have three BFFs. James-Lawson." She held up a finger.

"Right."

"Louisa at school." Another finger. "And you."

I stopped pushing my hair back from my face. "I'm one of your best friends?" I said.

She nodded solemnly. Obviously BFFs were serious business.

"Who are yours?" she said.

I brushed my hand across her perfect white knee. "Well, you, of course."

She dimpled.

"And James-Lawson."

"And Miss Wesley?"

I turned to Wesley, who stood waist-deep in the Cumberland River, holding her son's hands. In the past three days we had walked together down a path of topics that grew deeper with each cup of coffee, each feet-up-on-the-deck-railing, each promise to go shopping together when we thought we could safely leave the kids with someone else. We had passed from the comfortable distance of medical colleagues discussing the state of the health-care system to the intimate whispers of sisters sharing the funnies and fears of approaching middle age.

In our whole lives Sonia and I had never talked about the things Wesley and I had told each other in the two short weeks since we'd met.

"Yes," I told Bethany. "Miss Wesley is one of my best friends."

Bethany leaned in until her heart-lips were close to my ear. "Then will you tell her I don't want to go in the water?"

I stayed still. "I will," I said, "but will you tell me why?"

"Do I have to?"

"No. Only if you want to." I looked into her eyes. They were round with yearning. "But I've learned something, Bethie."

"Like I learn stuff in school."

"Right. I've learned that if you talk about something that scares you, sometimes it goes away."

She looked doubtfully at the water.

"Is it because of that day you went in where it's deep, when Judson and them were here?"

She shook her head hard. "I was scared before that."

"Did you fall in some other time? Did you hit your head or something?"

Her eyes became two limpid-blue pools of tears. "It's because I'm too fat," she said. "I'm so fat I'll sink to the bottom and never come up."

The pink hands went to her face, and she cried as if the heart inside her small self had broken.

I was sure it had.

I hoisted myself out of the water and sank down beside her, pulling her sweet softness against me.

"Listen to me, Bethie," I said, "and listen hard like you do in school. First of all, you are not fat. You are beautiful and wonderful. And second of all, people who *are* fat don't sink to the bottom."

Her head came up, and she looked at me with streaming eyes. "How do you know?" she said.

"Because I float like a beach ball, and I'm—"

I choked on the word. Bethany watched me, waited for me to shape her view of herself. I couldn't give her mine.

"And I'm thinking I could teach you to float with me," I said. "I would never let anything happen to you. I'm your BFF, remember?"

She searched my face until I saw the baby I had held in my arms. I was the first person she had ever trusted. And as she squeezed her arms around my neck and said, "Okay—teach me," I knew I was probably the only one.

So with James-Lawson demonstrating and Miss Wesley cheering and Aunt-Lucia-Mom-BFF holding her, Bethany Cabot let herself be carried into the water and laid on her back, like a fairy princess on the cloud bed she was entitled to. I never let my hands leave her, nor did I correct her when she declared that she was "swimming."

"You know what?" James-Lawson said when we were doling out the towels. "You're almost as good of a swimmer as me."

"Now if she could only be as humble, son," Wesley said.

She put her arm around my shoulders, and we followed the two Olympic hopefuls toward the house.

"This is a huge thing. You want to celebrate at Chuck E. Cheese? One night of junk food isn't going to hurt them." She winked. "I know how Bethany is about processed products."

I laughed. "I would love to do that kind of damage, but I have a therapy session tonight. With Dr. Crisp."

She stopped and stared at me. "Well, no wonder you're not beating down the door at PHV trying to take care of your sister."

"That is the last thing I want to be doing." I lowered my voice. "I think about her, and I worry. But I feel guilty because things are so much better without her."

Wesley sniffed. "Then you keep seeing Dr. Crisp until you get over that." She tucked her arms around mine. "I can't believe I've only known you for such a little while and I'm already talking to you like this."

"Come on, Wesley. I bet you talk straight to everybody."

"Unh-uh. I don't spend my straight talk on people who can't hear what I have to say. Only my sisters get that."

I closed my eyes to savor the words and the warmth and the rare contentment that touched me tentatively on the cheek.

But Wesley nudged me. "Look at that," she whispered.

I opened my eyes to see Bethany and James-Lawson on the deck above us, towels wrapped around negligible hips that bounced against each other. Bethany's hands were raised above her head. James-Lawson clapped out a beat with his.

"What are they doing?" I said.

"Baby, they're dancing."

"To what?"

Wesley moved her shoulders and with them her head. "To the music of their souls," she said. "Only I think we ought to show them how it's done."

I couldn't argue with Wesley Kane. Or with a long-ago rhythm that teased at my feet and set my arms afloat and turned my body like a feather. Like a fawn who didn't disturb a leaf.

"You can *move*, girlfriend," Wesley said.

Yes. By a miracle I decided to call God, I still could.

CHAPTER THIRTY-FIVE

Sully prayed before the session as always. After the amen, he added an unashamed thanks that Lucia had requested they meet in the breakfast nook instead of by the river so Bethany wouldn't be in the house alone.

God knew he was basically a coward anyway. He appreciated the break.

The nook actually provided a good place for a session, situated cozily into a bay window, cushioned benches forming a booth at the table. It was one of the few rooms in Sonia's McMansion conducive to easy conversation. Too bad he didn't feel especially at ease.

Sully pulled out his phone and checked for messages for the tenth time. He hadn't let the phone out of his sight for the three days since he'd left the message for Cyril and Una. Still no return call, and the possible reasons for that had finally taken over his attempts to stay focused on something else. Cyril and Una didn't remember him. They thought he was cavalier with Lynn and hated him for it. They had recently been abducted by aliens and taken Lynn's secret to an unknown planet with them.

All right. One more try before Lucia got there, just so he wouldn't go completely nuts. He dialed the number, but he hung up when it switched to voice mail. He could be tenacious—or just plain pathetic.

"Would you like some coffee or anything?"

Sully stuck the phone back into his pocket. *Time to shift, Dr. Crisp.*

"If I drink any now," he said, "I'll be prowling the grounds at 2:00 AM, and we both know where that gets you."

She nodded at his lip. "How's it doing?"

"I don't look as much like Mick Jagger now, so there's that."

Lucia smiled, and so did Sully. If nothing else, she shared more of her face now. Time to celebrate the progress.

"You seem good," he said. "Are you?"

She looked at the bay window as if the answer might be out there. "There haven't been any more weird things happening, so I guess the FBI was wrong about Bethany being the target. She loves school, which is huge. And we got her to go in the water. I personally felt like I'd walked on it, as much of a miracle as that was."

She turned to Sully with a tender ache in her eyes. "The only sad thing about all of that is that she is so much better when Sonia isn't here."

"And what about you?" Sully said. "You've just told me how Bethany is doing. How are *you* doing?" He propped his chin on his hand, ready for the resistance.

She redirected herself to the window again before she looked back at him. "I played *Dancing with the Stars*," she said.

Sully was surprised he didn't fall out of the booth. "You did?"

"I think Bethany and James-Lawson won, though."

"There are no losers in Game Show Theology. You play, you win." He felt his grin go past his ears. "Ding-ding-ding, Mrs. Coffey. How did it feel?"

"Good." Her voice went dry. "So I'm cured. Your work is done here, right?"

"You don't need to be 'cured,' because you aren't sick. *Healed* is more what we're going for. You ready to work on that?"

Again he steeled himself for the poker face and the folded arms and the bristling voice. Again she surprised him.

"I know what I want to be healed from," she said.

"And that is?"

"I want to be healed from hate."

Sully didn't attempt to keep his mouth from dropping open.

"Do I get a buzz for that?" she said.

"Absolutely not. Tell me more. And, Lucia—" He leaned into the table. "I want you to know that whatever you say, I'm not going to judge you. I won't think you're a horrible person or ask what you were thinking when you did such a stupid thing."

"You say that now. You haven't heard it yet."

"Try me."

She nodded, but studied the window for another moment before she went on. "I figured out that I hate a lot of things. And I hate that about myself."

"Tell me what you hate."

She folded her hands precisely on the table. "You know about my husband—that he basically became a drug addict."

"Yes, I do. Drug abuse in the family can make anybody hate."

"He was arrested and went to federal prison for two years. They took away his license to practice medicine, which means now he's working for some company that sells medical equipment instead of healing people, the only thing he ever wanted to do. I hate it, and what I really hate is that if it weren't for me, it never would have happened."

Sully put a foot up on the bench. "Can you tell me why?"

Lucia didn't want to, that was clear. She grew as still as he'd ever seen her. As much as he wanted to save her the pain, he let her wrestle with it.

"We had a great marriage at first," she said finally. "I thought we did, anyway. Sonia didn't think I should marry Chip because he wasn't a Christian. He went to church—we both did—but she said it wasn't real with him and I was risking eternity in hell if I took him as my husband."

"And your mother?"

She gave him a look.

"Sided with Sonia," Sully said.

"She didn't even want to give me a wedding, but my father liked

Chip, and he said I deserved as good as Sonia had." She rubbed her palms on her sleeves. "There is a point to all this."

"Take as long as you want."

"We had a nice wedding," she said, "and we bought a house in Havertown, and Chip tried to build up his practice. He was an internist."

"And what were you doing?"

"I went back to work at the University of Pennsylvania Hospital in obstetrics."

"*Back* to work. What were you doing before that?"

"I was in a nurse practitioner program, but we needed for me to work more hours while Chip got things going."

"Did you enjoy obstetrics?"

She almost smiled. "Most of the time everybody's happy in a newborn nursery. Except when something goes wrong. Anyway, things were hard for Chip—it's that way in any new practice—and I said we should go on a little vacation for our anniversary." She rushed the words like she was trying to outrun a train. "We were trying to have a baby, and nothing was happening, and I thought it was probably because of the stress."

"How long had you been married by then?"

"Just a year. We went to Cape May, New Jersey, and it was good. We got away from everything, and it felt like when we were first married."

She had lost her stillness, and she couldn't seem to get it back, even as she locked her hands together more tightly and stared at them.

"So we were on the beach one day, and I was acting stupid—"

Sully buzzed her.

"What?"

"If I don't get to judge you, neither do you. What were you doing that you think was stupid?"

"I was trying to get him to dance with me in the water."

Sully gave her a half grin. "That doesn't sound like stupid. That sounds like flirting."

"Well, in the first place, Chip can't swim. He's afraid of the water. And when he tried to pick me up and twirl me around, he fell and ruptured two discs in his back."

"Ouch," Sully said. "I guess that put a damper on the second honeymoon."

"It put a damper on our whole life." Lucia's voice took on an edge. "He couldn't afford to take the time off to have surgery, and they weren't sure it would help anyway, but he was in too much pain to work unless he took medication. I thought it was okay. The practice picked up—we weren't worrying about money anymore—but I didn't know he was addicted to OxyContin until long after I should have. And I didn't know he was selling it illegally until the FBI came to our home and took us both out in handcuffs."

Sully lowered his foot. "*You* were arrested?"

"They never charged me. Chip told them I wasn't involved, which they didn't believe at first. How could a wife not know her husband was abusing prescription medication when she was a nurse? They didn't have any evidence against me for dealing or any of the rest of the charges, so they let me go after twenty-four hours."

"Still—that had to be traumatic."

Lucia didn't seem to hear him. The story evidently had to come out in one piece, or not at all. "It was all over the news. One of our pictures was in the paper almost every day. The FBI came to my work so many times to ask me more and more questions, the hospital administration finally told me to take a leave of absence. They took me back after Chip went to prison, which was the only thing that kept the guilt from driving me crazy."

She stopped. Sully poured her a glass of water, which she took without protest, and he poured himself one too. He'd heard a lot of stories; few had made him as angry as this one. He wouldn't ask her another question until he could do it without threatening to shoot the man she was married to.

"You doing okay?" he said.

"No," she said. "I hate this. I guess that's my new favorite word."

"I think it's the right word for now. Lucia, tell me something. Which part of this whole thing do you think is your fault?"

"It boils down to what it always boils down to. If I hadn't been so disgustingly fat, Chip never would have hurt his back trying to carry me. He wouldn't have needed pain meds. He wouldn't have gotten hooked on them."

"Did your weight make him use pain meds to deal with stress? Was it because you were carrying a few extra pounds that he helped other people feed their addictions? Sold drugs illegally?"

"Don't," she said, lips barely moving.

"Why? Is there some reason why you want to take responsibility for something that is clearly not your fault?"

Sully could see her clamming up. Time to back off some. "So what happened while Chip was in prison?"

"I worked. Gained thirty pounds the first six months. I lost a lot during the trial and all that, but I gained it back and then some."

"Did your family help you?"

To his surprise, she gave a hard laugh.

"My mother had died just before Chip was arrested. My father basically went on the lam. I don't hear from him much."

"What about Sonia?"

"She refuses to have anything to do with our father."

"I mean, did she help you?"

Her eyes clouded. "I stayed as far away from Sonia as I could. I didn't want to hear 'I told you so' and 'This is what happens when you don't take everything to the foot of the cross and walk away free.'"

The bitterness spewed like venom.

"Do you know what she did? When she saw us on the national news, do you know what she did?"

Sully shook his head.

"She sent me a package—her video and book and workbook." She pulled a ragged breath through her nose. "*Faithless and Fat* was the title. She said she hoped it would help me prepare myself physically and spiritually for a new life now that I had been cleansed of Chip."

If Sully had been a swearing man, he would have done it then.

"I watched part of the video. It said something like, 'What would you think of our Lord Jesus Christ if you saw Him with a stomach that looked like He was nine months pregnant and jowls hanging down from His face?'"

Sully winced.

"I wasn't always *this* fat, but I've never been skinny like Sonia. And it never bothered me that much until after I heard how my excess fat was Satan robbing me of my life." Lucia licked at her mouth as if she'd just tasted something foul. "Since then, all I see when I look in the mirror is a hundred extra pounds of sin that God hates, because blubber means you're 'disobedient to His will.'"

Sully shook his head. "I hope you didn't believe that stuff. Salvation doesn't depend on your dress size."

"I told myself I didn't—while I was dumping the whole package in the garbage."

"Good."

"I didn't know it at the time, but I hated Sonia for that. I think it's one of the reasons I didn't divorce Chip when he was in prison: because she assumed that I would."

"It's interesting," Sully said. "In Sonia's 'Recapturing Marriage' program, or whatever it's called, she denounces divorce in almost every circumstance. I'm a little surprised she didn't tell you to stand by your man."

"She got around that," Lucia said. "We were never married in God's eyes anyway, because Chip had never really been saved. That's what she told me."

Sully bit his tongue. Literally.

"Doesn't matter," she said. "At the time, I convinced myself I stayed married to him because I'd promised for better or for worse, and it could have been worse."

Sully wasn't sure how, but he let her go on.

"I decided I was being noble and loyal to stand by him, and after the first year, I made up my mind that I was going to be a better wife when he got out so he wouldn't get into trouble again. I kept going over and over how many of the signs I'd missed when he was using. I just thought his withdrawing and snapping at me and forgetting our plans with each other was because of his getting sick of me."

Sully felt his heart shift. Some wise person once said being a therapist wasn't as much about what to say to a hurting person as it was about how much of her pain you could bear to hear.

"Would you tell me what happened when he got out?" he said.

She folded her fingers around the water glass. "When they said he'd be out in six months, I stopped going to see him, because I wanted to surprise him when he got home with how much weight I lost. I went on the South Beach Diet and took off forty pounds."

"In six months."

"Right. I had the house perfect, myself perfect, everything just right when he came home."

"How did he respond?"

"He didn't even seem to notice that I'd lost weight. He was just happy to be out—well, I guess *happy* isn't the word. It was like he'd forgotten how to be that."

"Prison has a way of doing that to a person."

"I think he tried to be who he was before, but sometimes I'd see this hardness around his mouth and in his eyes. Or he'd just have no expression at all. He couldn't get a job, not just in medicine but anywhere, because he was a convicted felon. He got depressed, and I became a wreck watching for signs that he'd gone back to drugs."

"That's understandable."

"Not to him. He said I was the one who drove him to them in the first place, and I would do it again if I didn't lay off him." She shook her head. "It was the pressure. I didn't blame him."

Why not? Sully wanted to say.

She rearranged her grip on the glass. Sully could see her fingers shaking.

"I know he broke the law, but he wasn't a serial killer. He didn't mean to hurt anyone, and yet he came out of the penitentiary as hard and cold as any of those men I saw in the visitors' room. That place sucked everything out of him that I'd loved."

"But you didn't leave him then, either," Sully said.

"No."

He waited and watched her. She stopped gripping, stopped breathing. He knew she was trying to stop feeling. This was the part he didn't like. The part when he had to push her to feel the pain all the way to its scathing center.

"What about after that?"

"I don't know if I can talk about this."

"It's all right. Just take a minute."

"I don't care how long I take, I can't do this! Don't you get that?"

Lucia stared at him, and Sully watched the horror come into her eyes.

"I'm sorry," she said. She struggled to stand up in the narrow space between the bench and the table, and dropped onto the seat again.

Sully spread his hand on the tabletop. "Don't be, Lucia. This is exactly what you need to be doing."

"I shouldn't take it out on you."

"Take it out on me all you want. It's better than taking it out on you, and that's what you've been doing probably your whole life. You're making everything your fault, and it isn't."

She closed her eyes. "You don't know all of it," she said.

"I don't know what you haven't told me, Lucia."

Her eyes opened, but she didn't quite look at him.

"If whatever this is was somehow your 'fault,'" Sully said, "we'll deal with that. Therapy isn't about making everything okay. It's about helping you come to terms with what is. No matter what it is."

He waited, the interminable wait that always happened at the crossroad—where there was no more room for coaxing or presenting arguments. There could be no pushing or tugging. There could only be holding his breath while she decided whether to keep feeding that Thing to keep it quiet—or rip it out and find out at last what it had to say.

"I got pregnant," she said.

Sully let out the breath. "This was after Chip got out of prison."

"He didn't want to try then, not with things the way they were, but I thought maybe if we had a family he wouldn't give up on himself and us."

She pushed her hands into her lap and rocked for a moment. Sully waited.

"I'm trying not to say that was stupid, because I know you'll buzz me."

"No buzzing right now," he said softly.

"Then how dumb was that? It never works to use a baby to put things back together, but I just wanted a child so much—and he always said he did, before."

"So he did agree."

"No. I just went off birth control without telling him. That was the idiotic part."

"Let's call it the last-resort part."

"Not that it mattered that much. Most of the time Chip wasn't that interested in me—you know—"

"Sexually," Sully said.

"It was mostly the drugs he was on for so long—that's what I told myself."

"And you were probably right. I take it you two didn't discuss your sexual problems."

"We didn't even discuss what to have for dinner." Lucia pressed against the back of the booth. "Anyway, one night things came together, and then I found out I was pregnant."

Sully tried to do some quick math, but he didn't have all the numbers. How long ago was all this?

"Again, stupidly, I thought once it was a fact, Chip would be happy. But like I said, he had forgotten how. My being pregnant just made things worse. All he could talk about was how we couldn't afford a child—and who wanted to grow up with an ex-con for a father? He was already so bitter about the insurance companies and the FBI and the courts and the prison system, and he couldn't figure out why I wanted to put more and more pressure on him."

Lucia looked at Sully, and her agony cut through him.

"He told me to have an abortion."

Sully's heart crashed. This—this was a thing he could hardly bear to hear. Only her desperate need to say it made him nod her on.

"It was the first time I ever said no to my husband. I couldn't terminate the pregnancy. That was what she was to him: a pregnancy. To me, she was our child, and I couldn't."

Her face worked, and Sully tilted toward her.

"It's all right to cry, Lucia," he said. "You have every reason to."

"I can't. Just let me finish." She flattened her fingertips to her temples. "I went to all the doctor's appointments by myself. The only time Chip even acknowledged that I was still pregnant was when I brought home the ultrasound picture that showed our baby was a girl. He said, 'At least that's one way she won't take after me.'"

"Was that his concern about having a child?" Sully said. "That his offspring would turn out like him?"

"I don't know. He wouldn't talk about it. He wouldn't talk about any of it, and I just kept working."

"You were still in obstetrics."

"Yeah, and I tried to keep things going at home and tried to suggest job possibilities for him . . ."

"What happened, Lucia?" he said. "What happened to the baby?"

"At twenty-four weeks, I started bleeding."

Her voice was so low and flat, Sully had to strain to hear.

"I had a placental abruption—where the placenta tears away from the uterine wall—and the doctor put me on bed rest. Chip nearly went out of his mind. I had some sick leave, but not three months' worth, and everything was falling apart around him."

She swallowed so hard Sully could feel the pain in his own throat.

"So when the bleeding stopped, I thought I could at least get up and cook him some meals."

No. Please, no.

"I was in the kitchen making lasagna—and I hemorrhaged. My baby died—and I—" The wall of tears she held back cracked through her voice. "The tear in my uterus was so severe and so infected they couldn't—I had to have a hysterectomy."

"Lucia, how long ago did this happen?"

"Seven months," she said.

Holy, holy crow.

Sully stretched his hand across the table. "Lucia, I am so sorry."

"Don't, please. I don't want to cry."

"Why? Why don't you want to cry when you've lost so much?"

"Because if I start crying, I'll never stop. I never will."

"You'll never stop hurting," Sully said. "You will stop crying, if you just go ahead and let it all out."

Lucia nodded even as her face collapsed. She put her arms on the table and wept into them.

Sully's soul wept with her.

CHAPTER THIRTY-SIX

I didn't know how long I'd cried when I finally pulled my face up from my arms, dripping snot and feeling like I'd just thrown up. Sullivan handed me a Kleenex and waited while I blew my nose. I thought I would have a hard time meeting his eyes now, but I found myself searching for them across the table. They were still kind, still safe.

"Is our time up?" I said.

"I stopped the meter a long time ago," he said. "Let's just sit for a minute, let you get centered."

I gave him what I was sure was a wobbly smile. "So I don't go break the mirrors?"

"People only break mirrors when they hold back."

"I definitely didn't hold back," I said. "I feel like I just vomited."

"Ding-ding," he said.

At least, that was what I thought he said, before it was lost in the slam of a door. We stared at each other.

"Were you expecting somebody?" Sullivan said.

"No."

We spoke in hushed tones, as if we were the ones who had just walked in uninvited. I could tell from the whiteness around his mouth that he was backpedaling from fear. I had already succumbed to it.

"Stay here," he said. He stood up and handed me his cell phone. "Call 911 if—"

"Okay," I said. "I think it was the door from the breezeway into the laundry room."

Sullivan moved toward the dark kitchen with painful slowness. I stayed frozen on the bench until he disappeared around the corner. Then I thought of Bethany.

I had to get to her. If this was that man coming back, I had to be with her.

I started inching my way out of the booth, then stopped when I heard Sullivan's voice bark sharply into the silence.

"Stop right there! Do it! Stop!"

Another male voice swore in surprise.

"I mean it—stay right there!"

After that I couldn't make out words. Something heavy hit the floor—and the cabinets and the walls.

With Sullivan's phone still clutched in my hand, I lunged for the hallway to the foyer, where the stairs seemed miles away. So did Bethany.

Dear God, please—please—just let me get past the kitchen without him seeing me.

I pushed away all the rest of the visions—including one of Sullivan being beaten to death—and focused on the foyer ahead of me. I had to get out of earshot to call 911. I had to get to Bethany. With my heart clawing its way up my throat, I made myself creep past the opening into the kitchen, forced myself not to look.

There was no need. Sullivan slid to my feet on his back. Someone else fell on him, one arm drawn back with his fist in a vicious knot. I couldn't see the man's face, but I knew the body.

"Chip! Chip—stop!"

He didn't until I screamed it twice more. Even then his fist remained suspended above Sullivan's face as he turned to look up at me.

He swore under his breath and drew back from the form he'd been pounding—and recoiled to his feet. Not, however, before I saw the cold, hard rage.

But the voice he finally spoke in was Chip's, though ripped at its edges. "Lucia, babe, are you all right?"

He reached out his arm, but I pushed it aside and knelt beside Sullivan, who still lay half-stunned at our feet.

"You okay?" I said.

"What is going on?" Chip said. "I come in here looking for you, and the guy jumps me."

I examined the skin under Sullivan's eye, which was already swelling.

"Get me some ice," I said.

"Lucia, who is this?"

"He's my therapist. Just get me some ice."

"Aw, man."

Chip dropped beside me and leaned over Sullivan.

"Man, I am so sorry. Are you hurt anywhere else? Can you move your—"

"I'm good," Sullivan said. "Just let me up."

I sat back on my heels and let him hoist himself to sitting. Chip offered his hand, but Sullivan ignored it.

"Chip Coffey," he said. "I'm Lucia's husband."

"This is Dr. Crisp," I said.

Sullivan massaged one of his own hands with the other. His face was blotchy, as if it couldn't decide whether to register red-hot embarrassment or ice-cold anger.

"I would have told you who I was," Chip said. "You didn't give me a chance."

He stood up and backed toward the refrigerator, where he opened the freezer and pulled out a bag of frozen blueberries.

"Try this on your eye," he said.

Sullivan planted it on the side of his face. He'd barely spoken a word yet, and when he did, I didn't hear the Sullivan Crisp I knew.

"You didn't act like somebody who was supposed to be here," he said to Chip. "I'm sure Lucia told you we had a prowler here less than a week ago."

"I saw it on CNN—which is why I came." Chip looked at me. "We need to talk."

"I'm going to go and let you do that."

Sullivan stood up and tossed the frozen package on the counter. When he walked away from us, I saw him favor his left leg.

"You sure you're okay, man?" Chip said.

"Good night," Sullivan said.

"Typical shrink," Chip said when Sullivan had let himself out. "Cold as a fish."

"How friendly did you expect him to be after you beat him half to death?"

Chip's eyes startled. "He came at me first, Lucia. What was I supposed to do?"

"You were the one coming in unannounced. We thought you were that guy coming back."

"Attack first, ask questions later."

"If he attacked you, why did he end up on his back on the floor with a black eye and who knows what else?"

I snatched up the bag of berries and flung them back into the freezer. When I turned around, he stared at me.

"When were you going to tell me you were in therapy?" he said.

"I don't know," I said.

"This guy must be pretty good. He does personality transplants. You're not the same Lucia." He took a step toward me. "Or are you?"

A smile spread across a face grizzled with a day's growth of beard. His eyes, faded blue and sagging with fatigue, crinkled at the corners.

"I've missed you, babe," he said. "Come here, would you? I want to hold you."

I didn't, so he came to me. I let him put his arms around me and stood with my face in his chest. The musky man smell wasn't there. He seemed clammy and stale.

"Why did I have to find out from TV about somebody trying to break in?" he said into my hair. "Did Dr. Crisp tell you not to tell me?"

"He doesn't tell me what to do."

"I'm teasing you. I gotta say, it scared the crap out of me." He held me away from him so he could look into my face. The rage had vanished. "This whole thing has gotten out of control, Lucia. I want you to come home with me. Now. Tonight." His fingers squeezed my shoulders. "I can't sleep—I can't eat—I can't concentrate thinking about you here with some crazy still trying to take Sonia down."

"She's already down," I said—for lack of anything to say that actually made sense. My mind careened.

"It's obviously not enough for this person that she's lost her whole ministry and pretty much her mind," Chip said. "He's obviously after something else."

"Like Bethany." I yanked myself away from him. "And you think I'm going to leave her here to cope with that?"

"We'll get her into state care. She'll be safer there."

"No."

"You can't protect her—you and Dr. Wisp."

"No. I am not putting that baby in foster care." I forced myself not to press my hand to my chest, where my heart threatened to hammer its way out. "I have to stay until Sonia comes home and is well enough to take care of her."

"Now that just makes me feel infinitely better." Chip shoved his hand across the top of his head, where the usually spiky hair was flattened in thin clumps. "Sonia coming *home*—right here—where all the targets will be sitting like ducks in a freaking shooting booth!"

"The FBI is watching the house."

My breath caught. If they were, why didn't they see Chip barging in?

He grabbed my arm and held on. "You have no idea what you're dealing with here, Lucia. The way this whole thing has gone down—it wasn't some ticked-off former employee who put this together. This is the work of pros. I lived with guys like that—I *know*. They don't stop until they get what they want. You want to hire a whole SWAT team for Sonia and Bethany, be my guest, but you are coming home with me."

Until then I'd been too stunned to pull away. Now I wrenched myself out of his grip and backed away, putting my hand up before he could step toward me.

"You're telling me what I'm going to do?" I said.

He gripped the back of his own neck the way he'd clamped onto my arm. "I'm just half out of my mind over this. I can't control what Sonia does, but—"

"You can't control what I do either."

We locked eyes for as long as it took for Chip to begin to breathe. I never looked away.

"Apparently not," he said finally.

"I'm going to check on Bethany," I said.

"I'll make us some coffee. When you come back down, we'll come up with something."

"I'm done talking for tonight," I said. I was already halfway out of the kitchen.

"Tomorrow, then," he said. "Lucia."

I didn't look back at him.

Sully took a shower and was in the leather chair with a bag of ice on his face before he remembered that Lucia had his cell phone. He was in no mood to talk to anybody anyway, and he thought his jaw might be broken.

He hadn't been in a fight since the sixth grade, when Billy Blakely had jumped him on the playground for beating him at Pac-Man. Now he'd been in two in a week's time.

Sully shifted the ice. Wiry little Kick Boxer had been one thing. All that guy had wanted to do was get away. The hulking Dr. Coffey was a different story. If Lucia hadn't intervened, Sully would have been lucky to get out of there without several broken bones and a brain hemorrhage. The dude was strong—and angry.

Sully gave a grunt. Why did it always seem like the wrong half of the couple was the one getting the therapy?

Not that Lucia wasn't benefiting. He hadn't even had a chance to process what she'd told him. He'd been busy being processed by her husband. When someone knocked on the door, he was sure it was Chip now, coming over to finish off the job.

"Who is it?" he said from the chair.

"It's Lucia."

Sully dumped the ice bag on the floor and hobbled to the door on his throbbing leg. Maybe the guy *had* fractured a bone. In any event, if Lucia had come to apologize for Chip, she and Sully had further to go in therapy than he thought.

"I'm okay," he said, even before he had the door all the way open.

She just put out the hand that held his cell phone.

"I didn't have a chance to give this back to you," she said. "I probably would have forgotten, but it rang, so I thought you might need it."

"You okay?" Sully said. "I'm asking you as your therapist—do you feel safe?"

"Yeah," she said. "Weirdly enough."

Sully felt his face soften, even around his throbbing eye. "Maybe it's not weird at all. Maybe it's just progress."

When she was gone, he dropped back into the chair, retrieved the ice, and looked at his missed call.

He sat up and gripped the phone. Cyril and Una's number. He glanced at his watch and saw with a groan that the crystal was broken. Another casualty of tonight's episode of *WrestleMania*. He could still see that it was only nine o'clock. Too late? He'd waited thirteen years. He could probably wait another ten hours.

Or not.

Fingers trembling, he made the call and prayed through the rings until a male voice with the faint trace of an accent said, "Sully."

Cyril flashed on Sully's memory screen. Pleasantly lumpy. Warmly argumentative on every topic Sully could bring up. Always with a twinkle somewhere on his face.

Sully heard none of that in the single-word greeting.

"Cyril," he said. "Long time no see."

Ugh. Lame.

"You have been a busy man," Cyril said.

So that was it. *You were so wrapped up in being the famous psychologist, you didn't have time for your old friends.*

"Too busy," Sully said. "I should have been in touch."

"No, Sully, you should not."

"Cyril." Sully cleared his throat. "How did we leave things last time we saw each other? I don't remember us parting on bad terms."

"No, no. You and I, Sully, we are fine. It's Una."

Okay, it was Una who hated him. Because of something she knew about Lynn that he didn't. Which was the reason for this whole agonizing search in the first place.

"I'm sorry there's bad blood between Una and me," Sully said. "I honestly don't know what that's about, and it may in fact help me to know—"

"You do not change one bit." Cyril's voice had warmed. "You still think you have all the answers. There is no bad blood, Sully. I just don't think it would be good for Una to talk to you. In fact, I have not even told her you called."

"I don't understand."

Cyril sighed into the phone. "Lynn's death was devastating to her. I could not console her for months. She finally had to seek professional help for her grief." Sully thought he heard him chuckle. "Too bad you hadn't begun your career yet then. Your work would have been perfect for her."

"Is she all right now?" Sully said.

"For the most part. I know the loss has deepened her ministry, as I'm sure it has yours. But to dredge it all up now, after so many years of grief . . . I can't allow that, Sully."

Sully tossed the ice bag and got himself up from the chair, but there seemed to be no place to go. He stood with his forehead to the glass door.

"I respect you being so protective of her, Cyril," he said. "I guess I just don't understand the depth of her grief."

"Then that would make the two of us the same. I have never understood it completely myself. But I do not want her taken down to it again, and I'm afraid seeing you would do that. I cannot take that chance."

"No, I hear you, Cyril," Sully said. *All too well.*

"So—you will not call again?"

"Of course not. You have my word."

"I would have liked to have seen you again myself. It is too bad, Sully. It is all too bad."

For the first time, Sully couldn't argue with him.

CHAPTER THIRTY-SEVEN

Harry the Heron was the only other being awake when I got up the next morning. I found him admiring his reflection in the glassy surface of the river. I joined him at the riverside with my coffee and offered him some. I took his relocation to the far end of the dock as a no.

"You're not missing much," I told him. "I'm out of whipped cream."

Although I was sure that, for once, no amount of pure fat and refined sugar could keep at bay what had driven me off of my futon at that hour.

"That's part of it right there," I said to Harry. "My husband came hundreds of miles to see me, and I didn't even sleep with him."

Harry remained unimpressed. He was obviously a loner. He knew nothing about relationships.

We had that in common.

"I believed every lie he ever told me," I said to Harry. "And now, when he actually might be telling me the truth, I can't even listen to him."

Chip *had* seemed generally concerned for me, beginning with the fact that he looked—and smelled—like an unmade bed. I had never seen him with patches of facial stubble or a plaster of unwashed hair, even on those gray Sundays when I'd gone faithfully to the prison to see him and sat among the pinched, weary mothers who were there to try and redeem their sons. I was one of the few wives. Most women didn't stay married to men who wrecked their lives. But I'd gone back over and over, looking for a glimpse of the

Chip I fell in love with, the Chip who couldn't imagine a world without me in it.

"Now he's here," I said to Harry. "Ready to go back to that time with me. And I don't know if I can."

Harry beat his wings, and with the obnoxious squawk I had come to appreciate, he flew to his favorite piece of tree that had lodged itself in the middle of the river. From there he accused me, right down the spear of a beak that gave him his noble profile.

"You know it, and I know it," I said. "I can't go back to that life—because I hate it. I hate every part of it. I hate it with everything that's in me."

My hands ached as I squeezed the coffee cup. Sullivan said I'd buried it. He didn't know about the times when I couldn't make it stay, and some of its rancid juice spurted out over everything. Its rot had started to spew the day I told Chip I was coming here, and I'd managed to drain it back down.

But, curse Sullivan Crisp—I didn't seem to be able to do that now. Not this time.

I flung the coffee into the river, and with it the next layer that wouldn't stay buried.

"I hate my fat. I hate the silence in my house. I hate my job. I hate the women in the hospital nursery who take their babies home. I hate it—do you hear me? I HATE IT!"

With a heave that brought up yet another stratum of pain, I hurled the mug downward and watched it smash against the limestone below. Harry squawked away. But I was no longer talking to him. In the tantrum of screaming and smashing and hating, I was talking to God.

I got my arms around my knees and pulled them to my chest. They didn't resist me; space had been made, and I breathed into a small nook of freedom.

Dear God—is that You?

"I brought you some coffee."

I wrenched myself around and grabbed for the edge of my rock perch to keep my balance. Chip stopped several feet away and shook his head.

"You're scarin' me, babe. Come back up here where you're not hanging off a precipice."

I could see steam still rising from the mug he held out.

"I'm fine here," I said. I turned back to the water and heard him pick his way toward me.

"Is this where that guy made his escape?" he said.

I nodded sharply.

"And you're out here by yourself."

I put up my hand and collided with the cup he extended. Coffee slopped onto the front of his shirt—a clean white polo that had replaced the slept-in look. I glanced at him only long enough to see that he'd shaved and returned his hair to its spikes.

Chip set the cup gingerly on the rock and squatted beside me as if he himself might also tumble. He lowered himself to his seat, arms shaking with the effort. One sandaled foot slid, and he jerked to catch himself. Several chips of limestone jittered loose and danced off the edge, and he shuddered visibly. A kinder woman would have suggested a different place for this nonswimmer to sit. Maybe a younger Lucia.

I felt like neither.

"I was lying awake last night, babe," he said, "thinking about what you told me, and I know where you're coming from."

"Do you."

I pulled my knees in tighter. It was one thing to hurl my hate at Harry. Even God. But I couldn't trust flinging it at Chip.

"When I'm alone and I'm making plans," he said, "I tend to forget that you don't know how much I've changed. We haven't had a chance to see what that's going to do in our marriage. I was living down here in Nashville—and then Sonia's crash—and then *you* came down here."

"I get that."

He had to hear my teeth grinding.

NANCY RUE & STEPHEN ARTERBURN

"I want that chance, Lucia. It isn't just about me being scared for you—it's about me missing you."

I watched Harry return to his tree and preen again into the watery mirror. I hadn't missed Chip much at all. When he touched the hair at my cheek, I smacked his hand away. He clutched at the rock.

"Look," he said, "I know how this place can get its claws into you."

"It isn't this place."

"You don't see it because you're right in the middle of it. I experienced that firsthand, and it's worse for you, because Sonia makes you forget you even have a life of your own."

"I don't!"

"That's what I mean."

"It's not what *I* mean."

I looked back at Chip—at the faded physician still sure that he had the diagnosis correct. I hated that too—that assumption that only he knew what was right for me—that down-the-nose belief that I would buy into what anyone told me about myself. I hated it, and God wasn't holding me back from saying it.

It was God who pushed me forward.

"Babe—"

"Stop. Just stop—or so help me, I will push you off this ledge."

Amusement lit up in his eyes like tiny birthday-candle flames.

"I am as serious as I know how to be," I said. "It isn't *here* that has its claws in me. It's *there*."

"Where, babe?"

"Wherever we are—you and I. I hate our life together—do you get that? I hate every single thing it has become, and it just makes me want to scream."

Which I was currently doing, in a voice topped only by the roar of a bass fishing boat flying past, its nose pointed arrogantly out of the water. I felt like that. I just wanted to go.

I even rolled to the side to start to my feet. Chip's hand came down over my arm.

"Let go of me," I said.

"I want you to listen."

"I don't want to listen."

"Babe, please—"

"Stop calling me babe! I hate that too!"

"Do you hate me?"

"What?"

He put his face close to mine. I could smell anxiety's breath.

"Do you hate me?" he said.

My heart slammed. "No, I don't hate you."

"But you hate our life."

I scraped his fingers from my arm. "Did I not just say that? Get off me!"

"If you hate our life, then I'll make us a new one."

"You will."

"I know that most of what's gone wrong has been the result of the bad breaks that have come to me. I didn't always make the best choices to deal with them, and that's why I have to be the one to lay the groundwork."

He put up his hand as if he were going to touch my hair. I stopped him with my eyes.

"Tell me what you want changed," he said. His voice pleaded. "Whatever it is, I'll make it happen."

"You can't."

"Let me try. I'll get us a new place to live, away from the bad memories, yeah? And I'll be somebody you can be proud of again. I've made some good money working for Mussen, and I've saved it for us. We can make any kind of new start you want."

Those were the promises I'd ached to hear when he was released from prison. Now they fell with empty thuds to the rock I sat on. I pried my gaze from the figure Harry cut against the now-brightening sky to find Chip's eyes straining against tears.

"We've lost so much," he said. "Please just give me a chance to get it back for us."

"You can't give me back what I want." I turned again toward the river, drained and spent. "Have you forgotten that we can't have children?"

"Uncle Chip?"

I was up and onto the lawn almost before Bethany's chirp reached me. She stood a few yards from the bank, bare feet on tiptoes as she clutched at the rag still hanging from her neck.

"Is that Uncle Chip?" she said. "He came back?"

"Hey, there's my princess!"

Bethany's face became an enchanted land of dimples. She took two tiny, pointed-toed steps before she broke into a run and flung herself into the big bear arms that reached down to pull her up. Her own chubby ones went around Chip's neck and squeezed as tightly as the eyes that crinkled closed in pleasure.

Chip engulfed her and found her cheek with his. "How's my princess?" he said.

"How's my prince?" she said back.

"Better now that I'm with you."

I could only gaze stupidly at the scene. I had just come upon a relationship already in progress. One I'd never known existed in this way until now.

"Do you know Aunt Lucia Mom?" Bethany said. She'd loosened one arm from Chip's neck and pointed a happily trembling finger at me.

"Aunt Lucia Mom." Chip grinned. "Know her? I love her."

Bethany nodded. "I do too. I love both of ya'll."

And then she stretched her pink, pudgy, hitherto stiff little arm out to me. When I went to her, she pulled me into her hug with Chip, and she held me there.

Sully was glad the podcast was audio and not video, because he looked like he was doing *The Jerry Springer Show*. He put down the microphone and went to the fridge for the last of the Frappuccinos, which he took onto the balcony. The air out there was hotter than the surface of the afternoon sun, but the room was closing in on him.

Just like everything else.

He poked his sunglasses onto his face and was about to flop into the canvas deck chair when movement by the river caught his eye. He had to blink to make sure he was seeing correctly.

Lucia was knee-deep in the water, pants rolled up, with Bethany beside her. They were splashing Chip, who crashed in after them, hoisted Bethany up onto his shoulder, and took off with her, to the tune of a full octave of happy squeals.

Sully watched, mouth open, as the brute who'd flattened him tossed a sturdy six-year-old in the air and called out, "Who wants to grill some hot dogs?"

Sully turned his eyes away. But the image stayed with him. Bethany was more Lucia's child than Sonia's in every way he could think of, and the mad wrestler had turned into every kid's dream of a dad. The irony of it pricked at him.

Now the guy was there, acting like a family man, just when Lucia had begun to see their past for what it was. Not that he would ever advise her to leave him; that had to be strictly her decision. Miracles happened. There could still be healing and family for Lucia. With a lot of ifs.

Sully propped his feet on the railing and took a drag from the bottle. For him the chance was gone. No matter what he did to change his life, no matter what he believed in, he was never going to carry Hannah on his shoulders or roast a weenie for her or watch her play a tooth in the school play. Lynn had taken that away forever. And he would probably never know why.

"That is a thing I know to be true," he murmured into the bottle.

Now *there* was something uplifting to release out there into cyberspace.

"J. Edgar!"

Sully pulled his feet off the railing and leaned over. Bethany ran toward the pug, who raced down the slope to meet her as if she were already holding one of those hot dogs. They fell to the ground together in such a tangle of tails—pigtail and canine—Sully couldn't tell where one stopped and the other began.

One thing he knew: Agent Schmacker wouldn't be far behind. She appeared, clad in mint green, just as Lucia joined the puppy pile. Chip was slower to approach.

"Sorry to interrupt the family gathering," Sully heard Agent Schmacker say.

"Oh, I don't think you're sorry at all," Chip said.

His face was congenial. His voice was not.

"How can I help you?" Lucia said.

But Schmacker had spotted Sully backing away from the railing.

"Dr. Crisp—perfect," she said. "Will you come down and join us? I have something to show you."

Three faces looked up at him: Bethany's shy, Lucia's startled, and Chip's as hard as the muscles twitching in his arms.

Sully nodded. *Dang.* He should have stuck to his podcast.

CHAPTER THIRTY-EIGHT

When Sully joined us on the deck, where I'd suggested we sit so I could keep an eye on Bethany with J. Edgar, Deidre Schmacker already had a manila folder open on the table in front of us. Chip stood behind me, and I could feel him glowering.

"Do any of you recognize this man?" she said.

She pointed a clear-polished fingernail at a mug shot. My instinct was to recoil from it, only because the scrawny character who glared back at me looked like every other wanted man whose picture I'd seen in the places I'd been forced to go. He was squinty eyed and surly lipped and not to be trusted. But this particular scumbag?

"No," I said.

"You're sure."

"Positive."

I could hear Bethany's happy chortles going up and down the scale, and I was missing it.

"Do you, Halsey? I'm sorry, I mean Chip."

"No. Who is he?"

Chip clipped off his words, but so far he hadn't threatened to throw her off the property. Still, my stomach churned.

"We found his fingerprints on one of the letters you turned in to us, Lucia," the agent said. "Which means you may have been instrumental in giving us a lead to the person—or persons—who tried to kill your sister."

"What letters?" Chip said.

"Some hate mail Sonia got," I said.

He muttered something I didn't catch. If Agent Schmacker did, she let it go.

"Anything about the shoulders or the shape of the head look familiar to you, Dr. Crisp?"

"You're referring to the guy I got into it with on the lawn?" Sullivan nodded. "He was built this way from what I could tell."

"Somebody want to tell me what we're talking about?" Chip said.

"What about the name Garrison? Derrick Garrison. Does that ring any bells for anybody?"

"Guess not," Chip said. He moved to the corner of the deck.

"I don't know anybody by that name," I said.

Sullivan shook his head.

Agent Schmacker didn't seem disappointed. "That's probably an alias, or he's using another one by now. He's made a career out of changing his identity to fit the crime."

"What crime?" Chip said. "Or don't you want to tell me that either?"

"Mr. Garrison is not currently incarcerated," Agent Schmacker said, hardly looking at him. "He bears some kind of grudge against your sister; that's apparent from his letter, so there may be motive. We can't link him to the crash yet, but we're working on that." She gave me the droopy eyes. "I hoped you had seen him at the airport that day."

"Haven't we been through all that?"

I could hear Chip trying to shift his voice into something less abrasive.

"Look, I don't mean to be a jerk, but we've cooperated with you—obviously my wife has, she's given you evidence—but we haven't been together for weeks, and we'd like to get back to our day."

"Wait," I said. I stared at the picture, and something about it poked at me.

"What is it?" Agent Schmacker said.

"Do you have another copy of this—I mean, could I write on it?"

"Of course. Do you need a pen?"

"Pencil."

"Lucia, what are you doing?" Chip said.

Sullivan caught my eye as Deidre Schmacker handed me a pencil. That made me brave.

"What are you *doing*?" Chip said.

"I just want to see something," I said.

I put the pencil to the chin of the man in the picture and sketched—a scrappy set of hairs here, another there. Fear came up in my throat like smoke.

"Pencil Whiskers," I said.

Agent Schmacker looked at the drawing and then at me. "What are you saying?"

"If this guy had whiskers like this, then I saw him the day of the crash. He was on the ground crew."

"You're certain."

"He opened the door for me when I went in the terminal, and he gave Marnie directions when she got off the plane to come find me. I watched him talking to her."

"Babe, how could you remember that?" Chip said. "A lot has happened since then."

"Mr. Coffey, please." To me, Schmacker said, "Why did you notice him, Lucia? Was he doing something suspicious?"

"No." I felt my face color. "He barely gave me the time of day when I came in, but he was all about chatting it up with Marnie."

"That would be Margaret Oakes, right?" Agent Schmacker said. "I'll get in touch with her again." She tapped the picture once more. "This is interesting—because this man was not on the ground crew."

"Then he *wasn't* there," Chip said.

"I didn't say he wasn't there. I just said he wasn't on the ground crew—not officially." She stood up and smiled at me. "I knew we'd make a good team, once we understood each other. Thank you. We could be onto something."

"Are you still watching the house?" I said. My eyes shifted to

Chip, who had turned his back to us, face pointed toward Bethany and J. Edgar.

"We are. It would help us if you would let us know of anyone new you're expecting, particularly at night." She, too, glanced at Chip. "The agent was about to accost your husband last night before he realized who he was."

If you find out who he is, I wanted to say, *would you let* me *know?*

I didn't look at Chip as I walked into the kitchen, honed in as I was on the sink full of supper dishes.

"Is she asleep?" he said.

"It didn't take long. She had a big day."

"She told me it was the best day of her life."

I wanted to inform him that Bethany said that every single night now, but I turned on the water instead. There was no point in starting him off prickling under the collar when we were already headed for the ugly conversation that had been brewing in his eyes since Deidre Schmacker left. Until then, we'd had a day that had given me a vague hope. Now he was brooding again.

"Give this to her, would you?" he said. "I forgot to do it before you put her to bed."

I shut off the faucet and turned to him. He held a small stuffed frog that bore a crown and a pair of glittered wings.

"She'll love it," I said. "Why don't you give it to her in the morning?"

"Because I won't be here."

He picked up the duffel bag I'd apparently missed on the way in.

"You're leaving right now?" I said.

"I have a meeting early tomorrow—in Memphis."

"On Sunday?"

"This is a major deal. It could mean the start of that new life for us." He touched my cheek and quickly withdrew his hand. "I just hope you want it as much as I do."

Before I could open my mouth, he put his finger to my lips. "I'm going to make it happen, Lucia. You will have everything you want—everything, I promise you that."

He hoisted the bag onto his shoulder and went for the door, stopping only to add, "I'll call you when I have it all together."

I didn't try to stop him. I just let him leave with a promise he couldn't keep. The way he'd been with Bethany made the pain of that bite harder.

"He'll be back," I told Bethany when she looked for him the next morning.

She didn't look as deflated as I thought she might. "He told me he would," she said, eyes round. "But I wish I knew how many more wake-ups."

Something in me said there might not be enough. Not for me.

"I have to ask you something, Porphyria," Sully said.

He could feel her smiling on the other end of the phone line. "Is this of a spiritual or a psychological nature?"

"Neither. Did you see it on the national news when the prowler came onto the property here?"

"No. It didn't make CNN or any of those. You told me about it. Why?"

"Just a question."

"Mm-hmm."

"Something Lucia's husband said has been bothering me, but never mind." He tried to put on a grin. "How about a little *Jeopardy*, Dr. Ghent?"

She groaned. "I don't guess I can stop you."

"Great quotes for five hundred. 'Freedom's just another word for nothin' left to lose.'"

"If I played your games, Dr. Crisp, I would say, 'Who is selling you a bill of goods?'"

Sully buzzed. "I'm sorry. That's 'Who was Janis Joplin?' You've never been very good at this, Porphyria."

"And neither are you if you believe that jive."

She so seldom treated him to a glimpse of her predoctoral self, he had to smile. He could tell, however, that she wasn't smiling with him.

"So you think you're at the end of the line," she said.

"The end of this one. The last door I know to knock on has been slammed in my face." He propped his feet on the balcony railing, then pulled them down. "I've been telling people for years: the whys will lead you to the 'what next.'" He paced back into the guesthouse.

"You've changed your mind about that?"

"Not entirely. If I had—" He pulled an imaginary microphone up to his lips. "The next item up for bid is this beautiful ministry! It can be yours, if the price is right!"

"Mm-hm. You want to get back on track, son?"

"That's just it." Sully flopped into the leather chair, which swallowed him into an awkward slump. "I don't know where the track is anymore. I just felt like I had more to do with Lynn and Hannah's death than just not seeing what was going on in my own house. And I was so certain that feeling was coming from God."

"Is God telling you that's not the case?"

Sully hauled himself out of the chair. "God's not telling me much of anything—I think I need to give up this quest I'm on."

"If Sullivan Crisp ever gave up searching for something he meant to find, I would start making the funeral arrangements, because I would know he was deceased. And you know what I've told you before."

Sully had to grin. "Until you're dead, you're not done."

"You're in a funk."

"Is that in the *DSM-IV-R*?"

"The answer is going to find you, Sully. Just get yourself ready."

He didn't ask how. That one he knew. When they hung up, he cupped his face in his hands and asked for the light he thought had faded to nothing.

CHAPTER THIRTY-NINE

Wesley arrived with James-Lawson before I left to pick up Bethany from school on Monday. She had news all over her face.

"If it's all right with you, I'm going to break my own rule and plug him into a movie for a minute," she said. "I need to talk to you."

With a sense of dread, I turned on a DVD in the backseat for James-Lawson, while Wesley climbed into the front. He gazed at the screen in rapture before *Shrek* even started.

"He thinks he's died and gone to heaven," she said.

"Am I going to hate what you want to tell me?"

"That depends. Your sister called me today."

I slammed on the brakes at the end of the driveway. "Why?"

"Because she was afraid to call you. She said you probably"—she glanced over her shoulder and mouthed the word *hate*—"her right now."

"Do you have any more bombs to drop on me before I pull out into traffic?" I said.

"Yes. She's ready to come home."

I let out all my air and steered the Escalade onto the road. "When Sonia's ready to come home and when her doctor says she's ready are two different things, trust me."

"You're not going to rear-end that Lexus if I say this?"

"Say what?"

"Dr. Ukwu is the one who told her to call someone and let them know. He said she had to do it herself. It's part of her therapy evidently."

I pulled up to the stoplight at Gallatin Road. "Don't take this the wrong way."

"Don't mean it the wrong way, and I won't."

"Why did she call *you*?"

"Because she wants me to come back and work with her when she comes home. She didn't come right out and say it, but I think she wanted to know if you were going to be here."

"I don't understand any of this."

"I would call Dr. Ukwu if I were you."

I swung into the school driveway. "I basically hung up on his nurse when she called to ask me to bring Sonia her pillow."

"She's probably afraid of you too. We all are." Wesley smiled her magnificent smile, but I couldn't manage as much as a lip curl.

"Now don't start feeling guilty because you don't want her to come home."

"Bethany is just starting to make progress."

"Mm-hmm. And so are you. The only person who can keep that from going away when Sonia walks in is you."

I jockeyed the car into my place in the school pickup line and turned off the ignition. "You don't know my sister."

"I don't know if you do either. She sounded like a different person from the queen that used to order everybody around like they were bees in her hive."

I leaned against the headrest. "You think she could have changed that much in two weeks?"

"Why not?" Wesley said. "You have. But I don't think it's so much changing as it is discovering what was already there." Her eyes shifted to look past me, over my shoulder. "Now, who's this coming up here?"

I turned to my window to see a blonde woman, Louis Vuitton bag hanging from her shoulder, jeweled fingers pulling off her Dior sunglasses. Georgia. Or was it Francesca? I never had been able to tell them apart.

Whichever one it was started to talk even before I opened the window.

"Lucia, honey," she said.

Francesca. Georgia called every woman *girl*.

"You look great," she oozed on. "Have you lost weight? Not that you needed to. Lose any more and you'll be too thin."

Give it up, Francesca. Your foot is too far down your throat as it is.

She pushed the sunglasses to the top of her head. Her eyes grew serious. "How is Sonia?"

How was I supposed to answer that?

"I don't have a right to ask," Francesca said. "We sort of abandoned her after that day with the boys and all."

When I didn't say anything, she went on, words tumbling out as if she'd been keeping them in a space too small for them.

"I can't speak for Georgia, but I just didn't know what to say to Sonia after a while. It was like she wasn't doing anything to help herself, and that didn't seem like what I always thought she believed in. I guess I had it wrong, you know, but I just couldn't sit there and agree that the doctors and the physical therapists and everybody was wrong, and she was the only one who knew anything."

She put her hand briefly to her mouth, nails shiny in the sun.

"I don't know if I should be saying this to you. I thought you'd get it, because it didn't seem to me like you supported that from the beginning." She put her hand on my arm. "I would just love to sit down with you sometime and hear about your faith walk. After this thing with Sonia, I'm so confused about God right now, and you just seem to have it together."

"Are you serious?" I wanted to clap my hand over my mouth, but it was no use. I couldn't un-ring the bell.

"I *am* serious," she said. "I'm so glad you're still here for Sonia. If there is anything, anything at all that I can do, you'll call me, won't you? And, again, I can't speak for Georgia."

She gave me a deep look, as if I were supposed to get something she wasn't saying. I was too stunned to absorb any of it.

"Thank you," I said.

She leaned in and kissed me on the cheek and saw Wesley at the same time. Her arm reached past me.

"Francesca Christie. I'm sorry to interrupt—ya'll looked like you were having a good girl talk." Her hand slid back to my arm. "I miss that. Please call me, Lucia."

I watched in a trance as her kitten heels tapped across the parking lot.

"You never told me about her," Wesley said.

"Yes, I did. She was one of the Designing Women who came to the hospital in Philly."

"Huh."

"What 'huh'?"

"She seemed pretty real to me—not the package—I'm talking about what she said."

I turned to face her. "Do you think she was genuine?"

"What do you think?"

"I can't believe I'm saying this, but I want to believe she meant that. She seems more sincere."

"She seems mixed-up." Wesley sniffed. "I'll take that over plastic any day."

"I see Bethany!" James-Lawson cried. "She's right there!"

"He is so in love with her," Wesley said. "We might as well just start planning the wedding right now."

I smiled at that, and at the sight of my niece bounding toward the Escalade with her Beauty and the Beast backpack flying out behind her. Miss Richardson caught my eye and waved, the signal that we'd made the handover safely. I felt a sharp pang as Bethany climbed into the backseat with James-Lawson. Handing her over to Sonia wouldn't be this easy.

I prepared as if we were marshaling troops for Gettysburg.

I contacted Dr. Ukwu, who assured me Sonia was ready for her outpatient treatment, of which her work with Wesley would be an important part. She'd done well with physical therapy in the hospital and was able to take care of herself "rather nicely." I was glad to live in a world where someone still said "rather nicely," but I couldn't quite apply it to my sister yet.

The rental company came and picked up the hospital bed, and the cleaning folks gave the house a sprucing up. The landscape people mowed the lawn, but they said someone else had already done a great job with the weeding and the edging. It seemed that Dr. Crisp had more than one talent.

I hit him up for his other one the night before Sonia came home. We had our session in the breakfast nook, even though I longed to be out by my river. Agent Schmacker called me daily to assure me they were doing everything they could to track down Pencil Whiskers Garrison, but I wasn't taking a chance by leaving Bethany in the house alone.

Sullivan propped one foot up on the booth seat, and I knew we were going straight for the hard questions.

"So what do we need to talk about before Sonia comes home tomorrow?" he said.

"You could be collecting Social Security before we cover all that," I said.

He grinned his one-corner-at-a-time grin. "Just hit the high points."

Wishing I'd written out a list, I studied the window.

"For one thing, Dr. Ukwu and Wesley are both saying Sonia's supposed to take care of herself, but I'm having a hard time believing she won't expect me to just fall right back into being her life-waitress."

"What if she does?"

"I won't do it."

"Ding-ding."

"But I don't think she'll know what to do with that."

"There's only one way to find out."

"But if I cross her, she's liable to kick me out, and then what happens to Bethany? Which is another thing. I tell her that her mom is coming home, and she doesn't even respond."

"That is pretty unusual. Most children adore their parents, even if they abuse them. From what you've told me, Bethany doesn't even seem to acknowledge that Sonia exists."

"I think Bethany's afraid of her," I said. My mouth went dry, the way it did every time I let myself visit this.

"That wouldn't surprise me." Sullivan put his other foot up on the bench.

We were going in.

"Let's try this," he said. "What do you do when you're afraid?"

"Run."

"Run how?"

I studied the tabletop, the window, the palms of my hands. Sullivan hummed the *Jeopardy* theme.

"Okay—I bury whatever I'm afraid of. Pretend it isn't there."

"Exactly. You think Bethany could be doing the same thing?"

"I do. So what do I do with that?"

"What are you doing with yourself now?"

"I'm not going to sit her down and try to get her to dig into her past with a little shovel."

"No—but you could give her permission to feel whatever she's feeling. That's what you did for yourself in our last session."

I closed my eyes. "You were wrong about one thing."

"Only one?"

"You said I was going to stop crying, but I haven't. Every morning after I take Bethany to school I'm down by the river, bawling my eyes out to Harry the Heron."

"It hurts, doesn't it?" he said.

"Like I'm being turned inside out, actually." Even now my throat ached.

Sullivan tilted his head. "I'm sorry life has brought you this much pain. But looking at it, talking to it—can you see what that's doing for you?"

I shook my head.

"You said it yourself. When Sonia comes home, you aren't going to be able to be her handmaiden. That isn't just a rational decision. That comes from learning to honor your own feelings and seeing yourself as a deserving person."

He seemed to consider something in my face before he went on.

"How do you think that might play out in your marriage? Have you given any thought to that?"

Only every waking moment when I wasn't gnawing on everything else.

"Care to share?" he said.

"I don't have it figured out yet," I said.

I got a buzz for that.

"What?" I said.

"You don't have to come here with everything figured out," he said. "I'd feel pretty useless." He spread his hands on the table. "This is the place where we put it out there and discover the answers together, remember?"

"I'm not used to that," I said.

"None of us sorts it all out alone."

"I thought I had to."

He let his smile dawn slowly. "I have a great game show for that, but let's get back to you and Chip. Any thoughts you want to put on the table?"

"He's promising me the moon, and at first I thought I didn't want it. But then I saw him with Bethany, and he was so—I don't know. He was like a real father." I could feel my throat thickening. "Part of me hates him even more because I see what could have been, and part of me wants to give him a chance and try to adopt—only who's going to give a child to a convicted felon?"

I shook my head. "There's still so much baggage. Can you ever get around that? I mean, should I just go ahead and divorce him?"

"You don't want me to tell you whether to do that or not."

"I have my moments," I said. "I don't know. Now that it doesn't seem like it's all my fault anymore, I have a choice. I didn't think I did before."

Sullivan nodded. "I will tell you this much: if you don't know exactly what to do, don't do anything yet."

"I don't think I can wait."

"Why? Is Chip pushing you to make a decision?"

I grunted. "He thinks he's already made it for both of us. Maybe that's what's holding me back. It might be different if we did it together—but he just wants to go out and make this life for us and then stick me into it. Just like always."

I could feel my face flushing as the words shoved their way out on their own. "I do want a relationship—a family—but I don't want it that way."

Sullivan leaned across the table, eyes shining into me. "That's because you've stopped thinking *they* and started thinking *I*—and not just *I*, but *we*."

"We," I said.

"You and Bethany, for starters. And the community you're form-ing with Wesley and James-Lawson. Sonia could be part of that. Maybe Chip. The point is"—he danced his finger toward me—"*you* can decide that. You can determine who your *we* is going to be."

He sat back and watched me. At first I'd hated when he did that. What the Sam Hill was I supposed to say? But now—now I had at least the faint shimmer of an idea.

"Ding-ding-ding, Dr. Crisp," I said. "Ding-ding."

That—and Wesley's phone call the next morning telling me that I could do this thing—got me to the front door when the hospital transport service brought Sonia home. She insisted on arriving that way, Dr. Ukwu told me, and he wanted to encourage her self-care.

She opened the door before I could even get my hand to the knob.

"Hi, *sorella*," she said.

Standing there in the rain, her voice was the same, creamy and rich as a mousse, but everything else was jarringly different. I had reminded myself with every toss and turn of the night that she would still be marred, but she had been transformed again, as if the first ravaging had not been enough.

The scars had set up like thick red yarn in some places. In others her skin was so flat and translucent I was sure if I touched it, it would dissolve on my fingertips. The ruins seemed less angry, and her eyes were brighter in the midst of them. With the rust-colored bandana wrapped around her head, she might have been a war-torn refugee arriving in a land she hoped would take her in.

"Welcome home," I said.

She nodded. She could nod now, and although her neck was still as gnarled as cypress bark, her chin lifted at least two inches higher than it had before she left. Yet as she gazed around the foyer, it seemed to sag from within.

I could not begin to imagine what she must be thinking, revisiting the scene of her madness—the mirrorless wall, the chipped marble floor, the echoing screams of "I hate God!" But I knew the pain that came with digging through that rubble, and it rose in my throat.

"Can I get you—"

"I want—"

We spoke over each other and choked on our words. Sonia was the first to try to smile, slowly, stiffly around her prosthesis, but surely.

"I have a long way to go, *sorella*," she said.

"No," I said. "We do. We."

Sully sat on the front porch with a glass of sweet tea and watched Lucia drive off through the rain to pick Bethany up from school.

"So far so good," she'd told him. "Sonia's asleep right now. She says the meds still knock her out."

"That's a common side effect," Sully said. "It should wear off after a while."

"I'm glad she's resting. I think this is all wearing her out—it's like she's trying so hard not to backslide."

Sully nodded to himself now. The kinds of transformations therapists and psychiatrists and counselors led their patients through were exhausting. He could use some decent sleep himself. He was lucky to get five straight hours on any given night, with Porphyria's words wrestling with his dreams: *It's going to find you, Sully, just get yourself ready.*

When the phone rang, he jolted so hard the tea slopped out of the glass and over his hand. What a waste. He pried the phone open on his chin while he swiped his palm on the back of his shorts.

"Sullivan Crisp," he said.

"You owe me."

"Anna?"

Sully tried not to sigh.

"You are going to be so glad that I can't keep my nose out of other people's business."

Sully doubted that, but he said, "Why am I glad?"

"After I gave you Cyril and Una's contact information, I couldn't stop thinking about them. All the old times, yada yada. I attribute it to being almost fifty."

"Uh-huh. Look, Anna—"

"No—wait. You want to hear this. I decided to call Una myself. I mean, who knew she was just down the road? I was like you: I thought they'd gone back to the Old Country years ago."

Sully shifted the phone to his other ear and took a long pull of sweet tea. He could be here for days. Decades. She was going to feel ridiculous when he finally had a chance to tell her that Cyril and Una had been a dead end.

"So I called and I said, 'Hey, Una, Sully Crisp looked you up, and I thought I would too'—blah, blah, blah—and imagine my surprise when she said she didn't know what I was talking about."

"I could have told you that," Sully said. "Cyril said he didn't want her to know I was trying to get in touch with her."

He waited for her to deflate, but she pumped up anew.

"She came to that conclusion like that." Sully heard Anna snap her fingers. "I guess when you've been married to somebody that long, you know that kind of thing. Not having had that experience myself—"

"Anna." Sully set the tea glass on the table and stood up. "What did she say?"

"You mean once she stopped crying? I had no idea she was still that torn up over Lynn's death. It was like it happened yesterday. She said she would have talked to you if you'd gotten her first, but—"

"Why are you telling me all this?"

"Cut me some slack; I'm going there. I said to her, what is the deal with the husband making this decision for you? Is that some kind of Eastern European tradition? Sully needs your help, and you're playing 1 Corinthians wife. Or was that Colossians? Anyway, I guess she got the message."

Sully put a stranglehold on the phone. "What do you mean, she got the message?"

"She just called me back and said she talked to Cyril, and he said she should do what she thought was right—hello!—and she wants to meet with you. She asked me to set it up."

Sully closed his eyes against the rain, the grate of her voice, the onslaught of doubt. The light was in there somewhere.

"Where and when?" he said.

"Forty-five minutes at Benton Chapel. She's at the divinity school for some church conference thing."

"Forty-five minutes from now."

"Yeah. Hey—Sully." Her pause was surprisingly tender. "Now that I've set this whole thing up—are you sure you want to go there? As upset as she is—this can't be good news for you."

"I have to," Sully said. "And, Anna? Thanks."

She gave him the gravel-filled laugh. "Like I said, Crisp—you owe me."

CHAPTER FORTY

I was a few minutes later than usual pulling into the pickup line in front of the school. My conversation with Sullivan had put me a little behind, but I didn't see Bethany out front yet. Maybe I should just get out my umbrella and go inside.

But I needed a few minutes to get myself centered before I took her home to see her mother. What I'd gotten out of Bethany the night before gave me hope, but there were still some eggshells to be walked on.

"Draw me a picture of a face," I'd said to her while I was finishing up the supper dishes.

"What kind of face?" she said, tongue and crayon poised.

"The face you want to make when you think about seeing your mom tomorrow."

Then I'd held my breath while she got still. Did a six-year-old even know what that meant? Maybe I should just leave well enough alone . . .

But the crayon had begun to move across the paper, and I pretended that getting macaroni and cheese off a plate was my sole purpose in life.

"Wanna see it?" she said when the scribbling stopped.

I turned and nearly fell into the dishwater. She'd drawn a round face, surrounded by a cloud of dark curly hair and wearing a blindfold. It couldn't have been clearer if it had been a photograph of Bethany geared up for her turn at Pin the Tail on the Donkey.

"Can you tell me about it?" I managed to say.

"It's me," she said.

"Why do you have your eyes covered?"

"Because I'm not allowed to see my mom without her face."

I knelt down in front of her, hands still covered in suds. "Your mom said that to you?"

She bobbed her head.

I couldn't even remember Bethany being in the same room with her mother since the hospital, and then their conversation had consisted of Bethany screaming as if she'd been stabbed.

"When did she tell you that?" I said.

"When I was five."

I tried not to let my mouth drop open. "Tell me that story," I said.

"It's not a story. I was in her room, and she was reading to me about Noah."

She touched the memory like a treasure she only handled with the tenderest of fingers.

"And we were almost done, and Miss Roxanne came in—and she said my mom had to change her makeup so she could be on TV, and my mom made everybody go outside."

Bethany blinked at me as if that were the end of the tale.

"Did you have to leave too?" I said.

"Uh-huh."

"Why?"

"Because she said nobody was allowed to see her without her face on."

A long moment passed before I could register that. When I did, the enormous relief spilled over into the urge to shake my sister's teeth loose.

Even with wet hands I took Bethany's shoulders and pulled her close to me. "Bethie," I said, "she was talking about her makeup. That was her fake face, and she just meant—"

That wasn't sinking in.

"You know what?" I said.

She giggled. "You sound like James-Lawson."

"I know, and you know what?"

"What?"

"Your mom has a face. It's just a different face from the one she had before."

She chanced a smile. "So I'm allowed to see it?"

"Yes, tomorrow."

She gazed down at the paper she held, while the small pink tongue worked at the corner of her mouth.

"Can I draw a new picture now?" she said.

I peered through the rain and turned on the windshield wipers. Still no Bethany, though I did see Miss Richardson, so she was probably in the line right inside the door staying dry. Within fifteen minutes she would be seeing her mother for the first time in who knew how long. Seeing her without being afraid that she'd be scolded for viewing that creature without her face.

I'd shown the new drawing to Sonia—a picture of a curly-haired-round-faced being with the tiniest of smiles on her face.

"I don't think she's going to scream this time," I said. "I don't know for sure, but—"

Sonia had put her hand on my arm. Her skin was icy. Fearful.

"Lucia," she said. "I know you can't do it *for* me—but can you teach me?"

"Teach you what?" I said.

"Can you teach me how to be a mother?"

I swiped at the tears under my eyes now. This was not the time to start crying, with Bethany moments away. Maybe I *should* just go in and get her.

I reached for the door handle just as Miss Richardson appeared on the passenger side, face surrounded by a hood. I rolled down the window.

"Hi, Aunt Lucia Mom," she said. "Did you forget something?"

I laughed. "I know I'm a few minutes later than usual, but her mom came home today." I waved myself off. "Is Bethany inside?"

I watched the color drain from the young woman's face.

"No," she said. "I'm confused. Did you bring her back after you picked her up?"

"I didn't pick her up. I just got here."

"But you drove up—and you waved—and she got right in the car." Her hand went to her forehead.

Mine clawed at the door until I got myself out. "She did not get in this car," I said. "That wasn't her you saw."

"It was! The windshield was fogged up, but she got in so happy—Oh my Lord—"

I had already gone where her mind was headed, shouting Bethany's name, pushing through the wide-eyed children against the wall, knowing I wouldn't find her there.

"Lucia—Lucia, what's wrong?"

Francesca Christie was at my elbow, and I snatched up her sleeve in my hand as I screamed into her face.

"Bethany! They've taken Bethany!"

Una Eremenko had changed less than anyone or anything Sully had seen since he'd returned to Nashville. Standing in the dark, wide-open vestibule of Benton Chapel, she was the same sturdy, bob-haired, clear-faced woman who had soothed their souls at SATCO thirteen years before. There was perhaps a bit of seasoning now in the slight forward roll of her shoulders and the shadow on her former blondeness, but she was still as hale and natural as a farm girl.

She was gazing up at a gaunt sculpture of Christ crucified. Only when Sully was close enough to startle her from her reverie did he see what *had* changed. The gray-green eyes had gathered wisdom. Whatever she had done with her life in the past decade, it had placed her among the sages.

When she saw him, her arms went around him, wordlessly, and she hung on until he realized she was silently crying.

"Sully, Sully, Sully," she said. "I'm so glad you still look like an overgrown boy." She held him out at arm's length, eyes streaming without embarrassment as she looked into his. "But I see you've grown up after all."

"I'm not so sure, Una," he said.

"I am. I see it." She squeezed his shoulders, still making no attempt to brush away her tears. "This world breaks your heart, does it not?"

Sully nodded. There would be no pleasantries in this conversation, no obligatory exchange of résumés while they privately tapped their mental toes to get on with what they had come to say. He was as grateful for that as he was unnerved by it.

"Let's go inside," she said. "It's empty."

The chapel itself was starker, had more rectangular lines than he remembered, though maybe back then things like warmth and hue hadn't meant as much to him. The stained-glass windows consisted of colored squares that inspired nothing. Only the smell of candle wax and worn hymnals gave it the feel of a place of reverence.

Sully followed Una to a back pew, where she sat in the dimness and patted the seat for him to join her. "I've hoped for years that I could talk to you," she said. "I think you and I loved Lynn more than anyone did."

"I . . . I didn't know you were that close to her," Sully said. "I sure didn't know you grieved so hard for her. I only started to genuinely grieve myself recently." He ran his toe along a kneeler. "I don't know if you knew, Una, but Lynn's death wasn't an accident. I know what the papers said, and what we didn't say at the funeral, but . . ." He trailed off as she drew her brows together.

"I knew. Is that why you wanted to see me? To tell me?"

"Partly. And to see if you knew anything that might help me understand why." Sully pulled his arms around himself to keep his heart from slamming through his chest. "Now that I'm here, I'm not sure I want to know."

Una cocked her head, sending the bob against her cheek. "I know your work, Sully. The only way out is through. In the *why* is the *what next*. Those are wise words."

"Until you have to use them on yourself."

"You don't think it was the postpartum depression?"

"You knew about that too?"

"I would have had to be blind not to. Sully—the shape she was in—what more is there to know?"

Sully steepled his fingers at his forehead. "I need to know if it was me too—if I wounded her somehow, so deeply that the depression took her over the edge."

"Sully, Sully, no. Lynn loved nothing in this world as she did you. Nothing. She lived for you, and you never failed her."

"Then why do I feel like there's more, Una?"

She pulled Sully's hands into hers. "I spent years—*years*—trying to understand why Lynn did what she did. I even read your books, hoping you'd show me. And do you know what I found out?" She squeezed emphatically. "I found out that I *can't* know. Only God knows. I had to leave it at that."

Sully shook his head. "Somehow, I can't."

She let the stillness press them for a minute before she said, "I'm curious about something."

"Yeah?"

"You seemed surprised that I already knew Lynn's death was a suicide. I knew it the minute I heard what happened." Her eyes flooded again. "That's why I avoided you. I thought you'd be angry with me."

"Why would I be?"

"Because I didn't stop her."

Sully shook his head. "How could you? She never threatened to take her own life. I had no idea she'd even thought of it."

Una put both hands to her mouth.

"What?" Sully said. "Did she say something to you?"

"She said she didn't really want to die, but she couldn't see how she could go on living the way she was . . . so imperfect."

"She told you that?"

"I thought she told you, too, Sully, I swear I did. Her therapist—I can't remember the woman's name . . ."

"Belinda Cox."

"Lynn said she told her to pray about it . . . that suicide was a sin, and she needed the power of God."

It was harsh, clear, and Sully pushed through it as he rose from the bench. "She knew? That woman *knew* Lynn was thinking of killing herself, and didn't call me?"

"Yes." Una's face seized as she stood up to face him. "I'm sorry, Sully. I'm so sorry."

Sully put his arms around her and let her sob into his chest.

"It's all right, Una," he whispered to her.

But he knew it would never be all right again.

CHAPTER FORTY-ONE

Those TV people are all over the place. I just caught one drippin' wet, trying to look in Sonia's bedroom window."

Deidre Schmacker turned from Sonia and me and drooped her eyes at Francesca. "I'll send someone out to tell them to back off. The local police are on their way to try to keep some order."

Francesca raked her fingers through her swing of hair. "Can I get ya'll anything? Water? Diet Coke?"

"Why don't you make these ladies some hot tea?" Deidre said.

I didn't tell Francesca that no amount of the tea she rushed off to brew could calm what throbbed in me. In the two hours since Nina Richardson and I knew someone had abducted Bethany, my heart had not stopped drumming the beat of terror. There was no pit deep enough to bury that in.

Beside me on the couch in the Gathering Room, Sonia still clutched my arm in the vise grip she'd had on it since Francesca and the FBI and I had arrived at the house. She'd said very little after the initial battering of horrified questions, but the fear she couldn't show on her face pulsed in her fingertips.

Deidre set her pad aside and squeezed the bridge of her nose. "The thing we have going for us is that her abductor didn't have much of a head start, and we have the make and model of the car, if it is indeed identical to your Escalade. We've put out an Amber Alert." She looked up at the doorway. "What do you have?"

Agent Ingram joined us, face showing nothing.

"I think Nina Richardson has told us everything she can," he said. "It was raining, so she didn't get a good look at the face through the windshield."

"Why didn't she make sure it was Lucia?" Sonia said.

"Bethany evidently got into the car with no hesitation. The teacher saw her smile at the driver. There was no reason for her to check."

"There was a reason! She knew Bethany was at risk."

"If it's anyone's fault, it's mine," I said. "If I had been there on time—"

"Both of you listen to me." Deidre's voice was mother-firm. "The fault lies with the person who went to the lengths to obtain a vehicle identical to yours, choose a day when visibility was low, and be at the front of the line when school let out."

She looked at each of us in turn. "We are talking about someone who planned this very carefully, someone determined to make it happen. Short of staring at the child 24/7, nothing that you, Lucia, or Bethany's teacher could have done was going to prevent it."

She glanced at Ingram. "If anyone is at fault, it's us for not being able to apprehend the perpetrator sooner."

"Then it's the same person who tried to kill me, is that what you're saying?" Sonia's voice rose. "Some professional assassin has my child?"

"No," I said. "I know Bethany. She wouldn't get in the car with somebody she didn't know. She wouldn't even stand in the doorway when the mailman came." My voice broke. "She told me, 'If someone wants to take you, they will.' And they did."

I jerked away from Sonia and staggered to the window, where I could choke down the sobs.

Sonia turned on Deidre. "If what you've been telling me all this time is true," she said, "it doesn't matter whether she knows him or not. I supposedly knew him, and he tried to kill me, so now he's going to kill her—"

"Stop it, Sonia. Just stop."

The three of them turned to me as one. I wrapped my arms

around myself to keep from flying out of my skin, but I didn't try to stifle what wouldn't stay back.

"They're doing everything they can," I said. "They have been for weeks, and you refused to do anything to help them. All you could say was that God's hand was in it."

"Don't talk to me about God." Sonia's voice was dead. "I devoted my life to Him, and He still allowed this to happen to me. I can't believe in a God like that."

Deidre gave me a full look before she turned her eyes back to her pad. Ingram cleared his throat.

"Let's not assume that our kidnapper is bent on hurting Bethany," he said. "He may be after money now. He could feel like we're closing in on him, and he wants cash to leave the country."

Deidre nodded with him. "We're set up in case either of you gets a ransom call. We need to go over what you're to say and not say."

"I will give him whatever he wants," Sonia said. "I'll call my accountant."

I didn't tell her that she no longer had an accountant or that a big chunk of her money was gone. Nor did I demand to know why she was suddenly willing to give everything up for her daughter, when until now she had let that baby girl sacrifice her whole being for her. That wasn't what tore at my throat and shook my soul.

I wanted Bethany on the floor at my feet, with her tongue at the corner of her mouth and her precious rag around her neck, drawing a picture of Harry the Heron. I groaned inside to have her look up at me and say, "Aunt Lucia Mom, do you want to see?" For that I would rip out my heart again and put her into Sonia's arms and this time teach my sister how to have what I had with her child—what I would give up once more and never have again, just to see her red bow mouth.

"Here's our tea," Deidre said. Her eyes sagged at the tray Francesca placed on the ottoman coffee table. "You ladies drink and try to rest. We're set up in the dining room if you need us." She touched

Francesca's elbow. "I'd like to ask you a few questions, Ms. Christie."

When they were gone, neither of us touched the teapot snuggled in its lace-trimmed cozy. Even the attempt at comfort caught in my throat. Was the kidnapper taking care of Bethany's needs? Did he know she liked warm milk with nutmeg before she went to sleep? Would he tell her how many more wake-ups before she could come home?

"Dear God," I said. "Dear God, please."

"I said don't talk to me about God."

I didn't look at Sonia. "I wasn't talking to you. I was talking to Him."

"Why?" Sonia folded her arms across her cave of a belly and rocked. "You can't trust Him. What is He doing right now?"

"He's stopping me from slapping you right across the face."

Her head came up.

"And," I said, "He's keeping me from losing my mind."

"Don't count on Him for that. He tried to take mine away."

Sonia stopped rocking and bulleted her eyes to the wall. I took a step toward her and, despite the palm she put up, another.

"What happened with God while you were in the hospital?" I said.

"I faced reality, Lucia."

"What reality?"

"That I am going to look like a freak for the rest of my life. That all the people I trusted have abandoned me. That one of them did this to me." She formed the misshapen smile. "Dr. Ukwu thought I'd made such progress in coming to terms with all of it. I thought I did too. I'm scheduled for my first autograft next week to try to create a face that won't drive people screaming from the room. I worked on my physical therapy so I could achieve some expression other than this zombiesque stare. I talked about my disaster of a childhood so I could learn how to be a decent mother."

She turned her eyes to me. "All because I finally discovered that God is going to do nothing for me. I thought He was in total charge, but I found out He wasn't—or if He was, He was a cruel, heartless being, and I could not let myself believe that. But now—"

Her mouth spread into a stiff slot. "Now I know He is. I was ready to make everything up to Bethany, and He took her from me." A long, deep growl tore from her throat. "And I can't even cry. My face won't let me. My eyes won't let me. God won't even let me cry, *sorella*."

"Then I'll cry for both of us," I said.

"You can't cry for me!" Sonia beat her fists against her thighs. "I can't make you live my life for me anymore!"

"I didn't say for you. It isn't all about you. I'm crying for *us*. For *our* Bethany. And if we don't see this through together, she has nothing worth coming back to."

Sonia's eyes fired at me. "And how do you think we're going to do that?"

"The same way I've gotten through everything else in the last month: by saying *Dear God* over and over until something comes out of me that makes sense."

"Pray? Look what praying did to me."

"I don't know anything about that," I said. I was crying so hard my words came out in agonized chunks. "I just know I'm still holding it together because God hears me."

Sonia dug into me with her eyes. "You don't really think God's going to send her back to us."

"I don't know," I said. "I just know He's with her."

Sonia fell against the sofa back. Turning her eyes to the ceiling seemed her only way to shut me from her sight. She wrapped herself in her own arms, and I went back to the window, where I sobbed a prayer for us. For *we*.

Sully didn't know how he'd gotten to the bridge, or how long he'd stood there pressed into the railing before its unyielding steel cut off his breath. Below him the Cumberland was brown and churning in the wake of the storm. He couldn't blame it anymore. It had only taken what Lynn had given it.

So. The turn down Why Road was the wrong turn all along. It led nowhere. He would never know—and perhaps Lynn couldn't even explain it if she came back at that moment. She was sick. She didn't have the help she needed to heal the pain she didn't understand.

Sully strangled the railing with his fingers. One thing he did know. For the first time, he understood why Lynn or anyone else would choose oblivion in a green, ugly river over this kind of suffering. Could he blame her for not being able to live with it, when right now he didn't know if he could either?

"Why couldn't you come to me?" he whispered to the water. "Why did you listen to that woman instead of to me?" A sob caught in his throat and would come no further. "Why did you believe everything was your fault?"

Why do you, *Dr. Crisp?*

Sully looked over his shoulder before he realized the voice came from inside himself—and yet not himself. He leaned over the railing, body tilted to the river.

The pain is in the blame, it said. *But there is no blame, Sully. There is only Me.*

Sully heard it, as clearly as the train whistle and the swish of a bicycle and the drip of leftover rain from the girders. As he pulled back from the railing, he knew. It wasn't the river's voice in him. It was God's.

"You all right, sir?"

Sully looked over his shoulder again and this time saw a young policeman who had pulled onto the overlook on a bicycle.

"Are *you?*" Sully said.

"Excuse me?"

"Are *you* all right?"

The boy-cop's hand crept not too subtly toward the radio on his belt. "I'm fine, sir. I'm more concerned about you."

"I'm not going to jump, if that's what you mean." Sully turned his back to the railing. "Stay fine, my friend. Hold on to *fine* as long as you can—because this world can break your heart."

"I'll do that." The officer beckoned to Sully with his fingers. "I'd feel a lot better if you'd step away from there."

"I think I will." Sully gazed once more into the Cumberland. "There's nothing more for me here."

He was almost to the Buick, with the policeman still keeping a cautious distance behind him on the bike, when his cell nagged from his pocket. Sully let it ring a second time. He was no longer waiting for information he thought he wanted to know. That itself was an empty realization that made him fish the phone out and answer it, just to fill the aching space.

"How is Sonia?" Porphyria said.

"Sonia," Sully said. He tucked the phone under his chin and pulled out the car key. "I didn't see her when she got home from the hospital. I'm headed back to her place now, but I thought I'd let her sort of reenter the atmosphere before I—"

"You don't know, then."

Sully stopped, key in the lock. "Know what?"

"I hope you aren't too far away," Porphyria said. "Because they're going to need Sullivan Crisp at that house."

The sunset silhouettes of journalists and their cameras set a surreal scene when Sully pulled up to the driveway. No less eerie was the police barrier that blocked his way, or the accusing light thrust into his face when he opened the car window.

"Mrs. Cabot knows I'm coming," Sully said. He shielded his eyes with the flat of his hand. "I called ahead. Sullivan Crisp."

"May I see your ID, please?"

As Sully fumbled for his wallet, a second voice barked from the other side of the flashlight. "We've got some guy out here, says he's Sonia Cabot's father."

"Is he for real?"

"I doubt it. He looks like a loser."

Sully nudged the arm resting in the car window with his license. While the officer examined it, he craned to see the person the second cop treated to the glare of another Mag light—a bulky man, perhaps formerly muscular but now spongy with age and inertia. His hard-gray hair curled over a forehead plowed into deep creases, and his eyes addressed the glare with a squint Sully suspected was more from half-mad worry than the insult of the light itself. The knot of a mouth cinched it. If he wasn't Lucia Coffey's father, he should have been.

"Sorry, dude," the officer said to him. "Mrs. Cabot didn't say anything about her father. You get permission from her and we'll talk."

"You're clear, Dr. Crisp," Sully's officer said. "Sorry for the delay. We just have to check everybody out."

"Of course."

The policeman shot the light away from his face and went toward the barrier. Sully leaned out the window.

"Mr. Brocacini?"

The bulky man jerked his head toward Sully. "Yeah?" His voice had the pinch of a man near panic. "Do I know you?"

"No," Sully said. "Do you want me to tell your daughters you're here?"

"Dr. Crisp, move on, please, sir."

Sully let the car drop into gear and looked in the rearview mirror. Tony Brocacini's face collapsed as he nodded.

Sonia and I were sitting across from each other in the breakfast nook, over a plate of fruit and cheese Francesca had assembled, when Sullivan brought Dad in and disappeared to the kitchen.

Though grayer and more lined than he had been at our mother's funeral, our father looked less beaten. I knew it was fear, not alcohol, that made his eyes seem unfocused.

"I'm sorry," he said. "I had to come."

Sonia only stared at him.

"I got something to say, and then you can throw me out if you want."

"I don't have the energy to throw you out," Sonia said.

"And I don't want to," I said. I slid further into the booth and patted the seat. "Sit."

Dad looked at Sonia. When she didn't protest, he fell heavily onto the bench beside me.

"I know this ain't the time to play the prodigal father," he said. "You got enough to handle." A sad something bleated from his throat. "I wouldna come if Chip hadn't called me."

"Chip called you?" I said.

"He does every now and again." He grunted. "Recovering addicts understand each other."

It was my turn to stare.

"He's all the way up in Oregon. He wanted me to make sure you were okay."

"Where were you?" Sonia said.

Dad studied his hands, which he'd spread on the tabletop, I suspected to control their trembling.

"I been here in Nashville since before you got home from Philly. Been staying at a motel."

There was no attempt in his voice to coax out guilt, but it stabbed me just the same.

"Chip just wanted me to tell you it's gonna be all right."

"I love these reassurances based on absolutely nothing," Sonia said. All the strain crowded into her eyes, because it had no other place to show itself.

"Why didn't Chip call me himself?" I said.

Dad winced, pinching the pleats beneath his eyes. "Said he didn't know if you'd be so happy to hear from him."

I couldn't hope for *happy*. But the thought of comfort swept over me like a wave of homesickness. I wanted Chip there to tell me a lie: that the passing hours of nothing did not mean that Bethany was lost to us forever. I would have believed him.

Dad pulled a battered receipt from his shirt pocket. "He gave me this phone number for you to call him when you're ready to start that new life."

I stared stupidly at the pencil scratchings. "This isn't his cell phone," I said.

"That's what he gave me."

"All right—we have some news." Deidre Schmacker swept into the room with Ingram behind her, spattering words like shotgun fire into his cell phone.

"We've picked up Derrick Garrison in Mount Juliet, just east of here." She nodded at me. "He's your Pencil Whiskers."

"Who?" Sonia said.

"Does he have Bethany?" I said.

Her eyes drooped. "No, but the good news is that there is no evidence so far that he ever did have her."

She left unspoken what I read in the grim lines flanking her mouth. We didn't want Bethany in the hands of Derrick Garrison.

"However, the fact that he was in the area at the time Bethany was taken may indicate that he is working with the kidnapper, and that is what we've suspected in terms of the plane crash as well. We're just still stumped about a motive."

"Lucia—what is she talking about?" Sonia said. "Who is Derrick Garrison?"

Her voice was shrill, but I stomped over it. "This doesn't bring us closer to finding Bethany, does it?"

Ingram closed his phone. "I'm going to question Garrison right now. If he knows anything, I'll find out."

For the first time I was grateful for the edge Agent Ingram kept honed like a butcher knife.

"We may need you to identify him," Deidre said to me. "Marnie Oakes too. Fortunately she's back in town."

"Whatever you need," I said. "Just bring Bethany home."

She turned to Sonia, whose frantic hands were climbing up my arm. "The press wants a statement from you. That isn't something you are obligated to do."

Sonia stopped her climb and searched my face.

Visions of gawking cameras chilled me, and I could see that same horror passing through her.

But she drew in a breath. "Does that ever actually help?"

Deidre grimaced. "The only time we recommend it is when we feel the perpetrator may respond to a plea from the parent. I don't know if that's the case here. If this person wants to see you hurting"— her eyes took their downward turn—"it might only make things worse. In that case, perhaps someone else should make the plea."

All eyes turned to me.

My blood turned to ice. "Are you saying I should go on camera?"

Ingram scraped his chin with his cell phone. "I don't know if it would be as effective. People respond more to the mother's situation and are more likely to keep an eye out, report anything they see. She's the one who has more at stake emotionally."

"I know what happens when people see me," Sonia said. "They can't think about anything but how grotesque I look." Her voice was thick. "No one loves Bethany more than Lucia, but she can't—"

"Can't what?" Deidre said.

"She hates the spotlight. She'll freeze."

"How about if I speak for myself?" I said.

Sonia's eyes widened.

Deidre's took on their liquid shine. "I wish you would," she said.

I clasped my hands to keep their trembling out of sight. "If there's even a small chance that it'll help," I said, "I have to do it. I'll do it right now."

"It'll take a little time to set it up," Ingram said.

"First thing in the morning would be better anyway," Deidre said. "See if we can use the studio in Mount Juliet—that Christian station. That way Lucia won't have to go so far." She put her hand on my shoulder. "I know you want to stay close in case we hear anything. I'll be right there with you."

When she left, my father stood up and buried his hands in his pockets. "I know I never said it enough. Maybe I never said it, and it's probably too late now." He looked at me and then at Sonia, eyes wet and red rimmed. "I'm proud of you both. They got to get that little girl home so she can grow up to be a woman like the two of you."

When he turned to go, I slapped my hand on the table. "Where do you think you're going?" I said.

"I'm going to get out of your hair." Dad ran his hand down the back of his head. "You know me. I always take off when I've screwed things up. Makes it easier on everybody."

"Yeah, well, we're all about putting our own issues aside tonight," I said. "The only issue that matters is Bethany."

"I don't deserve—"

"Shut up, Mother," Sonia said.

I jerked toward her, but her eyes had not gone wild.

"Sorry," she said. "I don't need the Mother voice in my head right now. Dr. Ukwu told me to just shut her up however I need to."

I filed that away for a time I hoped would come—when I could meet my sister for the first time. A time when Bethany would sit between us and we would peel away her layers of shoulds and can'ts and ought-tos—so the only voices she would hear were her own and God's.

"Dear God, please," I said.

Sonia said nothing. But my father said, "Amen."

CHAPTER FORTY-TWO

The sky was barely light when we walked into the WTBG building the next morning, but it didn't matter. I hadn't slept anyway. Francesca had put ice cubes on my eyes and then gone at me with the foundation and the concealer in an attempt to freshen me up, though it only made me look like an insomniac wearing too much makeup.

The effort was somehow calming at the time. Now that I was there, chilled by the air-conditioning and the thought of exposing myself to millions of viewers, I was beyond comfort. Only the little cherub face in my head and the constant *Dear God, please* in my breath got me to the chair a man in headphones led me to. I was vaguely aware that this was the set Roxanne had used for her prayer show. The thought was slightly nauseating.

"This is going to be a live feed," Deidre explained, while Headphone Man clipped a microphone to the lapel of the blue jacket Francesca had picked for me. I had no idea where she'd gotten it, but she said it was my color.

"You'll see Chelsea Bowles on the screen, so just talk to her like she's here in person, and the camera will do the rest."

"We need to clear the set," Headphone Man said to her.

She patted my hand and stood up. "This is brave of you, Lucia," she said. "Very brave."

I didn't feel brave, so I fought for numb, something I hadn't reached for in weeks. It was nowhere to be found. I was left with Headphone Man counting down on his fingers and a golf ball forming in my throat.

But this was for Bethany. And for the twisted people who had taken her from us. I swallowed it down and glued my eyes to the screen.

A stunning brunette with sympathetic eyes flickered into view and greeted me in a voice I almost believed.

"We appreciate your being with us this morning, Lucia," she said. "I know this is a difficult time for you and your family."

"It is," I said woodenly.

She nodded as if she wanted me to say more.

"But I had to do this," I said. "We have to find Bethany."

I could feel my face coloring, feel the sweat forming on my upper lip. I sounded so desperate.

But then, I *was* desperate.

Chelsea—was that her name? Chelsea?—nodded again. "You were the first person to discover that little Bethany was missing. Can you tell us about that?"

I nodded back and began to speak and tried to forget how many people were eyeing me. I said Bethany's name as much as I could, and that kept me moving through, kept me giving details that maybe, somehow, would nudge someone, make them think, *I saw that! I saw him!*

As I talked, I heard my own voice grow warmer, less stiff, more real. "Please," I said, "please, if anyone knows anything at all that might help us find her, please call the FBI."

"We have that number at the bottom of the screen," Chelsea said. "Lucia, how is your family handling this? You seem so composed, but I can see in your eyes that this is frightening. What are you doing to remain hopeful?"

I paused. Was I allowed to talk about God on national TV?

"I know Bethany's mother, Sonia Cabot, is influential in Christian circles," she said. "I would assume that—"

"We're praying," I said. "That's the only way we're getting through this."

Chelsea glanced down as if she were looking at notes. "Sonia Cabot has always claimed that God blesses those who are faithful to Him. Is she still able to maintain that in the face of yet another personal crisis?"

Beyond the camera, Deidre made slashing motions at her throat with her hand. Inside I moved toward that myself. I might have given a mechanical nod and ended the interview, if I hadn't noticed someone else behind her. Several someones.

Egan. Georgia. Roxanne.

Headphone Man snapped his fingers silently for me to focus back on the screen, but I couldn't take my eyes from them. The studio morphed from Roxanne's *Power Praying* set to a faraway hospital lounge, where a row of those same people, and others like them, looked at me with dismissal in their eyes and disgust in their curled lips. Just as they were doing now, as though a woman bloated with sin could not possibly speak for God.

Except that I was no longer that woman. And Bethany was never going to be.

"Thank you so much for being here this morning, Lucia," Chelsea Bowles said.

"I'd like to answer your question," I said. "About our faith in this crisis."

Her surprise was poised. "All right," she said.

In spite of Headphone Man's frantic motions, I looked straight at the trio, who looked as if they had just been jolted from a collective nap.

"I can't speak for my sister," I said. "But I can say for myself, and for Bethany, that we have never believed in the twisted version of God that Abundant Living Ministry propounded, and still claims, as far as I know."

Egan pulled his hands from his pockets in slow motion. I met his eyes.

"The idea that God only shows grace to those who toe the line is toxic Christianity," I said. "And believing that every tragedy that befalls us is either God's wrath or an opportunity for a miracle is dangerous."

I watched Roxanne march toward Headphone Man, arms swing-ing. I was about to be cut off. Wesley's words swam in my head, and Sullivan's, and Grandma Brocacini's. Roxanne had Headphones by the arm before I landed on my own. Mine and God's.

"I'm still holding it together because God hears me. I don't know if Bethany will come back to us. She's obviously being held by some-one who doesn't know a thing about that. I just keep crying out *Dear God*, knowing He's with her no matter what happens." I bored my eyes into Roxanne, who grabbed for Headphone Man's shoulder. "Nobody can know anything more than that. Nobody."

Chelsea Bowles broke in before the last syllable was out. "We can certainly appreciate your passion, Lucia, and we will all keep hop-ing that Bethany *will* be returned to you."

The screen went blank, with Roxanne still tugging on Headphone Man's arm.

"Excellent job," Deidre said. She was on me immediately. "Let's get you home."

"How dare you?" Roxanne pushed Deidre aside and stood inches from me, nostrils flaring.

Georgia was at her heels, wielding a BlackBerry like a weapon.

"How dare you disparage Abundant Living on national televi-sion?" Roxanne said. "You have no understanding of what we do here—I have known that from the first time I met you."

"Was that the first time when you said it was me and you and Marnie, saving the day?" I looked at Georgia. "Oh, this isn't Marnie. Sorry—you all look alike to me."

"Roxanne, leave it alone," Egan said. "You're not going to get anywhere with her."

"Her?" I said. "No, my name is Lucia. Not Lucy. Not Sonia Cabot's sister. Not the convenient nurse who will say what you want me to say. I am Lucia Brocacini Coffey—and I have a very clear understanding of what you're about."

Deidre let go of my arm and folded hers across her chest.

Roxanne breathed like a locomotive. "No," she said, "you do not."

"Yeah, I do," I said. "Because unlike the rest of you, who bailed out on Sonia one by one when your little formula didn't seem to be working, I stayed to watch it fail completely."

"If there was failure, that was Sonia's doing," Roxanne said.

"No, ma'am," I said. "It was yours—and yours—and yours." I jabbed a finger at each of them in turn. Georgia gasped. Egan turned his usual cowardly shade of pale. Only Roxanne looked ready to attack—but I didn't let her.

"God didn't crash that plane—some demented person did. But everything you stand for kept Sonia from taking the medical treatment she needed, or the psychological help, or the legal aid. Now she's more disabled than she would have been. She's mentally shattered and financially ruined—and you know what the worst of it is?"

I didn't wait for an answer. "Now she can't even stand to hear the name of God, because you gave her a God who is cruel and cold and takes people's children away from them."

I didn't realize until then, when Deidre put her hand on my shoulder and Roxanne's face distorted before me, that I was crying. Sobbing. Weeping out the truth.

"So don't talk to me about what I do and do not understand," I said. "And you know what? I'll be praying *Dear God, Dear God* for all of you—because that's all I can think to say on your behalf."

Egan folded his fingers around Roxanne's wrist. "Come on. Let's go."

"He's right, Roxy." Georgia took her other arm, and Roxanne let them pull her from the set, though she shot me through with her eyes until she was out of sight.

"Are you all right?" Deidre said near my ear.

"I think so," I said.

"Then let's go home."

"If you'll wait a minute you can have a DVD of this," Headphone Man said. "I've got the whole thing for you." He unclipped my microphone. "Including that last segment with the ALM crew. We won't be airing it, but you might like to use it sometime."

"For what?" I said.

He shrugged. "I don't know, as a PR clip for your next gig. You really know how to get to the bottom line."

I felt my knees buckle. "You're right, Deidre," I said. "We need to go home. I think I need some tea."

"I knew I'd make a convert out of you." She squeezed my arm. "I think you just made one out of me."

"That Francesca woman told me Dr. Sullivan Crisp was making sweet tea in here," Wesley said from the kitchen doorway. "'Course, she looks like she's been up all night, so she's probably hallucinating."

Sully turned from the stove. "I make killer sweet tea."

Wesley's eyebrows shot up to her hairline. "I hope whoever's clock you cleaned knows what time it is now."

"Wesley," he said, "so much has happened since then, I'd forgotten all about it."

She set a bag on the counter. "Miss Lucia is gon' need some fresh vegetables—and chocolate. She's got to have chocolate."

Sully gave the sugar water a meditative stir. "You're a sweetheart."

She put her hand to the back of her neck, and all humor drained from her face. "This goes beyond chocolate, doesn't it?" She blinked hard. "How is Lucia doing? How are they both doing?"

"As long as they keep talking they do remarkably well." Sully shrugged. "But what does *well* mean in a situation like this?"

"It means you don't rip somebody's lips right off or throw yourself in that river out there." She moved toward the coffeepot. "Where are they now?"

"They're up in Bethany's room with their dad and one of the FBI agents, going through Bethany's things to see if they can find any kind of clue."

Wesley stopped in midpour. "You need to back that truck up. Did you say *their dad*?"

"He showed up last night."

"And is that a good thing or a bad thing?"

"Good, so far as I can tell," Sully said. "I've only had a brief conversation with Lucia."

Which had amounted to her asking him to please stay close to her family. That in itself was healthy, but far more indicative of her progress was her appearance on CNN. At the end of the interview, Sully had let go of the grief that had been locked up in his own soul since the bridge the night before.

Wesley finished filling her cup. "Do you know if she's heard from her husband?"

"Indirectly. He's supposedly on his way here."

"And we don't know if that's a good thing or a bad thing either." Wesley put up her hand. "I know you can't talk about that. So—they're up there looking for clues?"

Sully shook his head at the coffeepot she offered him. "I think that's more to provide them with a distraction than out of any real hope they'll come up with something. Not unless they can find a motive."

Wesley sat at the counter with her mug. "Lucia and I have been over that so many times. Doesn't seem like Sonia's done anything bad enough that somebody would want to get this kind of revenge for it. Not that there's anything bad enough in this world that justifies taking somebody's baby."

"They just have to *think* it's bad enough." Sully kept his eyes on the tea syrup. "It's amazing what can make sense to a person when she's in pain."

"Do I smell sweet tea?"

Marnie's voice beamed into the kitchen. It was more nasal than Sully remembered, obviously due to recent crying, judging from the pink puffiness around her eyes. She lightened the room nevertheless, and Sully grinned at her.

"You start brewing a masterpiece and suddenly everybody's your best friend," he said.

"I'm so glad you're smiling. This is the worst day ever." Marnie dumped a slouchy purse, a wad of keys, and an oversized pair of sunglasses on the counter and put out her hand to Wesley. "I know we met before, but I was so stressed-out back then, I don't remember your name. Not that I'm any less stressed-out now. I can't even remember *my* name."

"You're Marnie," Wesley said, "and I'm Wesley. You better sit down, girl. You look like you're about to fall out."

Marnie lifted herself easily onto a stool and pushed back two hunks of brunette with her hands. "I just had to look at a criminal through a window that they promised me he couldn't see me through, but it's hard to believe that when he's looking right at it and you know he's tried to kill somebody before."

Wesley didn't ask her what she was talking about, for which Sully was grateful. That explanation could take more time than anybody had.

"Was it the guy you saw at the airport?" Sully said.

Marnie shuddered. "Yes. It was so horrible looking at him and trying to understand how anybody that knew Sonia would ever have anything to do with someone like him. I mean, when I worked for her, I got so disillusioned with her that I quit, but even then I, like, stayed four more days. I should have stuck with her instead of going to work for Roxanne."

Sully left his mixture on the stove and leaned on the counter across from her. "You went to work for Roxanne? At ALM?"

Marnie ducked her head. "She called me after I got to my parents' and asked me to come. I worked there for all of a week, but she was . . . Well, let me just put it this way." She lowered her voice. "Sonia was hard to work for after she got hurt, but Roxanne made her look like my fairy godmother. By the way, Dr. Crisp"—she widened her eyes at Sully—"I've been listening to your podcasts and, yeah, they make more sense than anything Roxanne has to say."

"I never trusted that woman when I saw her on the TV," Wesley said.

Sully smothered another tired grin.

"I shouldn't have either, when she was just, like, right there to step into Sonia's place after they were best friends." Marnie took a much-needed breath.

If she hadn't, Sully would have taken one for her.

"But it didn't take me that long"—she snapped her fingers—"to see that she doesn't have Sonia's integrity, or her compassion— hel-lo-o. The second day I was there, Roxanne fired this girl because she found out she used drugs, like, four years ago. She didn't care that the girl—who is so sold-out for Jesus, by the way—hasn't touched anything all that time. She just said she couldn't let her be associated with ALM." Marnie pressed a hand to her chest. "Then there's Sonia, who hired Chip *because* he was a recovering addict so she could help him. And that wasn't just out of guilt, either."

"Guilt?" Wesley said. "Why would Sonia feel guilty because her brother-in-law was a former junkie?"

"Because Sonia was the one who turned him in."

Sully's eyes clinked with Wesley's. Hers widened before she turned back to Marnie.

"Sonia turned him in to whom?"

"The medical board, I think. She did it anonymously—I was the only one who knew about it—and she only did it because she didn't want him hurting anybody else. That's just Sonia."

Sully switched the stove off. He wished he could turn off his rising anxiety as easily.

"Did Chip know she blew the whistle on him?" he said.

Marnie twisted a strand of hair around her finger. "I accidentally told him one night when we were talking. I thought Sonia had told him herself by then, so I was just talking about it, and then he acted all surprised and I felt bad. But he said it was okay—she'd done the right thing, and now he was on his way to healing." Marnie's eyes filled. "That's what she did for people, and even though sometimes she was hard on us and it just seemed like anything you did wrong or that went wrong was because you weren't right with God—and I'm not so sure about that anymore—but besides all that, she helped *so* many people who were *so* screwed up—"

Sully stopped listening. This could not have been there all along, right under the nostrils of everyone from the FBI to Sonia herself.

"Marnie," he said.

She put her hand to her mouth. "I'm sorry. I'm talking about all this stuff, and poor little Bethany—"

"Did you ever tell Sonia that Chip knew she was the informer?"

"Oh, gosh no! He and I made a pact not to, because he said it was all behind him and he didn't want her to ever feel bad. We bonded over that. In fact, right after that was when he started talking about how I was too talented to just be working for Sonia, and I should come to Philadelphia with him when he went home to Lucia, and he'd help me find a better job up there." She smeared aside the tears that pooled under her eyes. "What freaks me out is that I could have been burned or even killed on that plane too. I wouldn't have even been as hurt as I was if I'd gotten off with him. I still don't know what God was doing."

Sully didn't know what God was doing either. But with a sick heart, he knew what Chip Coffey was doing.

Marnie took the Kleenex Wesley pressed into her hand and blew her nose.

Wesley made what Sully knew was a pretense of joining him at the stove to check on the progress of the sweet tea. "I wish I didn't know that, Dr. Crisp," she said.

"Me too," he said.

"What are you gon' do about it?"

"The only thing I can do."

"Oh, Lord, Lord, Lord," she said.

He couldn't have said it better himself.

"Does this have any significance?"

I looked up from the Cinderella box I held on my lap on the floor and let out a cry.

"What, Lucia?" Sonia said.

I snatched Bethany's rag from the young FBI agent and pushed it into my face. "That's hers." I ached anew at the thought of Bethany trying to sleep without it. Of finding out that the "friend" she trusted enough to climb into a car with was not going to bring her home to get it.

"She loves this thing," I said. "She wrapped it around her neck when she slept, and I was always afraid she'd be strangled."

I felt a hand on my back as I sobbed into it.

"Do you know what that is?" Sonia said.

"It's one of her BFFs," I said.

"It's the baby blanket you brought to her when you came to take care of her for me. What's left of it. Every nanny tried to get rid of it, and she would just have a fit."

I felt Sonia lay her face against my spine.

"It was the one thing I stood behind her on. I have been the worst mother."

I pulled a program, still faintly sticky with some child-treat, from the box in my lap and twisted toward Sonia. "Do you know what this is?"

"That's from the circus," she said. "I took her in the spring when it came here." She ran a finger across a shriveled balloon and a paper rosebud whose pink had run onto the bottom of the box and left a stain.

"I took her to a little tea room for her birthday and we had a tea party, just Bethany and I, and Chip. She wanted Uncle Chip to come." Sonia worked to swallow. "He brought her home, and I went to the airport to fly off someplace. I was always flying off, Lucia."

I watched the spasm of grief go through her as she stared down at the few and tiny pieces of herself that her daughter had kept like precious stones. It was a grief I couldn't share with her.

"Could you please leave us alone for a minute?" she said to the agent.

He looked more than happy to get away from the estrogen.

When he was gone, Sonia seemed afraid to look at me. "Lucia, I'm sorry," she said.

"Whatever it is," I said, "we don't need to look at it right now."

"No—we do. I watched you on CNN this morning."

"Oh."

"I was so wrong about them—about me. Mostly about you."

I tried to pretend she was making sense, but I was worn too thin to pull it off. She sighed fretfully.

"You have always been smarter than me, *sorella*," she said. "And I have resented that all my life. But right now, I want you to be right. I think you are." Her voice teetered on a narrow ledge. "I have to learn to pray all over again. I have to learn to be a mother—if I even get the chance. I have to learn to let go of my feelings, like you did right on TV."

I pressed my fingers to my throbbing temples.

"You've already given up so much for me—don't think I don't know that," she said. "And I can't ask you to give up any more, but *sorella . . .*" She breathed so hard she could hardly get the words out. "The only person who can teach me to do that is you."

"Sonia. Lucia."

The tone of Deidre Schmacker's voice brought my head up, and Sonia's with it. She stood in the bedroom doorway, arms folded, rubbing one now-rumpled sleeve with the other hand. Her face was grave.

Sonia pulled the box to her chest. "Please don't tell us—"

"We haven't found her," Agent Schmacker said. "But I have something to tell you."

"It's not good, is it?"

"Not for Lucia," she said.

She put out her hand to help me up from the floor, but I got to my feet myself. I felt a sickening dread.

Deidre unfolded her arms, slowly, as if she would rather cut them off than say what she had to say. "Agent Ingram just called me," she said. "Derrick Garrison gave us the name of the person he was working for." She looked straight into me. "It's a man he knows as Kent Mussen."

The floor gave way beneath me.

"You know the name, yes?" she said.

I had to nod.

"You do?" Sonia said. "Lucia, who is that?"

Deidre shook her head at Sonia and turned back to me. "In addition to being the owner of a money-laundering operation disguised as a medical equipment company, Kent Mussen is an ex-con whose real name is immaterial now. The point is, Ingram has been interrogating Mussen for the last four hours, and he has given up the man who hired him to sabotage the plane."

I grabbed for the bedpost to stop the slide. *Please. Please, God, no.*

"It's Halsey, Lucia," Deidre said. "It's Chip."

The air left the room. In its place a suffocating fear closed over me.

"That makes no sense." Sonia was on her feet, hands groping for mine on the bedpost. "Why would Chip do that?"

Deidre Schmacker gave her a long, sad look. "Because you turned him in for dealing illegal prescription drugs, Sonia."

She could not have cut me more deeply if she had slit my throat. I sank to the bed and doubled over onto myself. Schmacker's words stabbed me, over and over, in places I'd covered with my blindness.

Chip vowing to take down the person who wrecked his life.

Chip pleading with Marnie to change her mind—to get off the plane.

Chip handing the pilot a cup of coffee.

Chip staying far away from the hospital.

They pierced me, those words, in my heart, in my gut, in my soul. Only one word pierced its way through my mind.

"Bethany," I said. "Then Chip has Bethany."

"That is possible," Deidre said. "Do you have any idea at all where he might be?"

"He told Dad he was in Oregon—but he told me he was going to Memphis."

My mind reeled. When I stood up to right myself, Deidre put her hands on my shoulders.

"I know this is too much to take in," she said, "but you have to try to think."

"I'm thinking! I have to call him."

"His mobile phone has been disconnected. The number he called your father from was a disposable cell. Is there any other way you know of to reach him?"

I pulled away from her and searched for my sister. She stood across the room from me, Bethany's rag clutched to her neck. Horror and hope cried out from her eyes.

For the first time in our lives, I could feel my sister's pain—for it was mine too.

I pulled the number from my pocket and handed it to Deidre Schmacker.

CHAPTER FORTY-THREE

I hated every word that came out of my mouth," Lucia said.

Sully only nodded. He couldn't trust himself to speak yet. Anger fired at will in his gut.

"It was all lies."

Sully had heard. Lucia's only argument to Agent Ingram's hard-core control of the phone call was that everyone be there with her when she made it. Under his steely, disapproving glare, Sonia, Tony Brocacini, Wesley, and Sully had surrounded her in the dining room as she dialed the number.

Sully got that. Only human contact could make a cold, bloodless task bearable. Lucia had carried it out with a poise Sully knew he himself wasn't capable of.

Chip hadn't answered, which was divine intervention in Sully's view, and Lucia had left the message Deidre Schmacker helped her craft. It was laden, as she said, with lies.

"Dad gave me your new number," she'd said. "He said to call you when I was ready for our new life—and I am."

Sully had watched her close her eyes and swallow.

"I need you. Bethany is gone—I'm sure you've heard that. I can't get through this without you. Sonia has her own people. You and I need to do this together."

When she hung up, Lucia had shoved the phone down the length of the table and careened out of the dining room. They'd all tried awkwardly not to listen as she retched in the nearby powder room.

She looked down now at the offensive cell phone in her lap. Agent Ingram had instructed her to keep it on her person at all times. He himself was a scant ten yards from their Adirondack chairs, should Chip return her call while she and Sully were trying to speak of the unspeakable.

"They want me to wear a wire if he agrees to meet me." Lucia clamped her folded arms to her ribs. "I feel like I'm on some bad TV show." She squeezed her eyes shut. "I didn't marry a monster. How did this happen?"

"Drugs can turn anybody into a monster. If that doesn't do it, prison will."

"It still doesn't feel real."

"That might be the only way to get through this part," Sully said. "It's all right to go through the motions until it's done."

Lucia looked him full in the face, eyes still their unyielding blue even through the swollen remnants of her tears. "And then what? What happens after I turn my husband over to the FBI—or after I find out he's done something horrible to Bethany—or after my sister shuts me out of her life forever? What do I do with all this pain after that?"

Sully rubbed the Adirondack arm. A year ago—even a day ago—he would have told her the only way out was through. That God would help her navigate this dark, dripping tunnel, and she could emerge scarred but healed. He still believed that, but as he stood here outside the tunnel at its other end, alone, he knew that wasn't all of it. Maybe it wasn't enough to build the rest of a life on.

"You don't know, do you?" Lucia said.

Sully looked up at her, ready for the disappointment in her eyes. There was instead a subtle melting of relief. "I don't know all of what I need to tell you, no," he said.

She began to weep, softly, with no fight in her face. "Do you know how glad I am to hear you say that?"

"You're glad?"

"If you gave me an answer you said was absolutely true, I'd have to try to believe it. I don't know if I can work that hard at this point."

"I hear you," Sully said. He leaned his arms on his knees. "Things could get a lot worse if you have to face Chip. We know that. But they're pretty bad right now. What's holding you up?"

She didn't hesitate. "You. Wesley. My dad, ironically enough. Francesca and her fruit platters—how weird is that? She said, 'Bless your heart' to me this morning, and I think I finally knew what it meant."

Sully gave her half a grin. "Dang. You want to tell me?"

"I think it means 'Your pain is so bad I don't know what to say to make it better.'"

"Does that help?"

This time she did pause. Sully waited—and hoped she had an answer for both of them.

"It makes me cry," she said. "It makes me touch people and sit with them and talk about how much this all hurts." She gazed at Sully in tearful surprise. "I haven't gone numb one time."

"Do you want to?"

Lucia slowly shook her head. "I used to think it kept things from hurting, but it was its own kind of pain."

"A pain you can't heal," Sully said. "But I don't think you could have taken the risk of feeling it before. You didn't have then what you have now."

"What's that?"

"You said it yourself. Wesley, your dad, the whole crowd."

A pang went through him, and left him with an answer that wasn't there before.

"You're finding something that a lot of us have forgotten we need," he said. "You're building community. You're not alone anymore, so now you can suffer without being afraid that it's going to take you down."

Lucia picked up the cell phone and squeezed it before her face. "Chip's trying to take that away," she said. "Dear God, please don't let him take that away."

"There's your final piece," Sully said. He had barely enough control left to get the last words out. "Keep saying, 'Dear God, dear God.' There may still be suffering—but keep touching those people, Lucia, and He won't let you suffer alone anymore."

Lucia nodded and turned her face toward the river.

Sully watched her cry silently to the water and the heron and the sunlight that embraced them both.

The same goes for you, Sullivan Crisp, it said to him. *Go back to touching God's people, so they won't have to suffer alone.*

And neither will you.

"He knows it's a trap," I said. "That's why he hasn't called me back."

In spite of the momentary, relative calm I'd felt after my talk with Sullivan, I beat back panic at the kitchen counter with a chef's knife and an onion.

"Girl, you are going to cut your finger off, and then you're gon' be no good to anybody." Wesley shook her head. "It's only been a few hours. Don't you be losing hope."

I kept chopping. I had no idea what these onions were going into, but I kept thrusting the knife into them, dicing them finer and finer.

"This isn't unusual," Deidre Schmacker said. She refilled Sonia's teacup.

Sonia looked up absently from the foot massage Francesca was giving her, and nodded.

"He thinks his plan is coming together," Deidre said, "and he's making sure every *i* is dotted, every *t* is crossed."

"Or he didn't believe me," I said. "How could I be convincing? I was lying through my teeth."

I picked up the second onion and sliced at it savagely.

My father reached across the counter and put his hand on my wrist. "I can help you with that," he said.

"I've got it," I said.

"No—I'm talking about with Chip."

Deidre Schmacker stopped stirring her tea. "What do you mean, Mr. Brocacini?"

Dad spaded his hands into his pockets. "Chip might not be using drugs, but once an addict, always an addict."

I stopped chopping.

"Go on," Deidre said.

"An addict has to have a fix, and if it's not drugs or booze, it's something else. He's got to have it no matter what it does to his body or his family or his job, because it puts him back on top." Dad ran his hand down the back of his head. "You got to figure out what fix he needs right now and give that to him."

"I thought she did," Sonia said. "I thought Lucia was his fix."

I listened for bitterness in her voice, but it wasn't there.

"I think I see where he's going." Deidre Schmacker folded her hands on the counter and leaned toward me. "What does he want that you can't give him, Lucia?"

I shook my head. I knew what he couldn't give me. But he'd said I was all he wanted.

"He wants what I took away from him."

We all turned to Sonia. She pulled her feet away from Francesca.

"He wants to be a doctor again," she said. "That's how this whole thing started. He thinks if I hadn't turned him in he'd still be practicing medicine."

I reached for the knife again. "I don't see how that helps. I can't promise to get his license back for him."

"So you call him up and tell him you got something wrong with you," Dad said. "Tell him he's the only one who can take care of you."

"I don't think so, Dad."

"You don't know what it is to lose your identity and your self-respect, Lucia. I do." Dad rubbed viciously at his head. "A man like us will do anything to get that back—to feel like somebody needs

him again. What did it take for me to risk having my butt kicked
back out on the street when I came here?" His voice was raw. "Chip
told me I could do something to help my daughter. I didn't care
what it was. I wanted it so bad I would have thrown myself in front
of a truck to get it."

"You did, Dad," Sonia said.

"Chip will too." My father looked at me with a face carved in
regret. "Let's face it, Lucia. You basically married me."

Deidre drooped her eyes at me. "Pick a disease, Lucia."

"I'm gon' put in my vote for high blood pressure," Wesley said.
"I don't even think that would be a lie right now."

She was right. My head throbbed, and my blood pulled through
my veins like barbed wire. I was probably pushing 180 about then.

"Can you help us with that?" Deidre said to Wesley.

Wesley made the list of symptoms I couldn't think clearly
enough to come up with, and once again my community gathered
around me while I poured a fabricated plea into the phone. Once
again we waited, while I whispered, "Dear God, please."

Only this time, the phone rang. Within thirty minutes Chip's
number was on my screen. At the sound of my hello, he was saying,
"Babe. Are you all right?" At the sound of his I was biting back a
scream.

Deidre Schmacker sat next to me, head bent to the phone so that
her hair mingled with mine. She motioned me forward with her
hand.

"No," I said. "I feel horrible. It's probably the stress."

"I don't want you stroking out."

The concern in his voice nearly choked me. Deidre squeezed my
arm.

"I need to get away from here," I said. "My head feels like it's
splitting open. I can't take this anymore."

Deidre pointed to the phone, and I gritted my teeth.

"I need you," I said. "Please get me out of here."

"I've got that worked out."

I closed my eyes—squeezed the phone so I wouldn't scream, *What about Bethany? What have you done with her?*

"Tell you what," Chip said. His sandpaper voice had a confidence that grated across my fear. "The news media and the cops are probably all over the front lawn, am I right?"

"Right," I said.

"So it's going to be easier for you to get out than for me to get in. Are you well enough to take a cab and meet me?"

My mouth went dry. "Yes. Meet you where?"

"Drakes Creek Marina, here in Hendersonville. Dock C. Slip 14. Are you writing this down?"

Deidre was.

"You're on a boat?" I said.

"It's all part of the plan, babe. It's going to be the new life I promised you."

He paused, and for a moment I thought he'd hung up.

"Chip?" I said.

"Look, Lucia . . ."

His voice dropped, and so did my heart. Was he changing his mind?

"Just come and let me take care of you. Don't tell Sonia or anybody else where you're going."

Deidre mouthed a *why.*

"Why?" I said. *Because you want to kidnap me too? Try to kill me too?* Fear rose like nausea.

"Because if we're going to start over, we have to do it without her. She'll wreck this life just like she did the last one."

I motioned frantically at Deidre. What should I say?

Chip saved me the trouble. "I know you don't get that," he said. "I'll tell you everything when we're away from here. And Lucia, just so you don't get caught up in guilt—Bethany is going to be all right."

My heart seized. "What do you mean? How do you know that? Do you—"

Deidre waved her hands in front of my face. I sucked in my breath and my panic.

"I just know," Chip said. "Trust me."

Deidre scribbled a note for me. I fought back the dread and read it out loud.

"What should I bring?"

"Just yourself, babe," Chip said. "All I want is you."

I hung up and handed the phone to Deidre.

"And all we want is you, Dr. Coffey," she said. "And our sweet Bethany."

"Do you think he has her, Lucia?" Sonia said. "Could you tell?"

"He says she's going to be all right. What does that mean?"

Deidre put her arm around my shoulder. "It means he's still playing the game. And right now you're about to get the ball back into our court. You ready?"

"Dear God," I whispered. "Dear God."

CHAPTER FORTY-FOUR

I stepped onto the dock at Slip 14 with a tiny microphone taped to the outside of my chest and a barbed-wire ball of anxiety clamped to the inside. The promised presence of an FBI unit on the water at the opening to the river and another in the parking lot kept my feet moving across the swim platform of a slim motorboat, like so many I'd seen skim past the house. The hope that Bethany waited for me there made me call out softly for Chip.

The cover was unzipped from the inside, and Chip put his arm out. When he pulled me in roughly through the mere slit he left me, I swallowed a scream. Was this going to be over before it started?

But he pulled me down onto a seat and folded me into his arms. I tried to breathe, slowly, evenly.

Pretend your fear is excitement at seeing him, Deidre had told me.

Don't rush him for an explanation, Ingram said. *If you can get him to confess, great, but we're more interested in you getting him out in the open.*

We've got your back. We won't let anything happen to you.

Chip turned me around and hugged me from behind, arms across my chest. *Dear God, please don't let him feel the wire.*

I searched the boat with my eyes—a tiny table, two white bench seats, two swivel chairs, one behind the steering wheel. No Bethany, and no place to hide her.

Don't ask for Bethany unless he tells you he has her.

"Whose boat is this?" I said.

"Ours. I traded Kent the Saab for it. And this is just our getaway boat, so to speak."

He forced me to face him again, and I tried not to stiffen.

"Where are we going?" I said.

"Someplace where they need doctors and aren't particular about their pasts."

"Oh," I said. *Don't push too hard.* "When are we leaving?"

Chip took my cheeks in his hands, bringing my fear right up to his face. I closed my eyes.

"Then you'll go with me?" he said.

I forced myself to nod.

"Look at me, Lucia. I want to see it in your eyes."

Dear God, please.

I looked at him and tried a smile. "I told you I needed you. My blood pressure . . ."

"I'll get you some medication," he said. "But I think getting away from that place is all the treatment you're going to need."

I'll tell you everything when we're away from here, he'd said.

It was a crack of light.

"You said on the phone that Sonia wrecked our life," I said.

"You don't even know." He looked at his watch. "We have to get started."

"Please," I said. I heard my own desperation. *Pretend your fear is excitement.* "You were right—it's been horrible at her place."

Chip arranged his face into a patient smile. "We have the rest of our lives to talk about this, babe. Once we get where we're going, you won't even want to think about it."

"She thinks she can run everyone's lives—and she takes them and crushes them." I sucked in a breath. "I found out what she did to you—to us. I wouldn't blame you if you wanted to kill her."

His eyes narrowed, and I knew I'd made a mistake. My heart slammed into my chest—into the microphone. *Don't push too hard—too fast.*

Chip studied my face for so long I was sure he could read what I was doing as if it were printed on my forehead. Then he said, "What if I did? What if I did try to kill her? Would you still go with me?"

Go through the motions to get through this part.

That wasn't Deidre Schmacker. That was Sullivan Crisp. Whatever it was, I hung on to it.

"Yes," I said. "I told you I need you. I want a new life."

Chip moved to the seat across from me and grabbed my hands in the gap between us. "I wanted her dead, Lucia. Not just because she turned me in, but because she could never let me forget that I was a criminal. And I wasn't, Lucia."

"No," I whispered.

"I was a victim, like all the people I tried to help. We were victims of the insurance companies and the justice system, just people in pain trying to make it in this world."

"You were," I said. "Sonia could never see that."

"She threw it up in my face every chance she got. Talked about it in front of her audiences. Used me for an example. I was her freakin' poster child for repentance and deliverance." His eyes were in ugly slits. "You see it now, don't you? I didn't know if you could, but you see it."

He pushed himself back on the seat and let his head fall forward. "She knew I was using, and she saw it as an opportunity. She turned me in, and then she waited for me to get out of prison, and then she brought me down here to use me to show the world that she was a miracle worker."

"I see that," I said.

What I truly saw was the frightening glitter in his eyes. I thought I'd witnessed insanity when Sonia smashed her own image in the foyer. But this. This was a twisted madness I was sure he would never come back from. If Bethany was here, I had to get her out. Were there compartments under these seats?

"So it was you," I said.

"It was me." He put his hands to his head. "Do you know what a relief it is to tell you—to know you get it?"

Chip stood up and went to the driver's seat, where he unzipped the cover. "I tried to poison her food. When that didn't work, I got in touch with a guy I knew in prison. Kent Mussen."

He stuck the upper part of his body out through the opening in the cover, and I looked around frantically. There was one door that looked like it led to a compartment large enough to hold Bethany. If I could just get a look in there.

Chip pulled himself back in, holding a line. "Mussen got a bum rap too. He said if I ever needed anything when we got on the outside . . ." He shook his head as he reached across me to the other side of the cover.

I looked longingly at the compartment as he pulled up the zipper.

"Otto never drank his coffee until at least five thousand feet—but he must have taken a sip before takeoff."

I got up from the seat. Chip caught my elbow.

"You're not in the way," he said.

"I don't mind."

He pushed open the flap and put his head through. I edged toward the compartment.

"If he'd waited, the explosives would have obliterated any evidence the crash itself didn't."

I was there, against the door. With my hand behind me, I felt for the handle. Chip emerged with another line, and I froze.

"Sonia would have been dead," he said with his back still to me as he lifted one of the seats and tucked the lines inside. I craned my neck—but the space was empty. "In a sense," Chip went on, "it worked out better this way. Now she has to live with a wrecked life just like I did."

The coldness in his voice was terrifying. I had to end this soon, because no amount of pretending could stanch my revulsion and fear much longer. I had to know if Bethany was in the compartment. My fingers hit on the handle, but they couldn't figure out how it worked. I was fumbling when Chip turned to face me. His eyes were like a pair of stones.

"It would have been easier for me to give you everything you wanted if she were completely out of the way," he said. "But in a way there is more justice in this."

He came to me and pulled my face into his chest. I had to let go of the handle—but my index finger caught in it.

"How do you figure that," I said into the front of his shirt.

"Because now Sonia knows she's losing everything—and you're getting it all."

I pushed myself back with my free hand. "What am I getting?"

Chip smiled down at me. "The child you always wanted."

Bethany? Was he talking about Bethany? I wrenched away from him and twisted to the compartment. My fingers clawed at the handle.

"What are you doing, Lucia?"

Chip's voice shot me in the back, but I yanked the door open and stared into a vacant hole whose only occupant was a box of trash bags.

Chip nodded toward the opening he'd dragged me through. "Untie that line," he said, "and I'll show you what I mean."

I couldn't read his face. He had turned it hard, and I felt myself panic. He wanted *me* to go outside this zippered cabin, not him. If he didn't know they were waiting for him out there, he was at least not taking any chances.

He followed me to the opening and unzipped it. "It's right there on the starboard side. There. You'll learn the nautical terms in no time."

I didn't care about starboard or port or anything else but Bethany. That kept me from running like the terrified rabbit I was as I crawled across the swim platform and untied the line with fumbling fingers. Chip already had the motor running when I came back inside. He pointed to the other swivel chair, and I dropped into it.

"Do you trust me, Lucia?" he said.

"Show me," I said. I just couldn't lie anymore.

He eased the boat out of the slip and cruised faster than it felt safe to between the two rows of other vessels, setting them rocking indignantly. By the time we reached the mouth of the marina, he had the bow up on step. We flashed past the sign that said 5 MPH—NO WAKE. I didn't have time to look for the FBI's boat, and I was afraid to. I was afraid to do anything except hang on.

But Chip's face frightened me even more. It grew harder and more intense with every ripple we bounced over. One thing I knew: I had to keep him talking, or his anger would burn a hole in this entire thing before I got to Bethany. If she was even where we were going. Something to say—something that wouldn't make him more suspicious.

"How did you learn so much about boats?" I shouted over the frantic flapping of plastic.

"Kent. I haven't been selling medical equipment, Lucia. I've been trying to get you out of that place." He made a hard right, and I thrust out a hand to keep from being thrown into the side of the boat.

"Sorry," he said. "That's why we're taking Kent with us. He's waiting."

No, he wasn't. He was in an interrogation room with Agent Ingram. Was that a good thing? Or was that hitch in the plan going to send Chip over the edge he already walked like a tightrope?

He gave me a harsh smile. "He's great with boats. Not so great with wife-snatching. He was a white-collar criminal, like me."

"Wife-snatching?" I said.

"He was supposed to 'kidnap' you and bring you to me, but Dr. Wisp aborted that mission."

"He was after *me*?" I said.

"When that didn't work, I came for you myself, but once again I was foiled by Dr. Wisp. What is that jerk's name, anyway?"

I didn't answer him.

"He put some bad ideas in your head, Lucia. That whole ministry crowd is like that." He jerked the boat to the left and sent us sailing hazardously close to a red buoy that swayed in alarm. "Don't worry—the boat we're leaving in won't do this."

I didn't say anything more as he made another fishtailing left and pulled back on the throttle. The boat bobbed like a cork, and I closed my eyes and fought back nausea. I opened them when it stilled and found us in a dark cove whose only occupant was a smallish yacht. Chip unzipped the cover beside him again and peered out.

"Yo," he whispered hoarsely. "Mussen."

There was, of course, no answer. I couldn't stay in the seat.

"Can we just go aboard?" I said. "I have to go to the bathroom."

Chip muttered something about Mussen, but he nodded. "You can get to the platform on the stern from the back of this one. I gotta drop anchor. Be careful."

I wasn't. The minute I got outside the cover, I crabbed my way across the platform and leaped to the bigger boat, setting the smaller one rocking like a cradle. I heard Chip swear as I tore at the latch on a glass door and slid it open. Shiny teak and white leather blinded me like a spotlight in my face, and I knew in that flash where Sonia's money had gone. How—when—it didn't matter. I called out Bethany's name as I hurled myself through the cabin, yanking open cabinets with brass latches on the way.

"Bethany! Bethany—are you here? It's Aunt Lucia Mom!"

The boat moved sideways, and for an awful moment I thought we were under way, until Chip's voice cut me from the door.

"Lucia—stop!"

He swore at me again, but I plunged ahead and pulled open a long hatch, so hard I felt a muscle tear in my shoulder. I stumbled forward into a bed that filled a cabin. Nestled into its satin pillows was a round child, curled into a motionless ball.

"Bethany!" I screamed.

She didn't move. Chip's arm came around my throat and jammed me against him.

"What did you do to her? Chip—did you kill her? Did you kill this baby too?"

"Shut up, Lucia! Shut up!"

His arm tightened at my neck and cut off my words and my breath. I tore at his skin and kicked until the black in my eyes flecked the cabin.

"Help us!" I screamed into my chest. "Help us!"

Chip's arm left my neck with a jerk, and I slithered to the bed. Before I could crawl to the too-still form on the pillows, Chip was on top of me, tearing at my shirt.

"Are you wearing a wire?" he shouted. His hand found the microphone, and he ripped it off, tape, flesh, and all. With his other hand he pinned me to the bed. "You too? You betrayed me too?"

I opened my mouth. Beside me Bethany stirred.

She was still alive.

That was the only reason I gave Chip one more lie. "They made me, Chip," I said. "Agent Schmuck, right?"

He went still.

"I just wanted to make sure you had Bethany. I knew she'd be safe with you."

"You're lying—just like your sister. Just like all of them."

He got to his knees and pushed the wires into my face. With a force that could only come from a mother bear, I brought up my knee and slammed it into his gut. With a yelp he rolled to the side and clutched his arms around himself. I snatched Bethany into my arms and staggered with her out of the cabin, through the galley, eyes on the glass door. Chip had left it open. I just had to get through it and they would see me—

But I only got as far as the stern platform when I heard Chip storming behind me.

"Help!" I screamed. "Help us!"

The cove answered with silence.

"Bethie—wake up, baby—wake up."

Bethany stirred again in my arms, but not enough. Chip flailed for me. As his hand caught my sleeve, I pulled her against my chest.

"We're going swimming, Bethie," I said. And with her dead weight heavy in my arms, I plunged over the side. As we sank below the surface, I could still hear Chip raving. But at least I knew he wouldn't come after me.

By the time we came up, yards away from the yacht, Bethany kicked and grabbed. Her voice was drug-thick as she screamed.

"Bethie, it's okay!" I shouted to her. "I won't let you go—remember—I'm your BFF! I won't let you go."

I believed in miracles at that moment, because she went limp in my arms.

"Good girl," I said. "I won't let you go."

"Can we float?" she said.

I didn't have enough air to answer her, but my nod seemed to be all she needed. Sleepily she rolled onto her back, and I held on. Beyond us a motor roared to life, and I whipped my head around in fear. But it wasn't the yacht. It was a boat with a guiding light easing into the mouth of the cove—with a squarish woman on its bow.

"Here! Over here!" I shouted with the last of my breath. "It's Agent Schmacker, Bethany—we're okay!"

Bethany just smiled. "I hope she brought J. Edgar," she said.

CHAPTER FORTY-FIVE

Sonia finally fell asleep, just as Bethany was waking up. The sun laughed through the rounded part of her window and teased at both their faces. I watched from the futon as Sonia's scarred one turned from it in exhaustion, and Bethany's cherubic one met it in sleepy glee.

"Aunt Lucia Mom?" she whispered.

"Yes, Bethie."

"I'm staying home now, right?"

I sat up and tugged at a dark curl and assured her she was—just as her mother and I had every time she'd awakened in the night with a startled cry.

"And you're not going away, right?"

That was a question I could only partially answer. At 2:00 AM Sonia had asked me to stay—as her sister, her friend, her baby girl's Aunt Lucia Mom. I didn't know if in the harsh realizations of the day the offer would still stand. There was so much for us to sort out. A lifetime of tangles.

"Not today," I said. "Shall we let your mom sleep and go get some breakfast?"

"May I look at her?"

I stopped halfway up from the futon. "You mean your mom?"

She nodded shyly. It came to me that she had not seen Sonia in the daylight in weeks. Since before she knew she was allowed to see her "without her face."

"Do you want to look at her?" I said.

Again she nodded.

"Then you go right ahead," I said.

Bethany gave me one more blue-eyed look before she leaned over her mother and pulled the covers from her neck. I held my breath. Had we come as far as I dreamed we had?

She didn't say a word. Like the rest of us, perhaps she could find no words for what she saw. But as I watched, she unfolded her chubby fingers from a pink fist and reached for Sonia's cheek. With a touch so light it could have been an angel's, she ran her finger along a rosy, raised scar. And then with her little red bow of a mouth, she kissed it.

I didn't move. I couldn't. I had just seen God.

Harry the Heron was guarding our river when I walked out onto the dock. He didn't lift himself from his perch, and I was grateful for that. I could use his wise, quiet company.

I'd left Sonia and Bethany discovering each other in the Princess Room.

Francesca had finally gone home, looking as drained and normal as the rest of us. When she said, "I'll call you, Lucia," I hoped she would.

Though Wesley phoned hourly, she was at her house, hugging James-Lawson at regular intervals. She said she was about to get on his last nerve.

Deidre and her team were gone until tomorrow, when the debriefing would begin again. For now they were satisfied with Chip's confession and had assured me that he would never see a day outside a prison. I hadn't even begun to process that yet.

I couldn't do it alone. Sullivan Crisp would help me for a while longer, he'd said. But he had to move on. He would make sure I had someone I could connect with. When he'd left for the guesthouse at dusk, he'd turned to me and grinned the one-side-at-a-time smile.

"I know you're in pain," he said. "But, Lucia, I hope you keep dancing with the stars."

I tilted my head back and looked for the stars now. A few were venturing into the evening sky, shyly at first, then twinkling with confidence.

"I want to dance, God," I whispered. "But I don't have a partner."

It came at me like a fist, that thought, but I thrust my arm up to ward it off. I hadn't had a partner for a long time. Maybe Chip had never been one. I had no tears for him. I had only a sudden, aching loneliness, and I closed my eyes and let myself sway with it.

"You always were a wonderful dancer."

I turned and watched the once-strong silhouette make its bulky way toward me on the dock.

"I wish you'd take it up again," Dad said when he reached me.

"I think I've started to," I said.

"What made you ever stop?"

"I guess I had the wrong partner," I said.

He grunted as only a disgruntled Italian father can do. "You were doin' the wrong dance," he said.

I looked at the life-weathered face, dimming with age and the twilight. "You were wrong, Dad," I said.

"You don't have to tell me that."

"No, you were wrong when you said I married you. You are nothing like Chip."

His head ducked. "Thank you for saying that."

"I think you just did what all we Brocacinis did. We were all afraid to be who we were, and we ended up doing somebody else's dance." I nodded at Harry, who still stood alone on his misplaced tree. "I think when you do that, you always end up dancing alone."

"You got too much love in you for that, Lucia Marie."

The pain rose in my chest again, and I rubbed at it with my hands. "I don't know where to dance yet, Dad," I said. "Or with who."

He watched me for a moment, hands parked in his pockets, before he pulled them out and held one toward me. "Will you start with me, Lucia Marie?" he said. "Because I would love to dance with my daughter."

And so, with the stars winking on and Harry the Heron watching with envy, I danced with my father by the water. Not like a fawn. Like a woman whose rhythm was merely *Dear God—dear God.*

"I'm going to miss you around here, Dr. Crisp," Porphyria said.

Sully grinned at her. "You know what they say about house-guests: after three months, they start to smell."

Porphyria smiled back at him, sunlight freckling her face through the leaves that canopied her veranda. "I think the saying is three days."

"Three months feels like three days with you." Sully swallowed the sweet thickness that had been gathering in his throat all morning as he packed. "I came here a broken man. You've helped me heal."

"Mmm—I think it was the good Lord and you this last month, Sully."

"It was the loneliest month of my life." Sully took a sip from the glass she'd put in front of him, carefully avoiding the mint leaf that sprang up between the ice cubes. That must have been the piece he'd missed in his attempts to make sweet tea like hers.

"Does that mean the Lord alone is not enough?" she said.

Sully saw the gleam in her child-wise eyes.

"It means the Lord shows up in people you wouldn't expect Him to latch onto. And if you aren't paying attention, you're going to miss them. And Him."

She nodded over her own tea glass. She was satisfied with him.

"So you're ready for the world again," she said.

"I don't know if the world's ready for me."

"Oh, I think the world is ready for another Healing Choice clinic. And whatever else you're going to stir up out there."

Sully set his glass on the table and leaned on his knees. "There is one thing I want to run by you before I go."

"You make it sound like you're never coming back. I do have a phone."

The thickness threatened to rise. "There is no substitute for talking face-to-face with Porphyria Ghent," he said. "I can't see your soul over the telephone."

She closed her eyes and nodded.

"I'm thinking of looking for Belinda Cox," Sully said. "You remember, she was Lynn's so-called counselor."

"You can't throw her in the Cumberland, Sully. They'll put you in jail for that."

"She's the one who should be in jail if she's still practicing therapy. I'm not doing it out of vengeance, Porphyria. I've seen what good that does."

"So you have."

"I just don't want anyone else to suffer what my family has—and what Sonia's family has—because of misguided dogma."

"You know you could have a big battle ahead of you," Porphyria said. "It won't be easy to prove she's unfit for the job."

Sully tried to grin. "When have I ever gone after anything easy, Porphyria?"

"Never since I've known you." She bathed his face with a long look. "Just keep your eyes on the prize, Sullivan," she said. "The real prize."

"I'll do that."

She stood up and put a warm, brown hand on his shoulder. "Are you leaving now?"

"I just want to do my last podcast before I go." Sully covered her hand with his. "How can I thank you, Porphyria?"

"By coming back to share your wisdom with me," she said. "The Lord be with you, my friend."

The thickness crept into his voice. "And also with you," he said.

When she was gone, Sullivan picked up the microphone and clicked Record. He let the birds take the first few seconds with their chatter before he joined them.

"Part Last of What I Know to Be True," he said. "God knows suffering, not because He created it, but because He experiences it with us. I know this as well as I know the piercing, biting, tearing pain of loss."

Sully tilted his face to the sun. "It is also true that although God knows suffering, He doesn't explain it. I waited and searched and beat myself up for that, and I know now that it just flat-out doesn't happen. God only walks us through it and out into a place where we can once again be free.

"He does this not because we believe some rigid this or that about Him. He does it because He believes in us. He doesn't ask us to go out into the world telling people why they suffer. Even if we knew why, it wouldn't hurt any less. What we need to know is how to help each other live with it, and live well." Sully felt the sweet thickness rise, and he let it come. "This I know as well as I know the sobbing, hugging, tea-pouring comfort of love," he said. "I have seen it. I will seek it every day of the life I have left. That, my fellow sufferers, is what I know to be true."

Sully let the birds agree before he clicked Stop.

But that wasn't the end.

That, he knew, was the beginning.

Ding-ding-ding, Dr. Crisp. Ding-ding.

ACKNOWLEDGMENTS

No one reads the acknowledgements unless he expects to find his name among the thanked, but in case you're the exception, please join us in our appreciation for the help of these generous people:

- Dr. Jeffery Guy, burn surgeon at Vanderbilt University Regional Burn Center, who gave hours of his valuable time, making sure we got it right. We hope you're pleased, Dr. Guy.
- Dan Ramage, LCSW, also at the burn center, who discussed Sonia with all the compassion he would give a nonfictional patient.
- The staff in the Nashville Room at the Nashville Public Library, who helped uncover more than we ever needed to know about the Shelby Street Bridge. We used it all.
- Carrie Daughtrey, Assistant U.S. Attorney, who kept us from depending on *Law and Order* and *Without a Trace* as primary legal sources. Sorry, Carrie, but we just couldn't follow your advice about leaving J. Edgar Pug out of the story.
- Marnie Huff, Margaret Huff Mediation, Nashville, who led us to Carrie and provided expertise of her own. If we misrepresent the justice system, it's through no fault of theirs.
- Dr. Dale McElhinney, Doctor of Psychology, whose painstaking attention to Sullivan Crisp keeps us from setting the practice of psychotherapy back fifty years—and keeps it moving forward.
- The brave, honest participants in Lose It for Life, especially counselor Elisa Marshall, and the God's Girls: Jennifer,

Melissa, Nancy, Linda, Ethel, Judy, and Peggy. Their courageous sharing brought Lucia to life.

- Sharon Hurt, Jefferson Street United Merchants Partnership, Nashville, who breathed into Wesley and made her real.

- Ken Feist, without whom we could never have gotten that plane off the ground, or crashed it, for that matter. Your attention to detail made the scene all too real.

- Luke Schurter, FF/EMT-P, who got us from the burning plane to the hospital. Space limitations wouldn't allow us to include all you taught us, Luke, but you gave us the voice of authority.

- Joyce Mocerro, who showed us the side of Philadelphia we needed to see.

- Nancy Feist, Linda Knause, Jennifer Thomas, and Melissa Craig, who read dreadful first drafts and steered us in the right direction.

- Amanda Bostic, our editor, who has no business being so smart and savvy and insightful at her tender age.

- L.B. Norton, our line editor, who is as good at putting up with whining as she is at tightening a manuscript.

- Marijean Rue, who gave us a peek at the Vanderbilt Divinity School—and a taste of SATCO.

- Jim Rue, who provided countless boat rides for viewing Sonia's house and gave her story many of its twists, as he so often does. Thank you, Jimmy, for being so un-Chip-like.

- Nan Allison, Nutrition Consulting, who models the kind of gentle, nurturing approach Sully uses with Lucia.

- Barbara Moss, Partner, Stites & Harbison, Nashville, PLLC, who shared both her professional expertise and her personal story, and inspired Lucia's courage.

- The Reverend Gordon Peerman, whose sermon on suffering brought Sully's struggles into perspective and shaped his podcasts. God bless you, Gordon.

God bless you *all*.

DISCUSSION QUESTIONS

You may answer the following questions if you promise not to treat them like a class assignment. These are provided in case you want springboards for thought and/or discussion. Otherwise, simply enjoy the story with our blessing.

Nancy Rue and Steve Arterburn

About Faith

1. Sully describes Sonia's idea of faith as "toxic." Do you agree? Do you see that concept applied in real life situations? With what results?

2. Do you think Sonia's faith was ever real? How did it disintegrate? What are her chances of gaining a truer perspective?

3. Can you follow the thread of Lucia's faith as it grows from virtually nonexistent to something her whole family can now stand on?

4. Can you follow the thread of your own faith's growth?

5. How do you account for Sully's ability to maintain his faith in the face of all he's lost? How about Wesley?

On Suffering

6. There are so many levels of suffering in *Healing Waters*, as portrayed by individual characters. How would you describe the suffering of

- Lucia
- Chip
- Bethany
- Sonia
- Sully

Where did it come from? How have they coped? What needs to change?

7. Sully has a, well, Sully-like view of suffering that he's able to paint through his podcasts. Do you agree with his treatment of it? Does your experience bear it out?

8. Have you ever been inclined to go with Lucia's view—that suffering is somehow based on how much God loves you?

9. At the end of the story, Lucia has begun to dig up what she's buried and fed for so many years. How do you think she's going to deal with what she has to face now?

In Therapy

10. Sully tells Lucia that whatever you bury (i.e. don't deal with emotionally), you bury alive and you have to feed it—literally as well as figuratively. Does that resonate with you in any way?

11. Lucia is so reluctant to talk about her past and her pain. Sound familiar? Why do we stuff it?

12. If you had to complete the assignment Sully gives Lucia—"I want you to be the *Family Feud* audience for your family and make a list of the first five significant things you can remember in your life with them," what would you include on your list?

In Life

Several of the characters are conspicuously flawed, and yet have much good in them—as do most of us. How would you describe the good, the bad, the ugly, and the holy in these folks?

13. Lucia

14. Sonia

15. Chip

16. Francesca

17. Agent Schmacker

18. Sully himself

19. . . . you

If you would like to do a more in-depth study of *Healing Waters*, you can download the curriculum from www.nancyrue.com. You can also visit our website: sullivancrisp.com.

Did *Healing Waters* shed light on anything for you? Get you to consider anything differently? Confirm what you know? Make you want to call us up and tell us we're nuts? If so, we would love to hear from you.

nnrue@hughes.net   sarterburn@newlife.com

With one flash of a camera, Demi's private life becomes public news. She doesn't know it yet, but her healing has just begun.

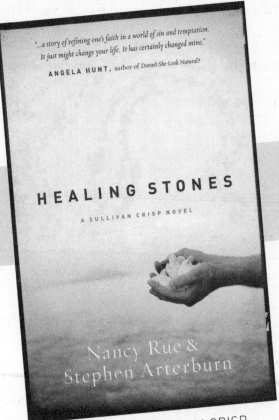

> "...a story of refining one's faith in a world of sin and temptation. It just might change your life. It has certainly changed mine."
>
> ANGELA HUNT, author of *Doesn't She Look Natural?*

HEALING STONES
A SULLIVAN CRISP NOVEL

Nancy Rue & Stephen Arterburn

For more from SULLIVAN CRISP, check out *HEALING STONES*

AVAILABLE IN BOOKSTORES EVERYWHERE

I sneaked down to the boat that night to say this couldn't happen anymore.

Mind you, I didn't want to. Ripping a man's heart out wasn't up there with things I relished. I don't know what I thought would come of things in the end, but I never envisioned this. "This" fell into the "have to" column. When you've made a mess so major you can't hope anymore that somehow things will turn out all right on their own, you have to fix them.

I made my usual way through the shadows, glancing back out of habit to be sure no one saw me. No one frequented the Port Orchard Yacht Club on late February evenings, and even I wouldn't have to anymore after tonight.

I sucked in damp Washington air and breathed out my urge to run from the pain. Then I slid my hand into the pocket of my P-coat, felt the key card waiting in its satin hiding place, and curled in on myself, plastic card digging into my palm.

Would everything that reminded me of Zach torture me from now on? This was just the key to the ramp. What was going to happen when I saw his face?

I managed to get the gate unlocked and then closed it behind me, clanging like a prison door. Yes, I waxed dramatic, but everything inside seemed to hold a piece of him. Zach always had a field day with the curled-up ad on the bulletin board asking for a stud for a Yorkshire terrier. Every time I picked my way in the dark down the puzzle grating on the gangplank, I anticipated his arms around me.

I started down narrow Dock C, the open-ceilinged hallway lined with cheerful doors that led to covered, inside boat slips, and I could hear Zach chuckling over the limp Valentine's Day wreath that hung over a faux porthole, reds and pinks oozing damply into each other. I belonged on this slender path to Zach's door. It always seemed to close behind me—holding me in that one safe place.

How, then, would I get out after I'd said what I came to say? My, my, Demitria. You sure know how to arrange things.

My hand was barely on the knob when the door to his slip came open and Zach filled the doorway, and me.

"Hey, Prof," he said.

Standing there with him so close I ached, I fought to remember how I'd steeled myself for this. I was doing it for Rich and our kids— because it was the right thing—because I couldn't do the wrong thing anymore.

Zach stood silhouetted with the boat rocking behind him until he pulled me through the doorway onto the enclosed dock—and into the intoxicating musky smell of his neck. Then he was too real.

"Okay, what's wrong?"

I couldn't answer, not with my face pushed into the black wool of the sweater stretching across his chest.

"You sounded stressed on the phone. I can feel it in you." He held me tighter and pressed his chin on top of my head. I didn't have to look at him yet, but I could see him all the same.

His dark thicket of brows drawn together. Blue eyes closed, I knew, squeezing the worry lines into fans at their corners. I tried to push myself away, but he cupped my face in his hands and soaked me in. I'd been right about his expression. The only thing I'd missed was the rumple in his wiry, almost-gray hair, where he'd apparently raked his fingers.

"You're scaring me, Prof." He tilted his head to kiss me, but I peeled his hands away and stepped back.

"Can we get on the boat?" I said.

I didn't wait for an answer but maneuvered around him and hurried down the dock to *The Testament*'s stern. Every squishy step of my rubber soles echoed like a taunt. *This is the last time. This is the last time.*

I stepped aboard and stopped to stare into the cabin. Candles dotted every horizontal plane, flames casting halos on the polished teak. I was walking into a sanctuary.

"You sounded like you could use a little candlelight." Zach eased the cabin door shut behind us. "What else do you need?"

What I needed was for him not to use that voice right now—the clear, bottomless voice that asked the right questions and gave me my nickname and always said if I wanted him to stop I should tell him before he wouldn't be able to.

"I need to talk," I said. "And I need you to listen."

"Always." Zach pulled me toward the pillow-piled seat that banked the corner, but I wriggled my hand free.

"I can't sit next to you for this."

"Okay, Prof." He ran a finger under my chin. "This is your meeting."

He swiveled the captain's chair to face me and perched on its edge. His long legs, clad in jeans that followed the commands of his thighs and calves, draped to either side.

"Rich?" he said. "Does he know?"

"Zach, let me—"

"If he does, so be it. You know I've got your back." He shrugged his squared-off shoulders. "I've been saying you should tell him."

I couldn't help smiling. I could never help smiling at him. "Am I going to have to duct-tape your lips?"

The lips in question eased into a grin. "I'm listening. Talk to me."

Of course I could talk to Zach. He would even understand this, which, ironically, had put me in this impossible situation in the first place: because I could talk to him like I could talk to no one else. There was never a need for caveats—and the undivided attention was as addictive as everything else about us.

Yet I had to say it.

"We have to end this. I mean us—we have to stop being us."

He didn't move.

"I love you—you know that. You're the rest of me that I could never find until you, and this place." I swept my gaze over the walls. The candle flames flickered frantically as if they registered what

Zach didn't seem to. "I want to be with you. I want the life I know we could have, only I can't have it all tangled in secrets and lies. I don't want anything about us to be wrong, and this is, and I can't anymore . . . Zach—say something."

"You told me not to."

"Do you always have to do what I ask you to?"

His face went soft. "One of the things I love about you is that you're the kind of woman who'll go back to her husband. I can't argue with your integrity, Demi."

I actually laughed. "What integrity, Zach? I'm a married woman and I've been having an affair with you for five months."

"Five months, three weeks, four days."

"That's not integrity—that's adultery."

"So you've said—at least one thousand and three times." He cocked his head at me. "But if you could see yourself. This is tearing you apart and has all along. A woman without integrity wouldn't care about right or wrong, especially after the way Rich has treated you—"

"He's still my husband."

"Exactly my point."

I pushed my hands through my hair. "I wish you would stop turning me into a saint. I'm trying to do the right thing here."

"I know. And I hate it and I love it at the same time." He leaned toward me, touching me without touching me. "It makes you even more beautiful."

I pulled my knees into my chest, the soles of my boots divoting the corduroy. *This must be what withdrawal feels like.*

"Prof, I can see into your soul. It's hurting."

"I don't care if I'm wonderful or scum—I still have to end this." I unfolded my legs. "I'm going to walk out of here, okay? And I'm not coming back."

He watched me. The liquid-blue eyes, the color of Puget Sound, swam, until I realized I was the one on the verge of tears. He made a move to come toward me, but I put my hand up.

"This is breaking your heart," he said. "I don't know if I can stand that—I want to help."

"We'll have to stay away from each other."

"How do you see us doing that? We'll be tripping over each other in the hall." He pulled his brows together. "No matter. I can't go anywhere on that campus without seeing you, even if you aren't there."

I watched him swallow.

"Our lives are too enmeshed for us to walk away from this," he said. "What about the Faith and Doubt project? That's a baby you and I brought into this world." His face worked. "We have students who would have completely turned their backs on Christianity if we weren't working with them. We have a responsibility—"

"We won't let that go," I said. "We're grown-ups, Zach—we can hold it together for the kids."

"I don't know if I can. A man in love isn't a grown-up." Zach leaned back. "At least not this man. He's a spoiled-rotten little boy who knows what he wants, and he won't be without it."

"You have to be without me."

"Forever?"

"I have to know if my marriage to Rich can work—"

"Haven't you tried hard enough?"

"Not enough to walk away from twenty-one years."

Zach pressed his palms on his thighs and wiped at his jeans. Zach Archer didn't do desperate, and I could hardly bear it. "A relationship needs two people to work," he said. "Do you think Rich is going to—"

"Zach, stop."

He did, just short of the line he'd promised never to cross.

"I'm sorry. I've never put him down."

"No, you haven't, Doc, and please don't start now."

Pain shot across his face, and I wanted to bite my tongue. I'd told myself I wouldn't use his nickname.

"You love me," he said. "I know you do."

"That isn't—"

"Then do what you have to do. I have to set you free for that."

I closed my eyes.

"But I have to say this one thing, and I want you to hear me."

He hesitated as if he were waiting for my permission. "This—what we have—this is true love, which will win out if we let it."

"But we can't let it *this* way." I opened my eyes. "If we put us before God, then that can't be true."

We both stared at the space between us, as if a third party had entered the cabin and spoken. The thought had curled in my brain like a wisp of smoke for—five months, three weeks, and four days. Longer than that if I counted the weeks watching him at faculty meetings, the days dreaming up reasons to drop by his office, the stolen moments I collected like seashells to hold later. Now that the thought was between us, it cut a chasm I couldn't walk around.

Zach leaped across and came to me. I straight-armed him before he could touch me and make God disappear.

"Please don't make it any harder," I said.

"Can't happen. I'm already in shreds."

"Then let me go—please—and we can both start to heal."

He brushed the hair off my forehead with one finger. "I'll never get over this, Prof."

And then he gave me the look. Our look. The look that destroyed me and threw me right into his arms—to the place where I didn't care what I was doing, as long as it felt like this.

Our clothes were halfway off within seconds. We had that part down to a passionate science. I was once more ripped from in-control to out-of-my-mind, lost again on the wave I wanted to ride all the way, no matter where it took me. I'd thought in every guilty-afterwards that this must be what a drug addict felt like.

I clung to his chest and let his mouth search for mine. He found it just as the cabin erupted with light. Over my heartbeat, I heard the unmistakable click and whir of a camera.

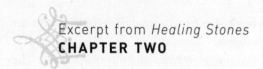

What? *Zach—what?*"

That was all I could say—in a voice whose panicked pitch couldn't possibly be mine. Another flash jolted my vision into misshapen rings of light—then another and another—while I found my jacket and tried to pull it over my face. The satin lining was cold against the bare skin on my chest but I couldn't get it turned around. I felt a flailing sleeve hit something. A flame zipped along the floor and grabbed at a pillow that had tumbled there, startling it to light.

"Go, Demi!" Zach called from somewhere.

The camera's auto-winder chattered like a squirrel as I snatched up articles of clothing and tried to hold them against me with one hand while I grabbed for more with the other. Parts of Zach jerked surreally as if he were moving through strobe lights, slapping at the fire. But it was Rich's voice that shouted in my head.

In a fire, you gotta move quickly, but don't panic. Stay low—don't run.

I lunged for the door and flung it open, my clothes in a bundle across my nakedness.

"That's enough," I heard Zach say.

I stumbled across the stern deck and hoisted myself onto the dock. Something slithered out of my arms, but I didn't stop to get it. I didn't stop at all until I was at the gate, tearing crazily at the handle. My hands were already so drenched in sweat they slipped off, and I fell backwards onto the ramp.

For an insane moment I considered throwing myself into the inlet and swimming for shore. It was only slightly less psychotic that I kicked my bra and camisole over the side of the gangplank, shoved my arms into the sleeves of my P-coat, and climbed the gate like an escaping ape. I managed to get myself into the Jeep and down Bay Street.

I'd passed city hall before the first rational thought shot into my mind. Two rational thoughts.

One—what was I running from? No one was chasing me. The clock on the hall read a quarter to nine. Drivers passed by on their leisurely way home from eating calamari at Tweeten's or picking up kids from basketball practice, but no paparazzi tailed me with their 35-millimeters hanging out the windows.

I slowed down.

Two—I'd left Zach alone, smothering a fire and dealing with— who? Who hid on his boat, waiting to take pictures of us—*half naked*?

I pulled to the curb and pressed my forehead against the steering wheel. I'd imagined our affair being discovered a hundred different ways—from Rich following me to *The Testament* and dragging me up the gangplank to my eighteen-year-old son hacking into my secret e-mail account. None of them had involved a photographer crawling out of the galley of the cabin cruiser and shooting us groping each other by candlelight.

Now whoever it was had pictures—of our last time together. I pummeled the steering wheel with my fists, and then I sat up. With chicken-claw fingers I buttoned my jacket. Zach wouldn't let anybody get out of there with that film. He'd sounded so calm when he said, "That's enough," as if it were going to be no trouble at all to disarm whoever it was. By now he'd probably already called the police, or brought the full power of the Dr. Zachary Archer charm and intensity to bear on the situation.

Zach wouldn't have hit the jerk. That was more Rich's MO. Back when he'd cared enough about anything to throw a punch at it

I pulled my cell phone out of my purse, which I'd left in the car, and turned it on. Pulling my lapels together with one hand, I was reaching down to turn up the heat when the tiny screen signaled one new voice message. Already dissolving into relief, I poked in my password.

"Hey, Mom?" It was the indignant tone only a thirteen-year-old girl can achieve. "Could you come get me?"

I could see Jayne's eyes rolling. But I could also hear the whine of uncertainty, even over the siren now screaming in the distance.

"Rachel was supposed to take me home from rehearsal, but I guess she forgot me. Could you call me when you get this?" The whine reached a peak and fell into a teeth-clenched finish. "Never mind. I guess I'll have to call Christopher."

I searched the screen. She'd left the message at eight—forty-five minutes ago. Fighting back visions of child abductors in black vans stalking Cedar Heights Junior High, I shoved the Jeep into gear, then shoved it out again. I dialed my home phone.

"You *so* owe me," Christopher said, in lieu of "hello."

"Did you pick Jayne up?"

"Like I said, you owe me."

"Is she okay?"

"She's in her room with the lights out and that music on that sounds like some chick needs Prozac." Christopher gave the hard laugh he'd recently adopted. "Which is what she always does, so, yeah, she's okay. Where were you?"

I was suddenly aware of the nakedness under my jacket.

"I had a meeting," I said. "Has your dad called?"

"I called *him* to see if he was okay."

"Why?" I said. My chest tightened automatically—the Pavlovian reaction of the firefighter's wife.

"Fire at that 76 station on Mile Hill Road. Heard on the radio on my way home from the library. They said it was contained, so I called him."

I told myself I was imagining the innuendo of accusation in his voice, the Why didn't you call him? I chalked it up to the overall attitude of superiority my son had taken on now that he was a college freshman and knew far more than his father and I could ever hope to. I was forty-two with a doctorate in theological studies, but Christopher Costanas could reduce me to the proverbial clueless blonde.

"He said they got another call and he's going out on it," Christopher said. "Even though his shift's over—you know Dad."

Thank you, God, I thought as I hung up. Although God helping me keep Rich out of the way until I could find out what had just happened wasn't something even I could fathom. Funny. All through my affair with Zach, I'd continued to talk to my God, asking His forgiveness over and over, every time I left the yacht club, knowing I'd be back. Now that I'd ended it, I couldn't face Him. In His place was a rising sense of unease.

Rich's Harley wasn't in the garage when I got home. Christopher answered with a grunt when I said good night outside his door. I tiptoed into Jayne's dark bedroom, but all I saw was a trail of strawberry-blonde hair on top of the covers and a rail-like lump underneath them. I kissed the cheek that was no longer plump and rosy, now that my daughter had abruptly turned into a teenager. She didn't stir, even when I whispered, "I'm sorry about tonight. We'll talk tomorrow."

Whatever "tomorrow" was going to look like. The uneasiness rose into full-blown nausea as I pulled on an oversized Covenant Christian College nightshirt and crawled into our empty bed. Tomorrow would be the first day of a new existence—without Zach to make me okay. When I woke up, I would be completely Rich Costanas's wife again, and nothing would be any different from the first moment when I'd admitted to myself that I'd fallen in love with someone else.

Tomorrow I would still try to be cheerful as Rich silently, sullenly sat like he was walled into a dark room he wouldn't let any of us into. I would kiss him on the cheek before I left for work, and he would mumble "have a good day." He would go to the station for the evening shift before I came home, leaving no note, making no phone call, giving me vague, monosyllabic answers when I called him. I'd stopped calling three months ago.

Tomorrow I would do the right thing: give up a relationship that made me feel alive and loved and necessary, and attempt to revive what Rich and I once had, before September 11, 2001, drained the life out of us. I'd found a reason to keep breathing. I wasn't sure Rich ever would.

And yet, tomorrow I would try. Only it would be a different person doing the trying. I was now a person who'd manufactured lies so she could meet her lover. A person who'd stripped herself down to betrayal, just to feel connected again. A person who'd been caught in the flash of a camera with her clothes on the floor around her.

I churned in the bed, tangling my ankles in a knot of sheets. I had to see Zach and find out what had gone down. And I had to make sure that he knew we were over—and I was really gone.

Though I pretended not to be, I was still awake when Rich fell into bed beside me, smelling of smoke and the Irish Spring attempt to wash it away.

"Hi, hon," he said.

I stiffened. Why did he choose this night to sound like the old Rich? His voice hadn't held that smushy quality for—what—two years? It sounded the way it used to when he wanted me to rub his head or make him a fried egg sandwich.

"How was your shift?" I said.

"I've got bad news for you."

My eyes came open. The answers I'd heard for months had tended toward *It was all right or The same as always.* They always implied that I'd asked a stupid question that was more than annoying. I propped up on one elbow and tried to sound sleepy. "What happened?"

"We hadda fight a boat fire—down at Port Orchard Yacht Club."

I curled my fingers around the pillowcase.

"Does your friend—that guy who took us out that one day—does he still own that Chris-Craft?"

He didn't know. He didn't know.

"Uh, yeah," I said—and then my heart clutched at itself. "*His* boat?"

"Had to be—total loss too." Rich punched at his pillow and wrapped it around his neck in his usual preparation for going into a post-fire coma.

But I had to ask.

"Is Zach—was he hurt?"

"Dunno. He wasn't around. I don't think he was there when it started." He gave a long, raspy sigh. "It was a mistake to ever leave New York."

I struggled to keep up. "Tell me some more," I said.

"I don't belong here, Demitria. I'm a fish outta water."

How many times had I turned myself inside out to get him to open up? Six months ago, I'd have had our bags half-packed already, willing to do anything to bring him out of his cave. Now I said nothing, because I felt nothing—except terror at the vision of Zach as a charred version of his former self, buried in the rubble of *The Testament.*

Rich sighed heavily and flopped over, leaving me on the other side of his wall of a back, the one I'd stopped trying to hoist myself over. "There's nothing we can do about it now," he said.

I sank back stiffly onto my own pillow. "Not tonight," I said.

"I didn't mean tonight."

There was the edge that implied I was of no help to him whatsoever, and why did I even think I could be?

I turned my back and moved to the far edge of the bed.

The next day couldn't dawn soon enough. Most of the night I watched the digits on the clock change with maddening slowness, and planned how to get to Zach before I lost my mind.

I was up, dressed, and making coffee by six thirty. Fortunately—and not surprisingly—I didn't hear a sound out of Christopher, but Jayne slipped into the kitchen in ghostly fashion at six thirty-five. Guilt scratched at me like an impatient dog.

"Hey, girlfriend," I said. "You're up early."

"Mom, I'm always up at this time. I have to catch the bus at seven."

I didn't see whether she rolled her eyes. Her face was already in the pantry, where she pawed at the cereal boxes. From the back, she was still a waif of a child, with little-girl-fine golden tresses and a penchant for long flowy skirts, an echo of the tiny days when she fancied herself a fairy princess. Her front was a different story, where late-blooming breasts and a well-rehearsed disdain proclaimed her as *teenager.*

"Silly me," I said.

"Unless you want to take me to school," she said into the cabinet. Her wistfulness slapped me in the face.

"I can't today, Jay," I said. "I have an early meeting."

I'd made up half-truths so easily until now, but this lie stuck to my tongue like a frozen pole.

"What happened to Rachel last night?" I said.

"I don't know. She ditched me, I guess."

"I'm sorry I didn't get your message right away. I had—a meeting."

Jayne turned and looked at me over the top of the Rice Krispies. "Is that all you do—go to meetings?"

"Sounds like it, doesn't it?"

"Whatever." She shook her hair back and turned the box upside down over a bowl. Two pieces of cereal bounced into it. She curled her lip.

"So—how was rehearsal?" I asked.

I tried to listen as I filled my coffee cup and twisted the lid on. If I didn't get out of there, I wouldn't get to talk to Zach before his eight o'clock.

"I got a different part," Jayne said.

I fumbled for the appropriate reply. "I thought you were playing Mary Warren."

"Mercy Lewis." She gave a disgusted grunt.

"Oh, so—who are you now?"

"Abigail Williams."

The sudden light in her always-serious brown eyes made me hunt through my faded memory of *The Crucible*.

"Isn't she a main character?"

Jayne nodded. The shyness that had disappeared with her twelfth year glowed on her face. I felt my throat thicken.

"Jay, that's amazing!" I said. "Congratulations!"

"Rachel didn't learn her lines and she kept messing around during rehearsal, so Mrs. Dirks bumped her and gave the part to me." She tilted her head like a small bird, spilling a panel of wavy hair across her thin cheek. "Maybe that's why she left me last night."

"Ya think?" I willed myself not to look at my watch. "Well, from now on, I'll pick you up from rehearsals."

"What if you have a meeting?" she said, adolescence slipping cleanly back into place.

"I'm not going to be having so many meetings from now on." The thickness hardened in my throat. I couldn't even say good-bye.

I'd just turned off Raintree Place when my cell phone belted out its disco version of the "Hallelujah Chorus," the ring tone one of my students chose for me. My heart sagged when the number on the screen wasn't Zach's. It was a college number though.

"Dr. Costanas, this is Gina Livorsi," said the California-crisp voice on the line.

Dr. Ethan Kaye's assistant. As in president of Covenant Christian College. My boss and my friend. So was Gina. My stomach tightened. Since when was I "Dr. Costanas" to her?

"Why so formal?" I said.

"Formal occasion." She sounded guarded. "Dr. Kaye wants to see you in his office. Soon as you can make it."

It was already after seven. Zach liked to be in his classroom by seven forty-five—

"I have a class at nine," I said. "I can be there after that."

Gina paused—uncomfortably, I thought.

"He says to cancel your class and be here at eight if you can."

"Do I have a choice?"

"Unh-uh."

"What's this about, Gina?"

"He didn't say."

"He didn't have to," I said. "You always know."

"Can you be here by eight?" she said.

My fingers tightened around the phone. "Yeah," I said. "Sure."

Why this summons? Something so secretive I couldn't even get it out of the secretary Zach and I had affectionately dubbed Loose Lips Livorsi?

I went cold.

WANT TO KNOW MORE ABOUT

NANCY RUE?

ancy Rue—the author of over one hundred titles for teens, tweens, and adults—has sold over one million books. Now get to know her as a speaker and teacher!

For information on booking Nancy for events, check out www.nancyrue.com or email her at nnrue@hughes.net.